Praise for Anna Castle's

Murder by Misrule was selected as one of Kirkus Review's Best Indie Books of 2014.

"Castle's characters brim with zest and real feeling... Though the plot keeps the pages turning, the characters, major and minor, and the well-wrought historical details will make readers want to linger in the 16th century. A laugh-out loud mystery that will delight fans of the genre." — Kirkus, starred review

"*Murder by Misrule* is a delightful debut with characters that leap off the page, especially the brilliant if unwilling detective Francis Bacon and his street smart man Tom Clarady. Elizabeth Tudor rules, but Anna Castle triumphs." — Karen Harper, NY Times best-selling author of *The Queen's Governess*

"Well-researched... *Murder by Misrule* is also enormously entertaining; a mystery shot through with a series of misadventures, misunderstandings, and mendacity worthy of a Shakespearian comedy." — M. Louisa Locke, author of the Victorian San Francisco Mystery Series

"Castle's period research is thorough but unobtrusive, and her delight in the clashing personalities of her crime-fighting duo is palpable: this is the winning fictional odd couple of the year, with Bacon's near-omniscience being effectively grounded by Clarady's street smarts. The book builds effectively to its climax, and a last-minute revelation that is particularly well-handled, but readers will most appreciate the wry humor. An extremely promising debut." — Steve Donoghue, Historical Novel Society

"Historical mystery readers take note: *Murder by Misrule* is a wonderful example of Elizabethan times brought to life...a blend of Sherlock Holmes and history." — D. Donovan, eBook Reviewer, Midwest Book Review

"The book is a compelling read and will keep readers glued to it with its suspense, intrigue and fast pace...An engaging murder mystery with a historical backdrop which makes it even more exciting." — A five-star review from Mamta Madhaven for Readers' Favorite

"Anna Castle combines humor with a complicated mystery to deliver a fun, satisfying read." — Starting Fresh

"The characters are well rounded as well as very memorable... The mystery itself was intriguing and really kept the reader going through twists and turns and yet in some cases it really surprised the reader." — Svetlana's Reads and Review

"Murder by Misrule is a highly entertaining story about murder, the law and politics; where none of which mix well together. This book is definitely a page-turner with very colorful characters. The storyline keeps you thinking to the very end." — Kinx's Book Nook

"It takes a talent to write a great mystery and also adhere to historical detail and this author has done just that. I'm thoroughly impressed... I'm recommending this book to anyone who loves mysteries." — A True Book Addict

"I loved Castle's humor and suspenseful writing. I highly recommend this book to any historical mystery reader or fans of the Elizabethan era of intrigue. If you like mysteries, you'll love this one. I'm looking forward to the next book in her series." — Oh, for the Hook of a Book

"I love when I love a book! *Murder by Misrule* by Anna Castle was a fantastic read. Overall, I really liked this story and highly recommend it." — Book Nerds

Praise for Anna Castle's *Death by Disputation*

"Castle's style shines ... as she weaves a complex web of scenarios and firmly centers them in Elizabethan culture and times." — D. Donovan, eBook Reviewer, Midwest Book Review

" I would recommend *Death by Disputation* to any fan of historical mysteries, or to anyone interested in what went on in Elizabethan England outside the royal court." — E. Stephenson, Historical Novel Society

"Accurate historical details, page turning plot, bodacious, lovable and believable characters, gorgeous depictions and bewitching use of language will transfer you through time and space back to Elizabethan England." — Edi's Book Lighthouse

"This second book in the Francis Bacon mystery series is as strong as the first. At times bawdy and rowdy, at times thought-provoking ... Castle weaves religious-political intrigue, murder mystery, and Tom's colorful friendships and love life into a tightly-paced plot." — Amber Foxx, Indies Who Publish Everywhere

Also by Anna Castle

The Francis Bacon Mystery Series
Murder by Misrule
Death by Disputation
The Widow's Guild

The Lost Hat, Texas Mystery Series
Black & White & Dead All Over
Flash Memory

A Francis Bacon Mystery — #3

The Widows Guild

Anna Castle

The Widows Guild
A Francis Bacon Mystery

Print Edition | October 2015
Discover more works by Anna Castle at www.annacastle.com

Copyright © 2015 by Anna Castle
Cover design by Jennifer Quinlan
Editorial services by Jennifer Quinlan, Historical Editorial

This is a work of fiction. Characters, places, and events are the product of the author's imagination or are used fictitiously and are not to be construed as real. Any resemblance to events, locales, organizations, or persons, living or dead, is entirely coincidental.

ISBN-10: 0-9916025-8-7
ISBN-13: 978-0-9916025-8-2
Produced in the United States of America

ACKNOWLEDGMENTS

As always, I must thank my critique group, the Capitol Crime Writers, whose comments always make my books better and whose conversation has made me a better writer: Russell Ashworth, Will Chandler,K.P. Gresham, Connie Norton, and Dan Roessler. This book was further improved by the sharp eyes and excellent taste of my editor, Jennifer Quinlan of Historical Editorial.

ONE

London, 29 August 1588

Francis Bacon sat at a scarred oak table in an interrogation chamber of the Tower, waiting for another prisoner to be brought up for questioning. He devoutly hoped this one would recognize the extremity of his situation and simply take the oath, surrendering a name or two. Then they could release him without further ado. The hope was not unreasonable; about half of the men they'd questioned so far had been eager to cooperate.

The other half had been hanged.

The loathsome chore of probing the loyalty of every known recusant Catholic in England had been appointed to Francis, along with seven other commissioners. His uncle, the Lord Treasurer, had offered him the post as a reward for past service — more work being the usual remuneration tendered by Her Majesty's frugal ministers. Serving on the recusancy commission was an honor, after all; everyone said it. The other commissioners were far senior to Francis's twenty-seven years, and several of them were knights.

And the work was necessary. English Catholics had in fact conspired to remove Queen Elizabeth from England's throne many times since her accession. This summer, the whirlwind of rumors, portents, and warnings swirling through Europe had in fact resolved itself into a real armada: over a hundred Spanish ships carrying an estimated thirty thousand troops, bearing down on England's sparsely defended coast.

The valiant English navy — and every Englishman with a boat — had dogged the Spanish fleet along the southern coast for most of July, nipping at their tails, keeping them at bay, while the whole country held its breath in terror lest the fragile defenses fail and ferocious Spanish *tercios* surge onto their shores.

Everyone knew King Philip had sent his awesome fleet to kill the queen, convert the populace at sword point, and swallow England into the over-swollen Spanish empire.

The English defenses had held. They'd driven the armada against the coast at Calais and closed in to strike. Sailors who witnessed the final battle on the eighth of August still spoke of it with a tremor in their voices and tears in their eyes.

England had won, or so it seemed. Her navy had driven the broken Spanish fleet north into the German Sea, but no one knew if or when or where they might stop to regroup. Drake thought they'd head for Denmark. Lord Burghley feared a landing in Scotland, where they might find friends, land their troops, and invade from the north, where so many English men and women continued to practice the old religion.

The queen wanted put the crisis behind them and let the people — especially soldiers being paid by the state — go back to their normal lives. She led a triumphant procession to St. Paul's Cathedral on the twentieth of August to give thanks for God's mercy in granting them the victory. The battles at sea had ended, but the streets now reeked from neglect. Sick and hungry men trickled in daily from the coasts, struggling to get home.

People snapped at each other, on edge, everyone's humors out of balance. The hangings of recusants over the past few days had helped somewhat to purge the city of fear and anger, like the catharsis of a Greek play. At least Francis hoped they served some purpose. There had been so many.

No one knew where the Spanish fleet was now or where it was going, but the security of the nation depended on knowing; hence the need for this commission, composed of clerks of the Privy Council, officers of the Tower, and experts in the common law. Every recusant — persons who refused to attend the services of the established Church of England — had to be examined. Francis shared the sense of urgency and accepted even the need for torture in times of imminent peril, but after every interview, he trudged home through the filthy streets with his stomach in knots. He knew in his bones that making fresh martyrs only prolonged the controversy.

"Did you hear Drake's report?" Sir Richard Topcliffe, Francis's co-commissioner, sat drumming his fingers on the tabletop in an irritatingly irregular rhythm.

"No," Francis said. He had not been in court that day. "But I understand the navy is exhausted and our coffers are empty."

Sir Richard said, "Drake wants to send a fleet to strike the Spanish hard, now, in their own ports, while they're weak."

The English were too. Drake would be hard-pressed to man even a single ship. "Did he have any news about the location of the armada?"

"We've seen the last of them," Sir Richard said. "They're staggering around the coast of Scotland, is my guess."

Everyone had their own guesses. "No word from Ireland yet, I suppose?"

Sir Richard barked a laugh. "Don't you trust my judgment by now, Mr. Bacon? I've been right about these prisoners of ours nine times out of ten, haven't I?"

More like five out of ten; a pathetic score, considering Sir Richard had gathered most of the names on their list himself in his capacity as a pursuivant for the Privy Council. He had spent the last year traveling through the

3

kingdom meeting bishops and justices of the peace to collect the names of those who failed to attend their parish churches on Sunday morning, as prescribed by law. Leading recusants, especially those with known associates on the Continent, were sent to Wisbech Castle in Ely, where they could be securely guarded. Gentlemen who convinced the authorities of their desire to cooperate were confined to their homes until the current crisis had passed. The lesser sort were brought to London and confined in prison cells to await their examinations.

Lord Burghley, a fellow Lincolnshire man, held Sir Richard in high esteem, but Francis knew him to be the worst kind of zealot. He loved to find men guilty — a dangerous bias when lives were at stake.

"Praise God for the news," Sir Richard's clerk said. He sat at the small table in the corner, unpacking his writing materials with the air of a man who had worked in far worse circumstances than this stuffy, stone-walled chamber. He rarely spoke, but often flashed a thin smile at a prisoner's reaction to his master's threats. He was a short, soft-bodied man with thinning hair combed over his balding pate, somewhere between Francis's twenty-seven years and Sir Richard's fifty-seven. His accent revealed his Lincolnshire origins.

Francis unrolled the documents concerning today's subject, one Thomas Howard of Suffolk. He suppressed a sigh. Would there be any of that surname left by the time the war with Spain had finally exhausted itself? The late and unlamented Duke of Norfolk, another Thomas Howard, had allegedly conspired with the late and less lamented Mary, Queen of Scots to dethrone Elizabeth and return England to the Catholic fold. Others of that family continued to foster Jesuit priests and disseminate Catholic pamphlets. They had to be stopped, one way or another.

Footsteps resounded outside the door. Sir Richard rubbed his hands together in eager anticipation. "This one is sure to need stretching — a little exercise on the rack. Not much doubt with that name, eh, Mr. Bacon?"

"Let us not pre-judge the case, Sir Richard. Our warrant constrains us to ask questions first and use harsher measures only in the obstinate cases."

"Ha! You're too soft, Mr. Bacon, too soft by half. Where there's smoke, there's fire, I say. Especially the stinking fumes of their idolatrous incense. You can smell it on their skin."

The guards ushered in a slight man wearing a dirty shirt and slops. They shoved him onto a stool and left. The man faced his interrogators with wary eyes hollowed by lack of sleep. His gaze shifted from Francis to Sir Richard, then settled on Francis, perhaps because he looked the less frightening.

Francis was slight, like the prisoner, with softly curling brown hair and hazel eyes. He wore his beard and moustache closely trimmed and dressed in simple yet well-tailored clothes of brown and black. His tall black hat bore only a plain gray band, though woven of silk. His barrister's gown declared his profession and possibly conveyed an assurance that the law prevailed even here in this fearsome stronghold.

Sir Richard, in contrast, dressed the part of an executioner, in starkest black with blood-red belt, garters, and hat band. His black hair and spade-cut beard were streaked with white. Thick black brows overshadowed his dark eyes, giving him a hooded aspect. He was tall and broad-shouldered, with a large round belly, and used his bulk to intimidate the prisoners.

Francis spoke first. He kept his tone level to signal the routine nature of the interview and put the prisoner at ease. "Good afternoon, Mr. Howard. We have a few questions to ask you today, nothing more. Then we'll administer the Oath of Supremacy, and you'll be returned to your cell to await further judgment."

"I'm not —"

"Wait for the questions!" Sir Richard pounded his meaty fist on the table, making both Francis and the prisoner jump.

Francis wanted to offer the man a smile, but he had learned not to. It only seemed to frighten them more. "Our pursuivants found a quantity of pamphlets written by Cardinal Allen in your house, evidently intended to be spread more widely. Where did you obtain them?"

"I never did! I wouldn't read such trash, nor ever let it into my house." The man shot a fearful glance at Sir Richard. "I'm not the one you want. Ask anyone. Ask my wife, I beg you."

"Ah, yes, your wife," Sir Richard said. "I well believe she's the one who bought those scurrilous tracts. Her so-called music tutor has been proved a seminary priest, hasn't he?"

"My wife has no —"

Sir Richard leaned across the table, thrusting his scowling face forward. The prisoner pressed his lips together and began to tremble from head to toe.

Sir Richard's deep voice fell into a menacing cadence. "You cannot hide behind your wife, Mr. Howard. She may be as guilty as you — more guilty, most like. Women are weak. They cling to their old superstitions. And they're sly, keeping their secrets inside their houses. We may not be able to prosecute her, but in its wisdom, the law makes you and she one person, with you the head — a head on a slender neck that can be stretched." He mimed pulling up a hanging rope. His clerk flashed an eager grin. "We hanged ten of your kind from Tyburn Tree this morning and watched them dance the hempen jig. Deny your foul seditious deeds and we'll stretch the rest of you too, by my good queen's virtue! If we must, I promise you, we'll get a warrant to bring your sneaking, traitorous wife here to answer questions as well."

The prisoner wailed. Francis smelled hot piss. He wished Sir Richard would let the poor man speak, not only to get his answers written down but to hear his accent. Something wasn't right.

"I'll tell you anything," the prisoner said, tears streaming down his unwashed cheeks. "Please, I beg of you, leave my wife alone. She's a good —"

Three knocks pounded on the door. Sir Richard called, "Come!"

A guard came in and sidled up to Sir Richard. He bent his head and murmured, "May I have word in private, sir?"

Sir Richard pointed a thick finger at the prisoner. "Sit there in your stink and think of every man — and woman — who has ever celebrated the devil's masses in that secret chapel of yours. Oh, yes! Don't think we don't know about it!" He rose, beckoning his clerk to accompany him. They followed the guard out the door, closing it behind them.

Francis seized the opportunity. He spoke in a low, urgent voice. "When he comes back, I'll offer to administer the oath before asking any questions. Take it, I beg of you, without fuss or disputation. There's something odd about this evidence against you, but I'm not sure what it is. Take the oath! And go to church, for God's sake, your own sake, and the sake of your family!"

"I swear to you, Mr. Bacon, I have never —"

Francis held up his hand. "It isn't so great a burden. Outward conformity is all that is required. Paint an attentive expression on your face and think whatever you like." He ventured a smile. "That's what I do."

"But, Mr. Bacon, I swear by —"

"Shh!" Francis heard the latch click and waved the man to silence.

The other men returned, leaving the door wide open. The clerk returned to his table and began packing up his writing desk. Sir Richard stood with his hands on his hips, looking down at the prisoner with a wry grin on his grizzled cheeks. He cut his gaze toward Francis. "It seems there's been a little mistake, Mr. Bacon. This gentleman here is not Mr. Thomas Howard of Suffolk. It seems the documents were miscopied. By the account of several of his cousins, all of whom are waiting in the yard below, he is in truth one Howard Thomas of Sussex and as good a Protestant as you or me." He chuckled as if it were a simple comical error, like mixing up the date or putting on the wrong hat, not one that had nearly sent an innocent man down to be cruelly tortured. "You're free to go, Mr. *Thomas.*"

His chuckle rose to hearty laughter as the prisoner fainted into the dirty straw.

TWO

Thomas Clarady pressed himself against a tapestry worth as much as his father's annual income, wishing he could slip behind it and escape this stifling chapel. He and his best friend, Benjamin Whitt, had been summoned to witness an event he'd hoped somehow might never take place: the marriage of their mutual friend, Trumpet, properly known as Lady Alice Trumpington, soon to be Lady Surdeval.

Her groom, Ralph Gumery, the first Viscount Surdeval, must have been three times her age. Or more; thrice nineteen made only fifty-seven. That doddering sack of puss could well be sixty. His hair was still yellow — what was left of it — but his eyes looked rheumy even from ten feet away, and his long nose had a crook in the middle. His spindly legs were too weak to hold him up by themselves; he needed a cane to stand next to his lithesome bride.

"Does he always look so crabbish?" Tom whispered to Ben.

"This is his third time around. I suppose the excitement wanes."

Ben's own habitual expression was that of a hound left behind while his pack mates raced out for the hunt. He was comely enough, or would be if he took more pains with his appearance. Taller than most, topping Tom by a good two inches, he tended to stoop to accommodate his companions. Dark brows overhung his sad brown eyes, shadowing the intelligence gleaming within. His brown hair and short beard were always neatly barbered, but he wore old-fashioned flat wool caps. He wore old-fashioned everything, being too thrifty to borrow money for clothes.

He did provide a countermatch to Tom, who always took pains with his appearance and had no qualms about running up bills at the mercers' shops. Tom had sky-blue eyes and curling blond hair with a stylishly pointed beard and thin moustache. He would have worn his best yellow silk and green velvet doublet this evening, with the yellow silk stockings, if he'd been given any warning. As it was, he'd come straight from pistol practice in his sweat-soaked shirt and dusty slops. He'd been allowed to grab his doublet, so he at least was decent, but he hadn't even had time to change his shoes and stockings.

Tom glared at the couple before the altar, gritting his teeth in a futile effort to stop thinking about what came after the wedding supper. He could not endure even the flicker of a shadow of the image of Trumpet in bed with that paunchy, onion-eyed fustilarian. She was beautiful on a bad day, even when dressed as a muddy boy. True, she lacked height and tended toward constant motion, but her emerald eyes shone in a heart-shaped face surrounded by glossy black hair. Her figure curved the right amount in all the right places, and she moved with a catlike grace.

Today she shone in triumphant splendor, radiant as a goddess, wearing the same pink and silver confection she'd worn on another day of bitter surprises in Cambridge last year. It made her look like an enchanted doll.

"We must stop this madness," he hissed into Ben's ear.

"Don't be absurd," Ben whispered back. "We spent months arranging this match."

"The man's a goblin! He's got one foot in the grave already."

Ben shrugged. "It's what she wants."

Tom snarled but couldn't refute that argument. Trumpet had always said she wanted a rich, titled husband, old and preferably on his last legs. He'd always assumed

she'd been joking. She couldn't have a very clear idea of
what happened on the wedding night or she wouldn't seem
so cursed pleased with herself.

She flashed him a grin that made his heart dance an
antic hay. He couldn't muster an answering grin; he could
only glare at her in dull disbelief. He whispered, "Why did
you bring me here to watch this travesty?"

"What?" Ben's deep voice sounded surprised. "We
thought you'd want to be here."

"Well, *we* were wrong."

When did Ben and Trumpet constitute a *we* without
Tom? Months of negotiation, was it? And not a word to
him — not so much as a hint — before they hauled him
into this airless den as a superfluous witness. They had a
second witness already; some relation of the viscount's,
judging by the crooked beak and pallid hair. The man wore
black from head to toe and looked about as pleased by the
proceedings as Tom. Perhaps they should get together for
a drink afterward and trade grumbles.

The priest intoned another section of the ceremony.
The viscount mumbled something and Trumpet
murmured her response. The priest nattered on again.

Tom didn't like him either. His robes vaunted too
much embroidery, giving him a decidedly Romish air.
Everything about the ceremony reeked of popery,
including this lavishly furnished private chapel, which
barely had room for its six occupants. Trumpet's dress
alone took up a quarter of the space. Catholic fripperies
cluttered every spare inch: silk tapestries, golden crucifixes,
ivory statues, silk-embroidered tablecloths. A gilt table at
his elbow held a copper box shaped like a sepulchre with
saints painted around the sides.

How could the viscount afford such blatant
noncompliance with the established religion? This
glittering trash should be melted down and converted to
something useful. And how could Trumpet marry a

Catholic? True, she had never been politically minded, and the queen must have approved the match. As the only legitimate child and heir of the Earl of Orford, Trumpet's marriage was a matter of state.

Months of negotiation. That phrase irritated Tom like a seed stuck in his teeth. Ben must have helped her draw up the marriage contract — legal work too complex for poor, dull Tom. Never mind that he too was a full-fledged member of Gray's Inn, the most important of Her Majesty's legal societies. He'd spent the last year studying till his wits curdled, under no less a tutor than Francis Bacon. He could draw up a marriage contract, he'd wager. Maybe not as clever as Ben's, but he could have helped. His handwriting was exemplary, even Bacon said so.

They'd kept their secrets mighty close; secrets evidently too sensitive for Tom the Blabber. Never mind that he'd spent the whole of last spring on a secret commission for the Lord Treasurer himself without leaking a word, not even to Ben and Trumpet. Somehow in the intervening year, he had evidently lost control of himself and become a prattling idiot.

Tom fumed through the rest of the service, wishing constables would burst in and arrest the viscount for recusancy, along with his dour-faced cousin and the priest. At last, the loving couple exchanged a kiss and turned to make their way out of the over-pomped chamber.

"Stay for supper," Trumpet whispered to him as she passed.

"As my lady pleases," Tom answered in the tones of an ill-treated servant.

Her eyes narrowed, but she proceeded at her husband's side through another small chamber into the great hall, where a hammerbeam ceiling soared thirty feet over their heads and a black-and-white chequered floor spread beneath their feet. A small table had been set up in a corner beside the carved oak screen. It held a small stack of papers, an inkpot, and a pair of quills. Ben went immediately to stand behind it. He reviewed the papers, running his finger down each page, nodding as if satisfied that nothing had been changed. He selected a page with room for signatures at the bottom and turned it toward the others. He dipped a pen and handed it to the viscount with a small bow. "My lord."

Lord Surdeval signed it with a flourish and passed the pen to Trumpet. She dipped it in the ink, signed, and passed it to the cousin, who signed in turn. Ben dipped the pen again, signed the page himself, and passed the quill to Tom.

"Me?"

"As a witness to the other signatures."

Tom blew out a breath. Very well. He would set his name to Trumpet's marriage contract for all of history to see. He manfully resisted the urge to scribble, "Although I strongly object to this ill-made match," underneath his signature.

Ben dusted the page, rolled it together with the others, and tucked the roll into his sleeve. Now for the supper. Tom hoped it would be equally brief.

A long table had been laid in the center of the hall, spread with pristine linen cloths. Candlelight reflected on silver plates and cups, even though the blue August sky still shone bright behind the high windows. The viscount sat at the head and Trumpet at the foot. Ben and Tom took one side, the crook-nosed cousin the other.

A liveried footman carried in a platter bearing a whole stuffed peacock, reassembled tail and all. The small party watched in silence as he placed the dish before the viscount and carved a portion for each guest. Other dishes quickly followed: broiled sardines, pork stuffed with apricots, bowls of fresh rocket decorated with beetroot and walnuts. The food was delicious and the wine excellent. Trumpet never stinted in such matters.

She kept up a stream of lively chatter, gallantly assisted by Ben. Lord Surdeval granted her a wrinkled smile now and then but mainly focused on slurping up a bowl of plain broth. Tom ate heartily — why not? — and glared at the viscount. The cousin nibbled and glared at Trumpet. All in all, it was the most dispirited wedding supper Tom had ever attended.

The viscount dried his white moustaches with his napkin and levered himself to his feet. "I'll leave you with our guests, my dear. I want to take a little nap before —" He broke off with what he probably imagined was a droll smirk. The expression made him look all the more like a goblin with a bellyache.

"Allow me see to your comfort, my lord." Trumpet hopped to her feet, shifting her belled skirts with a limber swing of her hips. She took his arm and led him through a small door at the back of the hall.

The three guests sat in silence while servants replaced the main course with an array of sugared violets, nutmeats, and tiny pastries shaped like hearts. They left the treats untouched but had their cups filled to the brim again. The silence deepened as they drank, gazes turned sightlessly toward the clutter on the table.

Trumpet returned in about a quarter of an hour, striding across the chequered floor like a Lord Lieutenant coming to inspect his troops, her habitual gait. Tom felt a pang of sympathy for the viscount. Could the man have any idea what he'd gotten himself into?

She did not resume her seat. Instead, she stood at the head of the table to address her guests with her hands demurely crossed over her stomach. "I thank you all for attending upon my lord husband and myself on this important day. I apologize for the suddenness of our arrangements, but as you know, my Lord Surdeval is anxious to restore his line, and we felt it wise to take advantage of his improving health."

They were being dismissed. Ben, perhaps with the benefit of advance notice, reached his feet before Tom and the cousin could hoist their arses full off their chairs. Trumpet met each guest in turn as they moved toward the exit.

"Mr. Whitt, I trust you'll make copies of the contract straightaway? We'll keep the original here, but I'd like you to keep two copies at Gray's."

"I'll see to it at once, my lady." Ben smiled down at her. He bent and kissed her on the cheek, murmuring, "I sincerely hope you know what you're doing."

Trumpet laughed gaily and batted her lashes, sending a shiver up Tom's spine. She only played the frisking minx when she had a scheme brewing and Trumpet's schemes often went awry. Ben crooked a grin at Tom and left without him.

She held out a graceful hand to the cousin, who lifted it to puff a kiss into the air an inch above it. "You must come to dinner tomorrow, Sir William. I'm *longing* to become better acquainted. We are family now, after all." She batted her lashes at him.

A waste of effort. The man was plainly half-blind. He muttered something and followed Ben out the door.

Tom's turn. Trumpet gripped his arm and looked up at him with excitement shimmering in her eyes. "I know you're not happy with this, Tom. I'll explain everything, I promise. Please wait here for a few minutes. Catalina will come for you."

Tom looked down into those twinkling green eyes, the eyes of his dearest friend. They'd been through some tough times together, not all of them her fault. He could wait a few minutes to hear her story. He nodded. "All right."

She bit her lip at the curt response. "Thank you." Then she left him alone in the echoing hall, but for a single servant stationed near the screen. Something about the man's posture suggested he was as eager for this evening to end as Tom.

Tom grabbed a bottle from the sideboard and returned to his seat. Then he got up and went to sit at the head of the table in the viscount's carved armchair. The servant watched him with disapproval but said nothing. Tom leaned back in the chair and lifted his feet to the table.

So Trumpet had married a gouty old goat in need of an heir. Did she truly mean to give him one or would she find ways to evade the marriage bed until he died? She wouldn't care about the continuation of the Surdeval line. He hoped that was her plan, because the alternative — the plan in which that withered ogre laid his hands on Trumpet's ripe, young body — was unbearable.

Tom drained his cup and refilled it. He gazed around the hall, wishing for some distraction. The oak paneling gleamed from a hundred years of hand-rubbed oil. Painted crests and banners hung here and there, separated by the heads of slain animals and off-color patches where armor ought to be hanging.

An old family like the Surdevals ought to have weaponry going back to Plantagenet times: pikes, flails, maces, halberds. Where was it? Most likely it had been confiscated by the Privy Council along with the horses. His Lordship must be a confirmed recusant; they'd want to prevent him from riding to the aid of the Spanish, if the Spanish should land, which they hadn't, thanks to God and the courage of the English navy.

The nobility got off with a slap on the wrist and confinement to their homes, not a hardship in a place as big as Surdeval House, one of the ancient buildings lining the Strand. It had probably been in the family since the time of John of Gaunt. Tom had seen it from the riverside, naturally, traveling upstream or down. The palaces along the Thames were one of the principal sights of London. He'd never been inside any of them until today.

He took a swallow of wine, fingering the golden pearl earring that dangled from his left ear. His father, the privateer, had brought the jewel back from the South Seas after circumnavigating the globe with Sir Francis Drake. Tom wore it to remind himself of where he came from, however far up the ladder he might climb.

He'd made it up the first rung last year as a result of the Cambridge commission, raising himself from yeoman to gentleman by virtue of a bachelor's degree and membership in Gray's Inn. People called him "Mr. Clarady" now or earned his scorn. But he could never raise himself high enough to reach Trumpet, no matter how hard he worked or how well he dressed. Not even if he got himself knighted for bravery — a private fantasy. An earl's daughter remained as far beyond his reach as the stars in the night sky.

When they'd met at Gray's two years ago, she'd been masquerading as a young lad learning the law. Tom had gotten used to thinking of her as someone more or less like himself. Things didn't change much even after he'd learned her secret, not for a while. They'd continued to sup together in commons and watch cases being tried in the Westminster courts. Shopping, fencing, idling in taverns, they'd spent the better part of their waking hours together as friends and equals.

Now, looking around at this great hall with its centuries-long accumulation of heraldry, Tom understood that she was nothing like him. Nothing at all.

The light falling from the high windows faded to gray. What time must it be? He and Ben had been summoned to appear at five o'clock and the ceremony had droned on for half an hour or so. That miserable supper might have lasted another hour. It could be nearly eight. It would soon be fully dark. Would his hostess be considerate enough to lend him a boy with a lantern to light his way back to Gray's?

He swilled the last of his wine and spat the dregs back into the cup. The swishing of silken skirts caught his attention. Catalina Luna, Trumpet's gypsy maidservant, glided toward him across the polished floor. She beckoned to him, black eyes flashing, a secretive smile curving her wide lips.

He followed her down a corridor, across a small interior courtyard, and up a stair winding through a narrow turret. They passed through a room furnished with odd shapes draped in canvas to a door at the rear of the house. Catalina opened it, revealing a sumptuous chamber with a wall of windows overlooking the Thames, open to admit the summer breeze.

Trumpet stood in the middle of the room. She had exchanged her wedding garb for a loose robe of deep red velvet that made her cheeks look like fine damask and her eyes glow like green fire. Her ebony hair hung loose to her waist. "What do you think?"

Tom had to swallow hard before he could speak. "About what?"

His words sounded harsh; he couldn't help it. Had she brought him here to flaunt her beauty on the very night she removed herself forever from his grasp? He knew she was beyond him. But he loved her, or he thought he might. He'd told her as much, or he almost had. She knew it, anyway. She'd told him she loved him in so many words a little over a year ago. He'd only seen her twice during that long and busy year, but now evidently things had changed.

Her chin tilted in that prideful gesture he knew so well. "What do you think about *me*? About this." She held out her hands to display herself. "About what you see."

"Ah." Tom pretended to consider it. "Well, I think you are the most perfect vision of maidenly beauty I have ever seen. I think they should hold a competition among the greatest sculptors in Europe to craft your image in marble

18

as a model for future generations of womankind to strive toward."

She blinked, and her mouth twisted in a complicated half frown. "That almost sounded like a compliment."

"It almost was one." They glared at each other. Then Tom said, "Why did you bring me here, Trumpet? Do you want some premarital advice? Catalina can give you that, surely. Or have you staged this display to taunt me?"

"*Taunt* you?" She cocked her head. "No, goose. I meant to please you." She bit her lip and began to untie the ribbons at the front of her robe, slowly, one by one. She spread the velvet folds open with both hands, revealing her body, naked beneath a transparent film of white gauze.

"Guh," Tom said as the air sucked out of his lungs. She giggled, and lightning lanced up his spine. His hands twitched with the need to grasp, but he stood his ground and mustered the strength to speak. "What?"

She nodded. "Don't worry about Surdeval. We gave him a sleeping draught. He'll snore merrily away till morning in his own room downstairs on the other side of the house. I gave the servants enough money to get stinking drunk and sent them off to celebrate their master's nuptials. We're alone, except for Catalina, and she won't interrupt us."

Tom noticed for the first time that the maidservant hadn't entered the room with him. They truly were alone, here in this moonlit chamber with an enormous bed draped in silk and heaped with tasseled pillows. He willed himself to keep his eyes on Trumpet's face and worked enough spit into his dry mouth to form another word. "Why?"

She clucked her tongue, a purely Trumpetarian expression of irritation. "It can't be that hard to understand. My lord husband wants an heir. I intend to give him one. But you may have noticed he's a thousand years old and ugly as a long-nosed toad." She grimaced, sticking out her pink tongue.

Tom's groin clenched. He took shallow breaths and cast a glance toward the door. "Your choice."

"Yes." She followed his gaze and moved to stand between him and his only escape. "My choice. My plan. He gives me this house, a generous jointure when he dies — which won't be long considering his failing health — and little interference in my daily life. In return, I give him sons." She padded toward him on her bare feet in the measured paces of a panther, letting the velvet robe slide slowly down her white shoulders. "Sons, Tom, which *you* will give to me. I want you to do the honors." She reached him, leaned into him, and raised her arm to curl her hand around his neck. Her breasts rose beneath the gauze, her small pink nipples pointed straight at his lips.

Tom had no more questions. He wrapped his arm around her slender waist and kissed her.

THREE

Tom lost himself for an uncountable span of bliss, his arms and hands filled with lush woman, his nose buried in rose-scented hair. Trumpet feathered kisses up his neck and along his jaw. Her curious tongue darted into his ear and set his loins on fire. He wrapped his hand around the curve of her bottom and pulled her hard against his body, backing slowly toward the bed, oblivious to everything but their rising passion, until his back came up against something hard and pointy. He stopped, blinked, and pulled his mouth free.

The bedpost. Thank God in all his glory for a grandiose, tree-sized, fully carved bedpost! Some ornate leaf stabbed him acutely in the small of the back. He blessed it for the pain. Trumpet, his dear old chum, was a virgin. Both her husband and her father were peers of the realm. This deed could only bring trouble thundering upon him from every direction.

Tom murmured, "Stop, sweetling. We must stop."

"No stopping." She nibbled his earlobe and drew him into another kiss. He leaned against the bedpost and let the unyielding oak prod life back into his wits. Freeing his lips, he turned his head, gritting his teeth against the tickling kisses she tongued across his collarbone. He tried to tug her arms away and found her legs wrapped tightly around his waist as well. She'd climbed him like a sailor climbs a mast.

Sailor. Mast. That was it. He'd spent a year between '85 and '86 on his father's ship, chasing Spanish galleons across the West Indies, seeking loot for the queen's coffers — and their own. They'd caught three, but not without cost. He could still hear men screaming and cannons booming. He'd seen a sailor's arm cut clean off not three feet from where he battled for his own life. Red blood had spurted everywhere as the man sank into the black smoke smothering the deck.

Tom focused his mind on the screams and the blood and managed to lower Trumpet to the bed without following her down. He struggled to disentangle her limbs from his trunk, but she kept twining them back around him. He cursed every minute he'd spent helping Trumpet-the-lad learn to wrestle. He finally had to use his full force to thrust her away. "No!"

"Yes," she crooned, half rising to tug at the laces of his doublet. "Yes, yes, yes."

"No, no, no." Tom backed away from the bed and turned to scan the room. He spotted a painted Italianate pitcher beside a matching bowl. He strode across and emptied it over his head, blowing into the stream like a horse after a hard gallop. Then he went to the windows and pushed the sash fully open, hanging out to catch the breeze on his face. The river-dank air cooled his fevered body, slowing his heart. He breathed deeply. Then, somewhat restored, he turned back to her.

Trumpet had lifted herself up on her elbows, back arched and breasts thrust forward — an unbearable pose. Tom snatched her robe from the floor where it had fallen and swept it over her.

"Hoi!" She shook her head free and sat up, draping the robe around her shoulders. She treated him to an imperious glare, green eyes blazing under beetled black brows, but Tom could withstand that far better than he could the vision of her nearly naked —

He shook his head and leaned out for another gulp of air.

"What's wrong with you?" *What's wrong with me?* she meant.

"Nothing." He smiled at her. "You are by far the most desirable woman I have ever seen."

That mollified her, a little. "Then what?" She stood and put the robe on properly, tying it closed and shaking the folds around her feet. Fully covered, from chin to floor. Thank God.

"Then what *what?*" He shook his head but softened the dismissal with a wry grin. "I can't do it, Trumpleton, much as it pains me to disoblige a friend. I'd dishonor both myself and you." And have his balls removed by the viscount's men, most likely. "I don't take virgins anyway. You know that."

She clucked her tongue. "That's exactly what Ben said you'd say."

"Oh, he did, did he? I suppose I should be flattered you found time to discuss my sexual policies among your important legal negotiations."

She had the grace to look a trifle abashed — as much apology as he would ever get. And in fairness, he would also choose Ben if he needed a lawyer. Besides, the Whitt family home was only half a day's ride from Orford Castle in Suffolk.

He let it go. "Why didn't you listen to him?"

"I thought I might persuade you."

Tom gave a short whistle. "You very nearly did."

Her eyes glinted and she did a little wiggle with her shoulders that raised the short hairs on the back of his neck. She pointed her high-arched foot, preparatory to taking one of those pantherine steps toward him.

He pointed his finger at her. "Not one inch closer. I'll tie you up if I have to." He rubbed his throat, as dry as if he'd run a marathon. "Do we have any wine?"

She flapped a hand at a small table near the giant fireplace. "We have everything, except your cooperation."

She flopped into a chair, folded her arms across her chest, and stretched her feet out in front of her in the posture of a discontented boy.

Tom breathed a sigh of relief. Crisis over — for now.

He found a jug of canary and a bottle of Rhenish amid plates of cheese, nuts, fresh fruits, sweets, and more of the heart-shaped pastries from supper, stuffed with sweet cheese and raspberries. A large bowl held fragrant roses. More roses adorned the mantel and the tables on each side of the bed. She'd laid out everything for the perfect tryst, complete with an intimate supper. Her wedding night, and he'd spoiled it.

He filled a cup and took a draught. Standing up was safer, so he went to lean against a faded tapestry of a hunting scene. The wine had been lightly sweetened with honey, just the way he liked it. Refreshing. He rolled another draught around in his mouth, savoring the wetness.

"Enjoy your drink," she said. "You'll change your mind in a minute."

"No, I won't." He stabbed his finger at her again. "And you stay where you are."

She tossed her glossy head. "You'll change your mind because your argument is specious."

"What argument?"

"You say you won't make love to me because I'm a virgin, but it's too late. I'm not a virgin anymore." She tilted her chin. "I experienced the rapture."

"No, you didn't."

"Yes, I did."

"No, Trumpet. Trust me. You did not."

"Then what do you call what just happened?"

"I call that bliss." He grinned at her. "Bliss times ten. But it was not *the* rapture. Rapture is —" How could he satisfy her curiosity without setting her off again? He scratched his head and came up empty. "Rapture is *more*."

"There's *more?*" She leapt out of her chair and onto his chest in a single bound, knocking the cup from his hand, twining her arms and legs around him again. She plastered her mouth on his in a ravenous kiss, and Tom's traitorous body responded in full.

His honor fought its way to the surface. *Screams. Blood. Smoke.*

He wrested his lips free and pressed them tightly together. Looking past her, he spotted a straight-backed chair near the bed and stalked toward it. She wriggled and writhed against him, humming and cooing and nibbling his ears.

Blood spurting. Men screaming. Smoke burning his eyes.

Tom pressed her into the chair and held her down with one hand while he yanked free the cord of the bed curtains, tearing part of the curtain away from the tester. He wrapped the cord several times around both chair and Trumpet, who kicked and cursed him like a pirate. He smiled through his teeth. Her raving only helped maintain his lust-reducing illusion. He knotted the cord securely behind her and scouted the room for more rope. He found a slew of silk ribbons and tested them for strength.

They would serve. He returned to his captive and bound her feet together at the ankles.

She screeched, "I'll have you whipped!"

"No, you won't." He found a footstool, added a pillow, and lifted her feet onto it. He stood back to regard his handiwork and stuffed another small pillow behind her back. He looked down at her with a grin. "I did warn you."

She groused and grumbled, but knew she'd brought it on herself. Trumpet was reckless, bold, ingenious, and implacable, but she was also fundamentally fair-minded. If the world were different, she would have made a formidable lawyer.

"Are you going to leave me like this all night? I gave Catalina strict instructions not to return until sunrise."

"I'll stay," Tom said. "I'd never find my way out of this labyrinth in the dark. Besides, you'd follow me, and we'd have to do it all over in some less handy place."

Her sly chuckle proved him right on that count.

Tom moved the most comfortable armchair over to where they could talk easily and found a small table to set beside it. He poured himself a fresh cup of wine and filled a plate with bread, cheese, and fruit, then settled in his chair with the small repast.

"Nothing for me?"

He walked over and held the cup while she drank, then went back to his own chair. "If you're good, I'll free one arm. Maybe after you start snoring."

"I don't snore!"

"Yes, you do." Tom restored his strength with food and drink. She watched him with an air of resignation. After a few minutes of restful silence, he said, "Your new husband's a Catholic."

"Only nominally. His wife was the devout one — wives, I should say. The second was the most religious. She's the one who repaired and furnished that chapel. I think she even had Masses said in there sometimes, by smuggled priests."

"That's outrageous! Why doesn't it bother you?"

"Why would it? She died last year, and Surdeval has proved his loyalty to the queen over and again." She laughed. "When the armada was sighted off the coast of Cornwall, he leapt on his horse and dashed to Richmond to offer her his sword, bringing his son and all his retainers. They accepted the son and the men, then sent my dear old lord home with heartfelt thanks."

"Gallant." Tom selected a hazelnut and chewed it well. "He has some qualities, then."

"He has many qualities. He loves books. I like books. He has a huge library, which he practically lives in now. It's closer to the stillroom and he doesn't like to use the stairs if he can help it. The son was killed in battle, which is why the queen consented to our hasty wedding."

"He needs a new heir."

"That he does." Trumpet gave him a meaningful look.

Tom shook his head. "It wouldn't work, Trumpet. People would notice that the newest Surdeval didn't look much like dear old Dad."

"I doubt it. He's fair, like you, with blue eyes. He's tall. The child won't have that crooked nose, but I have an ordinary nose, as do you. We'll say the nose came from my side. Surdeval's eyesight's not that good and no one else would dare to pose the question. Catalina says half the thrones in Europe are occupied by cuckoos."

Catalina had originated somewhere in Spain, the daughter of a gypsy chieftain. She had run away in Italy with a troupe of commedia dell'arte performers, where she met an English actor and followed him to London. He died, somehow leaving her in the care of Trumpet's Uncle Welbeck, who had sent her on to serve his favorite niece. At least that's the story she told. Tom thought it more likely that Trumpet had conjured her to supply the need for a conspirator with a flexible imagination, a gift for costuming, and few moral scruples. It would seem she was a fountain of dubious information as well.

"What will you do now?" he asked.

Trumpet shrugged as best she could inside her bonds. "I'll think of something. Catalina says it's easy to fake a pregnancy."

Tom snorted. "I think His Lordship would notice he hadn't performed the necessary service."

"Catalina says that can be managed too."

Tom had a vision of the two rascals drugging the old man and slipping a whore into his bed. He shook his finger at her. "I forbid you to do any such thing."

She laughed merrily.

Fair enough; he had no means to enforce any forbiddings. "It would be cruel; surely you can see that. Give the man an honest heir, for pity's sake."

"I will not surrender my body to that repellent old ruin."

"It won't be that bad, Trumpet." He gave her an encouraging smile. "Just close your eyes and think about what you'll gain."

"Never." Her face crumpled in a mighty yawn. "What time is it, do you think?"

"No idea." Tom yawned as well. He got up to grab a pillow and another stool for his own feet. "Can you sleep like that? Because I'm done in, but I won't close my eyes if you're loose."

"Go to sleep. I'm fine." She yawned again, shifted around a little, and closed her eyes.

Tom blew out the candles. Moonlight glowed behind the windows, turning her cheeks and forehead to polished ivory. He gazed down for a moment on his complicated friend, wishing he could help her, and not only for his own lusty reasons. She deserved a good husband — a handsome, kind young man who could love her the way she ought to be loved.

He kissed her on the forehead and settled himself for the night in his own chair.

"Traitor," Trumpet murmured.

He'd thought she was asleep. "Trollop."

She clucked her tongue. "Coward." He could barely hear her voice.

"Harlot."

He heard a soft snore and grinned into his pillow. He closed his eyes, grateful for the rest.

A loud boom woke Tom from a sound sleep. He startled and jumped to his feet to see Catalina Luna standing inside the door, panic on her dark features. "My lady! His Lordship! I think he is dead!"

FOUR

"Dead?" Tom rubbed his face and ran both hands over his scalp, waking himself up. Daylight streamed through the windows. They'd overslept. "What did you do to him?"

"Nothing," Trumpet said, squirming against her bonds. "We gave him his normal sleeping draught and left him alone."

Catalina moved far enough into the room to see her mistress tied to a chair. She glanced from Tom to Trumpet and back again, then treated him to one of those complex gypsy looks that clearly expressed her opinion of him as a man.

"Untie me!" Trumpet demanded.

Tom grabbed his knife from the small table and cut her bonds. He held out a hand to help her to her feet.

She shook each leg, rolled her neck and shoulders, and turned to her maidservant. "What's this about Surdeval? He can't be dead. We only gave him a bit more than his usual dose."

"I do not know, my lady. I go to see if he is awake before I come to you and find him stiff and still, covered with white sheet, like a dead man. I say, 'my lord, my lord,' but he did not move. I am afraid and run for you."

Trumpet set her hands on her hips and studied Catalina for a moment. Then she gave Tom a critical inspection. He'd gotten up in the night and removed his doublet and shoes. One of his garters had come loose. She cast a dim eye at her own soft robe and said, "Well, never mind. The servants are probably sleeping off their night of carousing.

We'd better hurry down and have a look for ourselves." She walked out the door.

Tom stuffed his feet into his shoes and grabbed his doublet. Odds were good this would be something bad and he'd be going straight out to fetch a physician. He followed the women through the maze of corridors and stairs.

"Why are you so late?" Trumpet asked as they hurried through a sunlit gallery. "It must be past seven."

Catalina said, "I sleep, my lady. I am sorry. My room is darker."

"Are the household servants back?" Trumpet asked.

"I do not know," Catalina said. "I have not seen one, but there is smoke from the bake house."

She led them to a corner of the ground floor on the street side of the house. This room had been transformed from a library to a bedchamber. The walls were lined from floor to ceiling with shelves of leather-bound books. Chairs and small desks occupied the wells made by the tall windows, but the dominant piece of furniture was a large curtained bed, flanked by night tables covered with the flotsam of an invalid. The room smelled faintly of medicine in spite of the fresh morning air wafting through the open windows.

Catalina stopped inside the door while Trumpet surged ahead with Tom behind her. The bed curtains hung open on both sides, gathered up against the headboard. The viscount lay in the center with a smooth sheet drawn up to his chin. His arms extended down each side, and his toes pointed straight up.

"Who sleeps like that?" Tom asked.

"Nobody," Trumpet said. "And look, his chest isn't moving. Is he breathing?"

"He is warm, my lady." Catalina moved to stand at the foot of the bed. "I touched his cheek. But no breath. Perhaps he is only newly dead?"

Trumpet stepped to the edge of the bed and laid a hand on his cheek. "He *is* warm."

"It's August," Tom said. "How long would a body stay warm after death?"

They exchanged a long look. They'd seen more than their share of unnatural deaths.

"I want to listen to his heart," Trumpet said. "Perhaps he's in some sort of swoon."

"Perhaps he woke in the night and took another dose." Catalina gestured at the night table with its litter of bottles and cups. "He had many medicines."

Tom doubted the answer would be so simple. "Don't touch anything yet. Mr. Bacon says we must observe the scene as it is before we alter it. Is this how you left him last night?"

"No. He was still awake." Trumpet glanced around the room and pointed at a large chest in a corner. "There are his doublet and shoes, right where I put them." She turned back to Tom. "I came in with him after supper to see him settled comfortably. He said he would rest for an hour while I made my preparations, as he called it."

"Building up his strength, no doubt." Tom couldn't keep the bitter note from his voice. "Did he have potions for that as well?"

She clucked her tongue. "It's not what you think. The difference in our ages embarrassed him more than me. I'm young enough to be his granddaughter. I also think he didn't want me to feel rushed."

Tom let it go. The unbearable prospect had been made moot. "What happened then?"

"I helped him off with his doublet and laid it on the chest. Then he sat on the bed, and I removed his shoes. Meanwhile, Catalina brought in some fresh wine and stirred in his sleeping draught. It's a mixture of valerian, chamomile, and mint. Nothing unwholesome. I gave him the cup and watched to be sure he drank it. He didn't know about the dose, but it was only a little more than his usual. I asked the stillroom maid about it, saying I wanted to learn how to care for my new husband. Then I took the cup and gave it back to Catalina. He kissed me on the forehead and said he would come up to me in an hour. And then I left."

"Could he have woken and covered himself with the sheet?" Tom asked.

Catalina shook her head. "No one can sleep with so smooth a sheet."

"Is anything else different about the room?" Tom asked, knowing Mr. Bacon would ask him.

"The coverlet," Catalina said. A heap of brocaded silk lay crumpled on the floor beyond the foot of the bed. She walked around to the other side. "And here is a pillow on the floor. I see no other change."

"I'm going to listen to his heart." Trumpet grasped the sheet on either side of the viscount's chin and pulled it straight back.

They studied him in silence for a moment. He still wore his shirt, hose, and stockings, although the stockings were twisted around his calves and ankles.

"Look." Tom pointed at two deep indentations in the plump mattress on either side of the viscount's body. "Like someone knelt over him."

Trumpet placed her hand on his neck, feeling for a pulse. She shook her head. "I'm not sure . . ." She climbed up on one side and pulled his shirt open. Then she gasped and sat back on her heels. "By my maidenhead," she whispered. "What's been done here?"

Someone had carved a cross into the center of the viscount's chest — two thin red lines, the long piece about two inches, the crosspiece about half that. The bright color stood out sharply on the viscount's pale chest. Dark smears, like bits of tar, clotted in the corners of the cuts.

"Murder," Tom said.

"But is he dead?" Trumpet knelt over him and set her ear against his chest. Tom held his breath while she listened. She straightened up again. "I think it's beating, but . . ." She shifted and bent her ear toward his nose. Then she bent her head to his chest again and listened for a long moment.

She clambered down from the high bed, shaking her head. "It was beating at first, but faintly. The second time, there was nothing. I think he must be dead. I wonder . . ." She felt beneath his pillow, reaching all the way under it. She straightened and shook her head. "He kept a rosary under his pillows. I noticed when I plumped them up for him. It seems to be gone."

"That doesn't sound nominally Catholic to me." Tom frowned, but he got down on hands and knees to peer underneath the bed. Standing, he said, "You've got good servants, my lady. It isn't even dusty. There's a small chest, like a money box, under the middle, but no strands of beads or crosses or anything up near the head."

"Then it's been taken." Trumpet met Tom's eyes, and they spoke together. "Mr. Bacon."

Tom said, "I'll go. He'll probably send me on to the sheriff. Who would do this? Did he have enemies?"

"How would I know?" Trumpet shrugged. "Those two little cuts wouldn't kill him, but I don't see any other wounds."

"A poison knife," Catalina said. "I have heard of such in Italy. They use venom of serpents to coat the blade. It kills you slowly, but first it turns your limbs to stone."

"Ah, my poor Surdeval!" Trumpet cried. Tom put his arms around her and she looked up at him with sorrow darkening her eyes. "I meant for him to sleep the night through and wake refreshed, to my loving greeting. I meant to give him strong, healthy sons to make him proud."

Tom patted her on the back, at a loss for comforting words. The viscount had been gallant even in his dotage; this was no way for such a man to die.

Trumpet blinked away her tears. "This is my fault. I left him here, drugged and helpless. I even sent away his servants. I did this, Tom. His death is on my head."

"Well do I believe it." A deep voice sounded from the doorway. The viscount's cousin filled the frame, garbed again in formal black. "I suspected you of some dark scheme from the start, Lady Alice. I knew I'd catch you with your henchman if I returned early enough this morning. And here you are, both of you, gloating over my poor cousin's murdered body."

Tom and Trumpet sprang apart as if they'd been pulled by giant hands, but too late. Tom could imagine how things looked from Sir William's point of view: him half-dressed in shirt and hose, with one stocking sliding off his knee; she half-naked in her night robe, barefoot, her long hair hanging down her back in tangled curls.

Sir William strode into the room, drawing his rapier as he walked. He pointed it straight at Tom's heart. He spoke over his shoulder to a servant who had come in behind him. "Find a footman and send for the sheriff. I want these two arrested for murder and taken to the Tower at once."

FIVE

Francis stopped at the edge of Holborn Road to wait for a flock of geese to pass. He wished they could be followed by a pair of sweepers to remove the hazards left by the waddling foul. He shouldn't have worn his new kidskin shoes, but his mother would have noticed and commented on it, forcing him into a conversation about his footwear before a group of ladies and gentlewomen.

He had been peremptorily summoned to attend upon a meeting of the Andromache Society: a sort of widows' guild composed of wealthy, influential women who met for dinner once a month at the Antelope Inn. The proprietress of the inn was Mrs. Jenifer Sprye, herself a widow of not inconsiderable assets. Her establishment on the Holborn Road lay conveniently between Gray's Inn and Lincoln's Inn and had thus become a favorite resort of judges and lawyers, creating a fruitful juxtaposition of clients and counselors.

Francis assumed the widows wanted to consult him about some legal matter. One of the society's principal functions was the monitoring of laws relating to women, particularly with respect to property. Having gained some credit as a legal scholar, as well as being a member of Parliament for the past four years, he had often been invited to deliver addresses to the society. He lectured on Acts of Parliament and discussed interpretations of judgments in the courts.

The ladies appreciated his scholarship, but that wasn't why they invited him rather than some other barrister. His mother and his aunt were founding members of the guild.

He hoped the questions today would be simple and brief. His work on the recusancy commission had exhausted him — spiritually as much as physically — and he had planned to treat himself to a day of light reading on his bed with the windows open to the breeze and a cool jug of spiced beer at his elbow. He'd been working his way through William Camden's *Britannia*, saving it for days like today when he needed some special refreshment.

The Antelope Inn stood three stories tall and spanned the width of three ordinary houses. It could accommodate dozens of guests and offered two private dining rooms upstairs in addition to the public room on the ground floor. The white plaster of the walls shone bright between the weathered oak beams on this sunny morning, as did the sprightly white antelope on the sign hanging over the entrance.

He walked across the graveled yard and climbed the stairs to the gallery. One of his aunt's liveried men stood at the door of the dining room. After being announced, Francis entered to find only half a dozen women seated at the long table instead of the usual twenty. The chair at the foot stood empty, but he did not attempt to sit. If he remained standing, it might encourage them to keep their questions short.

His aunt, Lady Elizabeth Russell, sat at the head of the table as the ranking member. Her late husband had been the eldest son of the second Earl of Bedford. Unfortunately, the son had died before the father, cheating his widow of the title. Nevertheless, she considered herself a dowager countess and insisted on the honors due that rank. Considered a beauty in her youth, at forty-eight her cheeks were still smooth, and her hair beneath the severe white widow's cowl still gleamed a tawny red. Her small, well-shaped lips held a characteristic tension of judgment as yet undelivered.

Lady Anne Bacon, Francis's mother, sat to her right. She greatly resembled her sister — and Francis — in coloring and build, though her features were sharper, especially her eyes, and her hair, like his, held more brown than red. Both women wore black from head to toe, relieved by touches of pristine white at the wrists, throat, and head.

They were two of the five brilliant Cooke sisters, renowned throughout Europe for their intelligence and learning. Their father, Sir Anthony Cooke, had been a tutor to King Edward VI. All the girls had married well. The eldest, Mildred, was wife to Lord Burghley, the queen's Lord Treasurer.

A woman Francis didn't recognize, rather younger than the usual Andromachaean, sat to the left of his aunt. Mrs. Sprye, with writing implements laid out before her, ready to take notes, sat on the other side of the new member. Three women of middling age sat across the table. Their somber dress contrasted starkly against the blue sky outside the windows, where late summer blossoms wagged on green trees behind the inn.

Francis extended his leg in a full court bow, then asked, "How may I serve Your Ladyships?"

"A matter of some urgency has been brought to my attention," Lady Russell said. "I summoned such members as have remained in town during this perilous summer to determine our best course of action. A request has been made specifically for your services, Nephew."

"My services?"

"Sit down, Francis," his mother said. She beckoned to a server standing against the paneled wall. "Have a cool drink after your walk. This may take some time."

Francis handed his hat to the server and took his seat. He made no attempt to speculate as to the nature of the emergency. His aunt regarded anything that touched her personal standing or the status of widows in general as an urgent affair of state.

The server brought him a cup of light Rhenish wine. He took a sip, more to mollify his mother than from thirst. "What services might I perform, my lady?"

Lady Russell lifted a sheet of paper from the table and showed it to him, as if he could read the thing from fifteen feet away. "Have you heard that Viscount Surdeval was found murdered in his bed yesterday morning?"

Francis blinked. "I have not."

"Well, he was. Quite a nasty business. His new bride — now his widow — has been arrested for the deed. She had the presence of mind to pen this letter to Mrs. Sprye before they took her to the Tower. A quick-witted girl. Most commendable." Lady Russell smiled. "She has her father's nerve, it would seem. She made the sheriff's men wait at the door while she wrote, and I have several pages here."

Lady Russell laid the single sheet atop the others, setting her palm firmly upon it. "I will give you the pith of the matter. The new Lady Surdeval was formerly Lady Alice Trumpington, daughter of the Earl of Orford."

Francis knew the name, if not the lady. Her cousin, Allen Trumpington, had been among his pupils at Gray's Inn two years ago and had recommended Benjamin Whitt when the lady found herself in need of legal counsel. Her Ladyship, like Ben's family, lived in Suffolk. Ben had visited her several times over the past year, working on marriage negotiations, planning nuptial contracts, and the like. He hadn't seen any money from it yet, but he had expectations. Francis hadn't spoken to Ben in private for a day or two; his friend had been so busy. Now he knew what had occupied him.

Lady Russell continued. "She and His Lordship were married at Surdeval House on the evening before last. She says she helped settle her husband for a nap after the wedding supper and then returned to her guests. It was an intimate party. The wedding itself had been somewhat hastily arranged, owing to a sudden change in His Lordship's tenuous health."

"He suffered from chronic infections of the throat and lungs," Lady Bacon put in.

"Thank you, Sister." Lady Russell shot her a quelling glance. "The guests consisted of a cousin, Sir William Gumery, and Lady Surdeval's legal counselors, Benjamin Whitt and Thomas Clarady."

Francis snatched his cup and took a hasty sip to cover his reaction to the idea of Tom in the role of legal counselor. Lady Alice would naturally have wanted her counselor to supervise the signing of the marriage contracts after the wedding. Ben, even more awkward in social situations than Francis, would have brought convivial Tom along for moral support.

"Sir William left immediately after the supper," Lady Russell said. "Mr. Whitt left at the same time in order to make copies of the marriage contract, a sensible policy. Lady Surdeval expected him to return within a matter of hours. Mr. Clarady stayed behind to review the properties designated for her jointure while they waited."

"I see." Francis doubted anyone would employ Tom to explain the intricacies of a trust. He could, however, easily imagine a young woman preferring the company of a handsome young man to that of an elderly invalid, even on her wedding night.

Lady Russell regarded him with a cool gaze. "We are assured that nothing untoward transpired. Mr. Whitt was detained and failed to return as expected. The happy couple had given the household leave for the evening so that they might also celebrate the nuptials of their master. Lady Surdeval disliked being alone in that unfamiliar house, so Mr. Clarady waited with her. They were attended at all times by her maidservant. Eventually, she fell asleep.

Mr. Clarady, reluctant to leave her unprotected, took up a station outside her door, spending the night in a chair with a book. In the morning, when they realized that Surdeval had never come to visit his new bride, they feared some accident. They went down to his room and found him dead. Mr. Clarady deduced that he had been murdered, but before they could summon the authorities, Sir William Gumery appeared and leapt to the wrong conclusion. He insisted that Lady Surdeval and Mr. Clarady be arrested and taken to the Tower. She returned to her chamber to dress for the journey and wrote this letter. Mrs. Sprye received it yesterday morning and naturally brought it to me for advice."

Francis took a moment to absorb the information. He could see how things looked from Sir William's perspective: a young bride, an old husband, and a handsome retainer. If he didn't know Tom, he might have made the same assumptions. However, he did know him and knew him well. Whatever might have transpired within the lady's chamber, Tom would never have been party to a murder.

"What led Clarady to suspect an unnatural cause of death?" Francis asked. "My lady mother says Lord Surdeval suffered ill health. Could he not simply have succumbed to excitement and an overly rich supper?"

"We have no details," Lady Russell said. "Obtaining them is part of your job."

An unpaid job, no doubt. "Is it Lord Surdeval's cousin who is pressing the charges?"

"Yes," Lady Russell said. "And with considerable adamancy." She glanced at the other women, who frowned in unison like a silent Greek chorus. "We hear that he disapproved of the match, ostensibly because of the great difference in ages but also, we suspect, because he is next in line for the title and estates and does not want to surrender the widow's third."

"Ah," Francis said. "Then he'll be eager for any excuse to invalidate the marriage. You're asking me to investigate Lord Surdeval's death, but cases involving peers of the realm are a matter for the Star Chamber. I have no legitimate reason to intervene."

"We don't want you to *intervene*, Francis," his mother said. "We want you to find out who did it."

His aunt said, "Lady Surdeval is one of us now. We cannot allow any member of our society to be treated in so peremptory a fashion." She leveled her basilisk glare at him. "You've done this sort of work before, Nephew. Our sister Lady Burghley affirmed that you and this same Thomas Clarady performed similar services for her husband last year."

"Perhaps I should seek permission from my lord uncle before proceeding," Francis said. Lord Burghley and wife had lost their only daughter to fever in June and remained disconsolate. His health had been further strained during the recent crisis to the extent that he refused to grant interviews to anyone for anything less than a national emergency.

"His Lordship told our sister he would be grateful to leave this matter in our hands," Lady Russell said. "He assures us that your work on the recusancy commission does not demand so much of your time as to preclude your assisting Lady Surdeval in her hour of need."

She had neatly forestalled his next objection. In truth, he could not refuse this task. He knew Tom was innocent of murder, if not of indiscretion. And he had to admit his curiosity was aroused. As far as he knew, Viscount Surdeval was a blameless, harmless old man. Who would want him dead?

The women regarded him with eager gleams in their eyes. Francis sighed. Camden's *Britannia* would have to wait. "Very well. I will do my best. The greatest likelihood is that Lord Surdeval died naturally in his sleep and that

Clarady simply mistook the signs. The coroner may already have discovered the error. This affair could be concluded in a matter of days."

"We are agreed to abide by your determination." Lady Russell gave him a knowing smile. "We will consider ourselves in your debt, Nephew."

He returned the smile. His aunt was one of the queen's oldest and dearest friends. That debt would come in handy one day.

He stood and waited while the women filed out of the room. Mrs. Sprye offered him a slice of almond tart and he sat down again to enjoy it with another cup of wine. He had almost finished when his mother and aunt returned. They sat on either side of him before he could rise and turned their faces toward him with bright intent.

"Finish your tart, Francis," his mother said. "And don't eat so fast. I hope that wine isn't too strong."

He had long ago ceased responding to her admonitions about food and drink, but he did chew the last bite of the delicious pastry slowly, observing the arch gleam in the women's eyes with a growing sense of impending peril. The Cooke sisters were renowned, true, but not for their fun-loving antics. His mother's idea of a merry pastime was devising multilingual spelling games based on the Polyglot Bible.

"Did you notice our newest member?" Lady Russell asked.

Francis shook his head. "I was intent on the problem being presented."

"She's very pretty," his mother said. "She has rather a Tudor look about her: fine red hair, pale skin, a proud nose."

"I'm sorry, I didn't notice." A comely *widower* with a Tudor look would have been more likely to catch his eye.

She narrowed her eyes, the playfulness gone. His lack of interest in women disturbed her, but the Cooke sisters were not easily deterred. "Her husband has been gone for many years, although his death was only recently confirmed. She has thus done her grieving and will soon be ready to marry again."

"Now, Mother, I am barely even —"

"You're twenty-seven; she's twenty-three. That's perfect. She has a son, so she's capable. I want a grandson, Francis."

"I have no income to speak of." Francis's mind raced to list impediments. He had no intention of marrying anyone. "I don't even own a house. Where would we live?"

"She's rich," Lady Bacon said. "Very. She has two houses, one in London and another in Exeter. You could sell that one and buy something closer to Gray's Inn, if you liked."

"Her husband was only a merchant," Lady Russell said, "if a successful one. But her mother was the youngest daughter of Baron Yeoford. Your mother and I have examined her antecedents and consider her acceptable."

"We'll introduce you to her next time, when you come to make your report," Lady Russell said. "A matter of days, I believe you said?"

"Ah." Francis grasped at that brittle straw. "I could be wrong. I often am. I have no information whatsoever as yet. Such a complex and mysterious death; it will probably take months to discover what happened."

SIX

Francis waited once again for prisoners to be brought to yet another interrogation room in the Tower. This one also had thick stone walls, a small barred window, and a plank floor dusted with broken straw. The furniture consisted of a long table with two backed chairs and two stools, with a smaller table and stool meant for a clerk next to the wall. These rooms rarely housed prisoners, being needed for questioning suspects. The affairs of England ran at such a pitch these days that they were occupied in that work all day long and sometimes well into the night.

Francis loathed these barren chambers with their echoes of past cruelties. At least this time he wouldn't have to listen to threats of future torments from Sir Richard Topcliffe. Today's prisoners were not recusant Catholics.

The door swung open. Francis rose to make a bow as a guard ushered in Lady Surdeval. She greeted him with a curious smile, then allowed herself to be seated at the table. Another guard brought Tom in, gripping him by the arm. "God's breath, am I glad to see you, Mr. Bacon!" He sat next to Her Ladyship. The guards stationed themselves beside the door.

"Wait outside," Francis told them. "I'll summon you when we're finished."

The instant the door closed, Tom and Lady Surdeval bounced to their feet and turned toward one another, reaching hands to comfort — or embrace? They shot swift glances at Francis and dropped their hands to their sides.

"Are you all right?" Tom looked Her Ladyship up and down as if searching for evidence of distress.

She appeared unharmed, unsurprisingly. No guard would treat a lady harshly. She seemed quite fresh, her green eyes bright, her black hair neatly braided under a clean white coif. Her simple dress of dark red broadcloth was unwrinkled, her ruff and cuffs white and crisp.

"I'm fine." She met Tom's worried gaze with a tender smile. "They've lodged me with the Lieutenant of the Tower and his family." She reached her hand toward him again but snatched it back with another glance at Francis. "How are *you*? Have they hurt you? What happened to your eye?"

"It's nothing." Tom bore a colorful bruise around his left eye. "The constable who arrested me made a rude remark about — ah — the circumstances in which they found us. We had a bit of a scuffle, but no one's bothered me since. I have one cellmate who went back to sleep after learning that they hadn't locked me up for religious reasons. The hospitality has been adequate." He grinned, but his appearance belied his words. Tom considered himself a man of fashion and took pains with his display. That ostentatious yellow pearl still dangled from one ear, but his ruff was missing, as well as several buttons from his doublet. His hose and stockings were grimy. He looked as though he hadn't slept in the two nights since he'd been arrested.

"Do they feed you?" Lady Surdeval's voice held concern. The two of them wholly ignored Francis. When had Tom come to be on such intimate terms with a noblewoman?

"Of course they do. Don't worry about me."

"I can't think of anything else." Lady Surdeval took a step closer to him, standing almost right under his chin. "This is all my fault."

"Please do not say anything of that nature again," Francis said. "Not even to me; not even if it's true."

That got their attention. They shifted a few feet apart. Tom asked, "We won't be in here much longer, will we, Mr. Bacon? You know we had no part in Lord Surdeval's death."

"I assume it," Francis said. "But my word will not suffice. Shall we sit? You must tell me everything you can remember about the events of that evening."

They complied. Lady Surdeval cocked her head, wearing that odd little smile again. Some private amusement sparkled in her vivid green eyes.

Vivid green eyes. Pitch-black hair. Unusual coloring, yet he'd seen it before, composed within an identical heart-shaped face. "Forgive me for staring, my lady," Francis said. "You resemble your cousin Allen as closely as twins."

She giggled, a sound not often heard within the Tower walls. "My cousin and I had many things in common." Her voice altered, dropping into a slightly lower register. The tone and timbre were strikingly like young Allen's.

"In common and in commons." Tom cocked his head at Francis, grinning broadly. "Don't you remember, Mr. Bacon? You looked down upon that face in the hall at Gray's twice a day for the better part of a year."

"A similar face, I grant you," Francis said slowly. He didn't like jokes, especially ones he didn't understand.

Tom turned to Lady Surdeval. "You must tell him."

"I suppose I must." She sighed. "That game is long over, in any event."

Francis said, "I can't help you if you keep secrets from me."

"I know," she said. "I apologize. I fear I must confess that I've deceived you. There is no Allen Trumpington; or rather, the boy you knew as Allen was me." She held two fingers across her upper lip to model a moustache. "Look familiar?"

Francis gaped open-mouthed, speechless, reappraising her face, the shape of her head, and the set of her shoulders while his understanding of the world regained its balance. "Remarkable." The shock subsided to be replaced by a sense of injury. "Did Ben know?"

The two of them grimaced sheepishly. Tom said, "They did share chambers for one term."

With extraordinary delicacy and discretion, it would seem. Francis's estimation of Benjamin Whitt's capacities rose, even under the hurt feelings. "The three of you conspired against me."

"No, no," Lady Surdeval said. "Never against *you*. Not against anyone. I wanted to study the law, that's all. As a woman of property, I must be able to protect myself. I could learn from books at home and engage a tutor, but without the moots and the other evening exercises, you never fully understand it. Practicing cases with real barristers is essential. I wanted all of that."

Allen had been a good student, quick to grasp the essence of a complicated statute or case in court. He could be argumentative, but that was not a defect in a barrister. Francis fully understood the desire to learn. He didn't like to be fooled, but he'd been told by others that he often failed to notice details about the people around him. One took the people one met as they presented themselves. One didn't peer into their doublets or tug at their moustaches.

That thought made him laugh, which surprised them. "I suppose your uncle planned it all." Her uncle, Nathaniel Welbeck, had been a barrister at Gray's until he'd gone too far with his clever schemes and been obliged to make himself scarce.

"My uncle helped," she said. "The plan was mine."

"Admirably executed," Francis conceded. Now he understood part of the intimacy between these two miscreants. They'd been close friends at Gray's, along with Benjamin Whitt, dining together in commons, studying together, attending the same fencing and dancing lessons.

Apparently, the friendship had continued after Her Ladyship's retransformation.

The scope of her deception outdid any of her uncle's extra-legal stunts. She must have nerves of steel. Her courage matched that of her noble ancestors, the Earls of Orford. Francis didn't blame her so much, nor Tom, who had proven his capacity for recklessness. But Ben should have let him in on the conspiracy instead of leaving him to play the fool for three full terms.

"This is not the time to belabor the past," Francis said. "The charges against you are very grave, and Lord Surdeval's cousin is determined to press them."

"He caught us at the worst possible moment," Tom said. "We had barely realized that His Lordship had been murdered —"

Lady Surdeval cut in. "We hadn't even had time to think about what to do when here came Sir William —"

"Looming into the doorway, leaping to all kinds of conclusions," Tom finished.

"I have his statement," Francis said. "He claims you were both in a state of undress and that he caught you embracing beside the viscount's expiring corpus. He further states that Her Ladyship declared her own guilt in unambiguous terms."

Tom shook his head. "We weren't embracing in the sense of *embracing*."

"He was comforting me," Lady Surdeval said. "Patting me on the back. You know."

"And of course Trumpet didn't mean 'I did it' in the literal sense," Tom said.

"I only meant that I was the one who left poor Surdeval in such a vulnerable situation. I gave him his sleeping draught and galloped off to my rooms on the other side of the house. I even gave the servants the night off, never thinking he shouldn't be left unattended."

"Tell me about the circumstances in which you found him," Francis said. "Neither your letter to Mrs. Sprye nor Sir William's statement has much to say about the manner of death."

"What letter?" Tom asked.

"I wrote to Mrs. Sprye when they took me upstairs to dress." Lady Surdeval turned toward Tom. "You should know what I wrote so we can both tell the same story."

"*Truth*," Francis said. "You must both tell the truth, if you're innocent."

"Of course we're innocent!" Tom said. Then he shot a conspiratorial glance at Lady Surdeval that contradicted his indignant tone.

Francis set his elbow on the table and pinched the bridge of his nose. He might be able to defend them from the charge of murder, but few things angered the queen more than dalliance with a noble virgin. She might clap them both in the Tower for a year if they didn't moderate their behavior before she heard the whole sordid tale.

One crime at a time. "Why did you decide His Lordship had been murdered?"

Tom said, "Someone cut a cross in his chest."

Francis frowned. "I don't understand."

"We don't either," Tom said. "But he had a small cross, right here." He made an X in the center of his chest. "The lines were ragged, maybe a coarse knife? With a blackish residue along the edges. Also little beads of blood, bright red. We didn't think he was dead at first."

"He wasn't," Lady Surdeval said. "I will swear to it. I put my ear next to his face and thought I heard a faint breath. I'm certain I heard a heartbeat when I pressed my ear against his chest. But he didn't move, not a twitch, not even when I touched his face."

"He was laid out properly too," Tom said. "Hands at his sides, feet together, with a sheet pulled up to his chin."

Lady Surdeval added, "When I pulled it back, Tom noticed impressions in the mattress next to the body, like someone had knelt over him."

"To make the cuts, I suppose." Francis shuddered. "Did you see anything unusual in the room? Signs of entry?"

They shook their heads. Lady Surdeval said, "The room looked the way it had when I left it the night before. My lord still wore the same shirt and hose. His doublet lay where I had put it; his medicines still stood on the night table. Nothing seemed out of place."

"No additional cups or bottles?"

She shook her head. "Only one thing was missing that I know of. Surdeval kept a rosary under his pillow; at least it was there when I settled him for his nap. Ebony and ivory with a gold cross."

"A rosary," Francis echoed. That formed a piece with the cross carved into his chest — a disturbing piece. "Nothing else missing? Any signs of a struggle or vomiting?"

They shook their heads again. Tom said, "His stockings were twisted, as if he'd kicked around a little, but otherwise, no."

"Hmm." Francis frowned. "There are poisons that cause paralysis, like wolfsbane, but I don't think they work so quickly. I would expect more mess."

Lady Surdeval said, "My maidservant lived in Italy for many years. She says they use serpent venom to poison knives. She thinks that venom could cause paralysis and a slow death."

Francis said, "The fact that your servant knows such things speaks against your innocence."

"We know it looks bad," Tom said. "Especially with me being there. I should have gone home right after —"

"I explained all that in my letter." Lady Surdeval smiled at Francis. "It made sense, didn't it, Mr. Bacon? My story?"

"Not to me. Even less, now that I know about your year-long masquerade. And please do not refer to it as a 'story.'" He caught their eyes in turn, striving to impress the need for absolute truthfulness with the seriousness of his demeanor. "Your explanation of Tom's presence is patchy at best. No one would believe it."

Although his aunt and mother, two women of prodigious intelligence, seemed to have done so. Could they have charged him with this indelicate case as an excuse to present him to their rich widow, the young woman with the Tudor air? Or were they so zealous in their defense of widows they would overlook the possibility of a marriage begun in cuckoldry?

Francis rubbed his temple; his head was beginning to throb. "Why did Tom stay all night? I must know the truth in order to help you. What you say to me will go no further."

They both spoke at once, their stories crossing and twining. One contradicted the other, then both backtracked to try a different approach. They were obviously inventing their tale as they went along. Worse, their tones, their postures, every little gesture, betrayed the very intimacy that formed the foundation of the charge against them.

Francis had hoped . . . he couldn't remember what he had hoped. He had expected, naively, that Lady Surdeval would be a somber, sober-minded widow of learning and discretion, like his mother and his aunt. The rash, ingenious madcap seated across the table from him now bore less resemblance to his respectable relatives than the erstwhile Allen Trumpington.

He had vaguely imagined that the lady would supply a fact or easily verified supposition that would clear her name and Tom's with minimal contributions from him. That hope now crumbled under the weight of their increasingly implausible protestations of innocence. They had most certainly not murdered the viscount, but their night together had been far from innocent. That suspicion alone would harm them both in ways they plainly did not understand.

Francis would have to start at the beginning and conduct a full inquiry. He'd have to visit Surdeval House to question the servants and poke his nose into the bed chamber. He would probably have to go into the city to consult the coroner and the sheriff. Somehow he'd have to discover the actual means of the murder and expose anyone who might benefit from the viscount's death.

He eyed his unwanted charges across the table, no longer bothering to listen to their nonsense. If he could get them released, he could at least make them do some of the work.

SEVEN

Francis brought a book with him to dinner at Gray's Inn that day to deflect the attentions of his messmates, if any should be offered, but he was left to think in peace. Reading at table was considered unsociable, but since he'd been promoted to the benchers' table at the top of the hall, no one seemed to care. The other benchers — the governors of the society — liked to rattle on about political intrigues or similar gossip and seldom asked for his opinions.

He had to shift the book as the servers delivered dishes of eels in jelly and baked eggs. His gaze shifted then as well, to the lower tables set perpendicular to the dais where the students and barristers ate. Ben sat in his accustomed seat at the top of his table, eyes on his plate, eating without interest in the food before him. Two years ago, Ben had had three messmates, all good friends: Tom, Allen, and the earl's son in whose train Tom had first arrived at Gray's. The young lord had found other games to play, and Tom had gone to Cambridge on his special commission, leaving only Ben and Allen. Then Allen had gone home to turn back into Alice.

Francis found it difficult to believe he had sat here for so many months watching that deceptive imp participating in the after-supper legal exercises without once suspecting he was anything other than what he seemed. He cautioned himself to be wary in future dealings with Lady Alice and to look twice when next he met a short person with bright green eyes.

Tom had returned from his Cambridge commission, taking up his old place in Ben's chambers and his seat across the table in commons, and so they had remained for the whole past year. They made a balanced pair. Scholarly Ben kept Tom's nose to the grindstone, while lively Tom got Ben out of doors to exercise the physical being.

Now Tom lay in prison and poor Ben sat alone, worrying, no doubt, about how the Surdeval business would affect his chances of being called to the bar in December. Lady Surdeval was his first important client. He'd been so proud of the work he'd done to negotiate a marriage settlement that satisfied all parties. This scandal threatened to destroy his achievement.

Further reason to solve the knotty problem as quickly as could be. Francis spooned eggs into his mouth and turned his thoughts in a more productive direction.

Assuming Tom's observations were correct, and he had trained the man himself, the murder had been committed by a curious blend of opaque and obvious means. If the murderer possessed a poison subtle enough to kill a man swiftly and silently, why advertise the deed by cutting an inflammatory symbol into his chest? Why not make a small incision in the bottom of the foot, for example, where it might go unnoticed or be attributed to some other cause?

Who benefited from the death of Lord Surdeval?

Not Lady Surdeval. That made no sense. A clever woman — and she'd amply demonstrated that quality — would wait a few months and be certain the marriage had been duly consummated. Whatever else had happened that night, Trumpet had apparently spent little time alone with her husband. The marriage would be invalidated, and she would lose her jointure. She should fight for it, of course. Ben could use the fees.

The Andromache Society had charged him with finding out enough to clear Lady Surdeval's name. Francis could think of no way of fulfilling that requirement without identifying the real murderer. Only that story would be exciting enough to supplant rumors about the young bride and her so-called legal counsel dallying through the wedding night while the groom lay dying in his bed. Gossip along those lines must have flown up the Strand before the constables had even handed Tom and Trumpet into the wherry for their trip down the river.

Francis helped himself to a serving of eels. The jelly had been barely seasoned; just the thing for his delicate stomach. This business would do his digestion no good. Especially discomfiting were the signs of a religious motivation for the murder. Or an attempt to suggest such a motivation?

More deviousness; excessive if the intention was to implicate the bride. What reason could she have to cut a cross in her husband's chest or steal his rosary? If she hated Catholics so much, she wouldn't have married the man.

His Lordship's death benefited Sir William Gumery more than anyone else. Always look to the heir. Francis had never met him nor heard anything unfavorable. Ben must know about the entailments of the title and estates; he could review Lord Surdeval's financial records to see if any other motives popped up. Perhaps His Lordship had cheated someone badly enough to inspire a vicious revenge. The religious business could simply be a ruse.

He'd have a word with Ben right after dinner and get him started. Francis would visit the viscount's home himself to speak with the steward.

* * *

The servant who admitted Francis to Surdeval House had either been trained not to answer questions or had arrived at that strategy on his own initiative. He merely shrugged his eyebrows when Francis commented on the

55

commotion emanating from the rear of the house, which sounded like furniture being roughly moved. When Francis tried to engage him in conversation about the night of the wedding, the man listened in courteous silence, then bade him wait and went to summon the steward. Tom would probably have elicited the life histories of everyone in the house, a gift Francis lacked.

The steward was a youngish man with glossy fair hair and a short beard circling his jawline. He wore black, but his extravagant taste countered any suggestion of mourning. His over-puffed sleeves larded with braids and his thickly padded doublet made him look as if he'd been baked, not dressed.

"Mr. Bacon of Gray's Inn." His eyes lingered on the velvet tufts on the shoulders of Francis's legal gown, the symbols of his status as a bencher. "To what do we owe the honor?"

"My lord uncle — Lord Burghley — asked me to inquire into Lord Surdeval's death. The strange nature of the crime, the distress of the young Lady Surdeval, and the putative involvement of a member of Gray's Inn brought the matter to his attention."

"Someone ought to make inquiries. This is the most appalling thing to happen in all my years of service. I suppose what you want is support for Sir William's testimony. I'll admit it's distasteful to prosecute a young lady such as her —" He broke off with a sour twist to his mouth. "Justice must be served."

"Indeed it must," Francis said. "May I see the room in which Lord Surdeval was found?"

The steward led him to a spacious and handsomely furnished library, an enviable place in which to read and study except for the bedstead positioned at one end. The wide bed had been stripped of linens and its curtains removed.

Francis surveyed the room, noting the tall windows looking onto a small garden. If they had been open, they would have granted easy access to anyone who got inside the walls. "Has anything been altered in this room since the night of the murder?"

The steward shook his head. "I had the bedding removed, naturally. And His Lordship's clothes, which were there on that chest. The windows were open, I'm told."

"You weren't here that night?"

"I was at the Surrey estate, on the course of my regular rounds."

"You didn't attend the wedding?"

"I didn't even *know* about it until afterward." The steward's lip curled under his fringe of moustache. "They — or rather, *she* — arranged everything in a rush. *Secretly.* I suppose her lawyers got the contract done up the way she wanted, and she needed to get it done before anyone changed their minds. The very haste smacks of impropriety, if you ask me."

Francis agreed, though he wouldn't say it. The circumstances implicated Lady Surdeval as surely as if they had been designed to do so.

Now there was a twist. Could she be a target as well as the viscount?

He dismissed the idea almost at once. Whatever wealth Trumpet possessed would go straight to her father, who would gamble it away in a month, if he had earned his reputation. Francis smiled, striving to emulate Tom's confiding manner. "I gather you didn't approve of the match."

The steward sniffed. "It's hardly my place to approve or disapprove. I thought the thing was overly hasty, that's all."

So much for the friendly approach. "My understanding is that His Lordship needed an heir after losing his son to the Spanish."

"His Lordship had an heir: his cousin, Sir William. An *exemplary* master. Sir William is a forward-thinking man. His estates are *thriving*. Lord Surdeval could not have chosen a better man to carry the family line forward. Far to be preferred to that — to *Her Ladyship*."

Sir William had an ardent ally in the household, and Trumpet had an enemy. That in itself was worth knowing.

"Have you heard from the coroner?" Francis asked.

"Yes," the steward said. "He had little to contribute. He ruled it a death by unknown causes."

"Did they find no injuries other than the cuts on the chest?"

The steward shrugged, his whole stiff costume rising and falling with the motion. "Not that I know of."

"Was there evidence of sickness? At the risk of seeming indelicate, did the servants find vomit on the bedclothes or the floor?"

"None." The steward's nose wrinkled. "And I know what you're asking: Were there signs he'd been poisoned? I thought of that, of course, first thing, since Her Ladyship admits to giving my lord his sleeping draught." He flapped his hand at the night table, still covered with the detritus of an invalid: small bottles, cups, and handkerchiefs. "I tested the remains of the medicine on a dog. The beast slept for ten hours but was otherwise unharmed."

"Well done." A vital element in Trumpet's defense, made more effective by being produced by this hostile witness. "I noticed a stir at the back of the house as I came in. Surely nothing is being removed while the situation remains undecided?"

"Of course not. I know my duty. It appears the chapel has been robbed in my absence."

"Appears?"

The steward pursed his lips. He didn't want to say it, but some essential honesty — or the Lord Treasurer's authoritative shadow — compelled him. "All the valuables are missing."

"What manner of valuables?"

"Oh, many things. Lovely things. Jeweled crosses, embroidered altar cloths, a very old reliquary. Her late Ladyship — the viscount's second wife — was devout." He lowered his voice to a whisper. "*Catholic.*" Then he placed his hand on his padded chest. "I am a committed Protestant, Mr. Bacon, I assure you. I attend the nearest church without fail every Sunday, wherever I find myself in the course of my duties."

"I don't doubt it. When did this happen?"

"On the same night His Lordship was murdered."

"The same night!" Francis frowned. More criminals wandering about in this supposedly empty house? "Where is the chapel?"

"On the other side of the house, behind the hall. Rather isolated. We might not have heard the burglars even if we had been home."

"Who could have known the house would be empty?"

The steward shrugged. "Most of the servants went straight to the Dog and Duck to spend their wedding largesse. Any rats who happened in that night would learn the cats were away."

"Was the gatehouse left unguarded?"

"No," the steward said. "Her Ladyship had that much sense. The chapel treasures must have been taken away by boat, but they'd need a key to open the gate." He plainly believed the bride had supplied that key.

"Was anything else stolen?" Francis looked around the room, noting a silk tapestry, silver candlesticks, and dozens of leather-bound books. Hundreds of pounds' worth of goods had been left behind. "Was anything taken from any other rooms?"

"Nothing at all." The steward poked a finger under his heavily starched ruff to scratch his neck. "Which is odd, when you think of it. The Surdevals are a very old family. This house is full of treasures." He sounded as proud as if the lineage were his own. Perhaps it was; stewards were often recruited from the cadet branches.

"It is odd. And oddities demand explanation. Why, for example, would Lady Surdeval steal from her own chapel? The family treasures are hers now."

The steward glared at Francis through narrowed eyes and licked his lips a time or two. "I can think of no reason."

Francis smiled. "Neither can I."

* * *

Francis stood outside the gates of Surdeval House in the shelter of the wall bordering the Strand, so lost in thought he barely heard the bustle of the busy street. Surdeval's chapel had been stripped of centuries of religious treasures. On the same night, the lord had been killed, his rosary stolen, and a cross carved into his chest.

"Mr. Bacon?"

The two deeds could not be unrelated; Occam's Razor would not allow it. Given two competing hypotheses, the one with the fewest assumptions was most likely to be correct. The simplest explanation here required that the same person or persons had executed both crimes.

"Mr. Bacon? Are you all right?"

Francis startled and focused his eyes on the world in front of him, only to find the Earl of Essex sitting in a painted coach, speaking to him through a small window in the door.

"My lord!" Francis bowed from the waist.

"I'm sorry to disturb you," His Lordship said, gracious as always. "You are clearly absorbed in some deep thought.

But I feared the traffic might not respect the demands of the intellect."

Before Francis could formulate a reply, the earl added, "Allow me to offer you sanctuary." He unlatched the door of his coach and slid to the far side of the seat.

How could anyone refuse so a noble a gesture? Francis climbed up and sat beside him. "Thank you, my lord."

"May I ask what captured your attention so completely? I notice you were standing at the threshold of my recently deceased neighbor, Lord Surdeval. Dare I presume you were making inquiries into his death?"

"I would believe Your Lordship to be a reader of minds did I not already know you to be both observant and swift of apprehension. Yes, my lord, I have been asked to look into the matter of Lord Surdeval's murder."

"So the rumors are true."

The stepson of the Earl of Leicester, Essex was the rising favorite of the queen. Not replacing Sir Walter Ralegh, for better or worse, but adding his youthful zest to court society. Not yet twenty-three years old, he had already become fully engaged in the business of government. Lesser scions of the nobility might idle their days away in frivolous amusements, but this brilliant man had more serious ambitions. He had learned some discretion as well; he'd demonstrated that quality at court more than once.

Perhaps he was the confidante Francis needed at this moment. "I wonder if I might enlist Your Lordship's aid, if only briefly, to help me think through what I have learned from the steward of Surdeval House."

"By all means." The earl rapped on the front wall to signal the coachman to drive on. He turned toward Francis, hands on his knees, his brown eyes alive with interest. "Your solution of the murders at Gray's Inn impressed everyone at court. In truth, I would love to learn more about your methods, Mr. Bacon. My first question is: Why do you believe Surdeval was murdered?"

Francis summarized the story Tom and Trumpet had told him of finding the viscount in his bed, heart beating faintly but unable to move. He skipped over their reasons for being together at that hour.

A smile flickered across the earl's lips, but he didn't interrupt. Then the expressive lips twisted in distaste on hearing about the cross carved in the old man's chest. "Who would do such a foul thing?"

"That is the essential question, my lord. Who — and why."

The earl said, "Rumor has it that Lady Alice, or Lady Surdeval, I suppose, did the deed. I don't know her well; she hasn't spent much time at court. Her father approached me about a match, but his terms were unacceptable. Orford thinks his title is a sufficient portion, but my sons will be earls on my own account." He held a hand to his mouth, pretending to whisper. "I need a wife with money."

Francis chuckled. "Such matters are multifaceted, are they not, my lord?"

Essex grinned with a roguish air that made Francis's heart skip a beat. "She is pretty and well educated, for a girl. But my impression is that if Lady Alice wanted to kill a man, she would stick a knife in his chest, not poison his sleeping draught. I can't imagine her — or anyone — kneeling over the victim to cut a cross in his chest. I find that aspect very odd."

"Exactly the word I used, my lord. *Odd.* Unnecessary, if the viscount's death were the only goal."

"I believe I understand you."

They fell silent, allowing the sounds of the street to invade the silk-lined sanctuary. The coach squeaked and rattled as it rocked up the street. People shouted at each other and at their animals; the animals added their distinctive cries. All part of the ceaseless rumble of London.

Francis had no idea where they were going and didn't care. He had never before sat in such close proximity to this potent and engaging man. He found the experience exhilarating. The earl's much-lauded beauty — his fine features and curling red-brown hair — could be observed from a distance, but close like this — thighs touching, shoulders meeting at every jolt, hands a mere hand's-width apart — one could feel the heat of the man's body, a palpable emanation of strength and youthful vigor.

The earl broke the silence. "A cross is a symbol, the symbol of the Christian religion as a whole. But Catholics make the sign of the cross over their breasts as part of their regular ritual, as I understand it."

"A valuable insight, my lord. That symbol might be the most salient feature. Although the cuts may have been the means of delivering the cause of death."

"You said they were shallow. Could the killer have used a poisoned blade?"

"The paralysis suggests a poison. The cuts suggest a poisoned blade, especially since the witnesses saw no other signs of distress, and the sleeping draught was tested and found harmless."

"Some type of arrow poison, I'll wager." The earl wagged his finger in no particular direction. "The savages of the New World and Africa use such things. You might search the less reputable apothecaries and pick up a hint there."

"An excellent suggestion, my lord!" The coach lurched sharply to the right, throwing Francis against the earl. He struggled to right himself without leaning on the noble person. "I beg your pardon, my lord." Embarrassed, Francis turned his face to the window while he recovered his composure. His wits were so rattled by the earl's civet perfume he didn't even recognize the street. He cleared his throat again. "There is another oddity, my lord, if I may continue."

"I insist on hearing everything." The earl smiled to soften the command. "I assure you, Mr. Bacon, that nothing you tell me about your investigation will go further than this coach."

"Your Lordship's discretion is beyond question." Francis told him about the robbery of the chapel.

"On the same night? The two crimes cannot be unrelated."

"I agree, my lord, although it is possible. Coincidences do occur, although they must always be regarded with suspicion. Most of the servants spent the better part of the night at a nearby tavern. It is possible that two criminals, intent on separate crimes, heard them celebrating. Realizing the house must be empty, each went forth to commit his particular deed."

"The people at the tavern should be questioned," Essex said.

"So they should, my lord." Another reason to get Tom out of the Tower as soon as possible. He would get more information from tavern wenches than Francis ever could.

Essex asked, "Nothing else was taken?"

"Only the rosary beneath His Lordship's pillow."

"I've been inside Surdeval House. That library alone is worth a small fortune."

They fell silent again, then spoke up at the same time, breaking off with a laugh. How easy this man's company was! An easy, intellectual accord.

Essex asked, "Who would steal only Catholic impedimenta?"

"My question exactly, my lord. Who? And again, why?"

"That's easy," Essex answered. "To sell it. Although it would be difficult to dispose of in England at present."

"Far more difficult than the books, which suggests that money was not the main objective."

"The chapel and the cross connect the two crimes," Essex said. "The underlying theme must thus be religion."

"I'm sure you are correct, my lord. Lord Surdeval was a Catholic."

Essex made a dismissive noise. "More by tradition than conviction. The queen considered him a loyal subject."

"Yet his late wife was devout. She furnished and maintained a Catholic chapel. She might even have kept a priest or helped one move through London."

Essex frowned. "An act of treason. Could our thieving murderer be a patriot?"

"If so, my lord, would we be able to convict him given the temper of the times?"

The coach stopped. Essex tilted his head toward the door. "Here we are."

"Oh!" Francis opened the door and climbed out. He held the door while the earl descended, then closed it behind him.

"I found this discussion most stimulating. I trust you'll keep me abreast of developments."

"I would be honored to do so, my lord." Francis bowed deeply. When he righted himself, he saw the earl moving toward a crowd gathered in front of a tall building. He blinked at the sunlight as he looked around, trying to orient himself. The tall building was the Curtain Theater. He was standing in Shoreditch, outside the northern wall of the city.

Francis sighed and began the long walk west, back to Gray's Inn.

EIGHT

The din of women's voices shrilled in Trumpet's ears. She'd been longing to become a member of the Andromache Society ever since she'd first learned about it. She'd looked forward to the monthly meetings in the stately dining room at the Antelope Inn, sitting alongside influential women like Lady Russell, listening to learned men of the law present illuminating cases for them to discuss. She hadn't expected it to come about so soon or in so brutal a fashion, and she had not anticipated this chaotic clamor.

This was her introduction to the guild and her first outing since she'd regained her freedom. Once Mr. Bacon had learned about the theft of the chapel goods, he'd persuaded the Privy Council of the absurdity of her stealing her own possessions. Arguing that the murder and burglary must be connected, he'd convinced them to release her into the care of her maternal aunt, Lady Chadwick, who had a house in Bishopsgate.

Tom had been shifted to Newgate, still under suspicion for murder. The chapel burglary added another motive for him. The injustice grated, but Ben had persuaded Trumpet to hold her peace. All she could achieve by pleading for Tom would be to confirm the rumors about their alleged affair. She'd have to find a way to make it up to him later.

A burst of high-pitched laughter pierced right through her skull. She winced, but she'd have to get used to it. She'd spent most of the past year at Orford Castle on the coast of Suffolk with only Catalina for company. She'd joined the court late in May, but those three months had not been enough to accustom her to the company of women. She preferred the tenor rumble of men during dinner at Gray's Inn, where she could argue with Tom about fencing or with Ben about forms of action.

At least the food at the Antelope Inn was always good. Mrs. Sprye had an exceptional cook. Once Mr. Bacon sorted out the current crisis and she obtained her jointure from the Surdeval estate, Trumpet could establish her own household in London with her own exceptional cook and fill her table with interesting men.

One step at a time, as long as each step moved her forward.

She spooned up the last of her compote and eyed the remainder in the serving dish. "Would you care for more raspberries?" she asked her tablemate courteously. As expected, the woman smiled and passed the dish to Trumpet. She scooped it all onto her own plate, along with the last piece of cobnut cake.

The gentlewomen of the Andromache Society ate next to nothing. But now that Trumpet was at large in her aunt's unfettered household, she could hire a dancing master and ride as much as she pleased. She needed the nourishment.

"It's good to see you have a healthy appetite," her tablemate said, "considering the ordeal you've been through. The Tower must have been horrifying."

"Mmm," Trumpet said through a mouthful of cake. She swallowed and added, "Not at all. They treated me with every kindness."

"Even so." The woman glanced toward the top of the table where the senior widows sat and lowered her voice. "You wouldn't have been able to practice your own religion."

"I don't have my own religion. What an odd notion! I attend my parish church or my aunt's. And I assure you, the Lieutenant of the Tower requires his household to pray together every morning and every night. I've practiced enough religion in the past few days to last me a month."

The woman frowned, a puzzled look on her pretty face. She made a portrait in pink with her pale red hair and a rosy blush on her white cheeks. "Aren't you a Catholic?"

"*What?* Me? Of course not. Why would you think such a thing?"

"But your husband, the late Lord Surdeval . . ."

"Oh, him!" Trumpet flapped her hand. "I suppose Surdeval may have done something a trifle Catholic once or twice, but he was hardly devout. Which never had anything to do with me."

"You astonish me."

So easily as that? Trumpet shrugged and returned to polishing off the compote, surreptitiously licking the bottom of her spoon, wishing for more. She settled for a gulp of wine and returned her attention to her tablemate. "We were introduced when we sat down, but there were so many names . . ."

"Too many at once," the woman said. "I'm Mrs. Palmer. Sarah. My late husband was a merchant in the Spanish Company. The Spanish took him prisoner two years ago. This spring, I learned that he died in their tender care."

"I'm so sorry." Trumpet wished she had something less conventional to offer in sympathy. The widows introduced themselves in terms of their late husbands' deaths, so one was obliged to murmur the same nothings over and over. "Were you married long?"

"Six wonderful years," Mrs. Palmer said. "Thanks be to God, I have a son, five years old, named Arthur for his father."

"He must be a comfort to you."

"Such comfort as can be." Mrs. Palmer smiled sadly at the tablecloth. Her sad smile was even more appealing than her friendly one. Her blue eyes held a hint of green, accented by the translucent blue stones strung across her linen partlet.

Young, pretty, and rich, with an assortment of attractive smiles. Trumpet vowed to make sure Tom never met her. "That's an unusual necklace. What are those stones, if I may ask?"

Mrs. Palmer touched the piece with shapely fingers. "They're opals from Peru, a region in the New World. My husband bought them in Spain."

A little bell rang, wielded by Lady Russell at the head of the table. The clamor of voices fell by half. She rang it again and got full silence. "Ladies and gentlewomen, it is time for the meeting to begin."

Servants cleared the table of dishes, withdrawing the soiled cloth and refilling cups on request. Trumpet was among the requesters.

Lady Russell waited until the servants left. She bent her commanding gaze left and right, gathering the attention of the dozen or so women seated around the long table. "I would like to start by welcoming our newest member, Alice Gumery, Lady Surdeval. She comes to us by recommendation of her aunt."

Trumpet blinked at the new surname. She hadn't thought about how dreadful it would sound. She should have added a pleasing name to her list of *desiderata*.

A round of excited murmurs arose, forcing Lady Russell to ring her bell again. "Ladies and gentlewomen, desist!" When they quieted, she said, "We will have no discussion of the unfounded rumors concerning Lady Surdeval's putative involvement in the mysterious death of Lord Surdeval. None whatsoever. The position of the Andromache Society shall be that her Ladyship is unqualifiedly innocent. We have engaged my nephew, Francis Bacon, to pursue the murderer and have every confidence in his abilities. Meanwhile, Her Ladyship now faces a battle for her property on two fronts. First, Lord

Surdeval's cousin, Sir William Gumery, is suing to have the marriage annulled."

Trumpet hadn't heard that. "How dare he? How can a third party sue to annul a lawfully executed marriage?"

"That is one of the questions that must be answered," Lady Russell said. "While the suit is a disagreeable inconvenience for you, it will afford our society an opportunity to study a rarely tested aspect of marriage law."

"I'm honored to be of service," Trumpet said, earning a wry glance from her tablemate. Mrs. Palmer had a sense of humor — and sharp ears.

"We will support you at every turn," Lady Russell said. "We cannot allow our marriages to be challenged in order to gain control of our estates. This is an extreme case — Lord Surdeval was murdered on his wedding night — but the precedent must not be set. How many nights must transpire for a marriage to be considered valid? We must draw the line here, and we must draw it now. I recommend you obtain the best possible legal counsel, Lady Surdeval."

"I have a counselor, Benjamin Whitt, a gentleman of Gray's Inn and a close friend of your nephew." She herself would act as his unofficial clerk. Where should they start searching for supporting cases? Marriage law was a matter for the church courts . . .

Lady Russell said, "The annulment suit strikes at the heart; the second attack pecks at your flank. Since your late husband was a recusant Catholic, the Privy Council may legally confiscate two-thirds of your jointure on the assumption that the wife shares her husband's religious views and would spend her wealth to promote those proscribed beliefs."

Two-thirds! That would leave her with next to nothing. The jointure, also known as the widow's third, consisted of properties meant to maintain the widow in a comfortable style after her husband's death, even if another heir should claim the bulk of the estate. Ben had helped her ensure that her jointure consisted of profitable farms and manors.

One-third of the Surdeval estate seemed little enough to ask. Reduce that by two further thirds and she'd have barely enough to pay her dressmaker. Her paltry leavings would never include the house on the Strand with river access, so convenient to Gray's Inn. Her dream of establishing herself as a leading patroness of the arts would wither before it formed a single bud.

Did Ben know about this perverse law? He must. But then, they hadn't expected her to be made a widow so soon. They'd assumed there would be time to secure her properties and even expand them while Surdeval was still alive to provide a legal shield.

Lady Russell rang her bell. "The Council may choose not to take such action in this case, but it is a risk. Surdeval's first wives were ardent in their practice of the old religion. Everyone knows religion passes from mother to child. I understand some members of Lady Surdeval's maternal family skate close to the edge of recusancy. That leaves her exposed to criticism, which gives the Council greater license."

Mrs. Palmer leaned toward Trumpet to whisper, "Twice tainted. You should have married a Protestant to purge your mother's stain, like I did."

Trumpet bristled at the slur to her mother. Before she could respond, her aunt spoke up in ringing tones. "Only my younger brother has ever been so considered and only by ill-wishers. The rest of the family is blameless. My late sister, Lady Surdeval's mother, faithfully attended her parish church at her husband's side throughout her marriage."

A few of the senior women cleared their throats or reached for their cups at that small untruth. Lord Orford attended church at his convenience, not his wife's — or the queen's.

Someone asked, "Yet is it not true that Lady Surdeval's grandmother was a Catholic?"

Trumpet sputtered. "Everyone's grandmother was a Catholic!"

Even Lady Russell smiled at that. She took a sip from her cup, then rang her bell. "Let us restrict our concerns to the present generation. Isn't Lady Surdeval's uncle the same Nathaniel Welbeck implicated in a wrongful death at Gray's Inn two years ago?"

"A conjunction of occurrences that led to no charges," Lady Chadwick said. "He remains a member of Gray's in good standing, although he now resides in Exeter."

"Nevertheless, the rumor of old scandal could rise like a specter to haunt Lady Surdeval's proceedings." Lady Russell rested her gaze on Trumpet. "We stand beside you, Madame. The protection of widows' rights is the foundation of the Andromache Society. Do you have any questions for us?"

"I do, my lady," Trumpet said. "My first concern is for my counselor's assistant, Mr. Clarady. He remains imprisoned merely for having been present in the house on the morning in question. He is blameless in every respect. I protest this injustice and beg you to use whatever influence you may have to obtain his immediate release."

Lady Russell frowned. "The criminal case is beyond our scope. We concern ourselves with questions of equity, wills, and other instruments for the conveyance of property before, during, and after a marriage. If he is innocent, I'm sure Mr. Bacon will secure his release in due course."

Trumpet recognized a brick wall when she ran into one. She'd have to find another way to help Tom. Perhaps her aunt knew someone who knew someone . . .

Lady Russell regarded her with a cool smile. "Your behavior must be beyond reproach, Lady Surdeval. I advise you to leave the criminal matters in my nephew's hands.

Now. Recognizing that the state of widowhood has its complexities, we have established a tradition of appointing each new member a mentor, always the next-to-last widow admitted into our society."

"Thank you, my lady." Trumpet looked around the table and added, "Thank you, all. I am proud to be a member of so learned and gracious a society."

Lady Russell nodded. "Your guide is Mrs. Sarah Palmer, who should be especially helpful since she is presently pursuing a case through Chancery concerning her late husband's estate."

Mrs. Palmer said, "I am happy to offer Lady Surdeval whatever assistance I can."

Lady Russell turned to answer some question from the woman on her left. Mrs. Palmer whispered to Trumpet, "I believe I know your uncle. Mr. Welbeck advised me on the sale of my mother's house in Exeter last spring."

"Did he?" Trumpet's uncle was a clever man, sometimes too clever for his own good. He loved intrigue and had enjoyed helping her deceive the men at Gray's. He preferred tricky cases with dramatic histories, but wills and widows were meat and drink for any lawyer.

"He's very handsome, isn't he?" Mrs. Palmer's whisper held a certain tremor that made Trumpet turn to face her with full interest.

"Some women think so." A rich wife could help curtail her uncle's taste for risky adventures. Trumpet hadn't seen him since he'd slunk out of Gray's in the dead of night two years ago, but he wrote to her from Devonshire now and then. Another benefit — if Uncle Nat married Mrs. Palmer, the pretty widow would be out of Tom's reach.

Then Trumpet could befriend her without strife. She would need respectable female friends in her new life as an independent widow in her own London house, especially ones whose respectability was flexible enough to include Nathaniel Welbeck in their circle.

Lady Russell cleared her throat, drawing Trumpet's attention back to the group. "Did you have any other questions, Lady Surdeval?"

"Just one," Trumpet said. "What grounds can Sir William put forward for annulling my marriage? I must prepare my defense."

"There is nothing to prepare. Since the queen approved the match and you are past the age of consent, the most probable grounds would be a failure to consummate the marriage. The court will order your condition to be examined by eight matrons of good repute."

"*Eight?*" Trumpet's mind boggled. Eight women were going to lay her on a table, hoist up her skirts, and discover whether or not she remained *virgo intacta*?

If she wanted that house on the Strand, she needed to get rid of that pesky maidenhead before another fortnight passed.

NINE

"How long do you plan to keep me in here?" Tom folded his arms across his chest, his glare as stony as the wall behind his back. He and Ben stood waiting for his cell to be made somewhat more habitable.

Ben hung his head like a scolded hound. "We're doing everything we can. At least we kept you out of the basement and got you into a cell up here, where there's a breath of air."

"Foul Newgate air." Tom spat into the filthy straw. "They brought me here in a cart, Ben! In broad daylight, right down the middle of Cheapside. People stood and shouted. They threw things at me, the idle varlets."

"I am sorry."

"You could have told me what Trumpet was up to." Tom knew he was being unfair, but his real targets — Trumpet and Mr. Bacon — weren't here. "A warning would have been helpful."

Now Ben had the guilty look of a hound caught with your gloves in its mouth. "She made me promise not to say anything."

"And heaven forbid that Lady Surdeval's wishes not be respected in every detail."

"That's not fair. Frankly, Tom, I expected you to turn her down and come straight home. You should never have spent the night in her room."

"I felt sorry for her, all alone on her wedding night, waiting for that old man to stagger up the stairs. I couldn't leave her." Especially not after he'd tied her to a chair. He shot Ben a rueful glance. "She doesn't know anything about . . . about anything."

"She's not supposed to. She's a lady. You must reconcile yourself to that simple fact." His focus snapped away. "You! Don't leave that there!" He went to argue with the guard supervising the prisoners doing the cleaning. One of them had swept the soiled straw into a heap at the foot of Tom's cot. Ben had that removed and new straw brought in, along with a clean sheet and a better blanket.

The cell was as comfortable as it could ever be. A man came up with a lumpy sack, which he unloaded onto one of the cots. Five bottles of wine, a round of cheese, two large round loaves of bread, a bundle of dried meat, and some pears. Tom fingered his earring as he contemplated his supplies. "How long do you expect me to be in here?"

"We're doing everything we can. At least the chapel burglary gives us a trail to follow."

Tom blew out a lip fart. "Oh, yes, that's encouraging. You and Mr. Bacon making the rounds of the dockside pawnshops in your legal robes, inquiring delicately about stolen goods. You'll have me out in no time."

Ben sighed, defeated. He left with a promise to return every day with more food and drink. Also to make sure the guards knew this prisoner had important friends.

Tom tucked his provisions beneath the cot and stretched out with his hands behind his head, staring at the mold-mottled laths of the ceiling. The mattress under him was so thin he could feel each individual supporting rope striping his back. He'd had a chance to clean up a bit and change into fresh clothes, but he still felt itchy and sour.

How could his so-called friends leave him in this stinking pest hole? Mr. Bacon was the nephew of the Lord Treasurer, for whom Tom himself had performed vital services. Did that count for nothing? Surely Bacon could petition to have him released if he wanted to.

But no; that would cost him a favor, one he might want for himself someday.

And what about the newly minted Lady Surdeval? Trumpet had been released in minutes and sent home to her aunt in Bishopsgate. No doubt she was there right now, sipping a cool cup of wine while her maidservant massaged her feet. She couldn't come visit him; it would only make things worse. Tom understood that. But she hadn't sent so much as a note. He didn't expect an apology — as well ask the rain to apologize for getting you wet — but she might have sent him a word of sympathy and a basket of fruit.

He listened to shouts and bangs echoing up through the tower from the yard. That racket doubtless went on day and night. Newgate Prison hosted neither torture nor beheadings in the yard, but the cells were far filthier than those in the Tower and were occupied by real criminals, not gentlemen of dubious religion. Some of the men in here wouldn't hesitate to cut him for one of his bottles of tinto.

Tom swallowed sour bile. After all the hard work he'd done to raise himself into the gentry — all those nights of study to keep his place at Gray's, all those months in Cambridge, where he'd placed himself in real danger in service to the Crown — he'd been carted through the streets like a common churl and left to rot in this ten-by-ten cell. Had the Clarady luck run out at last?

He opened one of his bottles and slumped at the head of his cot, back against the cold stone wall, staring at the door. He would drink all the wine and then sleep until Ben brought him a fresh supply. Then he'd repeat that cycle until they released him or he turned himself into a drunkard, in which case, he would no longer care.

The cell door opened, admitting a puff of rank air and another prisoner. The guard gave the newcomer a shove and jeered at Tom. "Didn't think you'd have this palace all to yourself, now did you, *Master* Clarady?" He swung the door shut and turned the key in the lock.

The newcomer hooked his thumbs into his narrow belt and grinned. Handsome enough in a roguish way, his ginger beard and hair needed trimming, and he'd lost a couple of teeth. His red and yellow doublet and hose bore the marks of several nights in the common hold, splotched and dusted with grimy straw. But his red cloth hat still boasted one wilting feather.

"Jack Coddington." He took a step forward and held out a hand.

Tom ignored it.

Coddington shrugged and sat on the other cot. He set his hands on his thighs and leaned forward, regarding Tom with lively interest. "People said there was a barrister in the house, so I bribed the guard to let me move up here with you. A pretty piece of silk embroidery I was saving for my *belamour*." He made a meal of that last word, ending with his wide lips puckered. Then he shrugged again, the philosopher of life. "Ah, well. The piece was too good for a whore."

Tom yawned into his palm to signal his total lack of interest in this man's prattle.

Too subtle, evidently. Coddington only grinned more broadly. "I knew a barrister would get the best of whatever's to be had, even in this rat trap. Nothing like a legal man for talking people out of or into anything they like. My master's a barrister, you see. I know the breed."

Tom was an inner barrister — a student — not qualified to argue cases or do much of anything else, but Ben had emphasized Tom's membership in Gray's Inn to the guards, wanting them to know this prisoner had friends in powerful circles.

"Lawyers make the best thieves." Coddington tapped his temple. "It's the organizational capabilities, that's what my master says." He pronounced the long words with exaggerated care.

Tom grunted and took a long pull on his bottle.

Coddington licked his lips. "People also said the barrister in question was the one that robbed the chapel in that palace on the Strand last week — Surly Vale House, they call it."

"Surdeval," Tom said. "I didn't do it."

"I believe you." Coddington's freckled face took on a crafty look. "As a matter of fact, I'm the one man in Newgate who knows you didn't." He waggled his ginger eyebrows, plainly wanting Tom to ask him what he meant.

Tom took another drink to cover his surprise. The only persons who could know with certainty that he was innocent of that crime were the men who had done it themselves. The Clarady luck still held, thanks to a generous God. This bragging fool might spill the whole story, if Tom played him right.

But gently, gently; he didn't want to appear to be too interested. "The authorities must think I'm an idiot as well as a thief. Who could sell Catholic trinkets in England these days?"

"Oh, you can sell it, if you know how. And *where*, more to the purpose. That's where your organizational capabilities come into it."

"I don't follow you." Tom kept his tone level, as if he was barely interested.

Coddington wagged his finger. "See, if I were the judge, I'd know at once you hadn't burgled no chapel. That's a specialty job, that is. Takes knowledge." He tapped his temple. "Those Catholic hideaways are secret and not all of them are worth the gamble. First, you have to know where the rich ones are. That's where your upright man comes into it. The one with the knowledge."

"The one with the organizational capabilities." Tom took another pull from the bottle and passed it across the narrow aisle. "But you're still saddled with a load of illegal goods. You can't tell me there are any pawnbrokers in London willing to risk the rack for a golden chalice."

"Chalice!" Coddington snorted. "A chalice is nothing. And gold's not the half of it. To loyal Protestants like me and you, that treasure's just a boatload of metal and shiny stones. But to the Romish tribe, those gewgaws have value far beyond the stuff they're made of. Sentimental, that's what they are. My master calls it 'religious signery' or some such word."

"Signification?" Tom asked.

"That's it! Adds to the profits, you see." He rubbed his thumb across his fingers. "That's the second job of your upright man: find the ones what cares and make 'em pay."

Tom reached under his cot for another bottle and pulled out the cork with his teeth. "Is that what they got you for? Stealing objects of religious signification?" He passed the fresh bottle across the narrow aisle to Coddington with a jerk of his chin, then settled back against the wall, staring at the door — a man with nothing but time to kill.

"Not me." Coddington mirrored his pose, cradling his bottle against his chest. "I never get caught at work. I go in and out like a cat." He shot a sidelong glance at Tom. "Nobody hears a thing, and nobody gets hurt. You make a racket, you wake the householder, next thing you know, there's murder added to the charges and more reason to chase you down. Sloppy planning, that is. That's what my master always says. In and out like cats, he says. Silent as shadows."

"Wise policy," Tom said. It made sense and fit with the little he knew about burglars. They hated conflict like cats hate water. Slide a long hook through the front window while the clerk was in the back of the shop; slip in the back door when everyone rushed out front to watch the diversion your fellow created. Thieves prided themselves on their invisibility.

Besides, Lord Surdeval had not been killed by burglars surprised in the act. They'd have left him on the floor, not tucked him into his bed with his sheet pulled up to his chin.

Tom yawned again. "You must've gotten caught doing something. Unless you have an odd taste in lodgings."

"I've been in worse." Coddington sighed deeply, pitching it to the gallery. "It's love what does me in. Love, and the jealousy that comes with it. I had a bit of an altercation, you might say, a couple of nights ago, with a whoreson knave who dared to lay a hand on my belamour's beautiful arse." He scratched his rumpled hair. "Things got a mite vigorous. But I won't be here long. My master will pay my bail when he gets back from —" His round face took on that crafty look again. "From somewhere."

Let him keep his secrets — for a while. Tom could feel Dame Fortune smiling on him again as she gave her wheel another spin. Coddington had either done the chapel burglaries himself or he knew who had. All Tom had to do was keep passing him bottles and pretending he didn't care. The blattering fool would tell him everything he knew.

TEN

"This one's for the rack," Sir Richard Topcliffe said. "He'll give us the names of every man and woman he's ever met, never you fear, Mr. Bacon."

Francis had no argument, not today. He'd realized almost at once this prisoner was a missionary priest. Certain turns of phrase betrayed training at the seminary in Rheims. The priest, named Amias Fenton, had smuggled himself back into England, where he had been passed from one Catholic household to another in the guise of a music master.

No one would hire him for such gentle pursuits now. He'd been wearing the same clothes for weeks, and Francis could smell his sour stink from across the room. Grime streaked his stubbled cheeks and bald pate, and his red-rimmed eyes sank into dark hollows.

As abject as he appeared, Francis could not pity him. The man was utterly recalcitrant. He scoffed at every question and spat at every name they mentioned until Sir Richard slapped him hard across the face. Then Fenton rubbed his reddened cheek with a satisfied sneer, as if he had finally achieved his goal.

Sir Richard remained standing throughout the interrogation. He liked to loom over the prisoners, his hands on his hips and his legs spread wide. Francis, in contrast, shrank into his seat, as far from the hostile pair as possible.

He glanced toward the small table where Benjamin Whitt sat opposite Sir Richard's clerk, his shoulders hunched against the rising threat of violence in the little room. Francis had brought him to take notes and for moral support. He hated being penned up with Sir Richard, especially when the prisoner of the day rivaled him in viciousness.

"I'll tell you nothing," Fenton said. "Don't you know they train us to stand up to your torture? Besides, I'm safer on your rack than I am in my own bed."

"What do you mean by that?" Sir Richard demanded.

"I mean I'm better off taking my punishment here. The ones you send home get murdered in their beds."

"Are you talking about Viscount Surdeval?" Francis asked. "That had nothing to do with this commission. His interview was the merest formality. His loyalty was never in question."

"Lord Surdeval, yes. And others." Fenton's gaze shifted between Francis and Sir Richard and back, another sneer twisting his bruised lips. "You really don't know, do you? You never bother to check up on the ones you let go."

"Why should we?" Francis asked. "They are no longer our concern. Their local justices will monitor their church attendance. We trust our conversation here will inspire them to greater compliance."

Fenton laughed out loud. Sir Richard slapped him again. This time the man spat blood. "Surdeval was the third that I know of, but there could be more."

"You lie!" Sir Richard raised his hand. Fenton didn't even flinch. That must have sapped the fun because Sir Richard lowered his hand.

"Three men have been murdered?" Francis traded worried glances with Ben. It had never occurred to them to search for similar deaths. "Who are the other two?"

"The first I know of was Baron Hewick. The next was Mr. Rouncey, the silk merchant."

"How do you know this?" Francis asked.

"Who cares?" Sir Richard bared his overlarge teeth at the priest. "Why bother asking? You can't believe anything these lying traitors tell us anyway."

Francis turned an exasperated look at his co-commissioner. "If we truly believed that, Sir Richard, we'd have no moral grounds for torturing them."

He pinched the pleats in his left wrist ruff while he absorbed the shocking information. Three peculiar murders of recusant Catholics, all of the better sort, all killed in their sleep while confined to their homes by the Privy Council? If their deaths were related, Francis's working suppositions about Surdeval's murder could be thrown out the window. Sir William Gumery would gain nothing from the deaths of an unrelated baron and a silk merchant.

"How do you know about these other deaths?" Francis asked again.

"I heard about Hewick in the Clink." Fenton bared his teeth at Sir Richard. "We have friends everywhere; you can never stop us. Mr. Rouncey's widow told me herself the day you picked me up. She had invited me to lodge with her for a few weeks, but when I got there, her house was being confiscated. She lost everything — the price of true faith. Even her prayer book was stolen, a beautiful treasure-bound volume that had been passed down from mother to daughter since your godless queen's great-grandfather held the throne."

Francis asked, "Was it taken from her chapel?"

"Along with everything else of value in Caesar's marketplace," Fenton said. "Beautiful, sacred, holy spaces, filled with objects bearing the history of true devotion, desecrated by your —"

The rest of his words were drowned out by the booming laughter of Sir Richard, who slapped Francis on the back, nearly knocking him from his seat. "Someone's doing our work for us, eh, Mr. Bacon? A pity we can't thank him for his services."

* * *

"He's even worse than you described," Ben said as they left the Tower through the gatehouse. "How can you stand to work with him?"

"Not here," Francis said. In these walls, the very stones had ears. Besides, he hated attempting to converse while walking in the city. Even a street as wide as Cheapside was fraught with hazards: slatternly housewives throwing night soil into overflowing kennels, dogs and pigs scavenging at just the right height to trip a man. One's full attention was required.

He turned up Petty Wales. Ben grasped his sleeve to tug him the other way, pointing toward the river. "Wherry."

Francis shook his arm free and tilted his head toward the city. "Guildhall. Sheriff."

"Why are we —" Ben hopped aside to avoid being jostled by two gentlemen in black gowns with document cases over their shoulders. Stepping back, Francis felt his heel sink into something unpleasantly soft.

"Walk, then talk," he said, suiting his actions to the words.

They marched in silence up Tower Street to St. Dunstan-in-the-East. There Francis turned into the churchyard and paused in the shade of a tall oak beside one of the gracefully arched windows. "We must go to the Guildhall —"

"To speak with the sheriff. I understand. If that foul-mouthed priest was telling the truth, Lord Surdeval's death is not unique."

"Two others," Francis said. "Possibly more. It's horrible to contemplate. I interviewed both of those men myself in the past month."

"Fenton could be lying. He seems an especially nasty piece of work."

"Seminary priests often are," Francis said. "They're motivated by deep resentments, some bitter sense of separation from the rest of society. Why else would they do what they do?" He watched the shadows of leaves dancing on the gray stone wall for a few moments as he reviewed what he knew of Englishmen trained in Rheims. They went abroad to become ordained as Catholic priests, where they also learned strategies for subverting and undermining the English church when they returned. Without them to foster the dream of a complete counter-Reformation, English Catholics would gradually, gently, and inevitably find their way into the fold of the established church. These missionary priests, of whom there were possibly more than a hundred in England at this very moment, stirred people up, prodding them toward acts of open sedition.

And to what end? Didn't they all worship the same God? What need had the English of a pope in Rome?

Francis shook his head. "I believe him. He seemed genuinely affronted that we didn't know about the other victims."

"We need confirmation," Ben said.

"The sheriff should be able to provide that. He may be in hot pursuit of this murderer even as we speak." There was a hopeful thought. Francis hadn't had time to visit the sheriff on Friday, and then he'd been obliged to spend all of Saturday on business for Gray's Inn. For all he knew, the proper authorities already had these cases well in hand.

Ben shattered that fragile hope. "If the sheriff knew the murders were connected, why would he arrest Trumpet and Tom?"

"He wouldn't. Fie. He must not know." Their eyes met and held. Somehow that link always seemed to double the strength of their mental abilities. "Perhaps the deaths looked notably different," Francis said. "Fenton connects the victims through the actions of their wives. The sheriff might not consider that aspect, especially if there was nothing overtly religious about the other murders."

"No crosses on their chest," Ben said.

"Precisely," Francis said. "We must review his reports, any interviews with witnesses, or other notes. It's possible the information is right there in his files and has simply been overlooked."

"Let's hope that's all it is." Ben gave him a grim look.

Sheriff's clerks typically spent a year or two at a university and perhaps another two at one of the Inns of Chancery, the lesser legal societies that served pettifoggers and tradesmen's sons unable to gain admittance to an Inn of Court. They could draw up simple documents and knew which ones went to which court, but their legal knowledge was shallow, and they weren't paid to be curious. Competent enough for ordinary purposes, they would not have Francis's ability to discern a pattern in a welter of seemingly unrelated facts. Few did.

"It might take some time," Francis said. "Perhaps we should have dinner first? There's a rather good ordinary across from the Guildhall."

"Let's go now," Ben said, "and at least find the dates of the other murders. That might be enough to get Tom out of gaol. He'd never forgive us if we left him in there for one more night just because our bellies were grumbling."

ELEVEN

Sheriff Skinner was a large man, both tall and portly, his girth evidence of his substance as a citizen. His dark red doublet set off the burnished gleam of the thick chain of office draped around his shoulders. He wore his yellow hair short, trimmed straight across the brow, and his six-inch beard cut square across the bottom, emphasizing the blocky shape of his face.

The windows in the spacious office stood wide open, yet still the room felt stuffy. The city was too cramped to admit breezes. A banner with the arms of the City of London, with dragons sinister and argent, hung limply against the plastered wall beside another banner displaying the arms of the Worshipful Company of Clothworkers, the sheriff's guild. That one had lions in place of dragons, with a teazel beneath and a ram on the crest.

Two clerks worked in this chamber; one seated at a long desk near the windows, the other poised nearby to run and fetch. That one was dispatched after Francis introduced himself and asked to see all records relating to doubtful deaths and burglaries of houses in the past two months. He explained that his aunt, Lady Russell, had asked him to look into Lord Surdeval's death.

The sheriff snapped his fingers at the waiting clerk and cocked his head to send him out for the files. Lady Russell's name had power. She lived in the city, in Blackfriars, and had made it clear over the years that she expected swift service from all city officials as her due.

Francis said, "I have recently learned of two other deaths that have some features in common with the

Surdeval matter. Baron Hewick and Mr. Rouncey, a silk merchant. Did you notice any similarities among the three cases?"

"Similarities such as religious allegiance?" The sheriff's tone held contempt.

He had noticed, then. And done nothing? "I meant, more specifically, the manner of their deaths. For example, did the coroner notice any unusual marks on the bodies?"

"He did indeed, Mr. Bacon. Same on all three. I suppose you already know or you wouldn't even ask — a small cross cut into each man's chest."

"Then the murders must have been done by the same man," Francis said.

"It might be one man, or it might be several. It could be a secret society, sending out a different man for each victim." The sheriff smirked at his own cleverness.

That idea had never occurred to Francis. Although highly improbable, it wasn't impossible. Even so, he would reserve it until all other options had been ruled out.

A third clerk appeared on the threshold, displaying a sheet of paper. The sheriff beckoned him over and scanned the document. He handed it back to the clerk. "Put the lot of them in Bridewell. Tell the gaoler to make room."

The clerk hurried off and the sheriff turned back to Francis with a weary air. "I've got clerks doing the work of marshal-men and barely a third of my usual complement of bailiffs. Now the city's filling up with men returning from the war, some trying to get home, some who never had homes to begin with. There's confusion in all directions."

"I understand," Francis said. He and Ben traded dark looks. They couldn't expect much help from this office. "Even so, the murders of three prominent men surely demand some attention."

"Attention!" The sheriff tilted his chin at the clerk behind the desk, who nodded, dipped a quill, and held it ready. The sheriff walked over and signed something with a flourish. "My attention's spread pretty thin these days. Unless a witness turns up with a name, there isn't much I can do."

The first clerk came back with a wire loop holding a set of documents. He handed it to his master and resumed his post beside the door. The sheriff handed the file to Francis. "These are the felony crimes committed from June to the present date."

"So many!" Francis passed the file to Ben, who began perusing the documents in order.

The sheriff lifted his beefy shoulders. "It's a big city, Mr. Bacon. Mind you, most of these cases are simple enough. A tavern brawl that goes too far, goods stolen by servants or apprentices. We do a good job of apprehending those responsible."

"And your work is appreciated, Sheriff. But whether there is one murderer or several, I think we can agree that these particular murders were instigated by the same motivating force. And since there are at least three victims, unrelated other than through their religion, it's extremely unlikely that my student, Thomas Clarady, had anything to do with them."

"Would that be the fellow we arrested at Surdeval House?"

"Yes. You must see now that he is innocent."

"I don't know about *innocent*," the sheriff said. "His excuse for being there at that hour of the morning sounded pretty feeble to me." He emitted a rumbling laugh. "If he wasn't *entertaining* the young bride, he must have had another reason for spending the night in the house. Why not burglary? His father's a ship's captain, you know. He could smuggle those fancy goods out to where they'd fetch a handsome price."

Francis could see the validity of that reasoning. Add to it a clever bride with a maidservant who knew about unusual poisons and the case was nearly made.

"Mr. Bacon?" Ben had his fingers laced through the file of documents, holding four places at once. "I have the dates for the Rouncey and Hewick murders, as well as two other burglaries of private chapels that don't seem to be associated with any deaths."

"Two other burglaries?" Francis reached into the string of files to turn up a page without interfering with Ben's fingers. He tilted his head to read the sheet upside down. "This is dated August tenth. That was the day before the recusancy commission was appointed. I remember that evening well because I spent it wondering if I'd be named or not."

Ben nodded. "I remember it too. I believe that's the first related incident. Another burglary occurred on the sixteenth. Mr. Rouncey was killed on the twenty-fifth and Baron Hewick on the twenty-eighth."

"The first recusants were tried at the Old Bailey on the twenty-fifth," Francis said. "You and Tom both went with me."

"I remember," Ben said. "We had a long discussion in the hall after supper about the trials. Everyone went to bed later than usual that night."

"The convicted men were hanged on the twenty-eighth," Francis said. "I didn't go. Sir Francis Drake came to court that day to beg permission to sail against Spain. Another long discussion." A heated debate, standing before the throne. Francis had much admired Drake's courage in the face of a stubborn queen, even though he agreed with her that the plan was pure madness.

"I didn't go either," Ben said. "Nor did Tom. He drilled the Gray's Inn militia that afternoon, twice as hard as usual. Everyone was angry that day, thinking about how close we came to losing everything. He made them practice in the yard after supper with slingshots, as I recall."

"I remember that. They broke a window!" Francis shook his head. "The hangings were meant to give the people a sense of completion, of victory achieved. I'm not sure it worked as intended. The mood at the benchers' table had as much bitterness as satisfaction."

Ben held up the ring of files, fingers still entwined. "Sheriff, I can vouch for Mr. Clarady's whereabouts on every one of these dates except the last. We share chambers at Gray's Inn. He could not have been gone long enough to commit these crimes without my noticing."

The sheriff grunted, pushing out his fleshy lower lip, doubtless pondering the additional work it would make for his overburdened clerks.

Francis tapped his foot. "I could ask my lady aunt to —"

"No need for that." The sheriff waved at the clerk behind the desk. "Write a letter for the gaoler at Newgate. Have him release one Thomas Clarady at his earliest convenience." He turned back to Francis with a tight smile. "Sir William insisted on that arrest. Let him argue with Lady Russell about the release, if he wishes."

Francis doubted he would. Sir William's objective would be better achieved in the bishop's court by annulling the Surdeval marriage, leaving him in full possession of the estate. He had no need to keep Tom in gaol in the face of any kind of opposition. It would help both Tom and Trumpet to have a better suspect take their place.

"I do have one other question, Sheriff. Has there been any attempt to trace the objects stolen from the chapels?"

"That Catholic trash? They won't be able to sell it in England." He held up a beefy palm. "And before you ask, no, I have not posted watchers on every quay along the Thames. I'm shorthanded, as I've told you."

"Three prominent Englishmen have been murdered," Francis said. "You can't let that go unpunished."

"Three Catholics," the sheriff said. "They might have been born in England, but they're not like you and me, Mr. Bacon, not by a long chalk." He moved toward the door, ushering them before him with his bulk. "Good riddance to them and their popish fripperies. Why should I waste my time chasing after a man no jury in England would convict?"

TWELVE

Trumpet and Catalina leaned on the windowsill of the bedchamber on the second floor of Chadwick House, watching the endless parade passing up and down Bishopsgate Street. They liked to study the clothes and accoutrements of the people — all manner of people — going about the business of the busiest city in the world. They'd gotten lots of ideas for improving their various disguises *and* they'd seen the most famous actors in London riding out to the theaters in Shoreditch.

Trumpet had whiled away most of the hours since she'd come back from the Tower at this very window, too restless to read and too itchy with worry about Tom to sit chastely in the parlor like a proper gentlewoman. At least Aunt Blanche had better sense than to expect her to do needlework. She could sew well enough when she wanted to, which was never, but considered it a spectacular waste of her capacities.

Not that anyone required either her intellect or her hard-won training these days. Ben had told her to be patient, as if she had any option. Well, all right, she had one. She could pace back and forth like a caged bear. Apart from that, she could dangle out the window waiting for news to be doled out to her in ladylike portions.

She hated being separated from her closest friends. Ben could come and visit whenever he wished, if he had the time, which he didn't, especially now that Mr. Bacon no longer had Tom to run errands for him. Ben had other concerns too, of course. He'd be called to the bar in a few months, assuming things went well, which he never believed things would. So he made himself study more and spend more time with the other men at Gray's, new-made barristers with perhaps a client or two they could spare. He'd need more money — lots more — once he was admitted as a barrister, because his parents would expect him to marry and establish a household. Trumpet could visit him then, but his wife would doubtless make a horrible fuss. They couldn't lounge by the hearth in their shirtsleeves spitting apple seeds into the fire.

And Tom — poor Tom! Trumpet's stomach clenched whenever she thought of him lying in a heap of stinking straw, cold and hungry, with vicious criminals lurking all around him. Ben had assured her his conditions were not that dire, but even so. He'd worked so hard to bring honor to his name with that commission in Cambridge. This past year, she'd hardly seen him; he'd been so busy taking charge of the Gray's Inn militia, culling the more egregious flounces from his wardrobe, and attending every session of the Queen's Bench. She wished more than anything that she could have spent another year at Gray's to watch him rise, and possibly even help.

She'd planned to work him gradually into her social circle as a newly married viscountess, always in the company of others at first, like Ben and maybe even Mr. Bacon, and always in the presence of her aunt and other respectable persons, if she could think of any she could tolerate. She could invite him for dessert or to musical entertainments, that sort of thing. Tom could be relied upon to be personable. In time, he could have charmed even her poor Lord Surdeval. He'd have had Aunt Blanche in his pocket after the first visit.

Now that lovely plan lay in ruins. She couldn't risk being seen in his company, not in her guise as her actual self, not for weeks. Months, possibly! She'd ordered gowns with Tom in mind, in the rich colors he loved, including an especially lustrous green satin she'd planned to wear with pink-and-green-striped sleeves. Now Tom was in jail, not that she could see him even if he weren't, and she was restricted to widow's black for who knew how long.

Forever, if the women in the Andromache Society were to be her guides.

The bell at St. Ethelburga's tolled the hour. Trumpet sighed and turned to her maidservant. "We'd better get me dressed."

She had been summoned to attend upon Lady Russell at her home in Blackfriars to receive the latest news about the murder from Mr. Bacon. He could have come to Chadwick House or sent Ben, but Lady Russell had arranged the meeting. She liked to get her news early and at first hand. Old friends of the queen tended to get what they wanted.

Bacon would undoubtedly deliver a carefully edited report. Trumpet wouldn't be able to press for details about Tom's well-being or hear any of the tentative theories, the tenuous threads that hadn't yet been followed. Still, it would be better than sitting here completely in the dark.

She hopped on the bed and extended each leg in turn so Catalina could slide on her fine black stockings and tie the garters. Then she stood again, raising her arms to let her farthingale be pulled over her head. While Catalina laced it to her bodice, she turned her thoughts to the upcoming meeting.

Mr. Bacon's news would be brief. If Tom were here, she'd bet him a pitcher of ale that Bacon would find an excuse to slither out as soon as he'd said his piece. Lady Russell's note had also said they would discuss Trumpet's forthcoming annulment suit, if she were so inclined. Indeed she was. These women knew more about marriage law than half the men at Gray's Inn. There must be strategies, some preparations she could make.

The essential question was whether or not the marriage had been consummated. If it had, it was legal, and she was entitled to her jointure as specified in the marriage contract. If not, the best she could do was sue for the return of her bride's portion, which would go back to her father. She'd get nothing for all her months of laborious negotiations.

She had to win. She wanted that house on the Strand or something comparable. She wanted an income she controlled herself. And she wanted to stop being treated like a child.

"How do they decide whether or not you're a virgin?"

"Mmm." Catalina took a pin from her mouth. "The women examine you within, my lady."

"When you say 'within,' do you mean —"

"Yes, my lady." Catalina gathered up the black satin kirtle and held it ready. "The matron feels inside to see if the maidenhead is whole." She cocked her head, her dark eyes moving as if searching the air for an explanation. "It's like a bit of waxy linen stretched over a soft bottle."

"Linen?" That description didn't help much since linen cloth ranged from gauze to canvas. "Is there any way to break the thing without, uh — without assistance?" Trumpet raised her arms again to receive the kirtle.

Catalina gently worked the skirt into place around Trumpet's hips. "Some say it may be broken by the riding of horses."

"Ha!" Trumpet snapped her fingers. "I rode every day at Orford, galloping as often as not. Wearing boy's clothes, as often as not. Perhaps mine's long gone."

Catalina shrugged, her mouth once again full of pins. She busied herself attaching the black-and-gray-striped forepart to the kirtle.

"Is it possible to have an intact maidenhead and not be a virgin?" Trumpet asked.

"No, my lady." Catalina paused in her work to look up at her mistress with a twisted sort of smile. "I do not know about the horses, my lady, but in the usual way, it works like this." She demonstrated the general form of action with her curved left hand and the index finger of her right hand.

Trumpet mapped the shapes to her own anatomy, remembering a drawing she'd caught a glimpse of once in Tom's chambers and adding other scraps of information she'd garnered here and there. "Oh," she said at last. And then again, "Oh! Ow."

"Only the first time, my lady." Catalina added the partlet and tied the bit of sheer linen under Trumpet's arms. Then she said. "Gown, please." She gathered up the folds of the fine black wool and pulled this final layer over Trumpet's head.

As her face emerged, Trumpet said, "That doesn't sound particularly delightful."

Catalina flashed a wide grin. "It is, my lady. Trust me. As much as you enjoyed the kissing, you will like this even better, after the first time."

Trumpet clucked her tongue. "Curse that Thomas Clarady! I could be pregnant at this very moment if he weren't so stubborn."

"It does not always happen on the first time. Nor even often, I think."

Trumpet moved to stand in front of the mirror over the dressing table and glared at her reflection. She couldn't rely on the chance of the horses; she needed something certain. "I must find a way to make Tom do the deed before this examination."

"I do not think he will, my lady." Catalina worked the partlet into place under the neckline with deft fingers. "He has honor, that one. It is why you love him."

"That's not why." She loved him for the dimple, the long legs, and the golden curls; at least that's what made her heart beat twice as fast whenever she saw him, even from a distance. Even more, she loved him for the way he'd shrugged, laughed at himself, and gone on being friends after finding out she wasn't a boy. "I need a new plan. How do they choose these eight matrons of good repute?"

"I do not know, my lady."

"I'll bet Lady Russell knows. She probably knows the judge who will appoint them." Trumpet considered her reflection in the mirror. She didn't care for black in general, but it did accentuate her unusual coloring. Would that be an advantage or a disadvantage in court? They never debated that sort of question at the Inns of Court, but she'd wager that the Andromache Society would have an answer.

"All right," she said, "let's imagine the horse riding did the trick and I pass the examination. How did my deflowering occur? I've said that I spent the night in my room alone with Tom gallantly guarding outside the door." She held out each arm to receive her sleeves — silk striped black and gray, to match the forepart of her skirt.

Catalina laced the sleeves and shoulder rolls to the gown with a thoughtful frown. Trumpet watched her in the mirror while she walked through the events of her wedding night in her own mind. They spoke together. "The nap."

"That's the only possible time," Trumpet said. "Luckily, I don't think I said much about that part. But I wasn't with my lord for long, and Sir William was in the house, waiting at the table. How long does the act of love usually take?"

Catalina grinned again. "That depends on many things, my lady. With an old man, I believe it is either very slow or much too fast."

"Too fast, then. I was only away from my guests for about twenty minutes."

"That is enough, I think." Catalina stood back to survey her handiwork and nodded in satisfaction. "If you will sit, my lady, I will do your hair."

Trumpet sat. She liked having her hair brushed. But she wished she had more facts about sex. Courtship and the arts of love were favorite topics among Her Majesty's maids of honor after they retired to their shared chamber at night, but since most of them were maidens, their information ranged from the dubious to the absurd. Trumpet had gathered what she could, but there was no substitute for experience. One might learn a great deal from a book about navigation, for example, but things would look very different on the deck of a ship in the middle of the wide blue sea.

After a few minutes of silence, Trumpet asked, "How about this? I went up with Surdeval to make him comfortable, leaving my guests in the hall. That much I said before. But now I'll say that as I unlaced his doublet, my Lord became inflamed with desire and insisted on possessing me right there and then. His passion burned so hot, the matter was completed quickly without the removal of any part of my costume, so I was able to return to the hall with minimal adjustment. Does that sound plausible?"

"I believe it could be so, my lady." Catalina began brushing her hair into a tight coil at the back. "And I can help this story. You wore your red taffeta farthingale that day and your smock with white embroidery around the neck. I will stain them with pig's blood and dry them in the sun. Then I will wash them, but not too well."

"What a clever wench you are!" Trumpet grinned. "I think this will work. No one will ask for details — that would be vulgar." Her gaze shifted over the bottles and jars on her dressing table while she rehearsed the new story under her breath. "Someone may ask why I didn't mention this before."

"You were too shy, my lady," Catalina said. "A gentlewoman does not speak of such things."

"That's good," Trumpet said, snapping her fingers. "I can be very demure, if I try. Watch this." She pouted and cast her gaze at her folded hands, batting her lashes.

Catalina watched her with a wry smile. "Perhaps with practice, my lady."

THIRTEEN

"Four days and four nights." Tom pressed his back against the door of his cell to peer sideways through the barred window and down the length of the stone corridor. Nothing to see but shadows; no sounds besides the echo of noise from other parts of the prison. No footsteps tromped up the winding stair, nor did a lanky figure appear bearing a satchel of food and drink.

Tom gave his cellmate a grim look. "They locked me in here on Friday, September 2nd, just before noon. I'm fairly sure today is Tuesday, September 6th."

"That's my best guess." Jack Coddington bore confinement with unflagging good cheer. He was warm, dry, and fed — better than usual, thanks to Tom. That seemed to be enough.

"Four days and four nights." Tom, in contrast, was ready to explode with sheer restlessness. He'd slept enough to last him a month and discovered that his limit for sitting and drinking was about two-thirds of one day. He wanted air, he wanted action, and, to his own surprise, he even wanted to get back to his books.

"Worse," he said, "it's now one night and nearly two full days since Ben brought fresh provisions. We're out of wine, if you haven't noticed."

Coddington shrugged. "It won't be long." He had infinite faith in his upright man, due any day to come bail him out.

But Tom knew how these things worked. At first your friends are contrite and concerned. "We're doing everything we can," they say. They bring you treats and comforts and visit you twice a day. Then little by little, they weary of the chore and your ceaseless grumbling. They come less often and bring fewer gifts. Next thing you know, you're alone and friendless, dependent on prison rations and the goodwill of the gaoler. Hunger and despair sap your strength until you fall prey to disease or worse.

"Be glad we're not in Bridewell," Coddington said. "Then those footsteps you're listening for might be coming to take us down to the basement and hang us in the manacles."

"We don't torture ordinary criminals in England," Tom said with authority. "That's on the Continent. We only use torture for matters of state, like treason." Francis Bacon had delivered a discourse on the subject a few weeks ago after supper at Gray's Inn, shortly after being appointed to the recusancy commission.

"A lot you know about it! I know a boy was whipped bloody to make him tell the names of his accomplices."

"Whipping isn't torture."

"Says the man who's never been whipped. They'll torture you whenever they please if they don't like the answers you're giving them."

Tom pointed at him, arm fully extended. "False. Whipping is punishment, not torture. Legally, those two things are distinct. Even on the Continent, torture must be ordered by a judge. In England, you have to get a warrant from the Privy Council to seek specific information, like the names of the co-conspirators in some specific plot."

He contemplated the space between the cots and decided he had room for a little fencing practice. Anything to beat back the boredom and give his muscles something to do. He adopted a sideways stance and measured the space with his arms, first front to back, then side to side.

Coddington had been lying on his back with his hands behind his head. As Tom's long arms extended over his cot, he pulled himself up to sit with his back against the wall. "I once met a man who'd been racked, poor bastard. His knees were ruined. He could never walk again without two sticks to lean on."

"Sad." Tom pretended to draw his sword and moved into *prime*, the hilt above his head with the sword pointing at his imaginary opponent near the door. His fencing master taught them that slow movements, performed with exquisite attention, trained the muscles to respond without thought, even in the mad heat of conflict. "Even so, I'd rather have the rack than the Little Ease. I loathe confinement."

"The Little Ease is barely four feet square, they say." Coddington drew up his knees and curved his arms to define the space around him. "Campion survived it for four days. Could you sit like this for that long?"

"I'd go mad." Tom shifted into *seconde*, imagining the weight of his thirty-three-inch rapier in his hand. "Although, the Little Ease wouldn't leave marks or break your joints. You might recover, in time. They say the manacles can pull your arms right out of their sockets."

"You'd never recover from that." Coddington rolled his shoulders as if making sure they still worked. "Nor the thumbscrews. That'd be the worst for me. I need the full use of my hands. I'm the one with the charm, you see." He fiddled his fingers in front of his face as if working some small mechanism. "Master of the dark art. The one that gets us in and out without a trace."

Tom suppressed a grin. He'd gained his cellmate's trust little by little — and bottle by bottle. He still hadn't gotten the name of Coddington's master, but he had learned the man was a member of Gray's Inn. There were over three hundred members, a hundred of them seldom in residence, but even so, Tom had an inkling of who it might be.

Ingenious crimes involving the smuggling of prohibited Catholic goods? He'd lay odds on Trumpet's uncle, Nathaniel Welbeck.

104

In fact, the more he learned about the chapel burglaries — Coddington had hinted at a number of others — the more he liked Mr. Welbeck as the upright man. He couldn't picture him kneeling over a body to carve a cross in its chest, but he could easily see him planning the burglaries. Welbeck loved deception, pulling the wool over everyone's eyes. He had friends with Catholic interests on both sides of the British Sea. And he'd been involved in smuggling prohibited materials in the past.

Coddington had bragged about his master's clever timing, hiding their crimes under the general panic caused by the Spanish armada. The war raised the odds of getting away with the theft of Catholic goods to a near certainty. Who would dare to declare them missing? And who would care if they did?

Tom shifted into *tierce*, his hand at waist height, supinate, blade pointing up. "I wouldn't worry, old chum. They won't torture you for picking locks."

"Thanks." Coddington nodded contentedly, then shook himself and said, "Wait, now. You say they torture men for ordinary crimes on the Continent. Does that include France?"

"Of course."

"Can they torture you for a crime you commit in another country?"

Tom turned full around on his heel and pointed his sword arm straight at his cellmate. "Are we talking about a theft in England?"

Coddington pushed the invisible blade away with one hand. "We might be."

"And the goods are sold in France?"

"That's where the Catholics are. The closest ones anyway."

"What part of France?" Tom barked the question, like a judge in a courtroom.

"Dieppe, the one time I went. We handed the goods on to another ship. We only spent one night, down by the docks. We left at sunrise the next morning. I barely set foot on the shore."

"Doesn't matter." Tom spread his arms in opposite directions, as if parrying thrusts from two opponents. "But why Dieppe? It's too close; too much competition. If it were up to me, I'd go farther, to Jersey or La Rochelle. Or even St. Jean de Luz."

"What do you know about it?" Coddington sounded a trifle indignant, as if Tom had cast doubt on his beloved master.

"More than you think. My father's a privateer, didn't I tell you?" He took two short, shuffling steps, right foot in front, then lunged forward, thrusting his sword toward the door.

"A privateer, eh?" Coddington sounded intrigued. "Isn't that interesting."

Tom glanced over his shoulder. "I was hoping you'd think so. The road I'm on isn't taking me where I want to go. I need new friends." He pulled in his arms, turned, and crossed his arms in front of his chest. "I could be useful to your master. I have chambers at Gray's, and my father is captain of his own ship. When we get out, maybe you could arrange a meeting."

When he got out, Tom intended to track down Nathaniel Welbeck by himself before mentioning the name to Mr. Bacon or Ben. Let them be left in the dark for a change! He could bring Trumpet along, dressed as a — whatever she chose. She'd mentioned once or twice that Uncle Nat had moved to Exeter, but he couldn't be directing these burglaries from that distance. He must be in London somewhere. Tom would need her help to find the wily barrister and besides, she had a right to know he'd planned the burglary of her husband's chapel.

If Coddington had picked the lock, there would have been two or three other burglars to carry the booty and row the boat. One of them must have killed Lord Surdeval for reasons of his own. Tom had probed as close to that subject as he dared. Coddington had steadfastly insisted that only incompetent burglars ever resorted to violence.

"In and out like cats, that's the first rule of the game. Don't leave a mess, that's the second. The household either sleeps through it all like innocent babes, or they're not home in the first place. Nobody knows a thing until next time they go inside their secret little church. By then, the goods — and us — are well out of reach."

Tom believed him, but he'd spent too much time with Francis Bacon to believe the thefts and the murders could be completely unrelated. With a little luck and a little guile, Tom intended to solve both crimes while Ben and Bacon chased fruitlessly around London. Neither of them could interrogate his own mother without Tom's help.

"I'll ask my master when I see him," Coddington said. "Not sure we're in need of a new man, but you never know. But what about France? Will they torture me to learn the names of my accomplices?"

"If they catch you, they might." Tom grinned. "My professional advice? Don't go back."

He swung full around again to face the door. He set his left hand on his hip and extended his right arm, making circular motions with his invisible blade. He imagined the door bursting open to reveal Mr. Bacon, hat in hand, stooping to beg his forgiveness on bended knee, clutching a letter from the Lord Treasurer demanding Tom's immediate release.

His lip curled at the idle dream. Why not imagine the queen rushing in as well, to kiss Tom on the lips? No, not the queen — Trumpet, in that pink and silver gown she'd worn on her wedding night. No, not the gown. That slip of transparent gauze she wore later, barefoot, with her hair gleaming like black satin hanging down to her —

His brain stopped while the shape of her perfect round arse formed in his hands.

"Hoi!" Coddington said. "Sounds like someone's coming up the stairs after all."

"What?" Tom heard a booming voice echoing up the stone stairwell, a voice he would recognize from fifty yards away in a howling gale. "Father!"

The door swung open and there stood Captain Valentine Clarady in the flesh. He looked thinner than he had last winter but otherwise hale and sprucely dressed in dark green with pale green linings. His satin hat sported a band of woven silk and two stiff feathers to emphasize its height.

The captain spread his arms wide and Tom walked into them, tears of relief springing into his eyes. He would rather have his father here than the queen and all her ministers.

Although he hadn't expected to see him anytime soon. He'd assumed the *Susannah* would remain at sea with the rest of the English fleet for many more weeks. He hadn't begun to come up with a way to explain his present predicament.

They separated with hearty slaps on the shoulders. The captain looked him up and down with a critical eye. "Well, well, me boyo! You don't look much the worse for wear, though you need a good barbering and a change of clothes. We'll attend to that while you tell me what in the name of the seven seas you're doing in here. Your lawyer friend just hums and mumbles when I ask him about it." He jerked his thumb over his shoulder.

Tom hadn't even noticed Ben looming in the background. "Am I free?"

"You are," Ben said. "Mr. Bacon got a letter from the sheriff." He waved a roll of parchment. "Your father caught me on my way here to get you out. You may be interested to know there have been two other murders and several other burglaries."

"More murders?" Tom shot a glance at his cellmate, who had risen from the bed. Coddington shrugged. *In and out like cats, the first rule of the game.*

Tom snatched the document from Ben, unrolled it, and read it quickly. A grin spread across his father's face, who loved watching his son doing anything lawyerly, even something as simple as reading a letter without moving his lips.

Tom rolled it up again and handed it back. "All right, then. I forgive you. But only because you brought my father with you."

"Forgive *me*?" Ben's dark brows knitted.

"Is there anything here you want to keep?" the captain asked, surveying the narrow cell.

Tom snorted. "Let Coddington have the blanket. Mr. Bacon did me a favor; perhaps the moon will turn blue and it'll snow tomorrow."

Ben frowned at him but said nothing. He gestured at the guard to move on so the rest of them could come through.

Coddington called, "It's been a right pleasure, Mr. Clarady. I won't forget what you said. Perhaps you'll let me buy you a drink once we're both at liberty again. You can find me at the Dolphin down by the Old Swan Stairs."

"I'll do it. Good luck to you!" Tom called as the door banged shut. They trailed the guard down and out.

Tom stood for a moment, appreciating the lack of walls. He felt like drawing in a deep breath of free, fresh air, but no place this close to the Fleet River smelled fresh at summer's end. He gave his father another hug instead. "We won!" Holding on to his father's shoulder, he grinned at Ben. "My father ran those Spaniards off with their tails between their legs."

109

The captain chuckled. "I had help." His smiled faded as he folded his arms and regarded Tom with an interrogatory eye. "That story can wait. I want to know how my son ended up in Newgate under an accusation of murder. And what's all this about the Earl of Orford's daughter?"

FOURTEEN

Trumpet sat in Lady Russell's private garden, struggling not to fidget. She was being subjected to an examination more intense, and more consequential, than any of the legal exercises she'd undergone at Gray's.

Lady Bacon fixed her with her penetrating hazel eyes. "Then it was melancholy that took you away from the court."

"I feel so foolish talking about it now." Trumpet dropped her gaze to her hands, which lay demurely in her lap. At least she'd chosen the right costume. The other three widows also wore black, relieved only by white cuffs and ruffs, even young Sarah Palmer, who had lost her husband years before. Widowhood defined them and their places in the world.

Their somber garb created a blot on the sunny flower garden. Their small table stood beneath an arbor shaded by a wide-leafed vine. More vines bearing white and yellow flowers climbed up the high brick walls. The late summer sun warmed the gravel paths that wound through an intricate pattern of clipped herbs. Lady Russell's garden defined the pinnacle of modern horticulture, or so Trumpet had heard. She added it to the list of things she would do with Surdeval House when she took possession. She wanted to sit in such a garden in the evening, sipping wine cooled in the river and listening to Tom play the lute.

But the battle for the house had hardly begun, which was why she sat here letting herself be interrogated by Francis Bacon's implacable mother. So far, however, she hadn't received any advice she couldn't have given herself.

Instead, the two elderly sisters had pried into every corner of Trumpet's history, starting with the terms of her marriage contract and working their way back. Whenever Lady Bacon detected some inconsistency, she pursued it with the tenacity of a well-trained hound. The woman had a nose for half-truths and evasions as keen as a dog's for sausage. No wonder Francis Bacon was so devoted to the truth!

Was this how the recusants felt when facing their interrogators in the Tower? The queen should have assigned these sharp-witted women to the commission — there'd be no secrets left in England. Trumpet would cast Lady Bacon in Topcliffe's role as the Fervent Believer. Lady Russell would then play Francis Bacon, the Staunch Realist. Funny how a man could look so much like his mother yet in character be so much more like his aunt.

Lady Russell blinked at her like an owl contemplating an uncooperative mouse. "I remember hearing at the time that you were leaving the court because your father objected to the expense."

"That was part of it." Trumpet drew the words out, desperately trying to remember which lies she'd told to whom. "Court is *so* expensive, as you know, Madame. The clothes, the gifts, the tips for the servants . . . it adds up so quickly." She sighed as if at a painful memory. "Then when the melancholy descended, I simply wanted to get away from all the commotion."

"I loathe the court myself," Lady Bacon said. "I wish my son could spend less time in that unwholesome environment, but without title or office, what choice has he? I consider it an especially unhealthy place for a girl. How did you treat your melancholy?"

"Ah." Trumpet batted her lashes while her mind raced. She had no personal experience of that malady, having always been more inclined to the choleric. Fortunately, she knew someone who frequently suffered from that complaint: Francis Bacon. "Regular sleep at the proper hours is the most important, and of course, a moderate dietary regimen. Then, I find an infusion of fennel, ginger, and licorice very soothing. If such simples are ineffective, I take a dose of poppy juice — the juice, not a decoction of the dried herb — mixed into a cup of wine."

"Exactly what I would prescribe." Lady Bacon's eyes narrowed.

"The episode came and went two years ago, Anne," Lady Russell snapped. "It has no relevance to the case at hand. I do think it was unwise of your father to remove you from court for such a minor complaint. There is no other marriage market of any worth in England." She shot a glance at Mrs. Palmer. "For a noblewoman, that is."

Mrs. Palmer smiled blandly into the middle distance. Trumpet admired the way the woman had perfected the art of seeming to hear only that which she ought and otherwise appearing to be contentedly absorbed by her comfit or the flowering vine.

Lady Russell persisted. "Who suggested Lord Surdeval? It isn't an obvious match."

Trumpet smiled humbly. "My father proposed it. He thought I would benefit from the steadying influence of an older man." In truth, she had been keeping her ears open for widowers who met her requirements. When Lord Surdeval had let it be known that he would pay in cold coin as well as in lands for a young virgin of good lineage, she had passed the news to her father. The earl leapt at the chance to barter his last unmortgaged asset. He'd set his price and left the negotiations to Trumpet and her counselor.

The sisters exchanged knowing glances. "No wonder you were so poorly suited," Lady Russell said.

Trumpet bristled. She thought she'd done rather well for the first time out.

Mrs. Palmer patted her hand. "Sometimes love may bloom where it's planted."

"That's right," Trumpet said, grateful for the idea. "My lord and I shared many things. A love of books and learning, for example."

"Oh?" Lady Bacon asked. "Who supervised your education? I understand your mother died when you were a baby." Her eyes gleamed. This was her domain of expertise.

"I was ten," Trumpet said, lifting her chin. "My father provided me with an exemplary range of tutors." He'd paid for them anyway. Her aunt and uncle had helped her hire complacent companions who let her do as she pleased and creative tutors who encouraged her expanding interests. Trumpet had essentially raised herself and she was proud of the job she'd done.

"Anne," Lady Russell said crisply, "we do not have time to review her entire curriculum. The issue at hand is her marriage." She returned her piercing gaze to Trumpet. "I should think you would have preferred a younger man."

"There were no younger men available who met my father's requirements." None willing to hand over a thousand pounds in silver with another four thousand in land. "Besides, my mother's first husband was much older than she — Mr. Joseph Dusteby of the Merchant Adventurers."

"My late husband was older as well," Mrs. Palmer said. "I admired him and found his guidance invaluable, especially in our early years."

"Mr. Dusteby and my mother were very happy," Trumpet said. "My aunt and uncle both say so. I think they must have been because he left her a portion large enough to attract an earl and another fortune bound up in trusts for any children she might have."

"*Trusts?*" the sisters asked in unison. They leaned forward, nostrils twitching, like hounds catching an alluring scent. "What are the terms? Who are the trustees?"

Trumpet smiled. Safe ground at last. Each of these widows had undergone lengthy battles in court after their husbands died. According to Ben, Lady Bacon had fought like a tigress to preserve estates for her son Anthony against the claims of his older stepbrothers. She hadn't been able to get much for Francis and had soured relations with the stepbrothers, but she'd held on to Gorhambury and learned a great deal about property law.

Lady Russell had brought many a suit to Chancery, having been widowed twice, with children from each marriage. She had ongoing disputes with her neighbors in Bedfordshire, zealously guarding and secretly expanding the boundaries of her estate.

But Sarah Palmer topped them both. Along with other widows of merchants murdered by the Spanish, she was suing the King of Spain himself, seeking compensation for the ships and goods he confiscated when he closed his ports and took their husbands captive. They could never win, but one felt bound to salute their faith in the law.

Trumpet explained that lands worth some thousand pounds a year had been enfeoffed to three trustees for the use of Trumpet's mother and the heirs of her body. Nathaniel Welbeck, her mother's younger brother, was one of the trustees. The other two were Mr. Dusteby's eldest sons from his first marriage. No lands could be sold without the consent of all three. Thus far, the income had been directed toward additional purchases. She had not received so much as a penny for herself.

"You could hardly do better than Mr. Welbeck," Mrs. Palmer said. "I have found him to be a wise and reliable counselor."

"So have I," Trumpet said. "I mean to consult with him soon, in fact. Now that I'm nineteen, I want to be given direct control over at least some of my property."

"No, no," Lady Bacon said, raising a long admonitory finger. "You mustn't do that."

"It would be most unwise," Lady Russell added. "You'll marry again within a year, I should imagine. We'll do better for you this time. But you must not expose those trusts to view. Let them remain hidden."

"Perhaps you don't fully understand how blind trusts work," Lady Bacon said. "Let us explain." She folded her hands on the table as if preparing to deliver a speech.

"I understand it perfectly," Trumpet said before the senior woman could open her mouth. She'd gone to great lengths to learn her law, after all. "Trusts such as mine are based on the doctrine of separate estate. My mother's first husband, in his wisdom, transferred ownership of the properties to three trustees to manage on my behalf — long before I was even born. Those three are the legal owners, but they have an obligation to act in my best interests. And so they have done; they've been exemplary trustees. Since the trust was established before my mother remarried, my father knows nothing about it."

Lady Bacon regarded her with a sour expression. She plainly did not like having her prerogative usurped. She sniffed and said, "If you understand the construction of the trust, then you must respect the intentions of its creator and your *exemplary* trustees."

"You have no need for an independent income at this time," Lady Russell said. "Leave your estates to grow."

"Save them for your widowhood," Mrs. Palmer suggested.

"I'm a widow now!"

Mrs. Palmer pursed her lips. The two sisters exchanged dubious glances.

Lady Russell said, "Sir William will certainly succeed in having your marriage annulled, my dear. By your own account, it was never consummated."

"But it was," Trumpet said. At last, the moment had arrived to present her revised story.

Lady Bacon said, "You told the sheriff's men that you spent the night alone in your room with your retainer outside the door."

"Yes, but I didn't tell anyone about what happened when I took my lord husband in for his nap. I was —" She ducked her head and batted her lashes, resisting the urge to peek at their reactions. "I was too embarrassed. It isn't something one talks about, is it? I didn't know at the time that anyone had any right to know. How could I?"

Sarah Palmer patted her hand again. "Of course you couldn't."

"What happened?" Lady Russell asked.

Trumpet lowered her eyes again and spoke in a girlish voice. She told them the story she'd rehearsed, but in stilted words and unfinished phrases, twisting her hands in her lap and never once raising her eyes. When she got to the end, she fluttered her hands in a helpless gesture and produced a sort of whimpering sniff.

"That will suffice." Lady Russell flicked her fingers at the servant standing in the corner of the arbor. The woman — tall, slender, and clad in somber gray — refilled their cups and moved a plate of comfits closer to Trumpet. She chose a square of painted marzipan and ate it in tiny bites, waiting for the response to her performance.

A long silence followed, broken finally by Lady Bacon. "She has no witnesses."

Lady Russell shrugged. "None could be expected under the circumstances."

"My maidservant preserved the petticoat," Trumpet said. "Wouldn't it show —" She broke off and dropped her gaze to her lap again.

"It might help," Lady Russell said.

"Sir William will insist that your claim be verified," Lady Bacon said. "Prepare yourself for the examination. It won't be pleasant."

This time, Trumpet's maidenly grimace was not faked. Mrs. Palmer offered her another comfit.

"If the consummation is confirmed," Lady Russell said, "the annulment suit evaporates. Then you face the contest over the will." Her expression was grim, but the fire of battle blazed in her eyes.

A footman clad in blue and gold entered through the wrought-iron gate and strode across the path to stand beside his mistress. "Mr. Bacon has arrived, my lady."

"Bring him to us here. Along with more wine, please."

Lady Bacon added, "Bring something savory for my son. Not too salty. Something dry, with no cheese. Or better, a cup of broth."

The footman bowed and departed. He returned shortly with a chair, followed by another servant bearing a tray of provisions. Francis Bacon followed them, waited patiently while they distributed the things they had brought, and then approached the table. He removed his hat and bowed deeply to the older women. "My lady mother, my lady aunt, I am happy to find you in good health." His lip twitched as he shifted his gaze to Trumpet, but he offered her a short bow. "Lady Surdeval." The glimmer of amusement faded as he turned toward Mrs. Palmer, but he inclined his head courteously. "Mrs. Palmer."

Trumpet admired his skill in executing four perfectly calibrated greetings without apparent thought — the benefit of a lifetime at court.

"Please be seated, Nephew."

Francis sat and accepted a cup of wine. His mother pushed a small bowl toward him. He lifted it, sniffed its contents, gave her an exasperated look, and set it down.

Lady Russell said, "Your note said you had good news concerning our commission."

"I do." Bacon smiled at Trumpet. "My Lady Surdeval may be relieved to learn that her counselor's assistant, Thomas Clarady, is being released from gaol today."

"Thank God!" Trumpet snatched up a napkin to cover her smile and coughed to excuse the napkin. Then she painted a demure expression on her face. "I apologize for my outburst, my ladies. But it pained me to know that gallant young man had been unjustly imprisoned on my account."

"We understand." Lady Russell's dry tone suggested she understood all too well.

"Have you apprehended the murderer?" Mrs. Palmer asked. Her lip trembled, as if afraid Mr. Bacon had brought the evildoer with him.

He gazed past her shoulder at the sun-streaked garden wall as he answered. "I confess we have not, but I have learned of two other murders so similar they must have been performed by the same hand. Chapels in each victim's house were robbed as well. These crimes were committed on nights when Mr. Clarady's whereabouts can be attested with certainty."

"More murders!" Mrs. Palmer turned even paler. "How horrible! Who were they?"

"Baron Hewick and a silk merchant named Rouncey," Bacon said.

The widows exchanged a round of glances and then a round of shrugs. Trumpet had never heard of either of them.

"What do you mean by 'similar'?" Lady Russell asked. "The men, or the methods?"

Bacon shot a glance at Mrs. Palmer, then another at his mother. "The methods employed appear to have been the same."

"Then you've learned something about the poison?" Trumpet asked. "And why is this the first I've heard about the chapel being robbed?"

"In regards to the second question: I don't know," Bacon said. "I only learned about it myself yesterday."

Then he should have sent her a note last night. Trumpet fumed inwardly. She hated being left out of things. The way he kept hesitating before answering told her he had information he didn't want to share in present company, probably similarities among the victims. They'd all been Catholics, she'd wager. What else could it be?

If he wasn't even going to send Ben to keep her apprised of developments, she'd have to learn what she could here and now, and a pox upon his hesitations! "With more victims, there should be more evidence. What steps will you take now, Mr. Bacon?"

"Francis's work is done," Lady Bacon said. "His charge was to obtain the release of Lady Surdeval and Mr. Clarady. That has been achieved."

"Quit now, with no real answers?" Trumpet let her displeasure show.

"I would also consider that unsatisfactory," Lady Russell said. "You should at least visit the other victims' houses yourself."

Lady Bacon sniffed at her sister. "I should think my son would be best qualified to determine when —"

"Did you speak to the coroner?" Lady Russell cut her off, earning an indrawn hiss.

"No," Bacon said. "It wasn't necessary."

"Not necessary?" Lady Russell's agate eyes sparked with impatience. "In a matter of death by unknown causes?"

Bacon frowned and began pinching the pleats of his wrist ruff.

"Stop that, Francis," his mother said. "You'll soil your cuffs."

Trumpet's patience wore thin. "You must have learned *something* to indicate why these particular men were murdered in so peculiar a fashion."

"The burglars must have done it," Mrs. Palmer said. "Dastardly brutes, who knows what reasons they might have had?"

Bacon looked skeptical but refrained from comment. He seemed perfectly willing to leave the whole matter unresolved.

"You can't leave it like this," Trumpet said. "Won't the wondering drive you mad?"

He met her eyes briefly, his expression opaque. "Many things cause me wonder, my lady. I've done what the Andromache Society asked me to do." He turned to his mother, who nodded at him with approval.

"I disagree," Lady Russell said. "Lady Surdeval may be at liberty in the literal sense, but as long as these crimes remain unsolved, suspicion will cling to her like a bitter smoke."

"That's true," Trumpet said. And it would be worse for Tom, who had no title to shield him. "Besides, the murderer will probably kill again. Why stop at three?"

Mrs. Palmer gasped at the brusqueness of the question. Trumpet shrugged an apology.

"Let the sheriff pursue him," Lady Bacon said. "I don't like you trotting about after a madman, Francis."

"Now that Mr. Clarady is free," Trumpet said, "he can do the trotting. But we cannot stop. I must know who murdered my poor Lord Surdeval and I want our names to be cleared beyond all doubt." Bacon didn't want to do anymore work, no doubt. Trumpet knew how to persuade him. "You might charge your expenses to the Surdeval estate. Sir William can't object without making himself look guilty."

Bacon's hazel eyes shone. He took a sip of his wine, obviously stalling so as not to appear too easily bought.

Then he smiled and said, "On those terms, I accept. Justice must be served, even in crimes against our enemies in times of war."

"Your commitment does you credit," Trumpet said wryly.

Lady Russell flicked her a glance to acknowledge the ironic tone. "You'll continue to report to the Andromache Society, Nephew." With a nod to her sister, she added, "You will naturally take every precaution."

"Of course," Bacon said. He took another sip of his wine and set the cup down with an air of finality. "If we're done . . ."

"Why don't you show Mrs. Palmer the orchard, Francis?" Lady Bacon said, as if the idea had just occurred to her.

"Oh, yes," Lady Russell said with the same artificial lilt. "It's especially lovely at this time of day." That much was true. The shadows were lengthening as evening drew in, bringing a cool breeze up from the river, though warmth still radiated from the brick walls. The bright sunlight had softened to a rosy glow.

"Ah." Bacon smiled through his teeth. "I do have a report to write, for the recusancy commission, you know."

"Nonsense," Lady Bacon said. "You could use the exercise."

Trumpet enjoyed watching her former tutor squirm under his mother's unrelenting eye. Now she understood why Sarah Palmer had been invited: not as a young companion for Trumpet nor as a widow with experience in Chancery, but as a potential mate for a bashful barrister in chronic need of funds.

She took pity on the man. He had been an excellent tutor, after all. She bounced to her feet and held out a hand to Mrs. Palmer. "I *adore* orchards. Let's all go." She beamed at the older women, batting her lashes at their smoldering glares. Let them smolder; she outranked them by birth and by marriage.

The three young persons passed through a side gate into the next garden. Here fruit trees had been trained in spreading patterns against brick walls and willow scaffolds. Bacon knew a great deal about gardens, to Mrs. Palmer's evident surprise and Trumpet's inner satisfaction. She and the other lads made fun of him behind his back, but they nevertheless took pride in his gifts. Francis Bacon knew something about everything.

They strolled around the neatly raked path while Bacon pointed out varieties of pear, plum, and apricot. Tiny limes formed under spent flowers on trees with waxen leaves. After one circuit, Bacon fell silent, his gaze darting constantly toward the gate. Trumpet could almost hear his nerves thrumming with his desire to escape, but she knew they had only used up a few minutes.

In all honesty, Mrs. Palmer would be a good match for him. She had a son already, so they wouldn't need to produce a child. She was rich, thanks to her husband's lucrative trade with the Spanish. Her mother had been the daughter of the cadet branch of a baronage, so she was more or less gentle by birth. She had an interest in the law and a sense of humor, both of which she would need.

Trumpet lifted her foot and began another circuit, forcing the others to join her. "Do you enjoy the theater, Mrs. Palmer?"

"Oh, yes! I go with my neighbor every Saturday. Have you seen *Tamburlaine*, Mr. Bacon? I thought it the most astonishing play I've even seen."

"I loathe the theater." Bacon's mild tone contrasted with the rudeness of his words. "Egregious nonsense served to a vulgar crowd." Now he had insulted them both, though he didn't seem to realize it. He fixed his eyes on the outer gate. "I really must go. I have an important —" He took three steps away from them, stopped, half turned around, and said, "Do forgive me." Then he turned again and fled through the gate.

They waited, listening for a reaction from the neighboring garden. Nothing.

"I believe he has managed his escape," Mrs. Palmer said. She and Trumpet grinned at one another, then began to giggle helplessly, their laughter rising until they were forced to cover their mouths with their hands.

"Mr. Bacon may not be quite ready for marriage," Trumpet said.

"Perhaps not quite." Mrs. Palmer gave Trumpet a conspiratorial look. "Would you happen to know if your uncle has any plans in that direction?"

"If he hasn't, he ought to," Trumpet said. "In my opinion, he could not do better than a woman such as yourself." She tucked her hand under her new friend's arm and began another turn around the garden. "I beg you to tell me the truth, Mrs. Palmer. Do you think the ladies believed my story about the nap?"

Mrs. Palmer laughed again, a high, short peal. She snapped her lips closed but couldn't repress another throaty chuckle. "Perhaps not entirely. But they have their own objectives. They'll support you to prevent Sir William from setting a precedent harmful to widows. We must protect our own, after all. Who else will do it for us?"

FIFTEEN

Francis left the city through Ludgate and passed the Old Bailey as he trudged up toward Holborn Bridge. He could feel his left garter loosening and only hoped he could make it home before the stocking descended and left him bare-legged in the street. To add to his misery, the stink of the Fleet River assailed his nose and the shame of that humiliating interview in the garden clung to him like a sour sweat.

His aunt and mother ought to have given him some warning. No doubt they assumed he would have made an excuse to avoid the meeting, and so he would have. He had no use for a wife. He'd managed to keep his debts at a manageable level in the past few years, and he'd rather borrow from Tom's father again than lock himself into a fruitless bond. He was comfortable in his house at Gray's Inn, which his own father had built. He liked living in a community of intellectual men. He had no desire to set up housekeeping in some little manor in Hackney or wherever the Palmer woman made her home.

His mother knew all that. The real problem was that, being no sort of a fool, she suspected he would never take an interest in any woman and she kept trying to force the matter. Lucky for him, Trumpet had been there to foil the plot. She'd done him a small favor by leaping in to defuse a tense moment and then deflect the widow's attention in the garden.

Did that place him in her debt? Francis paused briefly, tilting his hat to protect his ear from the sun's burning rays, and considered the question. No, on balance, he thought not. He'd gotten the lady released from the Tower, after all; a greater favor by anyone's standard.

He smiled as he turned up Holborn Road. He would do well to remember that Trumpet — absurd little minx though she might be now — would one day develop into a lady of influence, not unlike his formidable aunt. That day might come sooner rather than later if her next marriage could be arranged more astutely. Perhaps he ought to take an interest in that himself. He could keep his ears open and drop an appropriate word at the opportune moment. He resolved to retain her goodwill and maintain a healthy balance of favors.

When he reached the corner of Gray's Inn Road, he spotted the white sign of the Antelope Inn swinging temptingly up ahead. He wouldn't mind a few moments of solitary respite before going back to Gray's. Ben would be waiting to pepper him with questions about the meeting and who he might or might not have met on the way home, like the nagging wife he didn't want.

He stepped quickly across the road and entered the inn. Mrs. Sprye comprehended his distress at a glance. She led him upstairs to a private room, mercifully dim with curtains drawn against the slanting rays of the sun. He ordered a cup of dragon's milk, a potent ale he rarely imbibed. He felt the need of something strong to rebalance his humors.

The strong drink made him light-headed at first but sent a renewed vigor coursing through his veins. After a few minutes of rest, he felt sufficiently revived to call for a jug of spring water and a writing desk. He would make notes to guide the next steps of his inquiry into the recusant murders. He could send Ben and Tom, now that Tom was free, out to ask the questions.

He dipped his quill and paused to arrange his thoughts. Like a hunter, he needed tracks to follow. He wrote "Matters to pursue" across the top of the page and underlined it twice. The first item was obvious, deriving from the first question the villain or villains must have asked themselves. How could they gain entrance to the victims' houses?

Francis wrote "1. Ingress" and then paused again. The burglars must have left with sacks or chests filled with loot. Heavy, bulky burdens; they might not have gone out the way they came in. He added "and Egress" to the item. These facts might not uniquely identify the villains, but they would help him understand how events had transpired.

Once the burglars got away with their goods, where would they take them? Francis wrote "2. Disposition of chapel goods."

Where could proscribed objects of Catholic worship be sold in England in these fearful times? Selling them might be more dangerous than stealing them in the first place. This was another good trail for Tom to follow given his father's livelihood. Privateering and smuggling were two sides of the same ill-gotten coin, after all. Besides, there must be dozens of pawnshops in the London area; that meant days of dusty legwork.

So much for the burglary aspect. The third matter focused on the more heinous crime. He wrote "3. Poison" and began a search within his own well-stocked memory. What substances caused paralysis? Monkshood, also known as wolfsbane, would work, but its known symptoms did not accord with the description of the scene. He would follow the poison trail himself since it was as much a matter of natural philosophy as of criminal expedience. He would start with a visit to his own apothecary tomorrow.

What else? Francis reviewed his short list and realized that he hadn't begun quite at the beginning. Before considering methods of ingress, the villains must first have chosen a target. He wrote "4. Selection of victims" and stopped, holding his quill suspended over the squat inkpot while he took a sip of the strong ale.

This question troubled him the most. The killer appeared to be choosing recusants who had been questioned by Her Majesty's pursuivants and then merely confined to their homes until the crisis had passed. They were too rich or too well bred to be locked in a common prison yet deemed too tame to be sent to Wisbech Castle with the most dangerous peers. All three victims had been the milder sort of Catholic, with houses in the London area with private chapels and wives suspected of giving aid to seminary priests.

The victims formed an obvious class to Francis, but who else would see them that way? The public at large knew little about the recusancy commission until their work resulted in a hanging. Suspects who answered the questions satisfactorily returned to their homes without fanfare. Their names were ticked off the list and a mild eye kept on their activities; sufficient for the government, but not, apparently, for the murderer.

Who had access to those lists? Francis kept one; Sir Richard Topcliffe kept another. Sir William Waad, secretary to the Privy Council, kept the master copy. The commission's activities were confidential until verdicts were reached. Copies of those lists were not meant to be circulated. Of course, the clerks who made and kept the copies knew everything, as always.

Francis kept a close guard on his list; only Ben had seen it. Members of the Privy Council generally took pains with such documents. Everyone loathed torture, however necessary it might be in times of war, and sought to limit its use and public knowledge of same. Almost everyone — Sir Richard had boasted of his ability to pry secrets out of men by such measures.

Could the murderer arrive at those particular names by some other means? Did the victims have anything else in common besides their religious preference and their well-furnished chapels? Could their deaths somehow benefit the same person?

Francis doubted it. Only the chapels were emptied; nothing else was taken from houses filled with ancient treasures. That fact and the crosses carved in the victims' chests proclaimed the religious connection; indeed, the crosses declared a hatred for Catholics that went beyond mere wartime loyalty to queen and country.

A sour taste bubbled up from his stomach, not caused by the dragon's milk. Francis feared he knew where the fourth trail would lead: back around in a circle to the recusancy commission. He also feared he lacked the courage to follow it to the end.

A bustle arose outside the door. Some lively group was probably coming up to have supper in one of the other private rooms. They'd be noisy. He might as well go home. But his door opened before he could finish his drink, and in bounded Thomas Clarady, crying, "Here you are!" Behind him came a man who might have been his twin but older and more weather-beaten, dressed like Tom in gay colors. Captain Clarady, home from the sea. Ben brought up the rear, a tall brown heron shepherding two peacocks.

"What luck!" Tom said. "We came for a drink and Mrs. Sprye told us you were here. My father had hoped to speak with you, and he only has the one night ashore."

Francis glanced toward the windows, knowing there was no escape. Mrs. Sprye might have warned him; he could have slipped out the back. Too late now. He rose and answered, "Luck indeed. I thank God for your safe return, Captain Clarady. Any news of the Spanish fleet?"

"Of course there's news," Tom said. "News aplenty, and the truth for a change. But first let's get a fresh round of everything." He eyed the cup and jug beside the writing desk, then turned to the serving wench. "More of that, Dolly, whatever it is, and three pitchers of your best beer.

129

And let's have some savories — bread and cheese, whatever's handy. I'm too hungry to wait for supper."

"Another dragon's milk, Mr. Bacon?" Dolly asked.

Francis declined the offer with a wince as Ben and Tom traded amused grins. He withstood a hearty clap on the back from the captain and allowed his hand to be shaken almost free of his arm.

He had met Tom's father once two years ago, when Tom had first come up to Gray's in the train of the Earl of Dorchester's son. Tom had been placed at the clerk's table as befitted his station, but the captain had higher ambitions. Through his connections among merchants and port officials, he had identified a senior barrister with a substantial burden of debt; namely, one Francis Bacon. The captain had paid him a visit and a deal was struck. Tom had moved into Ben's chambers and up to the students' table in the hall. He and his chums had also become Francis's pupils.

Ben walked around him to move toward the far end of the table. "I was surprised to learn you were here, Francis. Why didn't you come home after your appointment with the widows? Did you meet the Earl of Essex again?"

"No." Francis frowned at the waspish tone. Ben had been harping on His Lordship as if some great personal bond had formed during that one short ride in the coach. A seed might have been planted — Francis hoped it had — but it was far too early for fruit. "I just wanted a respite from people and their endless questions."

They glared at one another, but Tom broke in with his relentless cheer. "Then you should have gone someplace where no one knows you, Mr. Bacon." He followed his father to take a seat on the opposite side of the table.

Ben slid past, ostentatiously averting his gaze from the half-written page of paper, and took a chair across from the captain. Francis resumed his own seat, arranging his list and his writing materials in orderly squares.

Dolly came back with a big tray, followed by a footman with an even bigger one. While waiting for the servers to distribute cups and plates, Francis regarded the two Clarady men. They made a handsome pair, each having the same clean-limbed frames and well-proportioned features on faces apt to smile, which displayed identical dimples in their left cheeks. Each had an abundance of fair, curly hair, although the captain's was a shade ruddier, especially his beard. He wore his beard and moustaches long while Tom preferred the more fashionable pointed beard with thin moustaches. Each wore a large pearl dangling from his left ear, an affectation that never failed to irritate Francis, ever since Sir Walter Ralegh had brought the fashion to court.

Tom met his gaze with a hint of challenge; from what cause, Francis could not imagine. He decided to ignore it. He smiled at his pupil. "Your time in Newgate doesn't seem to have done you any harm."

"So kind of you to take an interest." Tom's tone dripped with irony, earning him sharp looks from both Ben and his father. Ah. The lad had chosen to blame Francis for his recent predicament rather than Trumpet or his own poor judgment.

"Tush, Tom!" the captain said. "That cell looked better than your berth aboard the *Susannah*. A sight cleaner anyway, and I'll wager the food was fresher. That's thanks to your friends here. You owe them your freedom as well."

"I may be free," Tom said, "but I'm not clear. Until we catch the murderer, I'll be walking under a constant cloud of suspicion."

"I fear you are correct," Francis said. "Lady Surdeval said as much. In fact, she —"

As if summoned like a demon by the mention of her name, the door flew open and Trumpet appeared on the threshold. She made a striking figure in her widow's black, with the arching white widow's coif framing her face.

SIXTEEN

Trumpet's gaze flew straight to Tom. "You're free!" He grinned back at her, holding her gaze for a long, long moment, reveling in the simple pleasure of being together. A throat cleared and her attention shifted to the other side of the room, where Francis Bacon edged slowly toward the rear of the room, where Ben stood frowning at her.

Bacon asked, "Is that woman with you?" His pitch rose steeply.

"Who? Mrs. Palmer? Yes, she's here. She stopped downstairs to speak with Mrs. Sprye about a coach or something. She'll be right up." She tilted her head at Ben, smiling away his disapproving frown, which she knew had to do with her being glad to see Tom. As if she couldn't be *glad* without the world falling to pieces. "What a delight to find you all here! We came for a drink and —" She broke off as she noticed the fourth man in the room. Tall, fair, smiling, with a dimple creasing his cheek.

She strode forward with both hands outstretched. "You must be Captain Clarady! I've heard so much about you. I feel I've known you for years!"

"Good things, I hope." The captain bowed and kissed her hand. "And you would be . . ."

"This is Trumpet," Tom said. "Or rather, Lady Alice Trumpington. Or no, oops — now she's Alice Gumery, Lady Surdeval."

"That's a weight of names for so slender a maid." The captain smiled down on her. "Though I might have guessed, my lady. You're the spit of your father, my Lord of Orford."

"Do you know him?"

"What seafaring man doesn't! You're right glad to spot the Earl Corsair in the offing when you're caught between the devil and the deep blue sea."

"You are?" Trumpet blinked at him, bemused. She couldn't remember ever hearing her father praised. Usually, she caught knowing looks and gloved whispers about gambling, mounting debts, or other such faults.

She beamed at the captain as she moved toward the empty chair between father and son. What extraordinary luck! She'd invited Mrs. Palmer to join her for a cup of wine at the Antelope after being released from the elder widows' clutches. True, she'd secretly hoped Tom might choose to come to the inn for a well-cooked meal after a week of prison rations. But never in her wildest dreams had she imagined she'd get to meet his father!

Even better, now that the whole team was together, they could have a full and frank discussion of the murders. She wanted to know whatever it was Bacon had kept from his mother and aunt. They were old and quarrelsome; naturally, he'd hold back in their presence. But Trumpet wanted details. She wanted to know every single thing Bacon had learned so far and what he planned to do next.

Before she could sit, Mrs. Palmer appeared in the doorway. "Come in!" Trumpet cried. "Come meet my friends." She gestured across the table. "You know Mr. Bacon, of course." She introduced Ben, then Captain Clarady, and last, Tom, as if he were merely a minor participant. She didn't want the pretty widow paying too much attention to him.

Mrs. Palmer made a curtsy to each gentleman and murmured the conventional phrases. If she had any special interest in one or the other, she kept it to herself.

Trumpet pointed at the chair between Ben and Mr. Bacon. "Sit!" She seated herself between the Claradys and clasped her hands on the table before her. "We're going to discuss the murders."

"Oh!" Mrs. Palmer's hand flew to her mouth. She glanced at the door as if contemplating flight, then turned to Ben for some reason. "If you promise not to say anything *too* frightening . . ."

Ben somehow made himself taller and rumbled, "Your presence will be a bond for our good behavior, Mistress."

While he helped her into her chair and the other men resumed their places, an idea bloomed in Trumpet's mind — a splendid idea that would serve many purposes at once. Ben should marry the rich, pretty, young widow, not Mr. Bacon.

She'd always suspected Ben's preference for men had more to do with his circumstances than his fundamental tastes. Tom had told her some men turned to other men in colleges and Inns of Court and such, but liked women well enough once they moved out into the world. Ben always noticed pretty women and responded to them, puffing out his chest and lowering his voice. Bacon never did that sort of thing. Bevies of naked goddesses could frolic beneath his nose and he would merely sneeze at their perfume.

Mrs. Palmer's wealth would solve Ben's money woes once and for all, allowing him to pursue a legal career commensurate with his abilities. He'd adjust to marriage in time. He'd love the stability and the domesticity and be a good husband to both the woman and her estates.

Best of all, if Ben and Sarah had a house in London — perhaps even here in Holborn, handy to Gray's Inn — nothing would be more natural than for Trumpet to visit them frequently. Tom would do the same; he would naturally be a fixture in his best friend's house.

Yes, yes, yes! A marriage between Ben and Sarah would be ideal. She'd set to work on it as soon as the current problem was resolved. Yet another reason to get this sordid business behind them as quickly as could be. She pointed her chin at the papers on the table. "Were you making a plan, Mr. Bacon?"

"Yes," he replied. "I've listed four areas to be investigated. But Captain Clarady has only a short time to spend with his son. Perhaps he would prefer we postpone this discussion?"

"Not on my account," the captain said. He shot a wink across the table. "We're in for a real treat, Mrs. Palmer, getting to watch Mr. Bacon's gallant crew of intelligencers in action. Tom told me all about how they solved several ticklish murders at Gray's Inn during his first Christmas here."

"I look forward to it," Mrs. Palmer said.

Trumpet and Tom traded grins. The captain was Tom times ten! And she was a recognized member of the gallant crew. She asked, "What's first on your list?"

"The first question is obvious: ingress and egress."

Tom leaned across Trumpet with a wink and said to his father, "That's lawyer talk for how they got in and out."

Trumpet giggled, but the captain seemed unamused by Tom's impertinence. "Sounds like the right question to me. Were there broken windows or other such signs?"

"Not at Surdeval House," Francis said. "I don't know about the others."

"The windows in my lord's bedchamber were open," Trumpet said. "The night was mild."

"But the rest of the house must have been locked up," Ben said. "Could the burglars have come through His Lordship's bedchamber?"

"Why not?" Tom asked. "The viscount was deep in the arms of Morpheus. I doubt they did though. There must have been two or three to carry out all the booty. One of them would have been a lock-picker, most like. They'd come up the lawn from the river, where they'd leave their boat. You'd need a boat to carry away that much stuff. You couldn't very well leave a horse and cart standing about on the Strand, where every gate has a guard. They'd pick the lock at the bankside gate and whichever door they liked to get into the house. They'd go out the same way."

"I see you've given this some thought," Bacon said.

"There isn't much else to do in gaol." His tone was bitter. He probably blamed Bacon for his nights in Newgate. Unfair, if understandable. Trumpet shot him a sympathetic smile. At least he didn't blame her.

Bacon ignored the tone, or didn't notice it. He could be heedless of other people's humors. He said, "Baron Hewick had a house in Chelsea, I believe, although I don't know if it's on the river. I don't know where Mr. Rouncey lived."

Ben said, "In Bermondsey, south of the river, although his house might not be on the bank."

"I'll bet it is," Tom said.

"It would be worth finding out," Bacon said. "It might tell us something about our villains' capabilities. Ben, you and Tom should visit both houses tomorrow. Talk to the current householders. There might be other details about the crimes that the sheriff's men failed to note."

"That I can well believe," Ben said. "I'm afraid the sheriff is not overly concerned about these crimes."

Captain Clarady said, "If my son weren't involved, and Your Ladyship as well, I might not care so much myself. Three Catholics the fewer? Good riddance, some would say."

"Many, I should think," Mrs. Palmer said, then placed her hand over her mouth, as if she'd spoken out of turn.

Tom gave her a dimpled smile and answered his father. "That's the wrong idea, Dad. We can't let everyone go around murdering anyone they don't like. Where would it end? If people have grudges, they should bring them into the courts and let us lawyers work it out."

"For a handsome fee, eh, me boyo?" A huge grin spread across the captain's face. He winked across the table at Mr. Bacon. "'Us lawyers,' did you hear that? My son." He poked himself in the chest.

His unconstrained pride touched a chord of envy in Trumpet's breast. She couldn't imagine anything she could do to inspire such an emotion in her own father. In truth, the only person who had ever clapped her on the back to congratulate her for some achievement was Tom.

Bacon regarded his pupil with a wry look. "Your analysis is correct, Tom, if crudely phrased."

Tom leaned sideways to whisper in Trumpet's ear. "It could have been cruder." She giggled, but stopped as she caught the severe look in Captain Clarady's eyes. She didn't want Tom to get in trouble with his father.

The captain said, "I find it hard to understand, Mr. Bacon, how there can be any Catholics left in England, after what their masters in Rome and Spain have put us through."

"That's an interesting question, Captain." Bacon sounded pleased at the new topic. It was the sort of conversation he liked — abstract and political. "I wish I could offer you a simple answer, but if it were simple, we wouldn't need pursuivants or recusancy commissions. Most English Catholics don't see themselves as subjects of the pope. They love the traditions, the forms of worship they grew up with, the beautiful objects and music used in familiar rituals, and the connection to their own family histories."

"But fostering priests and spreading dangerous tracts only encourages our enemies," Ben said. "How can loyal Englishmen not recognize that as treason? I find that baffling myself."

"English*men* may recognize that such deeds put them outside the pale," Bacon said. "But these men believe their estates are theirs to govern as they please, within their own bounds. And let us not forget the English*women*: the wives, and more especially, the widows." He chuckled and took a small sip from his cup, making a face at the taste. "My mother is that sort of widow, as a matter of fact."

"Lady Anne Bacon is a Catholic?" Sarah Palmer's voice rose shrilly. "You astonish me, Mr. Bacon!"

"No, no. Heavens, no!" Bacon laughed. "Quite the contrary, I assure you. My mother is an ardent Calvinist. I only meant that she is in some ways like the Catholic widows who devote themselves wholeheartedly to their religious practices. Her Calvinism is the organizing principle of her life. Her household runs in accordance with the religious calendar. She summons her entire staff to chapel — a very plain chapel — for prayers twice a day, every day. She provides houseroom to visiting preachers, some of whom are so extreme they've been expelled from their own parishes. She spends hours a day translating religious tracts sent to her from the Continent, some of which might provoke the arrest of a man or a woman of lesser status. In short, she is the Protestant counterpart of Ladies Hewick and Surdeval — the late one, I mean." Bacon inclined his head toward Trumpet.

"It sounds exciting when you put it that way," Trumpet said. "These women are actively engaged in important affairs of state, even though it looks like they're just choosing the daily menu and deciding what should be read to the servants at meals. And of course all great houses have tutors in residence and other long-term guests; it's part of their function."

"Precisely," Bacon said. "Without such women, unapproved religions would find it hard to maintain any kind of foothold in our society."

"They're virtually untouchable too," Ben said. "Legally speaking. Since they have no standing, they can't be prosecuted."

"That's the part I like," Trumpet said, "though I don't plan to waste my time on religious conflict. I'm going to specialize in the law, like Lady Russell. When I have my own house, I'll fill it with poets and philosophers."

Bacon tendered her a curious smile. Had he never considered that one of these days she would become a woman of consequence? He needn't worry. Having Francis Bacon at her table would ensure its respectability and attract other men of intellect in one stroke.

"What's next on the list?" she asked.

Bacon consulted his page. "The disposition of the chapel goods."

"They'll be out of the country by now," Tom said.

The captain nodded. "France would be my guess."

"Dieppe, I'll wager, or St. Jean de Luz. Don't you think so, Dad?"

The captain snapped his fingers at his son. "Just the place for them! And I'm not surprised you remember it."

The two men shared a deep chuckle, plainly remembering some shared adventure.

"What's in St. Jean de Luz?" Trumpet snapped. Knowing Tom, the adventure had involved a brothel.

Tom waggled his eyebrows at her. "Nothing suitable for a lady's ears."

She kicked him under the table and he grinned.

"It has a vile reputation," Mrs. Palmer said, widening her pale blue eyes. "Although every merchant is obliged to avail himself of its services if he wishes to stay in business."

"I've never heard of it," Ben said.

The captain said, "It used to be just a fly speck down near the Spanish border. Then King Philip closed his ports to English ships, and merchants on both sides had to find another way to deliver their goods. St. Jean has a good harbor and port officials eager to be bought. You swap your cargo with a German or French ship to take it on to the final destination. Cloth and corn for Spain, oil and oranges for England. Most folks care more about what's on their backs and their tables than they do about what's said in their neighbors' churches, when it comes down to it. Trade must go on." He nodded at Mrs. Palmer, who nodded back.

Bacon said, "Those are basic commodities, bought and sold in bulk. Would you also sell small items of value and rarity in such a place?"

"You would," the captain said. "You'd need a special sort of buyer and you wouldn't get half their value, but you can sell anything in St. Jean de Luz." He flashed a smile. "When I take a ship, I take everything, right down to the officers' spare linens. I've sold crucifixes studded with pearls, Bibles wrapped in scented kidskin, all manner of gewgaws."

"How would you find this special sort of buyer?" Bacon asked.

"Depends on the goods, Mr. Bacon. Some things you can sell to anyone. A chalice is just gold and jewels once you melt it down. But some things are worth more than what they're made from. Those saint's boxes, for example — reliquaries, they call 'em. They can get to be part of the family, you might say. The owner will likely pay a smart sum to get that back."

Ben said, "Surely you don't go into Spain to sell them."

"Not me," the captain answered. "But I know a man who will. Jacques Le Bon, as slippery a Frenchie as ever you might hope to meet."

Tom laughed. "His name may be Le Bon, but there's nothing good about him."

"Nothing but his connections and his smooth talk," the captain said. "We've locked horns a few times over the years, but he's the first I'd ask about selling any especially tricky goods."

"He could sell water to a wherryman, couldn't he, Dad?"

"Or pomp to the pope."

The Clarady men laughed heartily, leaning back in their chairs. Trumpet basked in the reflected warmth of their mutual affection. She wanted to be part of it. She wanted both of them, somehow, someday; the one for a husband, the other for a beloved father-in-law.

Bacon also regarded the father and son with a wistful gaze. His father had been one of the most important men in the kingdom. He'd also had many other sons. Perhaps he hadn't had much time for the youngest one. Funny, Trumpet had never given a moment's thought to Bacon's relationship to his father before. At least Sir Nicholas had been an honorable man.

Sticking to the matter at hand, Bacon asked, "Who manages the English side of these transactions?"

"That's the job of the upright man," Tom said.

Bacon frowned. "Do you mean upstanding?"

Ben answered, "The upright man is the chief among thieves, the one who plans the swindle or organizes the job." Bacon raised his eyebrows and Ben shrugged. "The broadsides love thieves' cant."

And Ben loved the broadsides, the more scandalous the better.

"I believe our upright man may be a gentleman, probably educated, possibly even a lawyer." Tom said, a hint of challenge in his tone.

"Oh, surely not!" Mrs. Palmer cried.

Ben and Bacon made scoffing noises, but the captain held up a hand. "Tom could have the right of it. Not all gentlemen have the means to support their tastes, you know."

Bacon tilted his head. "I'll concede the possibility, but we must not allow ourselves to be misled by unsupported assumptions."

"Someone must be organizing these jobs," Tom insisted. "Someone with the authority to prevent the thieves from stripping the whole house bare. They only took what they came for; that shows restraint and planning." He gave them a tight-lipped grin that suggested he could say more if he wanted to.

Ben noticed it too. "I get the feeling you're not telling us everything you learned in Newgate."

Tom gave a hollow laugh. "I sincerely doubt you want to know *everything*. For example, were you aware that rats can actually —"

"I believe we can forgo the details," Bacon said. His tone made it clear that he would not indulge in guessing games. "I'm sure the experience was most unpleasant. Let us hope it inspires you to greater discretion in future."

Captain Clarady and Ben grinned. Trumpet pressed her foot against his to signal that she was on his side. She'd get whatever it was out of him next time they found a way to meet in private.

Tom kept his foot next to hers to show he understood. For the others, he leaned back and folded his arms across his chest. "I'll find the upright man; wait and see if I don't."

"It isn't a contest," Francis said. "We must work together." He returned his attention to Captain Clarady. "I had thought to send Tom and Ben out to survey pawnshops, but perhaps that would be a waste of time?"

"Not necessarily," the captain said. "While I agree with my boy here that the goods have probably gone south, they must have been kept somewhere for a time. You've got five burglaries, according to Mr. Whitt, spread out over the last month. Your thieves would have stored up their takings until they had enough to justify the journey. It can take a week or more to sail to St. Jean de Luz and that long to return. The Bay of Biscay has some fearsome treacherous winds."

"It's faster to sail in than out," Tom said. "And Dieppe is less than a day."

"If the weather's good. At any rate, Mr. Bacon, the lads might be able to find the place where they kept the stuff and pick up the trail from there."

"Thank you, Captain. We need trails we can pursue in England, or we're lost before we start."

"I'll be in Dieppe tomorrow night," the captain said. "I could poke around a bit. Le Bon might be around and in the mood to parley. If I find out anything, I'll send word with someone trusty."

"That would be very helpful, Captain," Bacon said.

Trumpet asked, "Won't you come straight back yourself?"

"No, my lady, not for a few weeks at least. I'm going fishing." He grinned, showing the Clarady dimple. "Our lads need food and medicine, commodities in short supply in England. But the Duke of Parma is still getting supplies for his troops in the Netherlands. I thought I'd see if I might relieve him of a cargo or two."

"We wish you the best of success," Mrs. Palmer said. "And a safe return."

"And a longer visit next time," Tom said. "You've got to see *Tamburlaine*, Dad; it'll purely amaze you." He patted Trumpet's foot with his. She took it as an invitation to join them. She'd fund another performance of the play herself for the chance to sit between the Clarady men!

Tom cocked his head at Francis. "Did you want us to tour the pawnshops before or after we visit the victims' houses?"

His father's tutted at the disrespectful tone, but Mr. Bacon always ignored their attempts to bait him. "After," he said. "Look for any place that seems to be dealing in religious impedimenta. You might try some of the less upstanding goldsmiths. Or should I say, 'upright' ones?" His eyes twinkled at the joke, but no one laughed. He had the worst sense of humor Trumpet had ever encountered — before she'd met his mother, that was.

He sighed and returned to his list. "The third item is the question of the poison we assume was employed to effect the murders. I'll pursue this myself. My apothecary has a broad knowledge of herbs and other medicines, as well as a fine collection of books on the subject. He might know something."

Captain Clarady said, "From what the lads told me, it sounds like it could be a sort of arrow poison."

"Why, yes. My Lord of Essex suggested that as well." Bacon shot a glance at Ben, whose lips had tightened. "He reminded me that the savages of the New World use such potions for hunting. Do you have any experience with them, Captain?"

"I'm sorry to say I don't, Mr. Bacon. To be honest, I'm not altogether convinced they exist." He wagged his finger. "I'll tell you who might know something — a new fellow in my crew. An Indian, as we call them. I picked him up in the Spanish Main this last time out. It's a pity you can't ask him yourself, but by the time we could send for him, it would be time for me to leave."

"I gather such poisons aren't easily come by," Bacon said.

"I've never tried." The captain fingered his pearl earring the way Tom did when he was thinking. "I'd start with an apothecary, as you say. One that collects the nastier potions." He chuckled. "I know a fellow in Amsterdam I wouldn't care to be on the wrong side of."

"Your apothecary is Dutch, Francis," Ben said.

Bacon chuffed. "And a perfectly respectable man. Although there are apothecaries of the other sort in London as well. Can you think of any other source, Captain? A chandler, perhaps . . ."

"I don't think so, Mr. Bacon. The stuff might be a myth, to my mind, like the fabled cities of gold. Something rare and dangerous that kills at a touch? Although if it's real, it would appeal to the sort of men who collect exotic weapons. You know the kind I mean."

"Lords," Ben said with a pointed glance at Bacon. "Men with great estates and great houses, who cultivate connections abroad."

Bacon gave him a dark look. "Persons whom we will certainly not be troubling with our intrusive speculations."

The two men evidently had some sort of ongoing quarrel. Trumpet wished they would leave it in their chambers. Their continual carping was making a poor impression on Mrs. Palmer. "What about the last item, Mr. Bacon? You said you had four areas of investigation?"

"Yes." Bacon tapped a finger on the paper, staring down at it as if unwilling to read what he'd written. After a longish pause, he said, "The last item concerns the selection of victims."

"I would have put that first," Tom said, earning another sharp look from his father. He shrugged. "I apologize, but it is first, logically."

"They're obviously choosing Catholics," Ben said.

"But only certain ones," Trumpet said. "And not the hottest by any measure."

"Rich ones with chapels," Tom said. "That's the key, for the burglaries at least."

"We can't separate the burglaries from the murders," Francis said. "We need one key that fits both."

"I don't see why," Trumpet said. "You could easily rob the chapel at Surdeval House without waking anyone if you were quiet about it and had your boat waiting, as Tom said. Why murder my poor lord, who must have been sound asleep?"

Bacon shook his head and wagged his finger at her. "No, Trumpet, it doesn't hold. The crimes cannot be unrelated. Occam's Razor won't allow it."

"I thought the men were poisoned," the captain said. "Did the murderer use a razor too?"

Bacon smiled at him. "It's a principle of parsimony, Captain. It means we must not postulate superfluous entities."

The captain's face went blank. Tom grinned. "He means we should pick the simplest answer, Dad, that's all."

Trumpet added, "If we have two crimes in the same house on the same night, we should assume one person or gang is doing both of them."

"That makes perfect sense," the captain said. "I hold with Mr. Occam."

Ben snapped his fingers. "Here's another idea that bridges the two. What if the thieves committed the murders to confuse the authorities? They've figured out that they can steal quantities of valuables from secret chapels without much risk of pursuit, assuming there's an upright man to coordinate their sale. But to cover their tracks even further, they commit these strange murders, seemingly motivated by religious hatred. That draws all the attention and sends any pursuers off in search of a lunatic."

Mrs. Palmer gazed at him in admiration. "You are a most ingenious man, Mr. Whitt."

"He's an exceptional legal counselor as well," Trumpet put in. "Easily the match of my uncle, in case you want a man in London."

"That is an intriguing idea, Ben," Bacon said, "although a shade diabolical."

Tom said, "These burglars would have to be far more ruthless than the usual variety. Usually thieves avoid violence." He gave them that tight-lipped smirk again.

Everyone fell silent while they pondered the implications of Ben's idea. Tom had obviously picked up some gossip about burglaries in Newgate. He might even have had a long conversation with a thief and now considered himself an expert. Trumpet wanted to hear every detail. Could she get the men to stay for supper? Or better yet, come to Chadwick House?

"I believe we all have our tasks for the morrow," Bacon said. "Ben and Tom will start by visiting the other victim's houses and make inquiries in a few pawnshops. I will visit my apothecary and learn what I can about poisons that cause paralysis."

"What should I do?" Trumpet asked. "I could visit pawnshops; many ladies do. My maidservant can help me concoct something Catholic-looking that I could try to sell."

Tom patted her foot with his to say he thought it a good idea. But the other men only frowned. Bacon said, "Your task, my lady, is to remain at home, presenting a portrait of perfect propriety."

My lady? It had been "Trumpet" a minute ago. "Do *nothing?*"

No one answered, not even Tom. If they thought she would sit at home twiddling her thumbs while they got to have all the fun, they had another think coming.

SEVENTEEN

The counterman plunked two mugs of hot ale laced with nutmeg in front of Tom and his father, then slid a wooden plate of warm bread toward their reaching hands. The Claradys were breaking the night's fast at a dockside tavern in Billingsgate that opened at the crack of dawn. In spite of the hour, the place was crowded with men waiting for the tide to turn so they could take the long ferry downriver to Gravesend, where the *Susannah* awaited its captain.

"Odd little man," Captain Clarady said, with reference to Francis Bacon. "He slipped away like that the first time I met him."

Tom took a wary sip of his ale — too hot. He followed his father outside, where a cool breeze rose off the river, strong enough to ruffle the hair curling under his hat. "Mr. Bacon finds sociability wearisome. He can only stand so much before he has to scuttle off to hide in a cool, dark room and recover." He chuckled, expecting his father to share the joke, but got a stern frown instead.

"He may be odd, but he's still your master, Tom. When he says froggy, you hop and hop lively."

"Aye, Captain." Tom dunked his bread in his mug and chewed it slowly, wondering what Mr. Bacon had said to his father last night. Mrs. Sprye had come in to ask about supper and they'd broken off their discussion of the murders. Ben had started collecting Mr. Bacon's papers and Trumpet had gone down with Mrs. Palmer, who said she had to get home to her son.

Tom had taken the opportunity to go out to the jakes. When he came back, he'd found his father and his tutor having a quiet conversation in the corner, which they plainly did not want him to hear.

Then Ben and Trumpet had drawn him into a dispute about where to eat. Trumpet wanted to bring them all back to Chadwick House, but Ben adamantly objected. He forbade Tom — as if he could — to so much as walk up Bishopsgate Street. He wanted to send Trumpet home at once. She flatly refused to leave, claiming she had as much right to have supper with Captain Clarady as Ben, which in all fairness, she did.

They'd finally agreed she could stay and sup with them at the Antelope, a perfectly respectable establishment. Mrs. Sprye was there, after all, and Catalina Luna was somewhere about. One of the grooms would escort the young women home afterward.

Bacon had slipped out sometime during their debate, presumably to take his supper from a tray in the soothing solitude of his chambers.

Now Captain Clarady strode to the edge of the wharf and peered down, gauging the rate and direction of the water's flow. One of the other men waiting for the ferry made some remark and they chatted for a few minutes. Tom watched them, his heart swelling in his chest. His father had always been his hero. Half of him wanted to toss his legal career into the Thames and follow him to sea, but the other half had learned that a court battle could be as exciting as one with steel blades once you knew the stakes and understood the tactics.

His father returned to the stretch of windowsill Tom had claimed as a table. "Should be here in a few minutes."

"When do you think you'll be back?"

The captain shrugged. "Depends on my luck, me lad, as always."

They watched a small boat pulling up alongside a ship down the other end of the wharf. Two men climbed up a rope ladder to the deck.

The captain said, "I'll pick up the gossip in Dieppe, sniff out who's carrying what for who. The Duke of Parma's suppliers are as like to be flying French or Danish flags. We need everything from rope to flour, but I'm hoping for munitions for a start."

"Is that likely?"

"Oh, I think so. Parma's so desperate for gunpowder he'd trade his own men for it if he thought anyone would take them. 'Course we are too. At any rate, I won't capture many ships with what I've got at present, so powder has to be first on my list."

Captain Clarady polished off his bread in two bites. Then he cocked his head and looked at Tom with pride warming his blue eyes. "I can see you're moving well along the path I set you on two years ago. Your speech is more Westminster than West Country now. I'll wager you're handier with a quill than a rope now too."

Tom winced. He hadn't realized he'd changed so much.

His father chuckled. "Aye, lad, you've grown into your new life. I'm well pleased. I took the first ship ready to sail when I set you up with Francis Bacon, but that's turned out to be a shrewd choice. I like this intelligencing game he's gotten you into. It's risky, granted, but it's already made your name known to the Lord Treasurer. Be careful, me boyo. Keep your wits sharp and your blade sharper."

"Always."

"Good lad. And you couldn't have chosen better than Mr. Whitt if you'd hired an intelligencer to spy you out the perfect chum. He's a loyal friend and a true, or you can hang me for a lewd cur."

"I trust him almost as much as I trust you." Except where Mr. Bacon was concerned. "I believe you've set me

150

on the right course, Father. I like my studies and I'm a fast learner. I acquit myself as well as most in the exercises in the hall these days. I'll be a great barrister one day, I promise you."

"That's what Mr. Bacon told me."

Tom's jaw dropped. He barely heard his father's booming laughter. Mr. Bacon usually treated him like a block-witted foreigner whose English was spotty at best. He'd never given a single hint that he regarded his unwanted pupil as anything but a burden.

Captain Clarady watched them load bales of wool onto the ship for a while, giving Tom a moment to absorb the unexpected compliment. Then he drained his mug and set it on the tar-streaked windowsill. "All that's well and good, me boyo. But I do *not* like the way you're carrying on with my Lord of Orford's daughter. That's a powder keg with a smoldering fuse and no mistake."

"I'm not carrying on with Trumpet, Dad. We're friends, that's all."

"She's *Lady Surdeval*, Tom, even in your own head." The captain grasped Tom's shoulder to catch his gaze and hold it. "Never forget it. The nobility, they're not like you and me. She may seem to be your friend. She may even believe with all her heart and soul that she's your friend. But she's the daughter of an earl and no more free to choose her friends than I am to choose which way the wind will blow. Her marriage is a matter of state. And so is her maidenhead." He jabbed his index finger at Tom's chest to emphasize each of those last words. "Touch her at your peril. One whisper of scandal and all we've built for you goes crashing onto the rocks."

Tom held his peace. He wouldn't contradict his father to his face, but the captain had some old-fashioned ideas. He would never understand.

His father wagged his finger in his face. "I mean it, Tom. No trifling with that girl. Promise me."

"I promise." Tom wouldn't dream of trifling with Trumpet; it would be far too dangerous.

Men began to cluster at the edge of the dock. The ferry must be pulling up. The captain tilted his head to sniff the breeze. "It's a good day for a sail." He always said that, even when rain fell in buckets on their heads. He flashed a dimpled grin, reached into the deep pocket inside his galligaskins, and came up with a large gold coin. He flipped it to Tom, who caught it in his palm and held it up to examine both sides.

"Minted in New Spain," the captain said. "I took it from the grandee's quarters on the ship we drove aground at Calais. Keep it for luck. You'll need it if you keep on with Lady Alice. Mark my words, Tom. She's her father's daughter, and I don't mean only her bonny green eyes."

"Thanks, Dad. I'll keep the coin in my pocket and the good advice in here." Tom tapped his chest.

"Let the one remind you of the other." Captain Clarady shot a glance at the queue, where some men had already started climbing down to the wherry. He threw his arms around Tom, clasping him close to his chest. "I love you, Son. And I'm proud of you." He gave him a few thwacks on the back to shake the tears welling into Tom's eyes, and he was gone.

* * *

Tom walked all the way home, knowing it would take forever to get a wherry going upstream at that hour. He wanted to stretch his legs anyway after a week in gaol and liked watching the city wake up. He passed a crew of men removing the heavy chains that had been strung across Cheapside and Tower Street to block the Spanish troops if they ever made it all the way to London. Some wards had laborers out forking heaps of rubbish onto carts to be hauled to the countryside. All manner of muck had been left to rot in the kennels during the long crisis, but Londoners were coming home at last and taking up their normal duties.

Tom walked up Bishopsgate Street to prove he could walk wherever he pleased, lifting his hat as he passed Chadwick House. He didn't bother to look up. Trumpet wouldn't be awake at this hour even if a Spanish *tercio* came marching past her door with pistols blazing. He strode out the city gate and up to Hog Lane to cross Finsbury Fields, enjoying the fresh smell of dewy grass and the view of fresh maids laying out linens to dry. Swinging back down Gray's Inn Road, he bought a couple of plum and raisin pies from the vendor outside the gatehouse and tossed one to Ben as he walked in the door of their chambers.

"Bless you, my chum." Ben, stark naked with his hair standing up in all directions, had obviously just staggered out of bed. He ate his pie where he stood. Then he found a cleanish towel and scrubbed himself from neck to knee.

"It's going to be another bright day." Tom stripped to the skin and gave himself a good rubdown with his shirt. He donned fresh linens and chose a nondescript costume for their investigations that day: dust-colored galligaskins, a brown linen doublet, and thin beige nether stocks. He chose a hat with a wide brim and plain leather band.

Ben nodded with approval. "Respectable, but not memorable." He always dressed according to that theme.

"And comfortable," Tom said. "We've got a long day ahead of us. Should we stop by Mr. Bacon's for instructions on the way out?"

Ben shook his head. "He won't be up until dinner, if then. Yesterday drained him completely."

They decided to visit the silk merchant's house in Bermondsey first while the tide still ebbed since it was downstream from their usual wharf. The journey took longer than they expected despite that advantage. Half the London wherrymen had joined the navy, offering their skills in defense of the queen. Everyone appreciated the gesture except when trying to get somewhere in something like a reasonable time.

When they finally made it down past London Bridge to Bermondsey, they found the Rouncey house without difficulty. It had been sold a few weeks ago by the Privy Council, exercising their statutory right to confiscate the property of a confirmed recusant. The agent who met them in the hall told them the widow had gone back to her family in Yorkshire, and the household staff had been dispersed to other positions. The children were grown and had their own establishments.

Yes, he could find out where, if they insisted, but he did have his own work to do. He knew nothing whatsoever about the murder, but as far as he knew, nothing outside the chapel had been stolen. It was just as well — he could hardly sell a house full of popish fripperies in these troubled times, could he? No windows or doors had been broken; he would certainly have noticed that.

"He wasn't much help," Tom said as they let themselves out the gate to the wharf.

"I wish we could have come earlier," Ben said. "The sheriff should have asked these questions while the staff was still in residence."

"Maybe somebody told him not to."

"I don't believe that."

"Don't believe it or don't want to believe it?"

Ben gave him a dark look but said nothing.

"I have the feeling Mr. Bacon's not telling us everything he knows," Tom said. His real question was: Did Ben know it too?

"Oh, I sincerely doubt you want to know everything," Ben said, echoing Tom's words from yesterday, thus effectively blocking another question.

Never mind. Let them keep their secrets. Tom had his own trail to follow.

He stopped to examine the old-fashioned lock on the iron gate. "God's bollocks, I could almost pick this myself."

The back gate was set into a brick wall about eight feet high. The wall stood well back from the river at the top of a long soggy meadow. With any kind of moon and the tide at flow, the thieves could have pulled their boat well up onto the grass, picked the simple lock, and slipped into an open window without making a sound or showing a light.

They paced back and forth on the dock, brushing gnats from their noses, speaking little until a wherry finally came. They stopped at a vendor by the bridge for sausage rolls and beer before heading onward up the river to Baron Hewick's small estate in Chelsea.

The new baron had already taken possession. Though busy sorting out his father's affairs, he granted them a few minutes in his library. The tall, slender man had been a member of Parliament and had recently led a good-sized militia to the muster in Wiltshire, where he had his own manor. His angular features mirrored those of the ancestor portrayed in a painting on the library wall, but he assured them that his religious views were faultlessly correct. He admitted to having been reared in the rituals of the Catholic Church, but then he'd spent a year at Cambridge and come home an ardent Protestant. His family never failed to fill their pew at the front of their parish church.

He'd volunteered all that before they even asked about the chapel or the manner of his father's death. Apparently, he had recently concluded negotiations with the Privy Council concerning his father's estate. He'd had to seal a bond guaranteeing his mother's good behavior in order to reduce the penalty they'd originally imposed.

"I've sent her up to Somerset to live with my sister and cut her allowance in half. I blame her for this, to be candid. That chapel should have been converted long ago — as should she." He smiled, a thin line cutting across his narrow face. "My sister has six children under the age of ten. Perhaps that will keep Mother busy enough to forget her intrigues."

When Tom asked if the old baron had kept a rosary under his pillow, the young baron startled. "How odd that you should mention it! It's the one thing that's missing from outside the chapel. It was quite valuable, with a large carbuncle in the center of the cross."

He showed them the chapel, which had been stripped to the linenfold paneling. "It's plain enough for my family now," he said with a wry smile. He told them that on the night of the murder, his mother had been visiting his younger sister. The baron's personal attendant had been ill and had confined himself to a room on the third floor. Baron Hewick had thus been left alone in his chamber on the first floor.

The baron walked them to the riverside gate, which looked even older than the one at the Rouncey house. They discussed locks and windows and the possibility of entering from the street. But who would bother, with the river lying so handy at the back?

They shook hands all around, preparing to leave.

The new baron said, "Tell Mr. Bacon I'm grateful that someone is doing something. My father was a good man in spite of a few old habits. He didn't deserve this. But Sheriff Skinner made it clear that the murder of a recusant ranked at the bottom of his list. I grant you, that was on the day sixteen Catholic priests were hung at Tyburn, but even so. A peer of the realm, murdered in his bed!"

They promised to let him know what they learned, if and when they learned anything of any consequence. Then they walked down the path to the pier.

Ben looked back across the meadow at the brick wall behind the house. "All three houses stand on the river, as we suspected. What does that tell us about the villains' capabilities?"

Tom set his fists on his hips and scowled at a wherry rowing past them with a full load of passengers. "They're not dependent on the Company of Watermen and Lightermen for transport; otherwise, not much."

"It might help us predict the next victim," Ben said.

"Yes, but I suspect there's a better way. That fourth matter on Mr. Bacon's list — the selection of victims. Did you notice how relieved he looked when you proposed your idea about the murders as distractions? He wanted to shift the talk away from the question of selection."

"I noticed nothing of the sort." Ben pretended to be fascinated by a dragonfly skimming over the reeds at the water's edge.

Tom almost laughed. His chum was a terrible liar. "I'll tell you what we learned today. We learned that the Privy Council is making a handsome profit from these murders. The Rouncey house is a juicy property, directly across the river from the Tower and all the major quays. They're getting a hefty fine from the Hewicks as well. How much are they taking from the Surdeval estate?"

"We haven't met with their agents yet." Ben frowned. "But I must say I don't like your implication."

"I don't like it either, but there it is. My father's right. We're fresh out of everything, the whole country: food, medicine, shot, powder. The treasury is empty but for a large promissory note. The queen owes the Merchant Guild something like fifty thousand pounds."

"Tom!" Ben gaped at him. "You can't think the Privy Council would stoop to murder in order to pay that note!"

"Not the councilmen themselves. God's teeth, Ben! Some of them are older than Viscount Surdeval. But a word here and another word there, they could get it done. They'd probably form a secret commission. What's more, I think Mr. Bacon has had the same idea himself." Tom watched his friend closely and saw a shadow pass across his face.

"I don't believe it," Ben said after too long a pause. "He would have discussed it with me."

"Are you so sure of that? Who else has lists of recusants with chapels and houses on the river, whose wives are suspected of harboring priests? That's a narrow set of considerations."

Ben shook his head. "There must be other sources. A disaffected Catholic, perhaps. And how does your educated upright man fit into this scheme?"

"I don't know yet. Maybe he bribed a clerk. Maybe he's the one they hired." A disaffected Catholic, eh? Nathaniel Welbeck might qualify under that heading. He had connections among Catholics in France and must know half the clerks in Whitehall and Westminster, having been a barrister for better than a dozen years.

Ben crossed his arms and turned his face to the river. "I refuse to countenance such nonsense."

"Refuse all you like." Tom would go his own way. As soon as he got a chance, he'd send a note to Trumpet to see if she knew where to find her uncle. Lady Surdeval might be housebound, but Alice-turned-Allen could come and go at will. They'd catch the villain and clear their own names before Ben and Mr. Bacon managed to agree on a story.

EIGHTEEN

Francis Bacon pushed open the door of his second favorite shop. No, his third. The first was a bookshop on Paternoster Row. The bookseller there was a crucial ally in Francis's quest for the truth. Also, of course, books were essential for the health of the mind. His second favorite was the draper's shop on the first floor of the Royal Exchange. He loved to fondle the silks and satins, even when he couldn't afford them, and the rainbow of colors made him feel deliciously light-headed. A courtier must stay abreast of changing fashions, even when restricted to the sad garb of a barrister.

Henrik Verboom's apothecary shop in Bucklersbury, under the sign of the blooming mugwort, had the advantages of both the others. The contents of the shop were nearly as intriguing as books but provided dual sensory stimulation by engaging the nose as well as the eye. Herbs and medicaments were essential for the health of the body — the foundation for everything else in life. There were nights when Francis would not be able to sleep a wink without a dose of Verboom's theriac, and without sleep, the mind ceased to function.

"Good afternoon, Mr. Bacon. I'll be with you in a trice." The apothecary stood behind his counter weighing out herbs for a woman in a plain blue costume. Two gentlemen waited behind her. One peered at a pamphlet, his nose almost grazing the page. The other stared absently out the small portion of window left unobstructed by the cluttered display of jars and bottles. Two assistants worked at a table in the rear of the deep, narrow shop, grinding and mixing simples.

"I'm in no hurry." Francis strolled up the aisle, studying the tidy rows of labeled jars arrayed on shelves spanning the long wall opposite the counter. Verboom kept the most potent drugs out of reach, either behind him or locked up in the back room, but even the accessible shelves contained an education in herbal lore. Francis appreciated the organization scheme employed — alphabetical by name rather than by use or season of bloom or some more idiosyncratic criterion.

Francis occupied himself by testing his memory against the display, walking back to the door to begin at Alder, for inflammations and ulcers of the inward kind. Angelica. Francis had that one in his garden at Twickenham. Chewing the root afforded some protection from corrupt and pestilential airs. Bay, leaves from trees that grew in Spain. It made a good physic for rheums of the chest and also a restorative after a course of opiate medicine. He wondered if the price had gone up in the past year.

Reaching the middle of the shop, he looked up to the topmost shelf and startled. A huge black bird with a fierce beak and a hungry glare loomed over him. He glanced upward again and chuckled; it was only Aegypius, Verboom's stuffed vulture, moved from his usual position over the door. He took a moment to locate Naja, the stuffed coiled cobra who usually occupied the top of the shelves behind the counter. Still there. He breathed a sigh of relief. That one still scared him after all the years he'd been coming to this shop. He noticed a new addition to the zoological display — a badger, posed in an upright sitting posture. The magical triumvirate was now complete.

"Mr. Bacon?"

Francis whirled around. "Yes?" He had the feeling Verboom had spoken his name several times to get his attention, a sort of echo in his mind's ear. The other customers had vanished. "Ah, yes. My apologies." He approached the counter.

"Are you wanting another packet of your theriac, Mr. Bacon?" Verboom peered at him through the half-moon spectacles perched on his nose. Shorter than Francis, his counter cut him off above the waist. "You're a week ahead of schedule, but we can mix up more in a twink."

"No, thank you, I have enough for the week." The medicine was a mixture of mugwort, opium, ginger, and other ingredients. Francis took a dose every evening, stirred into a cup of wine, as a general strengthener, and sometimes another one to help him sleep. "I'm only seeking a consultation today, although you may find my questions a bit odd."

Verboom cocked his square head and folded his plump hands on the counter. "Ask away, Mr. Bacon. I always find your questions intriguing."

"I have been charged with investigating the unusual death of Lord Surdeval. Perhaps you've heard something about it?"

"This and that. You know how rumors get about. They say the new wife's lover did it."

"No," Francis said. "Neither the wife nor the young man to whom the gossips refer had anything to do with His Lordship's death. The lad is my own student, as it happens. I have interviewed them both myself and am convinced of their innocence."

"That's good to hear." Verboom sounded doubtful. "Then how did His Lordship die?"

"He was poisoned, or so I believe from what Her Ladyship and my student reported. They discovered the poor man at the very moment of his death."

"How can that be?"

"That is the foremost question." Francis glanced at the door and then toward the apprentices at the back of the shop. "May I trust in your absolute discretion?"

"Of course." Verboom leaned his elbows on the counter, ready to receive a confidence.

Francis described the circumstances in which Lord Surdeval had been found, including the twisted nether stocks, the smooth sheet, and the jug of wine on the bedside table. He mentioned the cuts on the chest, but not the shape of the cross thus formed.

"The poor man." Verboom's round face wrinkled in disgust. "Then did he bleed to death? You'd think the broadsides would have picked that one up. They do love a bloody murder."

"No, the cuts were shallow. There was very little blood, barely enough to spot his nightshirt. I suspect the knife blade delivered some sort of poison."

"Ahhh. Then this is your question: What poisons can be applied through the skin?"

"That's the first question," Francis said. "The second is: What poisons cause paralysis? He was found in that condition. His heart still beat, if faintly, but his chest did not rise with breath, nor could he move any limb or feature."

Verboom frowned. "I know of only a few poisons that act through the skin. Some of what I've heard may be pure fantasy. But first I must ask about the more obvious possibility." He wagged his finger. "Many times have we discussed the error of concocting elaborate explanations, Mr. Bacon, when the simple answer lies beneath our nose. Are you certain His Lordship did not take too much of his sleeping draught?"

"The remains of the jug were tested on a dog and did the animal no harm. The level of the draught in its bottle was the same as when Her Ladyship last saw it. It was she who added the valerian compound to his cup before he went to sleep."

"Good, good. I must ask, you know. Old people often awaken during the night and take another dose of their medicine, forgetting they already had some. I warn my patients of this danger every day."

"Commendable." Francis met the apothecary's eyes. "I fear we may be forced to consider the fantastical explanations."

"If we must." Verboom scratched his balding pate under the rim of his round woolen cap. "Then let me ask another question: Are you sure the condition was paralysis, not stupor?"

"That's a good question," Francis said. "As I understand the terms, the condition of stupor is like sleep, in which case we would expect the chest to rise and fall with breathing, even if the extremities were insensate and immobile."

"That is correct, Mr. Bacon. Very good."

"My informants were very clear on this point: the chest did not move, even while the heartbeat could still be heard, very faintly, with the ear pressed against the body."

"Ah, then," Verboom said. "It is paralysis. Well. There is monkshood, or wolfsbane, which you know. But we would expect a great deal of vomiting. Was there any sign of that?"

Francis shook his head. "None whatsoever."

"Hmm. Well, monkshood can be absorbed through the skin, so I suppose it could be applied by a knife. It is sometimes used to make a poison for arrows. You apply an oil or tincture to the blade. Not too drippy nor too thick, or it would leave a stain around the wound."

"There was such a stain," Francis said. "A thin stripe of some tarry ointment at the edges of the wound. The center was bright red, very vivid, like fresh blood. Both witnesses remarked upon the color."

"That is striking, I agree. Also with monkshood, the extremities should be cold to the touch. Was this so?"

"No," Francis said. "Her Ladyship touched His Lordship's feet and his hands, I believe. She would have mentioned it if they had been an unusual temperature."

Verboom peered at him over the rim of his spectacles. "How well do you trust the observations of these young persons?"

"Very well indeed. How not? I trained them both myself."

"You have trained a young lady in such arts?"

"No, no." Francis held up both hands to erase the ill-considered remark. "Of course not. How absurd! I scarcely know her. Ha! Nonsense." He felt a flash of irritation at Trumpet for complicating his ability to make a simple remark without subterfuge. "I meant the student. I am responsible for his training, naturally. He has made some researches on my behalf before, and I have been satisfied with his work."

"Ah. That is good. Well, then, I think we may put aside the monkshood. Warm feet also rules out hemlock, although that must be ingested. If the feet and hands were very hot, we might think belladonna, though that must also travel through the stomach." Verboom paused for a long moment, his head tilted and his eyes moving as if searching for something invisible. "Alas, Mr. Bacon. I have no other suggestion to offer you."

"I have read stories of poisoned cloaks," Francis said. "Have you heard of such things?"

"Oh, you're thinking of Hercules. I am not sure I believe that story. Although one could soak a shirt in a solution of monkshood and cause much pain to the wearer. Death possibly also, but there would be convulsions and vomiting for quite some time. The room would be a mess." Verboom glanced up at Naja, with her great white fangs. "Perhaps the blade was coated with serpent venom. I have heard they do this in Africa and India."

Trumpet's maidservant had made the same suggestion. Francis was grateful for the confirmation. "Can one obtain serpent venom in London?"

Verboom flapped his hand. "Oh, you can buy anything in London if you know where to look! I don't sell such things, nor do I buy them. You won't find anything so rare and dangerous as that on a shelf, not even behind a counter, except perhaps in those unsavory alchemists' holes south of the river. It sounds like an assassin's tool."

They traded dark looks. The door opened to admit a well-dressed woman with a maidservant at her side. Verboom called a greeting, then turned back to Francis. "I'm afraid I cannot answer your questions after all, Mr. Bacon."

Francis glanced at the women. He hated to leave with nothing. "This idea of serpent venom tickles my memory. Something I've read, something to do with discoveries in the New World."

"Ah!" Verboom snapped his fingers. "I know the book you mean: *De Orbe Novo* by Peter Martyr. You've read it, Mr. Bacon. We've discussed it more than once."

"That's it," Francis said. "I can see the page in my mind's eye now, but I can't quite remember. Something about arrow poisons . . ."

"I have the book here in my shop. Let me have it fetched for you." He snapped his fingers to summon an assistant, then went to wait upon the gentlewoman. The assistant soon returned with a heavy folio volume, the original edition of the work in Latin.

Francis stood at the end of the counter paging through the book. Peter Martyr, though Italian by birth, had become a chronicler for the Spanish court earlier in the century. He gained access to the letters of explorers like Christopher Columbus and Vasco Núñez de Balboa and used them to write detailed accounts of their historic voyages, including marvelous tales about the places to which they traveled and the strange peoples whom they met. Since all explorers kept their eyes open for new spices and medicines, as well as gold and rare jewels, Martyr's book was full of notes about plants and their uses. Tobacco was mentioned, as were potatoes. Francis hadn't sampled either substance, though he'd been present when Sir Walter Ralegh had presented them to the queen.

He raced through the book, running his finger down the pages to help pick out the odd word to help orient him. He found the passage he wanted. "Here it is." Francis looked up and saw that Verboom had moved off with the women toward the back of the shop. Holding the place with his fingers, he continued to skim through the book, searching for a more detailed description of arrow poisons.

Voices passed behind him; the door opened and closed. Verboom reappeared behind the counter.

"I found it," Francis said. "That is, I found the passage I remembered. It doesn't say much, only that the savages in a place called Peru hunt with an unusual arrow poison."

"That is vague. Does it help you?"

"No." Francis closed the heavy volume, laying his hand on the worn leather cover. "But if this book was the murderer's inspiration, it might indicate a man who reads Latin." An educated man, in that case; perhaps Tom's idea was not so far-fetched. Sir Richard Topcliffe read Latin as well as Italian.

Francis sighed. "I suppose I'll have to reread this in hopes of finding more details. I'd like to have something more specific before visiting those alchemists' dens. I'd feel a fool babbling about paralysis drugs from New Spain with no more to go on than this book of fables."

Verboom wagged his finger. "Take a friend, Mr. Bacon. Or two." Then a smile split his round face. "If that fails, perhaps you should ask at the Spanish embassy."

NINETEEN

Tom and Ben spent the whole afternoon prowling pawnshops along the waterfront from the Strand to London Bridge. They were footsore and weary and almost ready to give up, although they still wanted to check the shops on the bridge. They'd learned nothing other than that London was overstocked with household oddments. People were pawning whatever they had to buy food and medicines to send to their menfolk on ships or in militias. Many of these men were stranded in Margate now, sick and hungry. The queen's treasure chests had already been emptied into the sea in the form of shot and powder, and the Privy Council clutched what little remained for fear the Spanish would regroup in Scotland and march down from the north or sail back around Ireland to try again.

It had been three weeks since the last reliable sighting of the Spanish fleet. Meanwhile, English soldiers and sailors lay starving all along the coast. Even Lord Admiral Howard had pawned the family plate to feed his men.

Tom and Ben hadn't expected to find incense burners and chalices laid out on shutters to entice the passersby, but they had hoped to catch a flicker of guilty knowledge in some pawnbroker's eyes. No joy. Some shopmen fairly pushed them back out the door. "If you're not here to buy, I can't help you. I'm all tapped out."

Now they stood in a goldsmith's shop on the bridge, waiting for the clerk to finish whispering across the counter to a woman draped in a gray veil. Tom had been here once or twice, searching for gifts to send home to his sisters. The shop had a specialty in stylish trinkets, catering to women who pawned gifts from one admirer to enjoy the cash until their next suitor redeemed them.

Tom elbowed Ben and whispered, "See? Trumpet could have helped out. That could be her now, for all we know. Those veils render a woman nearly invisible."

The woman raised her veil to examine a piece of jewelry more closely. She was twice Trumpet's age and nothing like as pretty.

"Not invisible enough." Ben shook his finger at Tom. "And I do hope she has sense enough not to try. Lady Surdeval, pawning her husband's valuables mere days after his death? We'd never see the end of this scandal."

"But it's all right for me, is it? The one accused of doing the actual thieving?"

"Don't be obtuse. You're a nob —" He stopped abruptly, then tried again. "No one knows you, not by sight."

You're a nobody, he'd meant to say. Tom chose not to take offense. It was true enough and not a bad thing under the current circumstances. But one of these days, everyone in London would know the name Clarady. With his wits and his father's wealth, he couldn't help but rise.

Tom spotted a pendant crafted of a band of gold around a disk of jade precisely two shades darker than Trumpet's eyes. A profile etched into the stone resembled Tom; at least it had a nose, a chin, and a crown of curly hair. He'd have a dimple carved into the cheek. She could wear it under her partlet. He chuckled to himself; then he could bribe the clerk to tell him when she brought it back to pawn it.

Ben followed his gaze and scowled. "I hope you're not thinking of that for Trumpet."

"What if I am?"

"You must avoid all communication with her, Tom. No notes, no gifts."

"You're vastly overstating the situation, *camerade*. But relax; I'll save it for later." Later this evening, when Ben was with Mr. Bacon. He'd send it in a packet marked "Gray's Inn." Any nosy servants or messengers would assume it was just another legal document.

They examined the other items displayed on shelves behind the counter but saw nothing they recognized from the chapel at Surdeval House. The wares included silver bowls and a jeweled cup but nothing with distinctively Catholic decorations. A few large crucifixes but nothing that couldn't appear in a Protestant family chapel.

The clerk finished with the lady in the veil and turned toward them with a smile. He lifted the jade pendant from its hook and draped it across his palm for Tom's closer inspection. "A lovely piece, is it not?"

Tom curled his lip. "The color's uneven. And what's that in the middle? Some sort of bird?"

They bargained for a minute without reaching a conclusion. The clerk replaced the pendant on its hook and turned to Ben. "Does anything catch your eye, Master?"

"I'm looking for a little cross for my grandmother. Something in gold, perhaps with a stone or two." He met the clerk's eyes. "Perhaps on a string of beads . . ."

"Certainly not!" The clerk leaned back as if Ben had waved a dead fish under his nose.

Tom jingled the purse in his pocket. "He's very fond of his grandmother."

The clerk's eyes slid left, then right. Then he lowered his head and murmured, "We do not keep articles of that kind on the premises. We might, on the very *rarest* of occasions, for one of our most *valued* patrons, accept such a thing in pawn, but we would pass it on immediately." He scratched his neck under the edge of his heavily starched ruff. "The long-term value is difficult to assess, you understand. And possession can be problematic in itself."

"Where do you sell them?" Ben asked. "If it's not too far, we might drop by this evening."

The clerk gave Tom a coy look. "One can't give away *all* of one's connections. Where's the advantage in that?"

"Perhaps I could have another look at that jade pendant," Tom said.

The clerk handed it to him with a smirk. He spoke to Ben in a low voice. "Our less popular items go to a shop in Southwark. I believe they send them out of the country. Cousins in France, one presumes." He sniffed. "In St. Saviour parish, just past the bridge, under the sign of the thistle. Don't mention my name."

Easily done, since they never learned it.

They bought mince pies from a vendor at the foot of the bridge and strolled into the warren of small streets and alleys on the right. Shadows spread through narrow passageways as the sun sank behind Winchester Palace.

They found the sign of the thistle down an alley barely wide enough for a handcart in a row of houses that backed up to the river. The shop, if shop it could be called, seemed designed to repel customers. Oily grime clouded the small panes of the windows, obscuring a dispirited display of moth-eaten draperies and clay jars covered with dusty cobwebs.

The man behind the counter had a weather-beaten face with a cloth patch over one eye. He wore a knitted cap that fitted smoothly over his skull. His good eye regarded them coldly. "How bist ye, gentlemen? Zummat I can do ye?"

His accent was thickest Dorset — an old sailor, and from Tom's native shore. This could be the luck he'd been waiting for.

"That depends." Tom looked around the dingy shop with a curled lip. "If you're in the game I'm playing, you're not very good at it."

"If ye've come to ballyrag, ye can turn yerself right around."

"Patience, man. I meant no insult." Tom murmured to Ben, "Let me talk to this churl alone. Might get more from him if he thinks we're fellow West Countrymen." Ben's accent was well-bred Suffolk, and the man had no ability to alter his speech. Besides, Tom wouldn't know how much of what he learned he wanted to share until he heard it.

Ben shrugged and turned to browse among the sad assortment of items in the front of the shop. He opened the lid of a barrel in the corner and dropped it again with a small cry of disgust.

Tom went up and leaned an elbow on the stained wooden counter. "That starched dandiprat at yon goldsmith's shop up on the bridge said you might be interested in something a bit out of the way." He took out the Spanish doubloon his father had given him and tapped its edge on the counter.

The man grunted, keeping his eyes on the gold piece. "I've seen such as they afore."

Tom flipped the coin under the man's nose, catching it and closing it in his fist. "This is just a sample of the sort of thing one finds in certain places under certain circumstances. There's plenty more, someplace safe. Things that got left out of the counting."

Everything taken from captured Spanish ships was officially required to be inventoried and delivered to the Lords Lieutenant to be sure the queen got her share, but a sailor with quick hands could pick up a trinket or two during the heat of the affray. They weren't likely to get any other wages anytime soon, so officers tended to turn a blind eye.

The man shot Tom a sidelong look. "I don't know ye or your fine friend. Ye'd best take yer fancy pieces back to yon dandiprat."

Tom opened his fist to consider the large gold coin lying on his palm. "Then what should I do with Señor

Doubloon and his mates? I've also got another curious item the former owner might pay a healthy sum to get back. You know the sort of thing I mean. A box, with bones in it . . ."

The counterman poked his tongue into his cheek and gave Tom a long, measuring look. Then he leaned closer and said in a low voice, "Talk with the Savoy Solicitor. If he reckons ye'll do, he'll send me word. Come back in a day or two and I might have zummat for ye."

The Savoy Palace! Tom knew at once that was the right track at last. What better place for a rogue barrister to hide than that ramshackle compound down on the Strand? The Savoy was a liberty — its own legal jurisdiction — which made it a favored residence for persons with a ticklish relationship to the law.

"I'll do that." Tom tucked the doubloon back into his pocket and turned to go. He watched Ben gingerly poke at a large book, then lean well back before flipping the cover open in a cloud of dust. Tom shook his head with wry affection. Naturally, Ben would be compelled to look inside a book, however rat-bitten and mold-encrusted it might be.

He didn't like the conflict that was growing between them, but he liked being treated like a newly signed apprentice even less. Until Ben and Mr. Bacon saw fit to include him in their game, he would keep his own cards close to his chest. Besides, Trumpet ought by rights to visit the Savoy with him. The solicitor in question was probably her uncle, after all. If so, she'd get more out of him than Tom could on his own and a far sight more than Bacon or Ben. Welbeck wouldn't tell Bacon if it was day or night.

"You certainly talked for a long time. What did you find out?" Ben's voice held a suspicious note.

"Nothing," Tom said, but the lie stabbed at his conscience.

TWENTY

Francis pressed his seal into the puddle of warm wax sealing the folds of a letter to his brother, Anthony, detained in France by the war. This letter was a copy, hastily written but covering the main points. He would send it by a different messenger in case the first one failed to arrive. He ought to send a third, but the message wasn't that urgent. *Come home, your mother misses you, and so do I.* He'd written the same words every week for years now.

He tossed the letter into the basket of correspondence ready to go out and snuffed the candle he'd used to warm his sealing wax. Two sharp raps sounded and the door swung open before he had time to call out.

Ben hastened into the chamber, fairly bristling with anxiety. "Francis, we must talk." His voice was still hoarse from all the shouting he'd done yesterday.

Thursday, the eighth of September, had been declared a national day of thanksgiving for England's deliverance from the dread armada. Eleven banners from defeated Spanish ships had been paraded up Fleet Street to St. Paul's. The men of Gray's Inn had gone together, wearing their best finery under their legal robes. Francis hadn't cheered, sparing his throat, but he had shared in the upwelling of gratitude and the simple satisfaction of being English still.

Francis said, "I was about to come down. Weren't we going to meet outside the hall at ten? The bell's only just struck." They were on their way to the bookseller's that morning to look for references to poisons from New Spain.

Ben stood before the desk with his hands on his hips. His agitation and the aggressive pose made him seem taller than usual. "The hour struck fifteen minutes ago, but I decided to come up. You won't talk while walking, and there's no place in the city quiet or private enough for this conversation."

"You're beginning to alarm me. What can have happened since breakfast?"

"Nothing, but I've spent the last hour pacing in my chambers, debating whether I should speak or hold my peace. In some ways, it's none of my affair. On the other hand, if we're truly working together as we used to, as I thought we were, toward a solution to the problems which strike more nearly —"

"Ben." Francis broke into the jumbled flow. "Sit down and compose yourself. What concerns you concerns me."

Ben subsided into a chair. "I think Tom's keeping something from us."

"Faith, is that all that's worrying you?" Francis laughed but cut it short as Ben's face darkened. "Peace, peace. I have no doubt Tom has some secret he regards as important, doubtless something to do with the night he spent with Trumpet. Those two did something they ought not to have done — that much is clear in their every gesture when they're together. Whatever it was, trust me, we should be grateful not to be told."

"I think it's more than that."

"Nonsense." Francis tried a soothing smile. "The queen won't hang him, if that's your fear. If the worst has happened and Her Ladyship is proved to be no longer a maid, she might be put in the Tower for a few months as a lesson. It won't do her any harm, and frankly, she could stand to learn some restraint. Then she would be sent home to Orford for a while, out of temptation's way. Tom might be packed off to the Continent on some lengthy errand; that might be wise in any event. I could send him

174

to France with letters for Anthony. I assure you, nothing worse will transpire. Her Majesty makes allowances for earls and their daughters. A story will be constructed and a bargain negotiated that allows the lady to retain her reputation while surrendering some of her property." He rose and collected his hat from the peg by the door. "Shall we go?"

"I appreciate all that, but there's something else." Ben drummed his fingers on his knee while he waited for Francis to return to his chair.

"Another woman? Where does Tom find the time?"

Ben ignored the feeble sally. "Tom had an idea while we were out visiting the other victims' houses. Did you know Rouncey's house was confiscated by the Privy Council? His widow was turned out. It's already been sold."

Francis shrugged. "I'm not surprised. They have the right and they need the money."

"Baron Hewick's son — the new baron — had to pay a substantial penalty in order to retain his hereditary estate."

"Again, I ask: Why does this surprise you? The Act of Parliament passed in 1581 declared it treason to reconcile with the Catholic Church. The property of traitors is forfeit to the Crown."

"You don't think it's a little convenient?" Ben asked. "That recusants with property are being killed and the said property being sold to replenish Her Majesty's coffers?"

"This is Tom's idea? That the Privy Council hired someone to commit these murders for gain?" Francis kept his tone level, but something in his eyes must have betrayed him.

"Aha!" Ben stabbed a finger at him. "You do believe it, at least in part."

Francis bit his lip. He wished he was a better liar. "I don't believe it, not in the sense that I have any real confidence in the proposition." He took off his hat and placed it on the desk. "Rather let us call it a foreboding or a suspicion."

"God's teeth," Ben said. "You *do* think the Privy Council is involved."

"I most certainly do not," Francis said. "At least not directly. But it's possible that someone said something to the wrong person, perhaps merely expressing a complaint, in the manner of King Henry the Second crying, 'Will no one rid me of this troublesome priest?'"

"Oh," Ben said. "I hadn't thought of that. That's nowhere near as bad as Tom's idea of a murderous conspiracy."

"No, but it isn't good." Francis sighed. "You've guessed that much. I might as well unburden myself of the rest. In truth, it might be helpful to discuss my fears out loud."

"You think you know who that wrong person is; the one who heard the innocent complaint."

"I might. But you must not repeat any of this to Tom. Not a hint. Not one word. I don't fully trust his discretion."

"That's why he's keeping things from us, I think. He feels he's being left out."

"Then he should conduct himself with greater circumspection. We are not the ones who got him sent to gaol, remember."

"I know," Ben said. "I agree. And I think I may know who you mean. You're thinking of Sir Richard Topcliffe."

"I am." Francis shuddered. "The name alone gives me a chill. Those flat black eyes, like some predatory beast. And the little smile when he reads a warrant authorizing torture. He enjoys it, every part of the whole ugly business."

"He fits everything we know about the murderer too."

"We know next to nothing," Francis said. Now that he'd passed his suspicions to Ben, he could play opposing counsel and argue against them.

"We know some things. We believe the man is educated. You think he may have read about the poisons in *De Orbe Novo*. Sir Richard is a member of Gray's Inn, and he reads Latin. We believe the killer is motivated at least in part by a fervent hatred of Catholics. Sir Richard is renowned for his hostility to papists. You suspect, as I do, that the victims are being chosen from your list of recusants. Sir Richard collected the original list. He would know exactly who possessed a house with a well-furnished chapel."

Francis had started shaking his head long before Ben reached the end of his list. "Houses large enough and old enough to have private chapels, situated on the banks of the Thames? They're one of the major attractions of our fair capital. Any wherryman will gladly call out the names of historic dwellings if you pay him a shilling. For a penny more, he'll throw in a brief history of their owners."

"Old houses, yes, but they don't all have private chapels. Or at any rate, not Catholic chapels. And you can't argue with the other points."

"I can," Francis said. "Easily. Although I agree that Sir Richard possesses all the relevant characteristics and is probably capable of such cold-blooded deeds. I despise his zealotry, and I'm more than a little afraid of the man. Which is precisely why I distrust my suspicions."

"I don't follow you."

"It is one of the greatest intellectual fallacies, Ben, to see only that which our personal fears and desires bring to our attention. We must be especially wary whenever we find our evidence singling out an individual we would be more than pleased to find guilty."

Ben smiled ruefully. "I would love nothing more than to see that odious man convicted of something —

177

anything. But the converse is equally true, isn't it? We can't allow self-distrust to make us dismiss our best arguments."

"You're right. We don't know enough yet to point our finger in any certain direction." He rose and picked up his hat. "Now shall we attempt to take one more step out of the darkness? The name of the poison might help us stumble a few yards farther along. I'd like to be back before dinner, if possible. Rumor has it there will be venison at the benchers' table today."

* * *

Francis's favorite bookseller traded under the sign of the owl on Paternoster Row. The shop was modest in terms of trade, but Oliver Brocksby had something of a specialty in philosophical works. His shop spanned fifteen feet along the street and extended the full depth of the row. Shelves ran up to the beamed ceiling everywhere except the front windows. More books loaded tables obstructing the aisles, so that one was forced to sidle past the tantalizing offerings. Michaelmas term was almost upon them; the front tables were well-stocked with ABCs and books of illustrated catechisms.

The bookstore occupied about a third of the building's length. The counter stood at the back of the store. Behind that, in the larger portion, Brocksby ran a printing press with his son. They produced mainly translations of Continental poetry and philosophy deemed likely to appeal to English readers.

Francis inhaled deeply as he entered the shop, savoring the acrid tang of potash. "I love the smell of ink." He smiled at Ben over his shoulder.

"I'm sure it's very unhealthy." Ben still seemed a trifle disgruntled at having been kept out of Francis's confidence, even for so brief a time.

Brocksby came forward to greet them. He wore a clean apron wrapped around his trim midsection, but his sleeves bore a few dark streaks. He must have been working at his press that morning. He smiled, showing teeth made gray from chewing type, and rubbed his hands together. "Mr. Bacon, what good fortune! Have you come to settle your bill?"

"No." Francis couldn't remember how much he owed. It couldn't be enough to warrant so much hand-rubbing. "But I'll take a look at it, if you like."

Brocksby's smile fell. "What can I do for you gentlemen this morning?"

Francis said, "We're not here to buy today. We want to have a look at your books about voyages, especially ones relating discoveries in the New World."

"Voyages?" Brocksby tipped back his cap to rub his brow. "Well, of course I have Peter Martyr's *De Orbe Novo*, but I believe you already own that one, Mr. Bacon. Were you wanting the English translation?"

"I didn't realize there was an English version." What a stupid oversight!

"Oh, yes. Richard Eden translated it years ago."

"So much for that small bit of evidence," Ben said. They frowned at one another. Every step forward took them another step back.

Francis asked, "Is that a popular book?"

"Oh, yes. It was one of my father's best sellers. I always keep a few copies on hand. Do you want one?"

"No," Francis said. "We didn't want that one, specifically. We're looking for similar works."

"There are many travel books, Mr. Bacon. Amazing discoveries every year and everyone keen to publish their own account." Brocksby guided them to a round table near the wall. "Here you'll find all the books I have about voyages and suchlike. You'll find quite a few in English, if that matters. It's a popular subject these days. Call me if you see what you're looking for. I'll just draw up your bill. Perhaps you could take that little look before you go."

Francis moved around the table, running his hand over the leather covers of the books on top. Ben did likewise, circling around the other side toward the shelves. His dark eyes shone, and his lips curved in happy anticipation, the first smile he'd achieved all morning.

Nothing balanced the humors of a scholarly man like the smell of ink and the touch of vellum.

Brocksby returned to his counter and began fussing with papers. He called, "Don't cut the pages!" As if they needed that reminder.

Francis and Ben worked in companionable silence for thirty minutes by the bells of St. Gregory's around the corner, opening volumes at whim to read the frontispieces. Some larger works listed their contents in a table at the front, a useful practice more printers ought to employ. They leafed through the most likely candidates, reading with a speed attained only by legal men and government clerks.

At one point Ben murmured, "We're just looking for references to arrow poisons, aren't we?"

Francis chuckled. "It is hard to stay on the track. Listen to this. It's a creature said to inhabit the coast of Paria. 'An extraordinary animal inhabits these trees, of which the muzzle is that of the fox, while the tail resembles that of a marmoset, and the ears those of a bat. Its hands are like a man's, and its feet like those of an ape. This beast carries its young wherever it goes in a sort of exterior pouch, or large bag.'"

"That can't be real!" Ben freed his fingers from the pages he'd been marking and came to read over Francis's shoulder. "It sounds mythological, like a gryphon or a sphinx."

"Doesn't it?" Francis closed the book and reached for another one. "We should take it as a cautionary note: whatever we find may be pure imagination."

Brocksby's reedy voice sounded almost in Francis's ear. "I would be grateful, Mr. Bacon, if you could pay any small part of your bill. The cost of paper has gone up, you see, with shipping to the Continent in such disarray. Any amount would help."

He handed over a slip of paper with a short bow and wove back through the maze of tables to his counter. Francis glanced at the bill and startled at the total. "Can this be right?" He passed the bill to Ben. "Two pounds, five shillings, and eight pence?"

"It says you haven't paid him in nearly two years." Ben's tone was a shade censorious.

"Has it been that long?" Francis had done Brocksby a great favor two years ago and been forgiven his bill at that time. He'd evidently lost the habit of thinking about it as a result. One must have books, after all, and he got through them so quickly he needed a constant fresh supply. "I suppose I ought to pay him something. Do you have any money with you?"

"No." Ben clucked at him. "I know better than to carry money when I go shopping with you."

"What's that supposed to mean?"

"Nothing." Ben turned his back and grabbed a book from a shelf too high for Francis to reach. He held it in the crook of his arm, opened it, and focused his eyes on the page.

Francis regarded him with pursed lips. He never borrowed money from Ben. He was too close a friend, and in truth, too poor. Francis's irritation abated as he watched him become intrigued by whatever it was he had found. He'd miss the man, and the closeness, when Ben moved on to the next phase of his life. That would happen soon after he was called to the bar in December, God and the governors of Gray's Inn willing. He wouldn't yet be able to argue cases in court, but the new status would attract more clients for wills and deeds, as well as allow him to raise his rates. His parents would expect him to start looking for a wife.

Now there was a thought! If Ben married the wealthy Mrs. Palmer, Francis would have a steady source of loans without having to alter his own living arrangements one whit. Or one Whitt, as the case may be.

He chuckled at his little joke, and Ben turned to him with shining eyes. "I found it!" He held up his book. "I grabbed this book just because it was the biggest." He set it on top of a stack on the table and opened at the place he'd marked with his thumb. "It's an account of the discovery of the Grand River by Captain Francisco de Orellana, translated by Richard Eden in 1560. And look — published by one Oliver Brocksby."

"That must be our Brocksby's father," Francis said. "Nearly thirty years ago. Anyone who likes this sort of thing might have a copy. Where's the Grand River?"

"In New Spain, the part they call Peru. It's very big and flows on into Brazil, which I believe is part of the Portuguese empire."

"Does it run through the region mentioned in the passage in *De Orbe?*"

"I think so," Ben said. "If it's not the same Indians, they must be very similar. They make a tarry ointment from the bark and leaves of a plant they call 'wourali' or 'curare.' They coat their weapons with it when they go hunting. It causes animals like monkeys to fall out of trees insensible and unable to move."

"Does it say how long it takes to act?" Francis leaned his cheek against Ben's woolen sleeve to read over his shoulder. "No, alas."

Ben flipped the page over. Francis read halfway down the next page until the story wandered to some other wondrous feature of that marvelous land. "They don't say how big the monkeys are either. I've seen one, at court, about the size of a small child. I should think you'd need different doses or different quantities of the potion for a larger person."

"There's no mention of convulsions or vomiting," Ben said. "That's hopeful."

"We mustn't confuse the absence of evidence with evidence of absence." Francis sighed. "At least we know the name of a drug that might cause the symptoms Tom and Trumpet observed. That's something."

Ben added, "There can't be many people in England who could obtain a rare poison from the New World. And we've discovered the means by which the killer could have learned about the poison. I wonder if Brocksby knows how many copies of this book he's sold."

They took the volume to the counter at the back. Francis asked his question and Brocksby said, "Oh, several hundred, I should think. I ran another printing of that book only last year." He regarded Francis with a weary look. "I couldn't tell you who bought them." He shifted his gaze pointedly toward the bill in Francis's hand.

Francis granted him a sheepish smile. "I'm afraid I've come without my purse." Perhaps Tom would lend him the money, even if his feelings had been a little ruffled lately.

No, wait! He had a better source of funds. Trumpet had told him to charge investigation expenses to the Surdeval estate. Why not include this bill? It had been presented as a clear condition for being allowed to stand reading — uncomfortably — in the shop instead of having all the books delivered to his chambers. Imagine how much his forbearance had saved the estate!

He explained the plan to the bookseller. "So you see, Brocksby, you'll be paid in full in a mere matter of months." He patted the Orellana volume and added, "I'll just take this one along with me since we're all settled up."

TWENTY-ONE

"What do you think?" Trumpet held the jade pendant against her chest, considering the effect in the mirror of her dressing table. Tom had sent it to her with a note early that morning, addressed "From Gray's Inn" in a packet of old notes about lawsuits.

Catalina leaned in for a closer inspection. "What are those scratches, my lady? Some kind of bird?"

"It's Tom, silly goose. In profile." She laid the piece in her palm and pointed at the tiny indentation inside the curve of the jaw. "See the dimple?"

"If you say so, my lady." Catalina returned to wiping paste from her eyebrows with a damp towel. She had coated them with a mixture of honey, lime juice, and cinnamon, trying to lighten her brown-black hair. Foreigners were not well favored in England these days. Apprentices followed them through the streets, hissing and spitting. It was unpleasant at best and especially troublesome if you were trying to avoid attention.

Trumpet's hair was even blacker, but her green eyes and milk-white skin declared her Englishness at a glance. Catalina had the disadvantage of dark brown eyes and an olive complexion, marking her as originating somewhere well to the south. Her self-transformation required continual effort.

Trumpet nodded at her maidservant's face in the mirror. "Your hair is definitely lighter. If only we could do something about your face."

"A touch of powder, but only a touch. I do not wish to look like a clown." She dusted her face lightly with a fluffy brush. Then she cast a critical eye at her mistress in the mirror and picked up a thinner one, opening a second small box holding a darker powder. "Here, my lady. Let me give you a smudge or two."

They were preparing to go down to the Strand again, but this time they'd be dressed as boys — the sort of ordinary, ubiquitous boys who performed small services for a penny or two. The note that had come with the pendant had suggested they meet him at an alehouse near the Temple Bar after dinner.

Trumpet could scarcely sit still while Catalina tugged her short wig into place. Seeing Tom at supper the other night had acutely whetted her appetite for him. She missed him with a palpable ache and knew in her bones he felt the same way.

The note said Ben and Mr. Bacon were keeping Tom on a short leash and that Ben had commanded him to stay away from Chadwick House. Trumpet giggled. Much good Ben's commands would do him. He'd treated her to a tart little lecture as well after supper. It wasn't that his arguments were flawed, exactly; he simply underestimated her ability to get around obstacles like prying matrons and gossiping courtiers. No one gossiped about street urchins, did they?

Ben meant well, but if he thought she was going sit around on her lily-white arse embroidering cuffs while everyone else got to rove the city tracking crafty villains, he had not been paying attention during the past two years of their friendship. Besides, these crimes concerned her more than anyone else. She had a right to help solve them.

She and Catalina donned wide-brimmed hats to guard their complexions. It wouldn't do to turn up in the bishop's court next Friday with sunburnt faces. Trumpet left word for her aunt that they might be late to supper, then they slipped out past the stable and blended into the crowds.

As they wove through the thronging streets, Trumpet took covert notice of the people they passed. There was a woman with heavy brows and a dark furze above her lips. That beardless man in the over-puffed hose had very slender shoulders. How many of these seemingly ordinary citizens had disguised their sex? What reasons might they have other than the pure fun of it?

Trumpet blinked as they entered the dark alehouse on Fetter Lane, east of the Temple Bar. She and the other lads used to come here sometimes when they wanted a drink but preferred not to bump into any senior barristers. The smoky den served cheap home-brewed ale and day-old pottage to laborers. Most men of the law preferred more fashionable venues.

Tom sat on a bench, a mug on his knee, watching them with that half smile that sent tingles dancing up and down her spine. Trumpet made straight for him, pulling up a low stool, while Catalina turned aside to get two mugs from the alewife.

"Well met, me boyos." Tom gave her a friendly clap on the shoulder. He shot a wink at Catalina to acknowledge her skill as a costumer. "Nice work."

Catalina accepted the praise with a flick of her eyebrows. They had learned a great deal watching out Trumpet's chamber window. Since Catalina was several inches the taller of the two, they made her the older boy. She had a spruce moustache and wore a reasonably well-fitted hose and doublet of a sturdy dark blue wool, with a soft cap of a somewhat lighter shade — the garb of a lesser servant in a large household. Trumpet wore the mismatched pieces of an urchin: blue hose that hung almost to her knees, tan stockings with a hole or two, a mustard-colored jerkin patched across the shoulders, and a small green cap.

Tom had dressed in a nondescript costume of beige and brown. From a distance, he could be any sort of tradesman; close up, the quality of the fit and fabric bespoke a higher status. They made a somewhat ill-assorted trio, but the odds of anyone in the bustling city bothering to stop and consider their oddity were miniscule.

"What's the game?" Trumpet asked. "You didn't give me much of a hint."

"I think I know who the upright man is," Tom said. He gave her a tentative grin. "I think it's your uncle."

"Uncle Nat? I don't believe it."

Tom shrugged. "At this moment, it's only a hunch." He told them about his cellmate in Newgate and the hints he'd dropped about a barrister of Gray's Inn. Then he told them about the pawnshop in Southwark and the tip he'd gotten about a man called the "Savoy Solicitor."

Trumpet drank a long draught of ale while she digested the new intelligences. "The Savoy Palace is the sort of place Uncle Nat would choose. Between London and Westminster, close enough to keep up with all the goings-on, but far enough from Gray's to go about without unwanted attention there. And I've known he wouldn't be content to molder away in Exeter forever."

Catalina's dark eyes widened. "Is Mr. Welbeck now so rich he may live in a palace?"

"It's not a palace anymore," Trumpet said. "It's more of a jumble of tenements with a hospital in the middle."

"That does not sound comfortable," Catalina said.

"I've never been inside," Trumpet said, "but the Earl of Oxford lives there, so it can't be too bad. It looks very grand from the river."

"The location isn't the main advantage," Tom added. "It's a liberty, the Liberty of Lancaster. Legally, it's in the jurisdiction of the Duchy of Lancaster, not the City of London or even the Crown. You can't be arrested for debt, for example, or served a royal writ summoning you to court."

"Ah," Catalina said. "That makes more of the sense. Your uncle is a clever man."

"Are you sure he's there?" Trumpet asked Tom.

"No. Or rather, I'm not sure the Savoy Solicitor is your uncle. But whoever he is, he's involved in trading Catholic goods abroad." He held her gaze, not smiling now. "Every new thing we learn about the burglaries points to your uncle."

"No, it doesn't. All you can do is connect this Savoy Solicitor to a pawnshop in Southwark that might be willing to buy ill-gotten goods to sell abroad. They probably buy well-gotten ones too. Even if this solicitor is my uncle, it only proves he gives them advice now and then."

"We know your uncle has smuggling connections in France."

"We know your father does too," Trumpet said. "His old friend What-d'ye-call-um, Jacques Le Bon. The one who can sell anything."

"He's no friend." Tom sounded nettled, unjustly. Her relative was the one whose character was being maligned.

"Regardless," Trumpet said, "you don't *know* anything. You picked up some gossip in gaol and leapt to the first available conclusion. You're just keen to come up with something Mr. Bacon hasn't thought of."

"That would be raisins in the bun, I'll grant you. But it's not the only reason. My gut tells me Nathaniel Welbeck is the upright man and you know I respect my gut."

So did Trumpet. But she remembered how their discussion at the Antelope had ended, with the grim suspicion that the chapel burglars had murdered elderly householders for the sole purpose of putting the authorities onto a false trail. Tom could never convince her that her uncle could ever have any part in such ruthless acts.

Tom was watching her with sympathy warming his blue eyes. He smiled now and said, "We go one step at a time, the way Mr. Bacon says. The first thing is to find out if there even is such a person as the Savoy Solicitor. The second is to see who the whoreson is. If he's your uncle, then let's see if we can find out where he's been the past few weeks. For all we know, he's been in Exeter, courting sixteen luscious widows who will gladly swear in unison to his attentions."

"Fair enough," Trumpet said. Her gut told her Tom's gut had it right: the pawnshop's solicitor would be her beloved Uncle Nat. What she wanted to know was how he could have sent his thieves to her new home on her wedding night. And what, if anything, did he know about the murder of her husband?

They finished their ale and went back out to walk down the Strand to the Savoy. The guard — or the man idling inside the gate — looked them up and down but offered them no challenge. A passage between two tall houses led them into a churchyard, where paths led forward, left, and right.

"Which way do we go?" Catalina asked.

Tom and Trumpet shrugged. "Let's watch for a while," Tom suggested.

They stood beside the flint-walled chapel as people came and went across the cobbled yard. Two boys lugged buckets down the narrow street on the left. A lady in a black veil and pattens clopped out of an alley leading south and crossed to the gate. Half a dozen men ranging from gentry to laborers strode or strolled from one place to another. The Savoy was a beehive inside a maze.

"We'll have to ask someone." Trumpet watched two men emerging from the same alley the woman had come from. Both men wore Dutch slops — longer and looser than usual — and short-waisted doublets. One man wore a tall red Phrygian cap. A gold circle glinted in one of the other one's ears. They both walked with a rolling gait.

"Sailors," Tom said. "I'll give them a try." He walked toward them, adopting the same gait. "Hoi, there! Might I ask ye lads for a wee favor?" His voice roughened into his native West Country burr.

Trumpet bit her lip to keep from laughing. He played the role to perfection except he was far handsomer than the average sailor. A sigh escaped her lips.

Catalina bent her head to whisper, "You know, my lady, *I* am not a virgin . . ."

Trumpet jabbed her with a stiff finger. "If you so much as offer to comb his hair, I'll send you back to Orford with a Calvinist gentlewoman to teach you proper comportment."

"No, my lady!" Catalina shuddered. "I will comport myself. But it does seem a waste."

The sailors stopped to listen to Tom's question. Then one of them sketched a path in the air while the other pointed with an arched arm toward the far corner of the palace complex. They shook hands all around and the men went on their way.

Tom showed off his rolling gait again as he returned to Trumpet's side. "They know the Savoy Solicitor, all right. And he's home — they'd just been up to see him. I let them think I was looking for work."

"Did they mention the solicitor's name?"

"No," Tom said. "We'll have to go see for ourselves." He laid his hand on her shoulder. "Are you ready?"

"How not?"

They found their way to a crenellated stone tower on the western edge of the palace and climbed the stairs to the first floor. The door stood open, so they walked right in. The large room was lit by windows on two sides and furnished like legal chambers, with a big desk for the lawyer, a small one for his clerk, a few plain chairs for clients, and shelves of books leaning against the walls. An inner door undoubtedly led to a bedchamber overlooking the Thames.

A pair of weathered leather satchels lay on the floor in one corner beside a glossy green ball and a sack with something yellow peeking out of the top. Shuffling sounds came from the inner chamber. Tom reached over her shoulder to rap on the outer door.

"God's teeth! I haven't even had time —" Uncle Nat strode through the door and stopped short. His eyes went first to Tom and narrowed. Then his gaze shifted to Trumpet and he smiled, shaking his head at her costume. "My darling niece. What a surprise!"

She and Catalina doffed their hats and bowed. He laughed and gathered her into a hug. Trumpet wrapped her arms around his waist and pressed her cheek against the fine worsted of his doublet. She closed her eyes, drawing in a deep breath. He smelled of travel: sweat, dust, and horses. She released him and stood back to study his face. He was tanner than when she'd seen him last, but he still wore the same curved moustache and short, rounded beard. His dark hair was still cropped just above his ruff. The Welbeck features — soft brown eyes, a little too close together, and a longish, broad-tipped nose — always reminded her of her mother with a bittersweet pang.

She sniffed at his doublet again. "You smell like horse, Uncle. Where have you been?"

"Exeter. I came in not an hour ago."

Tom grinned, or rather, raised his upper lip. "That's a long ride, and dusty at this time of year. What did it take you — about a week?"

"More or less," Uncle Nat said, eyes narrowing. "And I'd rather have dust than mud."

Something Trumpet couldn't detect underlay their travel talk. She hadn't ridden west since her mother died; perhaps there was something unusual about the road.

Uncle Nat peered past them out the door. "Where's the other one? That lanky hound, Benjamin Whitt. Isn't he part of your merry band anymore?"

"He's helping Mr. Bacon with something else today," Tom said.

Uncle Nat smiled through his teeth. "Leaving you free to play with the girls, eh? Tell me, did Bacon ever catch on to my niece's little game?"

"I told him," Trumpet said. "Recently. Things have happened, Uncle. How long have you been away?"

"Long enough." His expression turned sad. "The Earl of Leicester died on Sunday. Have you heard?"

"I suppose the war took its toll." Trumpet shrugged. "He was very old, after all."

"He was only fifty-six!" Uncle Nat ran both hands through his thick hair, perhaps to reassure himself he still had it. "I'll be forty in two years." He gave Catalina a lecherous grin. "I've never seen you in slops, Mrs. Luna. They flatter you, or rather you them."

She made a small bow, her answering smile equally warm. When the actor she'd been living with died, Catalina had turned to his friend, Nathaniel Welbeck, for help. He had sent her on to Orford, recognizing her as the ideal maidservant for an adventurous lady. Trumpet hadn't asked how well Catalina had known her uncle; it appeared they had known each other rather well and still had fond memories of one another. That could be useful if they decided to keep a closer eye on him.

Uncle Nat returned his scrutiny to Trumpet. "What happened to your sad little moustache? I always thought that was a clever trick." The scrawny appendage had been his idea.

"Smudges work just as well and they don't itch," Trumpet said. "But we're not here to show off our disguises."

"Aren't you? Then let's sit, shall we? I've had a long day already." Uncle Nat took the seat behind his desk. Tom and Trumpet drew chairs up to face him. Catalina chose a bench near the door.

A small silence followed. Trumpet looked at Tom, asking him with her eyes, *Where should we start?* He raised his eyebrows to say, *I don't know.*

Uncle Nat shook his head with amusement. "How did you find me?"

Trumpet glanced at Tom. They'd forgotten to prepare this part. He launched into an answer before she had time to think. "Lady Chadwick took pity on your niece, who has been longing to reassure herself of your continuing good —"

He broke off as Trumpet cleared her throat and glared at him, willing the word *no* through her eyes.

Too late. Uncle Nat sneered. "A waste of breath, Clarady. I know my sister would never violate my confidence, certainly not without warning me."

Tom tossed that off with a shrug. "I don't mind telling you the real reason. We've heard some intriguing rumors and came to see for ourselves if you were the one they call the Savoy Solicitor." He threw the words down like a gauntlet.

Uncle Nat only chuckled. "That absurd nickname! It isn't even accurate. It should be the Savoy Barrister, but that doesn't have quite the same ring, does it?" He smiled at Trumpet. "I do small favors for my neighbors, a bit of advice here and there. We've all sorts in the Savoy. It's one of the things I like about it."

Tom subsided, a disgruntled look souring his handsome features. Trumpet had expected something along those lines. They'd confirmed his hunch the minute they walked in the door. Her uncle could be the principal counselor for every back-alley pawnshop in London and it wouldn't prove he'd had anything to do with the chapel burglaries.

Uncle Nat said, "I've been keeping my eye on you, Alice dearest, from a distance. Your letters are always read with great interest, and my sister fills in some of the blanks. In fact, I found a letter from Blanche waiting for me when I came in today, about your overly hasty and all-too-brief marriage."

"Then she must have told you how it ended." Had he really only just learned about it? A wave of relief washed the tension from Trumpet's shoulders. He hadn't known; therefore he had not deliberately taken advantage of her wedding night to send in his burglars, if he even had any such. She was beginning to doubt Tom's whole construction.

"I'm appalled," Uncle Nat said, "and deeply grieved." What looked like genuine sadness darkened his eyes. "That poor old man! You know, Alice, I would have advised against that marriage if you'd consulted me. I thought you were using Surdeval as a counterweight in your negotiations. I never thought you'd actually marry him."

"I liked him," Trumpet said. "He was kind to me." She studied his face, which he allowed. That seemed a little odd. Was he deliberately showing her his grief? Toward what end? She shot a glance at Tom. He looked puzzled. He'd seen the sadness too, recognized its sincerity, and was being forced to rearrange his suspicions.

Her uncle had not been party to Lord Surdeval's death, she'd wager half her jointure on it.

"Why didn't Aunt Blanche tell me you'd come back to London? Why didn't *you* tell me?"

"I prefer not to attract attention yet. And I couldn't be sure where your loyalties lay after you took up with Francis Bacon and his boy here."

"Man," Tom said. "But no offense taken. He is my tutor, though I'm now a full member of Gray's on my own account. In good standing, I might add, unlike some."

"So I've heard. Service to the Lord Treasurer, how enterprising of you." Uncle Nat turned back to Trumpet. "Blanche also told me this *man* spent your wedding night in your bedchamber."

Tom spread his hands wide. "I would never touch a lady against her will."

"*Her* will is the one that worries me."

Trumpet repressed a smile at the memory of that brief but rapturous interlude. "Tom stayed to keep me company, Uncle, that's all. I didn't want to be alone in that big house, waiting for my husband to wake up and come to me." Never mind that she'd grown up in an ancient castle four times the size of Surdeval House.

"That's what Catalina's for," her uncle said. "To keep you company."

"She was sleepy."

Catalina yawned and stretched like an actress playing to the topmost gallery.

Uncle Nat watched her with his tongue poking into his cheek. "I am familiar with the word, thank you, Mrs. Luna." To Trumpet, he said, "Then you'll be proved *virgo intacta* and your ill-considered marriage will be annulled."

"No. I'm going to win." Trumpet told him the story of her fictional deflowering, glad for the chance to rehearse it before a male audience. She kept her eyes on her uncle, ignoring Tom's blink of surprise. She should have warned him about that too. This is what happened when they weren't allowed to communicate freely.

"No one's going to believe that story," Uncle Nat said. "The viscount was no sprightly youth. Apart from the unlikelihood of his being able to perform the said service in the time allotted, he was undoubtedly a man of fixed habits, like most old men. When nap time came, he would take his nap."

Trumpet clucked her tongue. "You don't know everything. And you won't be in that courtroom."

"It's for the best, Alice. You need a real husband; you more than most girls. We'll find you a better one next time." He jerked a thumb at Tom. "Not this knave; someone of your own rank, but young and well-framed. Trust me, a good husband is what you want. All girls do."

Nothing irritated Trumpet more than being treated like "most girls," especially by someone who ought to know better. She didn't want a husband; she wanted Tom. And a place where she could do what she wanted without everyone constantly yapping at her. "I want the house. I can't stand being stuck out in Orford with nothing to do or locked up at court with those wan-witted maids of honor. I want a house of my own, somewhere in London or along the Strand. Or possibly Holborn."

"You may not live alone," Uncle Nat said. "It is out of the question."

"If I'm a widow, I can." Trumpet crossed her arms across her chest.

"I have to agree with your uncle," Tom said. "It wouldn't be right. You'll have to wait until you're older, thirty or thereabouts. That's not so far away, Trumpet."

"Ten years!" She glared at him. Whose side was he on?

"Your opinion is not required, Clarady." Uncle Nat shook his finger at her. "And don't imagine you'll have me in residence as your guardian. I have plans of my own. I'll be moving back to Gray's as soon as I can contrive a decent set of chambers."

"That won't be easy," Tom said. "You left under a dark cloud, as I recall."

"So I thought at the time," Uncle Nat said. "But it turned out to be a mere wisp of Francis Bacon's fevered imagination. According to my friends — of whom I have more than a few — no word of blame has ever been uttered to connect me to the unfortunate events to which I believe you refer." He shrugged it off. "Besides, that was two years ago."

"At least I'll know where you are," Trumpet said. "I do have other reasons for seeing you, Uncle."

"I've missed you too, my dear. But I don't like Bacon peering into everything I do with those viperous yellow eyes of his." He looked down at his desk and flipped over a piece of paper. Then he asked, as if he didn't much care about the answer, "Did he send you here to find me?"

"Of course not," Trumpet said, but at the same time Tom said, "He might have."

Uncle Nat chuckled. "You two really should rehearse your stories in advance." He flipped over another piece of paper and paused to read the sheet beneath it. He had the air of a man who hadn't been at his desk for several weeks and needed to catch up with his correspondence. After a minute, he glanced at Trumpet again. "Was there something else?"

They hadn't even broached the topic of the burglaries, although she wasn't so sure it was necessary anymore. Trumpet caught Tom's eye and raised one shoulder half an inch. He tilted his head slightly. *It's up to you.* She knew he wasn't satisfied, but how to approach the matter?

Uncle Nat observed their byplay with a deepening scowl. "Wait a minute, Alice. You're not thinking of marrying *him*? It's out of the question! Absolutely, altogether, irrefutably out. Your sons will be earls. This churl is a nobody."

"I resent that." Tom sat forward, putting a hand on his hip near his sheathed knife.

Trumpet raised her eyes to the ceiling. Why did everyone think she needed reminding about the central fact of her existence? "Tom is a gentleman of Gray's Inn, Uncle. But of course I'm not going to marry him." Not yet, anyway. "On the subject of marriage though, I want control of my trust. I'm nineteen, a grown woman, even if I'm not yet proved a widow. And I need money, especially with this dispute over my jointure."

"You can forget about the jointure," Uncle Nat said. "Your marriage will be annulled without debate." He glared at Tom, who held up his hands, palms out. The coward.

"All the more reason to have control of my property," she said.

"You may be legally an adult, Alice, but your judgment is questionable." Uncle Nat granted her a half smile. "I suppose we might increase your allowance. If you're going to stay in London with Blanche, you'll need new clothes — women's clothes. I'll write to the other trustees to work out a suitable amount."

The other trustees were the two sons from her mother's first husband's first marriage — honorable, God-fearing men, prosperous merchants like their father. Trumpet barely knew them. She doubted they would understand her thirst for independence. Still, more money would be welcome, and it wouldn't hurt to remind them she had reached her majority and expected to participate in decisions concerning her property.

She said, "There is another question." She watched her uncle's face carefully. "If Aunt Blanche told you about my Lord Surdeval's murder, she must also have told you that the chapel was robbed that same night."

"She didn't. Were you there? My darling girl! Are you sure you're all right?" He looked shocked, but this time she didn't believe it. She shot at glance at Catalina, who fluttered her lashes to say she didn't believe it either. Uncle Nat was a gifted disputant, but no actor. He couldn't suppress the glitter of amusement in the back of his eyes.

"I was there to protect her," Tom said, "when others put her in harm's way."

199

"What others?" Uncle Nat grinned unpleasantly. "The only harm she's suffered is to her reputation and you're the cause of that."

Tom's eyes flashed. "Someone, not me and not Trumpet, murdered that old man in his bed that night. Someone also stripped his family chapel of its valuables that same night."

Uncle Nat ignored him. "I am sorry if you were frightened, Alice. I'm glad you're safely back in Blanche's house, where idle knaves will find it impossible to gain entry."

The two men glared at each other again. Trumpet had had enough of their manly posturing. "How could I have been frightened? I didn't know about it at the time, did I? But Surdeval House isn't the only one that's been robbed, Uncle, nor is my lord the only one who was murdered. There have been — how many others?" She turned to Tom.

"Five burglaries, three murders," he answered. Now he leaned forward, setting an elbow on one knee. "Curiously, the only things stolen from these great houses full of treasures were the chapel furnishings. Precious goods, but nearly impossible to sell in England these days."

Uncle Nat dismissed that with a wave of his hand. "Assuming that's really all that was stolen and that the things are being stolen for sale. I can think of a dozen alternative explanations, even supposing you've presented all the facts. Bacon tends to leap to conclusions. He's always eager to get the work over and go back to his philosophizing."

Suddenly, he slapped both hands onto his desk. "Wait a minute: He doesn't think *I* had anything to do with these crimes? I'll sue him. That's slander!"

"Not if it's true," Tom said. "I merely followed the trail leading from the chapel. I have my sources too, you know."

"I doubt the whores at the Two Bells would make good witnesses in a court of law."

Tom gave him a cool smile. "Catholic goods are something of a specialty, Mr. Welbeck. You can't sell them here, but you might in France. You have experience with that sort of thing, don't you? Importing banned Catholic pamphlets, for example."

Uncle Nat sat in silence for a moment, his lip curled. Then he shook his finger at Trumpet. "It won't work, my dear. Not this time. You're trying to apply a little Scottish blackmail to make me release your property to you. It only supplies further proof that you're not ready for the responsibility."

"That's not what I —"

"I have never set foot inside Surdeval House. If Bacon is implying otherwise, I'll sue him for slander and name you, Thomas Clarady, as his co-conspirator. Don't think I won't." He stood and walked to the door. "Now if you don't mind, children, I have letters to write."

They rose; the interview was over. Trumpet clasped her uncle in another hug and whispered, "I don't suspect you of murder, Uncle, and I don't much care about the burglaries. But I do want an increase in my allowance."

"That's my girl." He kissed the top of her head and let her go. Then he caught Catalina's sleeve and drew her into an embrace. He murmured, "Now you know where I am, come back sometime, without these two madcaps."

Catalina flashed him a warm look from under her thick lashes. "If my lady will allow."

Uncle Nat turned last to Tom. He stood before him with his hands on his hips and blocked the way. He had to look up to meet Tom's eyes, but Nathaniel Welbeck was a man in his prime, a barrister tested in the Westminster courts. Tom, years away from being called to the bar, had not even reached his majority.

"Lay one hand on my favorite niece — one hand, Clarady — and I'll recruit a gang of ruffians for the sole purpose of thrashing you so soundly you'll have to crawl back to your mother in Dorset to recover."

Tom pretended to cringe in mock terror. Then he grinned and pointed his chin at the bags in the corner of the room. "When you come to dinner at Lady Chadwick's, bring some of those lemons, won't you? I'm sure they'll be welcome. That muskmelon too. Fresh fruit from Spain is hard to come by this summer."

TWENTY-TWO

Tom let the women lead the way back through the Savoy to the Strand. He kept his eyes open for men or boys hastening up to the tower they'd just left and his ears open for a summoning whistle, but neither saw nor heard any sign of a reaction from Welbeck. Too soon. But the Savoy Solicitor would want to confer with his confederates now that he'd been discovered. It might be useful to know who was called and where they were sent.

The three stopped at the Temple Bar for a brief consultation and decided to choose a different alehouse to avoid being seen together in the same place twice on the same day. They walked in silence up Fleet Street to Water Lane and found another narrow cave selling bitter ale in clay mugs. This one boasted a small yard in the back which no one else seemed to favor — no doubt because it stank of stale piss, but you soon got used to that.

Tom ordered some bread, feeling peckish. The wench brought him a large dark roll so hard it nearly wrenched his jaw. He worked at it for a while anyway while Trumpet and Catalina traded notes about Welbeck's appearance. Trumpet seemed happy, glad to be reunited with her favorite relative, not worried about his probable involvement in any crimes. Somehow Tom had to make her understand that her beloved uncle was almost certainly a party to murder.

And he must talk her out of telling that preposterous nap story in court.

"The melon clinches it," he said when the women's chatter ran down. "Your uncle has been in France or southward, and recently. I'm betting he rode up from Rye today — not Exeter — after getting off a ship yesterday."

"What makes you so sure?" Trumpet asked.

"Lemons look a sight worse for wear after a week in a saddlebag and that melon would have been eaten. Nobody carries ripe melons around for a week."

Catalina nodded. "He is much browner than before, like a man who has been in places of sunshine." She sounded wistful.

"Melons aren't proof of anything," Trumpet said.

"He's the upright man," Tom said. "I'm sure of it. He might not go sneaking about with sacks of booty in the dead of night, but he plans the burglaries, engages the team, and handles the sale of the goods."

Trumpet got that sulky look that told him she knew she'd have to concede the point eventually but wasn't ready yet. "What we know is so much happenstance, Tom. Don't forget what an experienced barrister my uncle is. You may have noticed he never answered a single one of our questions directly. If pressed, he might admit that he's been on *a* ship, but not *that* ship. Or, oh, perhaps it was that ship, but only because an old friend in St. Jean de Luz got married and invited him to the feast."

"I grant you we're no match for him," Tom said. "He'll find it more difficult to argue with Mr. Bacon or the judges on the Queen's Bench. We're a long way from that, but I'm satisfied he's involved, at least in the burglaries. And I think you are too, if you're honest."

Trumpet gave him a long look, drew in a long breath, and let it out in a long groan. "I wish I knew what he was going to do next."

Catalina said, "I can help with that, my lady. I shall go back. Your uncle invited me. I shall go now before the evidence is disappeared."

"You want some of that melon," Trumpet said.

"Not only melon, my lady." Catalina's dark eyes flashed. "I like your uncle. Also, he likes me. I think he may let me stay while his henching men come and go."

Trumpet said, "Sounds like a good idea to me. Don't you think so, Tom? We ought to learn more about his men and how they plan their jobs."

"I'm in favor," Tom said. To Catalina, he added, "But only watch, listen, and remember. Don't ask questions. You'll put his guard up."

They agreed that she should go at once. She should spend the night, or even two. She left them with a smile of anticipation curving her wide lips. Tom found himself envying Welbeck and shook the vision from his head. He had no idea what Trumpet would do if she sensed he'd had lusty thoughts about her maidservant, but he could be certain he wouldn't like it.

Fortunately, her mind had gone in another direction. She said, "I'm stuck with Aunt Blanche all day tomorrow anyway. Her tiring woman might as well dress me too." She rolled her eyes. "We're having friends to dinner. Her friends."

Tom grinned. "Invite me. I'm longing to meet your aunt."

"I wish I could."

"Why can't you?" He gave her his most persuasive grin. "There isn't an aunt in England I can't charm."

Her eyes glowed with appreciation, but she said, "It isn't that. At my aunt's table, I'm Lady Alice, not Trumpet, and Lady Alice doesn't have friends like you."

Tom's grin fell. One day, everyone would want him at their dinner table, ladies included, but that day had evidently not yet come.

She watched his reaction with her tongue poking into her cheek. "Men, Tom. Young ladies do not have personal friends of the opposite sex."

"I knew that's what you meant."

He sawed at his roll, severing small pieces and chewing them slowly. A man could starve to death with this bread for his only food. He shot occasional glances at Trumpet, who ringed the top of her clay mug with one finger, deep in thought. He liked her in boy's garb, especially boys of the lower sort, with simpler costumes. That short black wig topped by the soft green cap emphasized the color of her eyes and the sweet shape of her face, and somehow the smears of dirt made her pale skin more luminous.

A fleeting worry crossed his mind. It might be a bit Baconish to like the way she looked in slops. He sent the notion flying. Once that cat had been let out of the bag, he could never again fail to see her as a woman. Especially not after that night in her bedchamber.

He caught her eye and raised his mug. "Here's to old times."

"Almost." She sounded sad, but then she flashed him that brilliant smile. "What do we do next?"

"Whatever you want. We could go watch the bears for a while and then have supper in that ordinary we like near Falcon Stairs."

"I'm not dressed for an ordinary. They'd think the worst of you, bringing a boy like me in off the street." She gestured at her patched jerkin. "I meant what's next in the investigation? What's Mr. Bacon doing?"

"How would I know?" Tom refilled their mugs from the pitcher. "They don't tell me anything anymore. I'm not trustworthy. I have shown poor judgment. Or maybe I'm not clever enough at philosophy to pursue the rare and mysterious poison."

"Oh, don't take offense at that. Bacons keeps secrets from everyone, even Ben. His policy is to tell the fewest people the least possible. It's from spending so much time at court."

"Or it could be from being born with his head up his —" Tom stopped short and popped a morsel of bread in his mouth.

Trumpet gave him a weary look. "I grant you permission to use the word 'arse' in my presence, Mr. Clarady."

He waggled his brows comically. "Arse."

They grinned at each other. The moment had come. They were friends, and friends did not permit their friends to make buffoons of themselves in public. "Don't tell that story in the bishop's court, Trumpet."

"What, the nap story? You don't like it?"

"I was there that evening, remember? But even if I hadn't been, I wouldn't."

That deep emerald gleam appeared in her eyes that never boded well for him. "You haven't left me much choice, Tom."

"It's nothing to do with me. I'm just the one that gets tossed in gaol after his friends treat him to a surprise he never asked for."

She crossed her arms and regarded him with an expression so absolutely, indisputably not boyish that Tom's eyes snapped to the door. This would be a bad moment for someone to come out to replenish their pitcher.

She noticed, wrinkled her nose, and relaxed her pose. "I want that house."

"There'll be other houses."

"When?"

Tom couldn't answer that. They drank their ale in silence for a moment of respite.

Then Trumpet leaned forward and spoke in a husky whisper. "Come to Chadwick House, late at night. Tomorrow night — no, the night after. We'll need Catalina. She'll let you in through the kitchen and keep watch in the corridor."

The fire in her eyes and that throaty thrum sent a jolt through Tom's loins. He could well imagine her bedchamber at Chadwick House. Not as large or as elegant as Surdeval House, maybe, but still lushly furnished with an oversized bed. A bed where Lady Alice waited for him, clad only in her damask skin and her silken waterfall of ebony hair.

He licked his lips. She whispered, "I need you, Tom."

He started shaking his head and waving his hands, erasing the vision. The fire in her eyes went out. "I can't do it," he said. "I can't altogether believe I'm saying this, but I can't do it. Especially not before your examination. If you're not proved a virgin by those eight matrons of good repute, everyone will assume I did the honors and another stretch in Newgate won't be the worst thing they'll do to me. You must be a virgin when you marry, Trumpet, and you can't marry me."

She chewed on her rosy lip for a moment, then asked, "Do you wish you could?"

"I'm not going to answer that." Tom stabbed his knife into the roll, pinning it to the table. "It would only give you another weapon."

"I'll take that as a 'yes.'" Trumpet snatched a piece of his bread and tossed it in her mouth, chewing it as if she'd won something. He supposed she had. Did she truly believe he'd let her take another man into her bed — even one as old as Lord Surdeval — if he had any power to prevent it?

They drank the sour ale and chewed the stony bread for a few minutes in a sort of companionable disgruntlement. Then Tom thought of a consolation, something they could do together without anyone unlacing anything. "My cellmate — Jack Coddington — said his upright man would bail him out as soon as he got back from France. That'd be another bit of evidence. Weak, I grant you, but —"

"Where can we find him?"

"At the Dolphin, near the Old Swan Stairs. We could go down there now, scout around a little."

"Yes." Trumpet sat up straight, a boy ready for a treat. "But not today; he won't be there. I can't imagine Uncle Nat rushing straight to Newgate after a long journey, especially not with Catalina sitting on his lap feeding him strips of fresh melon."

"True."

"We'll give them a few days, all of them. Catalina needs time to regain Uncle Nat's confidence and learn what she can learn. Uncle Nat needs time to decide what he's going to do now that he knows we suspect him. And it wouldn't look right to pounce on Coddington the day he gets out of gaol."

"I don't think he'd mind, but yes. Let's wait. I'll set a boy to watch for him at the Dolphin. Red hair, big mouth — shouldn't be hard to spot. We want to catch him before he gets himself arrested again."

"True," Trumpet said. "And that will give us time to come up with some suitable garb. Something more like a senior apprentice or a recently dismissed retainer . . ." She drummed her fingers on the rough tabletop.

Clean hands with well-shaped nails. A small flaw in her disguise. Her hands were one of his favorite parts though. Light, quick, and tender but surprisingly strong.

"What will we tell him?" she asked.

"Who?"

"Coddington. Are you going to sally up and say, 'What ho, me boyo! Look who's out and about?'"

Tom shrugged. "Why not? I'll pretend I want a place in the gang. Maybe I could suggest a likely target for the next burglary."

"Where?"

"I don't know. That's the big question, isn't it? How the victims are being selected. That's the one Bacon didn't want us to talk about the other night."

"I've been thinking about that too," Trumpet said. "At least in terms of my uncle. I wonder if they might have been clients of his at some time."

"Legal clients?"

"No, renters from his stable of whores." Trumpet rolled her eyes. "He's a well-respected barrister, Tom. And though he's not a Catholic, nor has ever been, he has some sympathy for them. My grandparents in Devonshire, especially my grandmother, hated to put aside the old religion. Their chapel at Winkleigh Manor must be stuffed full of reliquaries and the like, come to think of it."

"I suppose he has the grace not to steal from his own relations."

She clucked her tongue at him. He loved that sound. "My point," she said, "is that these old families know each other. My grandfather and Baron Hewick's father might have been pages together in old King Henry's court, for all we know. If my uncle did good work for one of them, they would recommend him to the next."

Tom's grandfather had been a Northumberland fisherman whose boat had capsized off the Dorset coast, where he'd been rescued by a smuggler's daughter. "Sounds plausible. How can you find out?"

"I'll ask my aunt. She might know about long-term or prominent clients."

Tom nodded. "What will you tell Aunt Blanche about today? Your uncle will probably say something to her."

She shrugged slowly, the corners of her bow-shaped lips rising as well. "I'll tell her the truth. She was a co-conspirator when I went to Gray's, but once I turned eighteen, she wanted me to stop playing, marry well, and settle down. She doesn't approve, but she won't hinder me. And she knows about you, a little, that we were friends when I was Allen. You might come to visit with Ben sometime. It would be a start."

Tom grinned. One goal achieved. "It would be a feather in our caps to figure out how the victims are chosen before Bacon and Ben get there, wouldn't it?"

"I'd love to see the look on their faces. It would teach them to keep their scoldings to themselves. Ben has been the most insufferable —" She broke off with a sharp rap on the tabletop. "I vow I would dismiss him if he weren't one of the only three lawyers in the world who can be trusted with the complexities of my circumstances. Mr. Bacon would charge too much for too little work and my uncle has a way of disappearing when things get hot."

"In a few years, you'll have me."

She pointed a slender finger at him. "Don't think I don't know it."

They smiled at each other. Still friends — best friends — but on different terms that had not been fully negotiated. Doubtless some terms remained to be revealed to him. Tom looked forward to them, whatever they were.

One more question remained to be asked. Then they could go down to Billingsgate and watch the ships go in and out. "Did your uncle collude in any way with the murders of those men?"

"No." She glared at him. "He couldn't have. First, he seemed sincerely grieved by Surdeval's death. You noticed it too — I saw you."

Tom nodded. But didn't some murderers repent their crimes?

Trumpet's eyes narrowed at the scant affirmation. "Second, and more compelling, your father said it would take at least five days to sail to St. Jean de Luz. That means another five to sail home again. If he only got back today, he must have been at sea on my wedding night. He could not have been in Surdeval House kneeling over my poor lord's body."

211

Tom nodded, pretending to be impressed. He had worked that out for himself days ago. She'd evaded his full question, not addressing the possibility of collusion.

He understood how much she loved her uncle. Welbeck was the closest thing she had to a father, though she hadn't seen much of him during her lonely youth in that dismal castle. Still, he was the one who brought her presents, encouraged her to go after what she wanted, and introduced her to the law.

But Tom saw a different side. He saw the man who held grudges — witness his constant harping on Francis Bacon. Tom always sensed the blade beneath the cloak of Welbeck's affable manner. Then again, the man was a barrister to his fingertips, more likely to fight his battles with words than knives.

Another silence grew, not so companionable this time. A shadow washed across the tiny yard. It'd be suppertime soon. Tom wanted more of Trumpet's company. He wanted to go out and look at things and eat coarse food in rough establishments for the daring fun of it, the way they used to when she'd been Allen and lived at Gray's. He wanted to debate philosophy and fashion and gossip about the barristers and the cases they watched in court.

"It's because I'm short, isn't it?" Trumpet asked.

"What?"

"You like tall women, like Clara and that preacher's daughter in Cambridge. You've written poems about their nymph-like figures. I'm short, so I'm not appealing."

Tom blinked at her. Now what? A man sat at a quiet table, innocently drinking his ale and eating his bread, when along comes a madwoman and drops an anchor on his head. "You're not short."

"I'm a full head shorter than you. More."

"Well, all right. Strictly speaking, you are short, in the sense of not tall. But trust me, Trumpet. It does not make you unappealing." He gave her his warmest grin, the one with the deepest dimple.

She did a kind of arching thing with her back that froze the grin on his face. "Then you'll meet me at the Two Bells tomorrow night. Remember that room you showed me, with the bed so big it nearly filled the room? I sent Catalina to ask about the price for a whole night. I'll pay with some candlesticks I took from Surdeval House. It's only fair since the cost of the room will be incurred in defense of my possession . . ."

Tom's mind glazed over with an image of Trumpet in that filmy gown, sprawled across the eight-foot bed at his favorite brothel. It had a slippery silk coverlet, gauzy pink curtains, heaps of pillows, and a never-ending —

"Meet me at midnight," she whispered. "I'll get there first."

"Oh, aye," Tom murmured, still lost in his imagination. She squealed, making him blink. "No," he said, returning to the world. "No, no, no. And again I say, no. Never, Trumpet. Stop doing that."

"You just said you would."

"No, I didn't. You tricked me, putting that vision in my head."

"What vision?"

He knew better than to answer.

She snatched up his knife and pointed it at him. "I only have one week, Tom, until I must submit to an examination of my intimate person by eight matrons. Eight, Tom. In *one week*."

Tom pushed the blade aside with his index finger. "I can hold out that long."

Another silence fell. The wench came out to offer them more ale, but they growled at her in unison and she skittered off. Gradually, the frustration leached out of Trumpet's posture. Tom held out his hand and she placed his knife in it, hilt first.

213

"I give up." She picked up her cup and peered into the dregs. She muttered, "Maybe the horses will do the trick."

"Not if you tell that stupid story," Tom said, knowing exactly what she meant. "And I beg you, my lady, please do not invite me to your next wedding supper. I intend to go out that night and get stinking drunk."

She blew out a lip-rattling sigh. He felt for her, he truly did, but everyone had a burden to bear. Hers was having to marry a man she didn't like and let him take her maidenhead. She might be in for a bad night, but only the first one and she'd survive it. Most women did.

"Don't tell Mr. Bacon," she said.

"About the Two Bells?"

"About my uncle."

That much he could do for her. "I won't, not yet. But I'll have to tell him eventually."

"I know."

He grinned at her. "Let's wait till we have something better than a bag of fresh lemons."

TWENTY-THREE

After chapel on Sunday morning, Francis went to his desk to jot a few notes about the sermon in his commonplace book. That reminded him of something else, so he got up to get his copy of Tacitus's *Histories*. He drew a line across the page and began to copy some useful quotations for his lord uncle to use in his next counterstroke against the vindictive lies being published by the Catholic college in Rheims. They fought this war with ink as well as gunpowder.

His servant, Pinnock flung open the door and dashed across the room waving a letter, disrupting Francis's train of thought. He scolded the boy absently while he turned the packet over, breaking off with a gasp when he saw the seal of the Earl of Essex pressed into the circle of red wax. He mirrored the boy's excited grin. "But mind you, keep this to yourself! Don't spread it about to the other servants."

"No, Mr. Bacon. I never!"

Francis opened the letter and read the note, savoring each word. His Lord of Essex graciously requested him to visit Leicester House that afternoon to satisfy his curiosity about the Surdeval affair. Thrilling!

He set Pinnock to brushing his summer barrister's gown — the lightweight worsted — and sponging his best — no, his second best — doublet, the black Milanese fustian. It wouldn't do to dress as if he was going to court. A step or two down was more appropriate for an informal visit on a Sunday afternoon. He could wear his velvet hat with the gold and garnet brooch.

He took a fresh sheet of paper and dashed out a summary of what he'd learned so far. Letters forming under his quill always helped to clarify his thoughts. He hadn't learned much, although he had made some progress on the matter of the poison. His Lordship would find that interesting. Perhaps Francis could engage him in a discussion of the means of acquiring rare plants from the New World. This educated earl would enjoy an intellectual pursuit more than the passive receipt of a dry report.

Francis reread his notes, dipped his quill in preparation to add one more thought, then cried, "Ben!" This was just the treat his friend needed to jog him out of his recent ill humor. Besides, it always looked better to have a retainer at one's side.

He told Pinnock to lay out fresh linens and warm some clean towels to rub his hair and then hop quick as a bunny across the yard to invite Ben to join him.

* * *

Combed and polished within an inch of their lives, Francis and Ben presented themselves at the gate of Leicester House on the Strand as the bells of St. Mary's tolled two o'clock. Leicester's only legitimate son had died in childhood, so his stepson, the Earl of Essex, was his heir. The steward ushered them into the great hall, an impressive region that had been refurbished by the late earl only a dozen years ago. The beams of the lofty ceiling were studded with enameled bosses in the Dudley colors of orange and white. An exceptional display of crests and weaponry hung upon the gleaming plaster walls.

Francis struggled to compose himself as they crossed the black-and-white-chequered floor. Excitement wreaked havoc with his digestion; he would pay for this tonight. It was worth it, though, to gain a private audience with a favorite of the queen. Especially one who seemed so favorably disposed toward Francis.

Now that Leicester had died, Essex would likely rise even faster. He was only twenty-three — Ben's age, as it happened — but had already been made Master of the Horse. His influence could only increase. Francis depended upon the goodwill of his uncle, the Lord Treasurer, but had thus far reaped a spare harvest from that stony field. His uncle held him at arm's length to make room for his own son. Francis was kept well supplied with work but granted neither honors nor offices. He needed a new patron, someone else to be his friend with the queen. Perhaps his Lord of Essex would be that man.

Ben dug an elbow into his side and murmured, "Look at those arrows."

"Arrows?" Francis followed his pointing finger and saw a whole section of wall devoted to the military arts. Bows of unusual material and design — large and small, some painted and decorated with feathers — had been hung with pairs of matching arrows. Crossed spears of equally varied design punctuated these assemblages.

The steward noticed their interest and led them over for a closer inspection. He gave them a concise lecture on the provenance of the collection. "My late lord received gifts from all over the world, not only from English explorers. Suleiman the Magnificent sent him those scimitars for his birthday many years ago. The Spanish ambassador brought him those hunting spears from Peru."

Didn't the Grand River described in Orellana's accounts run through Peru? Bless Ben and his sharp eyes! Francis would have walked right past that display, even after Captain Clarady had advised them to consider such collections as a source of the poison. He stepped in close to inspect the stone points of the Peruvian spears, but they had been polished clean. No oil or ointment clung to them now.

The steward cleared his throat and begged their patience while he went to see if his master was ready to receive visitors. As he clacked away across the polished floor, Ben hissed in Francis's ear, "Is it possible that Essex is the murderer we seek?"

"Shhh!" Francis glared at him. "What a preposterous idea!" Never mind that he'd just inspected the weapons for traces of poison himself.

"Look at all these things," Ben insisted. "Half of them are from the New World. What other dangerous trinkets might be squirreled away in this great house?"

"Impossible!" Francis's mind rejected the very thought. "Impossible," he repeated as his heart stopped racing. "These crimes are too small for a man of His Lordship's temperament, too ugly. And besides, I can't believe he would work in secret. He would want the queen to know he'd performed such an extraordinary service on her behalf."

As would Sir Richard Topcliffe, come to think of it. But Sir Richard wouldn't mind waiting for the credit to be revealed at some perfect opportunity. In fact, he would relish the private knowledge.

The steward returned and strode toward them. Francis gripped Ben's arm. "Do not give that unspeakable idea another moment of thought, and do not, under any circumstances, ever utter it aloud again."

Ben rolled his eyes but nodded to indicate compliance.

The steward led them to the library and bowed them through the door. His Lordship sprawled in a silk-cushioned chair before a wide bank of windows, open to admit a fragrant breeze from the walled garden outside. He wore very short hose and shining silk stockings, stretching his long legs out before him. He'd been reading a very old book, by the worn appearance of the binding. Clerks sat at two desks on the opposite side of the spacious chamber, each with a stack of books, scribbling notes on long coils of parchment.

"We're taking inventory," the earl said. He crooked his fingers for them to approach.

Francis performed the introduction. Ben bowed twice but otherwise acquitted himself well, apart from the deep blush rising up his sallow cheeks. His Lordship was too gracious to notice such a thing.

Francis composed himself in the balanced stance he adopted at court, where one might spend many hours standing in one spot. "An inventory of this important library is a laudable deed, my lord."

"Alas, I don't do it for the praise, Mr. Bacon. Everything in the house must be sold, right down to the inkhorns. My stepfather died owing the queen some twenty-five thousand pounds."

"Faith!" The sum put Francis's little book bill into perspective. "Her Majesty is the most generous of monarchs, but I suppose she must collect her debts."

The earl acknowledged the mischaracterization of the queen's parsimony with a swift grin. "So she must. But I mourn the loss of this library. Perhaps I'll find a backer and buy it myself."

"Then it could be preserved intact," Francis said. "Always desirable, if seldom possible." He looked at the overflowing shelves. His Lord of Leicester had been the chancellor of Oxford and a major patron of art, philosophy, and literature. Many of these books would bear his name as a dedicatee. There might be rare legal works here as well. Perhaps Gray's Inn could enter bids for a few volumes. He would mention it to the other benchers that evening at supper.

"But enough of these sordid business matters," the earl said. "Tell me what you've learned about Surdeval's murder."

Francis delivered his report, apologizing for its brevity. He highlighted the discovery of the name of the poison since that was really all he had.

"Curare," the earl said, pronouncing the word in the Spanish style. "A most *curarious* method, wouldn't you say?"

Francis and Ben laughed at the witticism.

The earl looked pleased at their response. He would doubtless employ the device again at court as soon as he could compose an opening. "It sounds too fantastical, however. A substance capable of rendering a grown man insensible with no other signs of distress? I wouldn't believe it if we hadn't seen so many marvels brought home in recent years. Who could have imagined a pineapple, for example, without ever having seen one?"

"An astute observation, my lord, and an apt example." Francis admired the swiftness of the earl's comprehension. "I confess I'm not certain how the poison works, or even it really was this curare that Orellana mentions. Nor have I discovered a source for a New World poison, and to be candid, I don't know where to look. Spears and arrows might be hung on walls, but a bottle of tincture or a pot of paste would not make so gallant a display."

"Ah, but it would make a most impressive gift! Think of it: the queen could bring down a wild boar by herself with such a poison on her darts." A speculative look stole into the earl's brown eyes. "You'd keep something like that quiet until the right moment. You wouldn't want every stray traveler who wandered into your hall to see it. You'd keep it in your treasure room and only show it to a select few, those who could appreciate the tale of its acquisition."

"I'm sure Your Lordship is correct." Francis hoped he hadn't inadvertently begun a fashion for exotic poisons. Surviving the twists and turns of the court was difficult enough with unvarnished barbs. "Although I'm not sure how I can pursue that trail."

"I'll see what I can learn." The earl smiled at the shadow of doubt that crossed Francis's face and added, "Never fear, Mr. Bacon. I shall exercise the utmost discretion." He paused with that indefinable air noblemen adopt to dismiss the present topic, then plucked a piece of paper from the small table at his elbow and handed it to Francis. "This is the other reason I asked you to come. A sack of coins was delivered here yesterday, accompanied by this note."

"Coins, my lord?"

"A substantial sum. About five hundred pounds."

Francis read the note aloud for Ben's benefit. "Those who would murder our Sovereign Queen and overthrow the right and lawfully established Church of England must pay for their criminous affronts with their own goods, the chattels of popery. However humble, however weak, all loyal English must sustain the battle against the viperous traitors who infest our very homes. I beg Your Lordship accept this first payment exacted from the slaves of Rome, to be spent in aid of the piteous yet valiant sailors and soldiers who rose to Her Majesty's defense in her hour of greatest need."

He turned the paper over, then held it up to the light of the window.

"We couldn't find any sign of who had sent it," the earl said. "The sack was delivered by a boy who disappeared at once."

"Even if we could find him, my lord, he probably couldn't tell us much. No doubt he was given the sack and the note by a gentleman in a hooded cloak who spoke in a whispery voice."

"That was my assumption," the earl said. "It's all the more intriguing now that you tell me there have been other chapel burglaries. What do you make of it, Mr. Bacon?"

Francis studied the note more carefully. "This writing is odd. It seems to be deliberately distorted." He couldn't say if it resembled Sir Richard's writing in any way or not.

"I thought so too." The earl sat forward in his chair, an eager look on his face. "You see how it slants in different directions? I thought the writer might have been using his left hand, though he's by nature a right-handed man."

"What sharp eyes you have, my lord!" Francis had noted the same irregularities. "The author must have been trying to disguise his hand."

"Doesn't that suggest someone who would be known to me?" the earl asked.

"Or to your secretary," Francis said. "Or it merely indicates a high degree of caution and forethought. If we had any idea who it was, we could compare some other sample of their writing with this note."

"Forgive me, my lord," Ben said, bowing unnecessarily. "But to be perfectly clear: Are we assuming these coins are part of the profits from the sale of the stolen chapel goods?"

"I believe we are, Mr. Whitt." The earl smiled patiently.

"But, my lord," Ben said, "can it be possible that the murderer of these three men acted out of love of country?"

"So it would seem, Mr. Whitt," the earl said. "Like you, I find the idea repellent, though I love my queen and my country as much as any other man. Even while I despise the source, I will see the money is spent as intended. God knows we need it." He tossed the note onto the table. "So, Mr. Bacon, does this tell us anything to help us apprehend our villain?"

Francis sensed that the interview had reached its conclusion. "I'm sure it must, my lord, although I will need to consider it further." He knew better than to share his tentative theories with the earl, who might be unable to resist the impulse to speak of them at court. "It does tell us our villain is not an ordinary criminal. The motive appears not to be personal gain or even personal retribution. I have my assistant tracking the chapel goods. And I will continue to seek the source of the poison. My hope is that those two trails will converge."

He had a horrible feeling he already knew where they would meet: in the home of Sir Richard Topcliffe on Mincing Lane.

TWENTY-FOUR

Francis tossed and turned all night, struggling to think of a way to find out if Sir Richard Topcliffe had pots of New World poisons or a secret collection of stolen rosaries or any other damning possessions without approaching the man, his house, or his servants. It couldn't be done. He must summon the courage to visit the house. But what excuse could he offer Sir Richard for wanting to inspect his library?

Francis knew himself to be a man of exceptional discretion, but he was not skilled in deception in the flesh, as it were. He made a better spymaster than an intelligencer. Fortunately, he had someone with the desired qualities right across the yard.

He found Tom and Ben in the hall, finishing their breakfasts of bread and ale. He slid onto the bench next to Ben and told them about his dilemma. Tom offered to go in his stead, but Francis considered a visit from a total stranger even less likely to be accepted as unremarkable. And he wasn't sure what he expected to find, exactly. He would have to see for himself.

Tom said, "Well, the first thing is that you don't want to go when he's at home. Can you think of a time when he's certain to be out?"

Francis hadn't considered the idea of visiting a man known to be elsewhere, but of course it made sense. "He'll be at the Tower at eight o'clock to interview our next prisoner. But I should be there as well."

"Be late," Tom said. "That's the ideal time."

"I can't just walk in the door of his house," Francis said. "What pretext will I give the servants?"

Tom snapped his fingers. "I know! Bring Sir Richard a book. Say you wanted to drop it off to spare him having to carry it home. You're a bookish man; anyone would believe you had a few spare volumes you wanted to pass around."

"I suppose that's true." Francis didn't much like being called bookish — an ill-made expression — but he let it go in the interest of expediency.

"Take Ben," Tom said. "He goes with you to the Tower sometimes, so it's plausible."

Ben said, "I'm willing, if we don't linger. I must file a document in the bishop's court this morning for Trumpet's case."

"You won't have time to linger," Tom said. "You can get in and prowl around a bit, but that's all."

Francis frowned. "How can we prowl around with the servants watching us?"

"You'll create a diversion," Tom said. "That's why Ben should go with you."

"Me? What can I do?"

"Pretend to sprain an ankle or get a sudden cramp in your belly," Tom said. "Anything that draws the servants' attention away from Mr. Bacon for ten minutes or so. Get them to walk you to the jakes or the kitchen or somewhere."

Francis and Ben exchanged doubtful glances. Ben said, "I'm not sure I could be convincing enough."

Tom sighed and rolled his eyes. "It does require a little acting ability. You have to *believe* your ankle hurts too much to walk on." He fingered his earring. "All right. I'll come with you. But only long enough to start the diversion. I'm drilling the militia this morning, and we had no end of trouble agreeing on the time. We're participating in a review of the troops before Her Majesty in two weeks, and we're nowhere near ready. Three of my men still can't remember to light the fuse *before* they pull the trigger."

Francis asked, "Won't it be more suspicious for me to bring two men along just to drop off a book?"

"They won't see me," Tom said. "Oh, and you're going to want to inscribe the book, which is why you'll ask to be shown into the library. Draw it out; make a fuss." He raised his mug. "Fear not, gentlemen. Sir Richard's servants won't be anywhere near you while you tear apart his library."

Ben and Tom walked behind Francis on the way into the city, engaged in a disjointed conversation about firearms. They didn't seem to mind the constant interruptions caused by the hurly-burly of the streets, where persons of arbitrary size and disposition might erupt into one's path at any moment. Francis preferred to keep his eyes on the ground, watching for bits of refuse that might ensnare his feet, and his mind focused on the task of navigation.

When they reached Mincing Lane, Tom stopped at the corner to rehearse them in their story. Francis had a copy of the *Genevan Book of Common Order* his mother had given him — a plausible gift for a man of Sir Richard's zealous tastes. Tom checked the first page to be sure it hadn't already been inscribed. Francis hadn't thought to do that; luckily, his mother hadn't thought of it either.

Church bells everywhere began to clang, sounding the quarter hour. Tom said, "I'll watch until you go in, then give you a couple of minutes to get into the library. Work fast; I can't guarantee more than ten minutes."

"How will we know when you're ready?" Ben asked.

"You'll know." Tom's grin sent a chill of foreboding through Francis.

The plan worked. Sir Richard had left for the Tower half an hour earlier, as expected. The servant who opened the door seemed suitably impressed by the name Bacon. Francis flourished the book, explaining that he didn't like to bring it to the Tower for fear of soiling it. Ben had the bright idea of reaching over his shoulder to open the cover and exclaim, "Oh, you ought to have written a personal inscription since this book is intended as a gift."

The speech sounded stilted, but the servant let them into the house without demur. Sir Richard's home was substantial, though scarcely a rival to Lady Russell's establishment in Blackfriars. They entered into a sort of screens passage, a partially closed-in area meant to protect the main rooms from drafts and prying eyes. Two doors punctured the floor-to-ceiling paneling. One presumably led to the service area. The other, through which they were conducted, opened into the great room.

The servant marched across the rush-strewn floor toward a staircase with a carved newel post, leaving the smell of crushed tansy rising in his wake. Francis turned to observe the small display of crossed pikes on the wall, topped by Sir Richard's family crest. If he possessed a larger collection of weapons, it must be at his house in Lincolnshire.

The library had pride of place at the front of the house on the first floor. Wide windows hanging over Mincing Lane let in an abundance of light, a treasure in itself for a house in the center of the crowded city. The windows were open to catch what little breeze managed to straggle through the narrow streets. The view consisted entirely of the family parlor of the house across the street. That room seemed empty at the moment, but they would need to keep an eye in that direction as well, assuming they were left alone at all.

The library was handsomely furnished with carved oak chairs and tables, beautifully polished by well-trained servants, but there were fewer books than Francis expected. Sir Richard presented himself as a man of learning; perhaps he kept his books in Lincolnshire as well. The servant gestured to the writing materials on the largest of the tables. Francis raised his eyebrows at Ben, who raised his twice in reply. He had no more idea than Francis what Tom had planned.

Francis dallied, turning to the single stand of books. "I do hope Sir Richard doesn't already have a copy of my humble gift." He shuffled roughly through the neat stacks, feeling like a veritable pirate. He found only a blameless selection of Protestant works and useful volumes like *The English Secretary*, along with a few predictables like Thomas Hoby's translation of *The Book of the Courtier*. Every gentleman in England kept those books in his house.

"Ah!" The small cry of discovery startled Francis; he hadn't meant to make a sound. But here was one thing he'd been hoping for: Eden's translation of *De Orbe Novo*. He pawed through the rest with wanton disregard for their original order, but found nothing else concerning New Spain or other voyages.

Did the absence of Orellana's book count in Sir Richard's favor? No; Francis deemed it inconclusive. The pursuivant could have learned about New World poisons from a Spanish prisoner, a merchant, or a member of the Spanish ambassador's household. Sir Richard moved in the same court circles as Francis and had also traveled the length and breadth of England in search of crypto-Catholics and the secrets they kept. Besides, he could have borrowed the book from a friend and long since returned it.

Ben had been chatting with the servant with an increasingly desperate tone in his voice. Francis could think of no further reason to delay. He walked to the table, set down his book, and opened it to the frontispiece.

An echoing bang exploded in the street. Tom's voice shouted, "Spaniards! After them!"

Chaos erupted. Feet pounded, men shouted, women screamed. A series of loud clacks resounded as someone slapped the shutters across the windows of the house opposite. Sir Richard's servant cried, "God save us!" and dashed from the room.

Francis and Ben froze where they stood for one long moment, then Ben laughed. "An unmistakable signal indeed."

"I hope no one gets hurt." Francis turned in a circle, fingers twitching, wondering what to do first. He saw nothing worthy of note in this room. Furniture. Books he'd already examined. A fireplace, swept clean, with paintings of dour-faced ancestors, one male, one female, on either side. A small tapestry hung on another wall.

Then he spotted a narrow door in an awkward corner to the left of the stairs. A storage area, perhaps?

Ben had spotted it too. He opened the door and they gasped in unison at what they found inside. The windowless closet, about eight feet square, had one small writing desk covered with neat stacks of paper, one set of shelves leaning in the corner, and one small chest set atop a larger one. These were unremarkable. Any man might utilize such a room for a private secretary or even himself if his house was filled with noisy family and visitors.

The gasps had been provoked by row upon row of files, strung on wire rings and hung from pegs, each bearing a label in Sir Richard's clerk's neat hand. Francis glanced over his shoulder to be sure the servant had not returned, then stepped inside the closet. Ben followed him.

Beginning at opposite sides, they quickly examined all the files within reach. Ben asked, "Do you recognize any names?"

"I recognize all of them. Fitzherbert, Neville, Manners: all part of his cousinage; some on his side, some on his wife's. Some of these families are Catholic by tradition, though none have ever been charged with anything specific. It looks as though Sir Richard has been collecting notes about them for decades."

Francis leafed through the pages strung on one file, careful not to pull at the holes. "Look, he seems to have made a note of every place this Fitzherbert has ever been and everyone he's ever done business with. It's appalling — even a little mad."

"Here's a ring with all known recusants with residences in the London area." Ben thumbed through the documents. "This is bad, Frank. All our victims are here, with notes about the commission's interviews. This one has writing in the margin in a different hand, saying 'Should have racked him, the lying turd.'"

"That's Sir Richard." Francis frowned at the vulgarity. "Still, nothing here is evidence of crime; at least none of Sir Richard's doing. What's in those chests, I wonder? Can you take a quick look?"

He went back out into the library and jogged to the window. The shutters were still closed in the house opposite. Francis looked down into the street and almost laughed out loud to see two men running pell-mell in one direction while two women skittered shrieking in the other. A man in an apron tiptoed across the lane with a stick raised in one hand. He bent double to peer beneath an overturned bushel basket, as if expecting to find a tiny Spaniard huddled beneath. Sir Richard's servant was nowhere in sight. The silent house felt empty.

He returned to the closet to find Ben holding an iron ring with a thick chain dangling from it. A manacle.

"God's breath," Francis said. "Why would anyone keep such a thing in his house?"

"There are three more, of different sizes, inside that chest. And look at this." He put the manacles back and lifted up another instrument made of oak and iron, shaped like a small vise with two screws. "If I'm not mistaken, this one is called a thumbscrew, or pilliwinks."

"Pilliwinks? It sounds like a children's game." Francis touched it gingerly. His thumbs ached at the mere sight of it. "Is it possible he uses these cruel devices here, in his own home?"

"One more thing." Ben pointed into the chest.

Francis peeked inside, fearing to see an even more terrifying instrument of torture. What he saw was worse: the colored beads and crosses of a pair of rosaries, tangled among the iron chains of the manacles. Articles of faith entwined with the instruments of torture. Was this what their religious Reformation had brought them to?

TWENTY-FIVE

They let themselves out of Sir Richard's house and walked quickly to Tower Hill. Ben said, "I don't like the idea of you going back to work with that man. I could file Trumpet's papers tomorrow without postponing her hearing more than a day or two."

"No, no. Don't delay on my account." Francis summoned a brave smile. "I'll be all right. And don't forget to add the five pence for the wherryman to your expenses." He watched Ben's tall figure disappear into the crowds on Tower Street, then turned to walk down Petty Wales.

Ben assumed Francis would be afraid to meet Sir Richard now, after what they'd learned. And he was, a little. He had known the man enjoyed threatening the prisoners and relished the idea of torture. He had not known that Sir Richard enjoyed it so much as to collect the devices in his own library. The thought of the man applying those thumbscrews to someone right there in his home appalled Francis so deeply his chief fear was that he wouldn't be able to face him with his usual manner.

What if Sir Richard suspected that Francis knew about his secret cache? What would he do? Francis's thumbs twitched. He drew a deep breath to calm himself.

Underneath the riffle of fear, however, lay something else — something buoyant, almost a sense of exhilaration. That puzzled Francis until he traced the sensation to its source. He had just successfully completed his first act of subterfuge. He had learned something pertinent to his investigations and he had not been caught.

Francis bounced a little on his toes as he waited for the guard to pass him through the gate. He smiled as if in cheerful greeting, but the smile was for himself. It would seem he had a bit of the spy in him after all.

He found Sir Richard and his stoop-shouldered clerk standing outside Wakefield Tower talking with one of the liveried guards. After exchanging greetings, Francis asked, "Are we waiting for Sir William Waad?" He doubted it; the Privy Council secretary used every excuse to avoid the actual work of the commission.

"Come and gone," Sir Richard said. "Another engagement. You're late, Mr. Bacon."

"I do apologize. There was a commotion in the street."

"Begging soldiers, I'll wager."

"I heard a shot fired," Francis said. "It caused a bit of a panic."

"There are even more of them this week," the clerk said. "With no money to pay their wages, some have no way to get home."

"Sad but true, Mr. Kemp. Sad but true." Sir Richard had the air of a man waiting patiently for some pleasurable event. "Pity we can't use the top of my list in our commission, isn't it, Mr. Bacon? The fish we net in the prisons are poor lot as a rule, yet we're obliged to let the great whales swim free. If I had my way, we'd stuff my good queen's coffers so full of coin she'd cry my name out again and again."

He and his clerk shared a round of chuckles while Francis struggled to mask his disgust. The man was even more vulgar in a good humor. Still, he did seem inclined to chat. His servants would be sure to mention Francis's visit; best he said something about it himself first.

"I took shelter in your house, Sir Richard, as it happens. During the disturbance."

"How's that?"

"I dropped by to leave you a book. *The Genevan Book of Common Order*, which my mother sent me. I thought you might find it interesting."

"Why, Mr. Bacon! That's very thoughtful of you. Do thank Her Ladyship for me. I hope my servants treated you well."

"In every way," Francis said. "You'll find the book on your desk when you get home." He wanted to ask Sir Richard about arrow poisons but couldn't think of a way to introduce the topic.

A guard strode across the yard, handed a letter to Sir Richard with a short bow, and returned to his post. Sir Richard unfolded the letter, read it with a grunt, and tucked it into his sleeve. He cocked his head toward Francis, a measuring look in his eyes.

"Is anything amiss?"

"Perhaps," Sir Richard said. "Perhaps not. Some accidents turn into strokes of luck." He clapped his hands together, making Francis jump. "Let's get to work, shall we? Mustn't waste the whole morning."

Francis turned toward the door, ready to go upstairs.

"Not that way, Mr. Bacon. We're in a different venue today."

"How is that?"

"The prisoner we meant to question died of a fever in gaol last night. God's judgment precludes ours — and saves us a bit of work." Sir Richard gestured toward the White Tower, looming in the center of the castle enclosure. He started walking, so Francis fell into step beside him. The clerk followed at a pace behind.

Sir Richard smiled, deep wrinkles creasing around his eyes. "It's just as well. Now you can join us in the second round with Amias Fenton. You remember him, don't you?"

"Of course." Fenton was the snarling priest who had first told him about the other victims. This could be an unexpected opportunity. "Do you think he knows more about the recusant murders?"

"I think he knows more than he's told us about many things," Sir Richard said. "Let's probe him to the marrow, shall we?"

Francis didn't like the sound of that. Nor did he like the door Sir Richard now opened, leading down to the basement instead of up to the administrative chambers. He hesitated on the threshold, but Sir Richard grasped his elbow.

"Come along, Mr. Bacon. It's time you took a full part in our examinations. Who knows? You may find you have a talent for it. The cool ones usually make the best practitioners."

Francis met his hard black eyes, then blinked and tried to turn around, but the clerk closed in behind him, pressing him forward. He swallowed hard and let himself be herded down the stairs.

Wooden vaulting supported the high ceiling of the windowless basement. Widely spaced torches threw shifting shadows across the vast space. Huge barrels were stacked three high against the walls. A rectangular contraption with ropes and large spools, like a bed frame with no canvas, leaned against one of the stone walls. The rack, most dreaded of the instruments of torture, was roughly made of unpolished wood and pitted iron. What craftsman could take pride in constructing such a machine?

Two men in workman's garb fiddled with the ropes, testing the play of the metal pegs that supported the spools in the iron frame. A liveried guard held Amias Fenton in his meaty grip. The recusant's hands were bound before him. He stood with his eyes closed while his lips moved rapidly and soundlessly.

"I can't —" Francis tried to turn back toward the stairs, but Sir Richard used his bulk to block his way.

"First time's the hardest. You'll get used to it." He turned Francis back to face the rack. "You know that this is done, Mr. Bacon. You know it must be done. An honest man would want to know *how* it's done."

That shamed Francis. How could he sit smugly in his comfortable chambers, never giving another thought to the men he had recommended for "further questioning"? This was where they went, he'd always known it. Perhaps he did have a moral obligation to face the result of his judgments, at least once.

The workmen lifted Fenton up and laid him on the rack, arms over his head. They secured his wrists and ankles to the rollers. "Silence!" One of the men slapped him hard across the face to stop his praying. The crack echoed into the dark corners.

"We're ready, Sir Richard."

Francis pressed his lips together and willed himself to stand still, though he couldn't bring himself to watch directly. He kept his eyes open but tilted his face toward the floor.

Sir Richard handed his hat to the clerk and stood at Fenton's head. He bent to look his prisoner in the eyes. "This doesn't have to take long, Amias. The sooner you answer my questions, the sooner these men will return you to your cozy cell."

Fenton spat in his face. Sir Richard laughed. "I thought that might be your answer. Good! Let the game begin!"

The men set to work. Sir Richard wanted the names of any householders who had sheltered Fenton and other seminary priests. Sometimes he shouted the question, sometimes he crooned it. "Names, priest. I want their names."

Fenton's only answers were groans of agony and muttered Latin prayers.

Francis's stomach roiled in disgust and pity. This man would never yield. They should hang him and be done with it. He tried to speak, but his voice sounded thick. He cleared his throat and tried again. "Let him go, I pray you. Take him back to his cell."

"This obstinate cur? Not yet, Mr. Bacon. Not until he gives over at least one of the juicy widows who succored him while loyal Englishmen died." He rapped his knuckles on the iron frame. "Tighten it up! Let's make this man a little taller. Maybe that will loosen his tongue."

Metal slid across metal and ropes creaked. The prisoner's moans rose in pitch, broken by the fleshy *pop* of a joint being pulled from its socket.

"That's got it!" Sir Richard crowed.

The prisoner's screams filled the cavernous chamber. Francis doubled over and vomited into the straw.

TWENTY-SIX

Dirimara Montoya de la Torre stepped off the gangway onto the wharf east of the fabled bridge of London. Sailors had told him about it, but he'd never seen the like. It looked like a town suspended over the water on mighty pillars, tall buildings with glass-filled windows covering every inch from end to end. Clearly, it had been built by powerful people. He hadn't thought the English capable of such monuments before.

He inhaled deeply, savoring the rich stink of the city. The smell of life, invigorating after months at sea. London: great capital of Inglaterra, the native land of his dearest friend in all the world, Captain Valentine Clarady. If only his friend were still alive to share this occasion.

Dirimara stood for a while watching the cranes on the wharf load bales of wool onto a ship. He much admired the efficiency of the cranes but was grateful not to be the man trapped inside the wheel, walking the same short course all day to keep the mighty engine moving. He felt sorry for that man, but he had an even crueler job to do himself today, if he could find the boy.

One of the sailors clapped him on the shoulder as he passed. They'd become friends on the long voyage from New Spain last year and had fought side by side during the recent battles in the British Sea. "I hope you're going to be all right here, my friend. The English don't much like strangers." He looked Dirimara up and down, his gaze lingering on the waist-long braid of blue-black hair and the shark's-tooth earrings. "And you're a sight stranger than most."

Dirimara grinned, showing the gap between his teeth. "I have been in worse places than Inglaterra."

"England." The sailor shook his head. "You could let someone else deliver the bad news."

"No," Dirimara said. "The duty is mine. When we came here and entered the battle with the Espaniards, my captain said to me, if I die, go find my boy. My Tomás. Tell him what happened, and he will look out for you."

"All right," the sailor said. "May God protect you, then."

"*Vaya con Dios*," Dirimara replied. He turned away from the sea, his home for more than a year, and faced the enormous city. He decided to start with the dockside taverns. Someone there would surely know of the famous Captain Clarady and where to find his son. And they might be less alarmed by his strange appearance.

The first place was nearly empty at this late hour of the morning. Dirimara smelled something savory cooking and decided to eat a meal. He had enough coins, thanks to his captain, and needn't worry about food or lodging in this cold city of stones beside its broad, gray river.

The wench brought him a bowl of fish stew, a chunk of dark bread, and a mug of ale. She was pale as a ghost and her hair was a demonish red. Were all the women in this country descended from devils? The thought frightened him more than the caged man under the crane.

The food tasted wonderful after meals of stale biscuit soaked in sour beer. When he finished and she returned for his plate, Dirimara said, "I seek a place called Grace Inn. Do you know it?"

She screwed up her face, as if squeezing the thought from her brain. Then she shook her head. "Up toward St. Paul's? The big church with the broken spire?" She pointed toward the north.

Dirimara thanked her and left. San Pablo, the grand cathedral of London. The sailors had told him about that place as well. They said a man could learn anything there, but he must be wary of thieves. He had a large knife in the scabbard on his black belt and knew how to protect himself.

He turned his back to the river and walked up through narrow lanes shadowed by overhanging houses. He could barely sense the location of the sun and had to navigate by pure instinct. At least the people gave him space to walk, sometimes crushing each other against a wall to avoid him. Dirimara appreciated their generosity. Their bodies stank of sour milk.

Men worshipped animals here. He had learned as much from his shipmates, who told him there were more sheep than people on this small island. They ate their God on feast days in the form of bread, which Dirimara found both mystifying and disgusting. It made more sense to feed your gods than to eat them.

He came to a broad street and saw a tavern fronted with wide windows filled with gleaming glass. He'd seen quantities of glass on almost half the houses, sometimes even on the upper stories. He wondered why these Londoners wanted so much glass when there was nothing to see but other houses and the dull gray sky.

The tavern was filled with gentlemen, richly garbed in round hose and padded doublets. One wore a shade of bright canary yellow that Dirimara found irresistible. Perhaps when he found the son of Captain Clarady, he could buy such a doublet with puffed-out hose to match. His long striped slops made sense on board a ship, where a man spent as much time climbing ropes as walking and met few people who were not members of his own crew. Here in London and on the Continent, when he continued on his way, he would rather look more elegant, like a grandee.

The men turned to stare as he entered their domain. He met their unfriendly gazes without offense. "I seek the son of Captain Valentine Clarady. He abides in a place called Grace Inn."

"Grace Sin?" The canary man frowned beneath his long moustachio. "Those are contraries. Is it a riddle?" His eyes narrowed as he looked Dirimara up and down. "We don't want Spaniards here, sirrah."

"I am no Espaniard." Dirimara drew himself up to his full four feet ten inches. "I kill the Espaniard, many of them, to help the English. I sail on an English ship, but I am Yagua. You would say, an Indian of Peru."

The canary man tucked his chin in surprise. "Are you, now!" The other gentlemen displayed equal portions of bafflement and curiosity. Curiosity won.

"You won't find grace in a tavern," said a man with a fluffy white feather in his high-crowned hat. Dirimara determined to buy himself exactly such a feather once he had found the boy.

The others laughed, and Dirimara realized they did not understand him. They thought he meant *gracia*, like the favor of a god or a gift for music. He sighed. His shipmates had told him his English was perfect. It seemed they had been more polite than factual.

He tried again. "Not *gracia*. I mean the color, like the sky. *Gris*."

"Grease isn't a color," the canary man said.

"Some places it is," the feather man said. The other men laughed.

"There's the Grease Pot near Aldgate," another man said. "They'll do you an apple dumpling that's as near to grace as you'll come in this life."

"He don't mean 'grease,'" another man said. "He means 'grass.' Like the Grass Harp."

"That's an ordinary," the canary man said. "He's looking for an inn. He wants lodgings."

The gentlemen broke into a heated debate about the merits of various London establishments. They clearly had no idea what he wanted. Perhaps Capitan Clarady had told him the wrong name for the place where his son lived. Or perhaps he had remembered it wrong.

He slipped away from the bickering gentlemen and walked west, steering toward the broken spire of the great cathedral. The sailors had told him the spire had been struck by a bolt of lightning and burned. The English wisely left it in that condition, as a reminder of the swiftness of God's wrath. But other spires poked up from every corner, as if in defiance of that wrath. They were plainly confused about their role in the universe and their relation to their God.

Dirimara found himself constantly looking up as he walked — at the glass, the spires, the painted signs dangling over doors. At sea, your eyes remained at a level, scanning the horizon, gaze probing the infinite blue. In the dense jungle from which he had come, your gaze shifted constantly up and down, but mostly only a few feet ahead, ever vigilant for snakes, jaguars, or mounds of deadly ants.

He saw a coach roll under an arch and followed it into a square yard surrounded by four stories rimmed with galleries. They had such places on the coast of France as well. They were inns, where a man could find a bed for the night, and sometimes a woman to share it with him. He might try that, but he wouldn't want one of the devil women. There were women of all colors in St. Jean de Luz. He might go back there one day, perhaps to stay.

He found the public room and made his way to a counter at the back tended by a man in a dirty apron. Dirimara squeezed in between two men. One talked rapidly in staccato bursts, his voice so rough Dirimara couldn't tell if it was English or not. The other sat on a tall stool staring gloomily into a tankard, as if reading some dire portent within its depths.

The counterman raised his eyebrows at Dirimara to ask what he wanted. Perhaps he'd learned not to bother with speech in this place.

Dirimara placed his hands flat upon the counter and spoke as clearly he could. "I seek Clarady."

The man on the stool shot him a dark look. "Don't we all, mate," he said mournfully. "Don't we all."

TWENTY-SEVEN

"I cannot pursue the pursuivant," Francis told Ben. "I can't do it, and not solely because he terrifies me." They were in his chambers discussing his upcoming meeting with the widows of the Andromache Society. He'd sent a message to Lady Russell saying he was ready to deliver a report. He intended it to be the last one.

"I agree," Ben said. "In fact, I think you should avoid Topcliffe altogether. Tell the Privy Council you're unable to continue with the commission due to ill health. With all these sick soldiers wandering about, you might easily have caught something. They'll understand. You won't mind spending a few weeks holed up in here reading."

Ben sat in the armed chair in front of the desk. Francis couldn't bring himself to sit. He paced back and forth across the rush matting, pausing to fidget with the Venetian glass and silver plate displayed on his oak cupboard or to straighten the always tidy stacks of books on his shelves. He'd made his decision while stumbling home from the Tower yesterday, sick in both mind and body. He hadn't left his chambers or eaten anything since, even though Ben kept sending for tempting tidbits like a cup of warm broth or dish of cool blancmange.

"I can't risk them learning of my suspicions," Francis said. "Not even Tom can know. He'll want to do something, make up some mad plan to expose Topcliffe in the act."

"I won't breathe a word. And you don't need to inform the widows of your speculations. Just tell them you've reached an impasse. Your hands are tied and the matter is closed."

Francis wished it were that simple. He'd wrestled with the decision all night. He knew his reasons were sound, but he couldn't stop rehashing the argument. He had first accepted the task to please his lady aunt and to gain the debt of one favor. He had wanted Tom to be released without blemish, knowing the lad to be incapable of murder and also intending to make use of him as an intelligencer again someday. The same combination of loyalty and self-interest motivated his desire to help Trumpet. He did not want her to suffer from scandal, both for her sake and for the sake of her future influence.

This was the way the world worked, how the webs that connected people were formed. Similar considerations bound Sir Richard to the Lord Treasurer, from their mutual origins in Lincolnshire to their long-standing service to the queen. Sir Richard's grandfather had served the queen's mother with the kind of loyalty Her Majesty never forgot — another strand in the web.

The queen and the Lord Treasurer might believe Francis — or at least not disbelieve him — but never say it in so many words. Nor could he be certain they didn't already know and in some covert fashion approve. But if they didn't know and didn't believe him, the sheer presumption of his proposal was certain to offend, which would have an incalculable effect on his hopes of advancement. Not even the Earl of Essex could redeem him from so grievous an error.

Sometime in the wee hours of the night, Francis had untangled himself from his damp sheets and risen to take a dose of valerian. He'd plumped up his pillows and lain down again. While waiting for the medicine to take effect, he'd remembered another reason he'd accepted the commission from the Andromache Society: his curiosity had been stimulated by the strangeness of the crime. The paralysis in particular had intrigued him. Then, when he learned that more murders had been committed, all with the same ugly signs of religious hatred, his sense of duty had been aroused. Someone must investigate these crimes if the authorities would not.

Science and duty were the two driving forces of his life. They animated his every step, informed every choice he made. They had propelled him forward in pursuit of the murderer until he struck an immoveable obstacle: a villain he feared more than he loved truth.

There was the rub, the reason he couldn't settle on this decision. He hated knowing that he could be defeated by his own baser nature.

"It isn't just the fear," Francis said out loud.

"Of course not," Ben said. "You could never prosecute him, not without absolute proof. He's too well respected. You'd need at least two reputable eyewitnesses; better than burglars, even if we had them in our clutches at this moment."

"That's true." Francis stood beneath the portrait of his father that hung over the mantel. The late Lord Keeper, pragmatic enough to flourish under four Tudor monarchs, would doubtless advise him to leave it alone. He turned back to Ben, spreading his hands in supplication. "If we had proof, I could bring it privately to my lord uncle and lay the whole matter in his lap. But all we have are concatenations of unlikely events and a certain harmony — or disharmony — of intent. Sir Richard could have done these deeds. He has the ability, the knowledge, the will, and the desire. But he also has friends among the very highest, including my uncle. Many would applaud his results, if not precisely the methods. The queen herself protects him. His grandfather, Lord Burgh, was our queen's mother's chamberlain, did I tell you that?"

"Twice," Ben said. "And yes, that makes it worse. Neither should you discount your fears. Given what we saw in his library, fear is a sane and sensible response, worthy of serious consideration. What good would reckless courage do you or anyone else? You've said yourself that boldness is the child of ignorance. Knowing what we know, the only rational course is to withdraw."

Francis asked one last question, the only one that mattered. "What if he does it again?"

Ben's dark eyes met his with a bleak look, but he had no answer.

* * *

Trumpet stared at the painted cloth on the wall in the dining room at the Antelope Inn. The interlocking red and gold shapes had been drawn by two different painters, or by one painter who had been drinking steadily over the course of the day. She'd never noticed how the lines drifted westward before, but then she'd never spent so much time in this room with nothing else to do.

She'd been invited to an irregular meeting of the Andromache Society along with half a dozen widows: Lady Russell, Lady Bacon, Mrs. Palmer, and several relics of merchants whose names she had forgotten as soon as they were uttered. Mrs. Sprye sat ready with her quill and inkhorn to record the report about to be delivered by Francis Bacon, who was now late by a good half hour.

Lady Russell sat to her right, at the head of the table. Lady Bacon's stern visage faced her from across the board. Trumpet would rather have sat farther down, where she and Mrs. Palmer could chat freely, but as the highest-ranking woman in the room, she was obliged to sit at the top.

Her eyes met Lady Bacon's by accident, then pride compelled her to hold her gaze in spite of the eerie sensation that she was staring into the eyes of an older Francis Bacon. They had the same unusual amber-toned irises and the same deep well of ceaselessly active intelligence. Trumpet felt a giggle rising in her throat but was saved by Lady Russell, who tilted her head to whisper something to her sister.

"Perhaps he isn't coming," Mrs. Palmer murmured. She sat on Trumpet's left and had also been watching the formidable Cooke sisters.

Trumpet blinked her eyes several times to refresh them. "He would have begged off if he had nothing to tell us. He wouldn't want to walk all the way here."

"It's less than a quarter mile! Is he so very lazy?"

"Not lazy. He doesn't like to waste effort, that's all."

"You reassure me. I would hate to marry a lazy man."

Trumpet looked directly at her. "Are you truly thinking of marrying Francis Bacon?"

"His connections are impressive. And he is a bencher at Gray's Inn." Benchers were the governors of the Inns of Court.

"So he is." Trumpet bit her lip to keep from saying more. She doubted Bacon would consent to wed, however wealthy the bride, so there was no reason to burden her new friend with details such as chronic debt and a preference for his own sex. "I thought you were interested in my uncle."

"Oh, I am! I like him. But he is rather old, as you pointed out. And Lady Russell has been very persuasive about considering all my options."

"She has her own objectives, as you pointed out," Trumpet said. "I suspect you'd be happier with my uncle. He's quite fit and not yet forty. Or someone else entirely. Mr. Bacon is . . . well, he . . ." She cast about for something inoffensive yet discouraging. "He studies a great deal. Sometimes to the exclusion of everything else, including his duties at Gray's."

"You seem to know him well."

"Oh! Do I?" Trumpet emitted a small laugh. "Not so very well, really." She kept mixing up Allen's knowledge with Alice's. "My lawyer, Benjamin Whitt, is a student of Mr. Bacon's. He talks about him, you know, the way men do."

"Nothing but gossip!" They shared a smile at the absurdities of men.

"Speaking of Mr. Whitt," Trumpet said, "you seemed to get along well the other evening at supper."

"He's very nice," Mrs. Palmer agreed, but without the note of enthusiasm Trumpet had been hoping for.

Now a servant opened the door to admit Francis Bacon, followed by both Ben and Tom. Why had Bacon brought supporters to this meeting? Had he caught the murderer? She hadn't heard anything from anyone since Tom had left her at the corner of Bishopsgate Street last Friday night. Being on the outside rankled desperately. Two years ago, she would have been in the thick of whatever was brewing; now she had to sit with a bunch of dreary widows, hands folded in her lap, waiting to be given the same news everyone else would hear.

Bacon gestured the other men to a bench against the wall. Ben sat down immediately, but Tom couldn't pass a group of women without some flourish. He swept off his hat and bowed, hand across his waist, then winked at Trumpet before taking his place on the bench.

"I do admire that young man." Mrs. Palmer sounded slightly breathless. "What was his name again?"

"Clarady," Trumpet said. "He's a nobody. A mere inner barrister." She shot her companion a sharp look. She could not allow this tasty widow to develop an interest in Tom. "He's comely enough, I grant you, but he's a terrible bore. He can't talk about anything but clothes."

Mrs. Palmer hummed doubtfully, but her further response was cut off by the ringing of Lady Russell's silver bell. The women fell silent and turned attentive faces toward the foot of the table.

"We bid you welcome, Mr. Bacon," Lady Russell said. "We hope you have good news for us today."

"I do, my lady." Bacon bowed to each side of the polished board. "I am happy to report that thanks to my efforts, Lady Surdeval and Mr. Clarady have been released from custody without let or hindrance, with no lingering stain or suspicion."

Trumpet frowned. This news was neither new nor good enough. Suspicion would linger until the murderer was hanged. She could weather it, though her next husband must die a demonstrably natural death, but the clouds would darken Tom's path for years to come.

"Then you've identified the murderer?" Lady Russell asked. "Well done, Nephew!"

Some of the women began to applaud, but Bacon held up both hands to stop them. "No, my good ladies and gentlewomen, I must admit I have as yet no proof sufficient to bring the murderer to justice."

"But you know who it is," Lady Russell said.

Bacon pinched the pleats in his left wrist ruff while his gaze wandered over the tops of the women's heads. Trumpet recognized the evasive mannerisms. He either didn't know or he wasn't going to tell them. He would babble pompously for a few minutes and then run away.

"Suspicions have evolved in such directions as to preclude any definitive verification of culpability."

"What in God's name does that mean, Francis?" Lady Bacon snapped.

Bacon sputtered and stuttered, producing a spate of legal terms and Latin aphorisms that furrowed the other women's brows. Trumpet stopped listening.

Mrs. Palmer murmured, "Does he mean that he knows but doesn't want to say?"

"I think so. It sounds like he's afraid to."

"Can he be such a coward?"

"He's not a coward," Trumpet said. "Or, yes, physically, I suppose that's fair. But if someone threatened him, he would hide in his rooms and send a letter to the sheriff. It must be something else."

"What sort of something else?" Mrs. Palmer asked. "What could induce him to conceal the identity of a murderous fiend?"

Trumpet shook her head. "He must think it's someone powerful, or someone protected by someone powerful. Someone too big to bring to justice." Someone who frightened him, judging by the sheen of sweat on his brow. Ben had told her, with an uncharacteristic whine of jealousy, that Bacon had spoken with the Earl of Essex regarding the Surdeval matter. She could easily imagine Robert Devereux accepting money from stolen goods without a qualm, but she couldn't see him committing murders in secret. Where would be the advantage?

"Who could be too big for justice?" Mrs. Palmer asked.

Trumpet shrugged. Every member of the Privy Council, for a start. Did Ben know? Did Tom know? She caught his gaze and furrowed her brows. He raised one shoulder slightly and gave his head one tiny shake. He was equally in the dark. Ben refused to look at her.

Lady Russell rang her bell and Bacon stopped babbling. She frowned at him. "You're repeating yourself, Nephew. I comprehend that you wish to terminate your commission without presenting a conclusion. I must say I'm disappointed in you."

"I'm not," Lady Bacon said. "I never liked the idea of my son chasing violent criminals. That is the sheriff's job, and Francis has wisely decided to leave it to him."

"He said nothing of the sort," Lady Russell said.

"He implied it," Lady Bacon retorted.

The two sisters glared at one another while everyone else held their breaths. Lady Russell blinked first. "Very well. I will personally make certain the sheriff performs his duties to my satisfaction. And I will have a private word with you, Nephew, immediately after this meeting." She looked around the table and rang her silver bell. "We are adjourned."

All of the women rose except Lady Bacon, who crooked her finger at Ben. She liked to interrogate him about her son's eating and sleeping habits whenever she got the chance. Lady Russell gripped Bacon's arm on her way through the door, drawing him out with her. Tom rose and bowed as she passed, then remained standing.

"You must introduce me again," Mrs. Palmer said with a thrill in her voice. "Individually, not as part of a group."

"What?" Trumpet wanted to follow Lady Russell and Mr. Bacon. She had as much right to know the full story as anyone. But a clot of widows in wide farthingales blocked the doorway, each gesturing politely to the others so no one could move forward.

Tom smiled at Trumpet and nodded once to signal that he meant to speak with her before he left. Good. They needed to plan their next outing.

Mrs. Palmer sighed dramatically. "A little boredom would be endurable with a smile like that to compensate."

Trumpet turned to her and realized with a start where she had fixed her attention. Tom noticed too. His eyes took on that extra sparkle he gave to beautiful women.

This had to be nipped in the bud at once. "Take my advice and stay well clear of that man." Trumpet crossed her fingers in her lap. "He's as skit-brained as a sparrow. He snorts when he laughs and he farts incessantly." She put her hand beside her mouth and whispered, "And I rather suspect that he prefers boys."

TWENTY-EIGHT

Tom wove through the throng in St. Paul's Cathedral, eyes open for Trumpet and Catalina, cursing himself for a crack-brained nidget. Why had he let her choose Duke Humphrey's Walk for their rendezvous? The place was always crowded and the crowd was notorious. He'd kept one hand over his pocket since he'd entered the dim, echoing cathedral. All manner of thieves and prostitutes prowled the aisles in search of prey. Although in fairness, Tom's friends were most unlikely to be cozened by a lightskirt.

He turned at the top of the aisle and began to walk back, openly inspecting faces like a man keeping an appointment with someone he'd only heard described. A pair of young rogues leaned against Duke Humphrey's tomb, trading scurrilous remarks about the passersby. One of them caught Tom's eye with an insolent smirk as he walked past.

Tom's head turned, then his feet followed. "Trumpet, God rot your sly bones! I almost didn't recognize you."

"You passed us twice without a glimmer." She punched him in the arm. "I practically had to wave my hat at you."

Catalina said, "I could have taken your purse easily, Mr. Tom. You are so helpful to tell everybody which pocket it is in."

"Nobody picks my pockets." Tom shifted his hand to his hip. "All right, fair's fair. You fooled me proper. But it's dark in here and I didn't know how you'd be dressed. It won't happen again, I promise you."

"We shall see." Trumpet blinked at him — that slow, infuriating cat's blink.

They had business to attend to, otherwise he would do something about her lingering smirk. "Coddington's out of Newgate, and he's at the Dolphin, all right. I paid a boy to keep an eye on the place. He's been there every afternoon since Monday, sometimes all evening. It's his regular haunt, him and his fellows."

"Let's go," Trumpet said.

"First I want to hear what Catalina learned about your uncle. It might help." Tom jerked his chin at a recess behind the tomb and they shifted into it, turning their backs to the traffic in the aisle. They looked exactly like a trio of pigeon pluckers devising a snare for their next victim.

Catalina spoke in a near whisper, making her accented phrases harder to parse. "He has a new ring, very expensive, I think, with a big red stone. Some men, five or four, come visit him. He make me stay in the bed when they come, but I peek. Two came more than once. They argue. One thing they argue is Mr. Bacon. What he knows, what we should do. Mr. Welbeck sent a man to go and watch him. Another thing they argue is murder. No good for us, says Mr. Welbeck. They must stop."

Tom asked, "Stop what? Stop burgling or stop murdering?"

Catalina shrugged, raising both hands. "I think he mean stop burglary." She said it *burgulare*. "The two who come every time say, 'but it is so good money.' Mr. Welbeck say, 'no, no, we must wait, or go outside of London.'"

Tom snapped his fingers. "That's good, that last part. Because that's how I'm going to get in with Coddington. I'm going to offer to locate likely targets out in the country." He pointed at Trumpet. "I'm thinking about your grandparents or people like them. Off in the

254

hinterlands, with chapels stuffed full of valuables, waiting to be robbed."

"That might work," Trumpet said. "If they were really talking about robbing chapels. Catalina told me they never said anything that explicit, not even in my uncle's chambers."

"Never," Catalina said. "They talk about clients and fees and goods to barter."

"He's a close one, your uncle," Tom said. "But it's no use, Trumpet. We know he's our upright man. Everything points to him and nothing points anywhere else. Why would he send a man to watch Mr. Bacon if he had nothing to hide? And why did that churl in the pawnshop call him the Savoy Solicitor and send me to him for approval?"

"You're right, I agree. I just wanted to give it one last try." Trumpet tilted her chin at her maidservant. "Tell him about Sunday."

"Yes, my la — Mr. Allen. On Sunday, Mr. Welbeck dress himself very nice, a red doublet and round hose lined with cream silk. Many slashings, much fine work." She paused as if fixing the design in her memory for future use.

"Less detail, please," Trumpet said. "We mustn't tarry."

"Yes, my — Mr. Welbeck went to dinner in his fine clothes. He do not say where, and he bade me stay inside the rooms. 'Do not follow me, my dear,' he said. Of course I did. But he had a man watch me, one of the two who argue yes to more *burgulares*. That man catch me and bring me back to the Savoy. When Mr. Welbeck return, he seem worried and also sad."

"Sad?" Tom asked. "What does he have to be sad about?"

"It could be something unrelated," Trumpet said. "Maybe he's been courting some gentlewoman and she turned him down. Or maybe he lost a client."

"I do not think so, my lady," Catalina said. "He seem sad more as if he lose a great friend or a loved dog."

They stood and thought about that for a moment. Trumpet stroked her moustache with the tip of her finger. Tom understood that gesture now, which had been habitual with Allen. She was pressing it into the glue, always worried it would come loose.

"The sadness is an oddity," he said, "and Bacon taught me to be wary of oddities. But for the moment, I can't imagine what it means. Let's go talk to my old cellmate. Let's get him to tell us how they choose their jobs."

They made their way out of the church and found the Dolphin on Old Swan Lane, not far from the river. Shutters obstructed the bottom half of the windows so the patrons could not be seen from the street. Inside, the tavern seemed clean enough, with moderately fresh rushes on the floor and air not too fusty with smoke and stale beer. A group of Germans sat at a round table by the windows, drinking from enormous tankards and jabbering over a set of knives in a lined case. Smaller tables stood scattered about the room, some sheltered by high-backed settles. Most of these were occupied by men of varying degrees with their drabs.

A scrawny boy in torn stockings hailed Tom as they stood inside the door getting their bearings. He'd been sitting atop a barrel where he could watch everyone who entered. He jerked his head toward the back of the room, past the winding staircase in the middle. "Red hair, big mouth, name of Coddington? 'E's 'ere, all right, with a few of his mates." He held out his hand, and Tom dropped a penny into it.

Tom told the tapster to bring them a couple of bottles of his best wine and five cups, pointing to the table at the back. Two men came off the stairs, arguing about something in low growls. Catalina abruptly turned full around and sneezed into her hat. Tom shifted position to cover her, giving the two men a casual inspection as they walked around him to speak to the counterman.

Tom murmured, "Welbeck's men?"

Catalina nodded. "I must go. He has seen me in this moustache."

They consulted in swift whispers and decided Catalina should walk straight out the back door. Tom and Trumpet stood side by side to block the view from the counter, bickering about whether ale was more nourishing than beer. Catalina clutched her belly as if taken with a sudden ache and hurried toward the back door. She ducked her head as she passed the last table, pretending to sneeze into her fist.

Tom and Trumpet waited until the door had closed behind her, then strolled toward the table where Jack Coddington and another man sat playing cards, their backs against the wall. Both of them wore pleated hats with crisp feathers in the shiny bands. Brass buttons glinted on Coddington's doublet. Signs of new prosperity, most of which would doubtless end up in the tavern-keeper's cash box.

Coddington spotted Tom and crowed, "Why, it's my old friend Thomas Clarady!" He rose to give Tom a shoulder-clapping hug. He introduced his companion as Sam Pratt.

Tom started to introduce Trumpet, but stumbled on the name. She thrust out her hand. "Allen Underhill. Pleased to make your acquaintance."

Coddington invited them to sit. Since the two thieves had the choice positions, Tom and Trumpet were obliged to sit with their backs to the rest of the tavern. Tom shifted his chair sideways so he could look toward the counter with only a slight twist. Trumpet put her elbows on the table, fist in palm, and grinned at the thieves as if she had never met anyone more intriguing.

They traded pleasantries for a few minutes, then Coddington's freckled face broke into a grin. "Brace yourselves, lads. Your hearts are about to be broken."

"That's not all they'll break," Sam Pratt said, winking broadly at Trumpet.

Two buxom wenches with red hair escaping from their coifs swung toward them with loaded trays, skirts swishing. Two pairs of blue eyes shone from two identically round faces. Twins, by the grace of a benevolent God!

Tom let out a low whistle, earning a smile from one of the twins. Then he jerked his leg as Trumpet's shoe cracked against his ankle. He met her green eyes and grinned. "Too much for you?"

"We're here on business," she said.

"A crafty man can mix work and pleasure," Coddington said. "Why do you think we meet here?" He tried to persuade one of the twins to sit on his lap, but these wenches had each other for support and were proof against flirtations.

After they left, Tom filled cups and passed them around. "I'm glad to find you here, old mate. I've been thinking about our conversations back in Newgate."

"Ah, the old cell." Coddington raised his cup to Tom. "I'll tell you, friends, Clarady here has influence. I ate better in Newgate as his cellmate than I do at my landlady's table." He took a sip of wine and smacked his lips.

"Happy to oblige," Tom said. "Now perhaps you can do me a good turn. My partner here and I want in on the chapel game. It costs a pretty penny to keep up appearances at the Inns of Court, as I'm sure you gentlemen know." He flattered them by that appellation; they plainly liked it.

Pratt said, "I can appreciate your difficulty, Mr. Clarady, but we've got all the men we need. Although from what Jack here has told us, you could be useful. Your father's a ship's captain, is that right?"

"He is indeed," Tom said. "A privateer, I don't mind telling you. But the takings aren't what they were, with the cursed Spanish armed to the teeth and always on the lookout. I need another source of revenue. We don't come looking for charity." He jerked his thumb at Trumpet. "My friend here had the bright idea of expanding the venture into the country. Lots of rich pickings out there on isolated estates. Get out of London before things get too hot."

"Interesting you should say that," Pratt said. "Our upright man's had the same idea. It hasn't been decided yet, but there's been trouble lately." He gave his mate a doubtful look.

Tom took a small leap. "The murders, you mean."

Coddington shook a finger at him as he said to his friend, "What'd I tell you? He's a sharp one, he is. I'm telling you, we should take him to Mr. Welbeck."

Tom kept his face still as he reached for his cup, resisting the urge to glance at Trumpet. Her foot touched his. She set her index finger on the table, making a strong point. "We won't do the murder part — we want to make that clear. We're strictly set-up men. We locate the best targets and get in with the servants to pick a good night when everyone will be out. That's all we do."

Tom repressed an admiring grin. She must have thought of that ploy as they walked down from St. Paul's. He'd been watching the people go by and noting new temptations in shop windows while she had been strategizing, the clever wench. They'd make the ideal team for that job too, especially with Catalina's arts to alter their appearance from town to town.

He'd more than half convinced himself at least.

"We had nothing to do with the murders," Coddington said. "I didn't even know about 'em till the master bailed me out. But you must have known something, Clarady. You were in for doing that Viscount What-d'ye-call-um. Surleyville, was it?"

"Surdeval," Trumpet said. She spoke in her low Allen voice, which now sounded husky to Tom's ears. "Didn't you know whose chapel you were robbing?"

Coddington shrugged. "Who cares? All we need is the date and a map."

"We don't even need the map most of the time," Pratt said. "Those old chapels are almost always attached to the hall."

"For the record," Tom said, "they cleared me of all charges. Wrong place at the wrong time, that's all. But I've heard a man's been killed everywhere a chapel's been robbed. I reckoned it must be one of your gang."

"We don't object," Trumpet put in. "We hate Catholics too."

"It was never us," Coddington insisted. "We're thieves, not murderers. In and out like cats, remember? Murder causes too much fuss."

"But how could you not know?" Tom asked.

"Well, it's a mystery, isn't it?" Coddington scratched his head behind his ear. "They must've snuck in behind us, or come in a different way."

"It's nasty to think about," Pratt said. "Some raving assassin creeping about while we're doing our work. I tell you, it's not safe for honest thieves anymore."

"They probably followed you in," Trumpet said. "They must have known you were going to be there."

Tom shook his finger to underscore her suggestion. "Maybe they got hold of your list. Or paid the same clerk your — what did you call him? — your Mr. Wallbeak paid."

"Welbeck," Coddington said. "No, the clerk gets paid after the goods are sold. And the master has another —"

"Who's this, Coddington?" The man Catalina had recognized loomed up behind Tom. "They're asking a lot of questions."

"This is my old cellmate," Coddington said. "Him what's father is a privateer. I told him to look me up and so he did." He introduced the newcomer as William Buckle.

Buckle was a cut above his fellows, by his clothes, his accent, and his manner. He snapped his fingers at Pratt to move over and give him the choicest seat, where he could watch both the front door and the red-haired women behind the counter. He leaned back against the wall and gave Tom and Trumpet an unwelcoming glare.

Tom displayed his most congenial grin. "You'll be wanting something better than this swill, I'll wager." He shouted at the tapman to bring them a bottle of the very best. Then he turned again to Buckle, enlisting his counsel. "Is anything in this place fit to eat?"

Buckle frowned but managed to allow that the bread was usually fresh, and the cheese could be eaten without distress. When the twins brought the wine, Tom ordered plates of food to share around the table.

He waited until everyone had eaten and drunk a little. Trumpet told some bawdy stories, making everyone but Buckle laugh till the tears flowed. Then Tom brought the conversation back around to the central topic. "It's sheer genius, if you ask me, robbing Catholic chapels. It's like privateering, only on land. Safer and better lodgings when you're done for the day."

He realized the truth of the words as he spoke them. Privateers raided Spanish ships, in part for funds to fight the Catholic threat. How did these men's raids on Catholic chapels differ from what his father did?

Then he remembered: the victims were Englishmen.

Pratt nodded. "It's like stealing gold from pirates. Who're they going to complain to?" He took out a silver toothpick with a carved head and put it to use.

"It was good while it lasted," Buckle said. "But I'm afraid you've come too late. These murderers, whoever they are, have spoiled the game. They attract too much attention."

"There's got to be a way around it." Tom refilled Buckle's cup. "We have to get out ahead of them, is what I think. Separate the two acts, if you follow me. Who's next on the list?"

Too abrupt. Buckle's eyes grew stony. "I've got a question for you: Who was that person you came in with? The one who left as I came down the stairs?"

"Who?" Tom shrugged. "Oh, nobody special, just a fellow we happened to —"

"Because I'm certain now that I recognized him. Or should I say *her?*" Buckle set his hand on his hip near the sheath of his knife. "Who are you working for? Francis Bacon? I warned the master he'd set spies on us."

Before Tom could answer, Trumpet shifted position so awkwardly she tipped over a bottle of wine, causing Pratt to jump out of his seat. Tom laughed loudly and pointed at him. Then he leapt out of his chair, tipped up the whole table, and raced out the back door into a tiny yard, with Trumpet close on his heels.

The yard reeked from an overused privy. They paused long enough to catch each other's eyes and trade nods. Then they ran together toward a half-open door that led them into a workshop strung with long lines sagging under skeins of wet yarn in a rainbow of colors, stinking of fresh dye. Apprentices in aprons shouted at them as they pushed through the sopping masses, heedless of the stains streaking their doublets.

They burst out of the dyer's shop into an alley so narrow Tom could barely see the sky between the jettied upper stories. He couldn't tell north from south and had no sense of where the river lay. "Which way?"

Trumpet shrugged. "Let's go left."

Tom had barely taken two long steps before he heard her shriek and wheeled around. Pratt had caught her from behind, circling her small waist with his beefy arms. She kicked and cursed, hindering him, but not much. He lifted her off the ground and started backing toward the dyer's shop.

Tom leapt up and grabbed the iron bar supporting the sign over the shop door, swinging his legs out to kick the knave in the head. The new hat went flying. Pratt roared and let go of Trumpet but turned the wrong way at the same time as Tom let go of the bar. He landed on Pratt's shoulders, legs astride his neck.

He pounded him on the head while Pratt turned in circles, shouting, "Get off me, you poxy swine!" Pratt struck at Tom's legs, pulling on them so Tom couldn't get free. He kicked his heels against the man's padded doublet with no effect. He pounded on the knave's shoulders and tugged at his ears, making him yowl, but not bringing him down. They were at an impasse unless Tom could steer him under the iron bar again to pull himself off.

Trumpet, once free, did not run away — unlike most girls, some boys, and one or two men Tom could name. Not the Earl Corsair's dauntless daughter. She turned back to her assailant and drove her knee hard up into his egg sack. When Pratt doubled over with a howl, Tom slid off his shoulders. He caught Trumpet's hand and they raced down the alley, shouts rising behind them.

They ran as fast as they could on the rubbish-strewn cobblestones. When the alley took a sharp curve, they spotted an impassable obstacle and had to bang into a wall to stop themselves. A large donkey stood tethered to a post chomping straw from a barrow, blocking the whole passage. He rolled his eyes at them and twitched his ears but kept eating as if he hadn't been fed for days and didn't know when he might get so rich a meal again.

"Clarady! Stop right there!" Buckle's deep voice echoed off the plaster walls.

Tom and Trumpet looked at each other and shrugged. They took a few steps back to get a good start and then ran forward. Tom vaulted over the donkey while Trumpet slid under. He reached down a hand to help her up and their eyes met. She grinned and nodded. He grinned back. Two minds that thought as one.

She loosed the donkey's tether while Tom swacked it on the backside and gave it a good shove. The beast jolted toward their pursuers, piteous brays emerging from its mouth while balls of shit dropped out the other end. He picked up speed, knocking Coddington down as he came around the curve. Buckle skidded on the slippery shit but didn't fall. He had his knife drawn, ready to cut or throw.

Tom and Trumpet ran. The alley curved again and then opened onto a wider street. Water shimmered at the end of the lane — the Old Swan Stairs and safety. Neither donkeys nor thieves blocked their path; just one small figure in a long cloak walking down toward the river.

Buckle shouted, "I'll chase you to hell and leave you there, Thomas Clarady! No quarter for spies!"

Tom threw a glance over his shoulder as he ran. The man was only a few yards behind. He picked up speed and crashed right into Trumpet, who had stopped altogether for no good reason. They tumbled down in a tangle of arms and legs.

"I've got you now, Clarady, you sneaking whoreson!" Buckle reached them as Tom struggled to his knees. He reached for his knife and twisted to face his attacker, only to see Buckle's eyes widen in horror. "A demon! Save yourselves!" Buckle staggered, caught himself with a hand on Tom's shoulder, turned, and ran the other way.

Tom made it to his feet and was nearly knocked down again by Trumpet, walking backward, a weird keening sound issuing from her lips.

He looked over her shoulder and gasped. There at the end of the lane, standing between them and the safety of the river, stood a dreadful figure, short but solid, as swarthy as a man burnt by the fires of hell. His eyes shone black as ravens' wings and his black cloak billowed behind him. His legs were clad in long canvas slops striped in red and white. Shark's teeth hung from his ears and a curved knife hung from his belt.

He stared at them, then stalked toward them, raising one arm to point straight at Tom's heart. "You are Clarady!"

Tom screamed, "It knows my name!" He flung Trumpet over his shoulder and ran past the frightful apparition, down to the Old Swan Stairs. A wherry had pulled up to let a passenger off. Tom shoved past him and tossed Trumpet into the boat, clambering in to sit beside the startled wherryman. Tom wrapped his hands around the oar on his side and shouted, "Row, man! Row!"

TWENTY-NINE

Tom and Trumpet were halfway up the stairs to Tom's rooms at Gray's Inn before they remembered that she shouldn't be there, especially not dressed as a young rogue. Too late. They were as likely to be seen going out again as they had been coming in and besides, they needed a safe haven. She could hide inside until dusk.

"We're in for a scolding," Trumpet warned as they mounted the last of the four flights of stairs. "Ben will not be happy to see me."

"I'm less afraid of Ben than I am of that — what was that thing?"

They hurried each other through the door and locked it behind them. Ben looked up from his desk, blinked twice, and started in. "She mustn't be here! What are you thinking? Why is she dressed like that?"

"Relax, *camarade*," Tom said. "We have good reasons. But give us a minute." They stood inside the door, catching their breaths.

Trumpet looked around the study chamber with her hands on her hips. "It's tidier than it was when I lived here."

These rooms on the fourth floor of the building behind the kitchens used to belong to her uncle. Trumpet had lived in them, sleeping in a trundle bed and dressing behind a screen, during her year at Gray's. Tom lodged with Ben for his first term in rooms across the yard. Welbeck had departed abruptly right before Christmas, leaving Trumpet alone. When Tom went to Cambridge, Ben had moved in with her. Recognizing that her legal education must come to an end, she'd left Gray's at the end of Easter term. When Tom returned from Cambridge, he moved into these chambers with Ben. Full circle.

"We have the cleaners in three times a week," Ben said. "Neither you nor I could afford it." His words were pleasant enough, but his leveled gaze made it clear he was still waiting for an explanation.

"Anything to drink?" Trumpet asked. "I feel like my throat has been scoured with sand."

"All that screaming," Tom said, grinning.

"That was mostly you."

Trumpet pushed aside a stack of clean linens and hopped onto the narrow bed against the inner wall, stretching her feet out with a sigh. Tom found three cups that looked clean enough and filled them from a small cask. He handed them around and then took his usual chair behind his own desk, which stood back-to-back with Ben's in front of the windows.

Ben asked, "Are you going to tell me, or do I have to guess?"

Tom and Trumpet traded considering looks. "How much can we tell him?" Tom asked.

"I would tell him everything," Trumpet said, "but I'm not sure —"

Ben's eyes and mouth turned down, his expression mournful. "Not sure of what? When did you two stop trusting me?"

"We trust you," they cried together. Trumpet added, "Mostly."

Tom said, "We stopped telling you everything when you started passing things on to Bacon. He's my tutor, Ben. I have to be able to keep things from him sometimes, or the whole student-teacher relationship collapses."

Ben did not appear to agree fully with that proposition.

"Besides," Trumpet said, "every time we see you, you scold us about being friends. We're tired of it, old chum. Surely you can understand that."

"I only have your best interests . . . All right. I'll stop. Or I'll try. And I won't tell Francis anything without your permission unless —" He held up a stern finger. "Unless I sincerely believe your health or well-being is at risk."

"Fair enough," Tom said.

Trumpet raised a cup and they sealed the new bargain with a drink.

"Now," Ben said, "will you kindly tell me what's happened?"

They told him the whole story, beginning with the pawnshop in Southwark and moving right on to their visit to Nathaniel Welbeck at the Savoy. While Trumpet told that part of the story, Tom admired the lawyerly way Ben managed to listen in silence, giving her his full attention. He sat with an elbow on his desk, his cheek resting on his thumb with his index finger across his mouth. It probably helped to block the urge to raise objections.

Tom picked up the tale at their meeting in Duke Humphrey's Walk. When he got to the end, where the demon had blocked the lane, Ben's eyes popped. "God preserve us! Who was it?"

"Or what," Trumpet said. "Could it be a demon, do you think?"

Tom shrugged. "What else could it be? It came out of nowhere."

"It can't have been a demon," Ben said. "Fiends from hell do not stalk about London on a Thursday afternoon. There'd have been a whole crowd of people, including churchmen. Maybe even the bishop." He waved his hands. "No, I cannot countenance that idea. I won't tell Francis, but I can imagine what he would say. The fellow was probably a sailor. Didn't you say he was wearing an earring and striped pantaloons?"

"Yes," Tom said. He considered that possibility. "Ships do pick up all manner of men."

"It could have been a Moor," Trumpet said. "Or a Turk. Did you see how black it was?"

"I don't think Turks are black," Ben said. "And don't they all wear those little red hats?"

"Whoever he was," Tom said, "why did he know my name?"

"If he's a sailor, he might know your father," Ben suggested. "He might —"

Three loud knocks on the door were followed by the voice of the under-butler. "Mr. Clarady? You have a visitor."

"No," Trumpet said. "It can't be."

The three friends exchanged a round of wary glances. Tom's stomach clenched; he knew what waited outside the door.

Trumpet got up and slipped into the bedchamber, pulling the door almost shut. Ben went to answer the door, opening it wide. There on the poorly lit landing stood the under-butler, the gatekeeper, and the demon.

He looked less terrifying in this context. His black cloak fell in quiet folds, hiding the curved knife. He looked even shorter than before, his head barely reaching the shoulders of the under-butler, who was nowise a giant. He gazed around the room as if he'd never seen such an unusual abode. When he turned his head, he displayed a nose as hard and angular as the blade of an axe.

He gave Ben a brief inspection and then turned his gaze to Tom. He removed his cap and bowed from the waist. Then he said, "I come with news of your father."

Tom didn't rise; his body had become too heavy all of sudden. He nodded, meaning to say, "Come in," but his throat wouldn't work. News delivered by demons could never be good.

Ben ushered the small man inside and closed the door, leaving the under-butler and the gatekeeper out. He moved the spare chair into place before the two desks and offered the demon a cup of beer. Then he returned to his own seat. Trumpet came out and returned to her spot on the bed.

"*Gracias*," the demon said. He drank all of it and set the cup on the edge of Ben's desk. He looked at Tom, his dark eyes unreadable. "I am Dirimara Montoya de la Torre. I am a sailor on the ship of the great Captain Valentine Clarady." He smiled and a gold tooth glinted in his brown teeth. "Or I was, until Sunday."

Tom took a breath. "What happened on Sunday, Mr., ah, Tohray?"

"Dirimara," the demon said. "I am not a master." He began to speak in a voice thickly accented with Spanish and some other language with a musical quality. The *Susannah* — the ship named after Tom's mother — had sailed out of the Thames last week and gone across the British Sea to Dieppe, where the captain hoped to pick up supplies and news. They had spent three days there. The captain managed to find a supplier with many barrels of gunpowder who would accept a promissory note in partial payment.

"That was lucky," Tom said.

"The supplier was Jacques Le Bon," Dirimara said.

The captain's old rival. "Not so lucky," Tom said as his heart froze.

Trumpet whispered, "Oh, no." Ben folded his hand around his mouth and shook his head.

Dirimara nodded once and went on with his tale. The powder had been loaded onto the *Susannah*, along with water, biscuit, and other necessaries. The wind changed and the sky cleared. The captain said they would sail on Sunday after dinner. He left the boatswain in charge and took Dirimara into town for a good meal. When they finished, they walked to the wharf, but the master gunner told them that the boatswain had gone to say good-bye to his wife.

Tom knew the man. He had a second wife in Weymouth and a third in St. Jean de Luz. The boatswain believed in holy matrimony but found the usual rules too restrictive for a man who traveled for a living.

Captain Clarady had sent Dirimara back into town to roust the boatswain. Then he stepped into the ship's boat waiting at the wharf. That was the last time Dirimara saw him. He found the boatswain in his wife's cottage and hurried him back as quickly as he could, but they were too late. Or perhaps some god had chosen to spare him.

They had almost reached the wharf when the *Susannah* exploded with a resounding boom and a flash of fire. More explosions followed, columns of flame rising in a row, revealing where the barrels of gunpowder had been stowed. Smoke billowed skyward, engulfing the ship.

Dirimara and the boatswain reached the wharf, now crowded with horrified onlookers, screaming and pointing. They pushed through to the wharf and found the wharfman staring wide-eyed at the disaster, pulling at his hair with both hands.

"The captain?" Dirimara had asked, but the man could only shake his head and stare.

No one could tell him anything. Two other ships pulled out of the harbor, anxious to avoid the wreckage. Dirimara and the boatswain spent hours roving up and down the wharf, meeting the few sailors who had managed to reach the shore. They all agreed that the captain had been in his cabin, studying his charts. Powder had been stored beneath it. He would have gone up in the first blast.

Dirimara had gazed blankly out the window throughout the telling of his tale. Now he turned his eyes to Tom, who met them, peering into their obsidian depths. A bond formed between them; a sense of mutual loss, and something harder.

The Indian had described the explosion as an accident, but Tom knew that Jacques Le Bon lay behind it; why, he couldn't yet imagine. Let the others believe it was an accident for now. He had no desire to debate the matter.

First, he would grieve. He could feel sorrow welling up from his heart and knew it would soon overcome him. But someday — not soon — he would track down Jacques Le Bon and kill him, slowly. As he stared into the unfathomable black eyes of the strange messenger, he knew the Indian would gladly join him in that quest.

Tears flowed into Tom's eyes now, and he let his head sink onto his folded arms. Sobs rose, shaking him from the core. Trumpet rose and came to stand behind him, wrapping her arms around his shoulders and laying her head on his.

Silence fell. Nothing remained to be said.

THIRTY

Francis Bacon passed a cluster of barristers standing in the yard with their heads together, chattering excitedly about some scandal. The news spread quickly from one man to the next, but he had no desire to learn what it was. He had fresh troubles of his own.

He had just concluded a distressing interview with the widow of Sir James Lambert, who had been murdered in his bed sometime Tuesday night, or perhaps early Wednesday morning. Lady Lambert had been visiting her daughter in Essex and come home to find her husband quite cold, laid out as if asleep on his back, with a small cross cut into his chest. She had summoned the sheriff, who had sent her to Francis. Lady Lambert was rightfully outraged and had relieved her feelings to Francis at some length.

Furthermore, while the lady admitted that she and her husband preferred the old religion — although she hoped they loved their queen as much as Francis did himself — they did not maintain a private chapel in their house in Hackney. They had sometimes worshipped with friends — years ago, she hastily added — and otherwise made do with a temporary adjustment to her husband's study. Nothing had been stolen from the house except for the rosary Sir James kept under his pillow. It had belonged to his grandmother and was very valuable.

Francis had expressed his sympathies and promised to do what he could, recognizing with a sinking heart the futility of his attempt to evade the responsibility the widows had placed upon his shoulders. "Murder will out," he murmured to himself as he climbed the stairs to Ben's chambers. And this one's ousting had fallen to him.

He knocked once on the door and opened it. "Ben, you will not believe what has happened . . ." Both words and feet came to a halt as he took in the scene inside the room. Ben sat behind his desk, as expected, in his usual seat. But his expression was that of a man who'd just experienced a terrible shock. Tom also sat at his desk, but with his head buried in his arms. He didn't bother to look up. A young man stood next to him, clasping his shoulders, his cheek pressed into the top of Tom's head. The man raised his face, revealing brilliant green eyes. *Trumpet.*

She shouldn't be here, nor should she — the reproach vanished as Francis noticed the fourth person in the room: a small hawk-nosed man with a braid of blue-black hair hanging to his waist. The reddish tinge of his brown skin reminded Francis of the Indians Ralegh had brought from Virginia in 1585 to meet the queen.

"Come in, Francis," Ben said. He raised his eyebrows at Trumpet, who nodded. "You might as well hear it from the source. The news will be all over Gray's by now anyway. I'm sure the gatekeeper and the under-butler stopped to listen at the door."

Ben introduced him to the stranger, who was indeed an Indian of the New World, with the lyrical name of Dirimara.

The Indian rose, bowed, and offered him his chair. Francis took it, feeling as if he'd stumbled into a dream. He listened to the appalling story of Captain Clarady's demise with a growing sense of futility. When hostilities between nations grew hot enough to flare into open conflict, the flames licked far and wide, sparking up again weeks later to destroy another cherished life. This senseless accident would never have occurred if King Philip had kept his armada in his own harbors. Now Tom had lost a father and England a gallant captain. When would it end?

At some point during the retelling, Tom raised his head to watch the storyteller. Trumpet remained at his side throughout with one hand on his shoulder. When the tale was told, Francis struggled to find words to express his sympathy. He understood the enormity of Tom's loss from his own painful experience. He'd lost his father nearly ten years ago; now that grief returned as sharp and bitter as if no time had elapsed.

"I offer my deepest condolences, Tom. If there's anything I can do . . ." An empty offer. What could anyone do at such a time?

Silence fell. Trumpet's feet shifted in the rushes on the floor. Voices rose from the yard below. Ben cleared his throat with a gulp, then winced at the loudness of the sound.

Francis contemplated the display of weapons on the inner wall — not heraldic, merely those the lads employed in regular exercise, but perhaps more impressive on that account. Both men owned longbows, whose use was still encouraged by conservative men like Ben's father. Both men owned rapiers, which they were forbidden by the rules of Gray's Inn to wear in public. The rules did not prevent members from taking fencing lessons, nor indeed from wearing the things as they pleased and paying the fine. Tom owned two pistols, taken from a Spanish ship by his father some years ago. Recently, he had also acquired a longer instrument called a harquebus, which appeared to be a sort of cannon small enough to be carried by a man.

The chapel bell rang the quarter hour, jolting everyone out of their private thoughts. Tom looked at Francis and said, "What's happened?"

Everyone stared at him blankly. "Tom?" Trumpet peered at him, placing her palm across his brow.

He shook it off. "Go sit down, why don't you? I'm fine." She quirked her lips, but went to perch on the edge of the narrow bed with her hands on her knees. Tom said,

"When Mr. Bacon came in, he was saying Ben wouldn't believe what has happened. So what is it?"

Francis waved his hands. "Nothing for you to worry about now. There's been another murder, that's all. Ben and I will cope with it tomorrow somehow."

"I'll help," Tom said. "I want to work. What can I do?"

Ben said, "No, Tom. You must go home. You must go tell your mother."

"Ah, my mother!" Tom clapped both hands to his face in dismay. "She doesn't know yet!"

"She knows," Dirimara said, "unless there was a storm. The boatswain found a boat Monday morning that go to Weymouth, where lives his second wife and other wives of our crew. He said he would speak to the wife of our captain first. He would see her yesterday, perhaps the day before. I lost two days in search of you."

"You should go anyway," Francis said. "She'll need your comfort."

Tom stared at him with narrowed eyes, but his gaze seemed focused inward. Then he turned his face to the window and stared at Bacon's building across the passage. Finally, he turned back to the others and said, "No. I won't go. It's the fifteenth already; term starts in two weeks. I can't get home and back in two weeks, not and do more than kiss my mother once and turn right around. She has my sisters and their families, as well as her own sisters and Uncle Luke. Her house will be packed with friends and relations and sailors' families for the next month." He pounded his fist on his desk. "I mean to stay at Gray's. I'll stay the course my father set for me. I'll work harder than ever and I'll excel. Mark my words. I'll be called to the bar the first day I'm eligible and I'll be knighted before I'm thirty."

Francis understood what drove his determination. Might his will persist and his hopes be fulfilled! Francis's father's death had inspired him to fling himself into the study of the law and made him equally resolved to succeed at court. He hadn't yet, but he hadn't turned thirty yet either. He smiled to think that Tom, of all people, could have shown him the silver lining on that omnipresent cloud.

"Let's have some more beer," Tom said. "Let's get this murder business sorted out once and for all."

Ben asked, "Are you sure?"

Tom rolled his eyes at him. "Of course I'm sure. Do you think I want more deaths on my head?"

Francis agreed. Work was better for a man of Tom's vigorous nature than lying on a bed in a darkened room. "I applaud your commitment, although I'm not sure what our next step should be. A step of some kind must be taken, however. I've had a visitor this afternoon as well, though not as interesting as yours." He glanced at Dirimara, who had settled on a stool beside the brick-lined hearth. "Mine was one Lady Lambert, whose husband Sir James was murdered in his bed on Tuesday night, in a manner that sounds identical to the other cases we have met."

"What about the chapel?" Trumpet asked.

"They had no chapel," Francis said. "Nor was anything stolen other than Sir James's rosary."

"Another rosary," Ben said.

"But no burglary?" Tom cocked his head at Trumpet. Their eyes met for a long moment while they conducted a silent debate. It ended when Trumpet shrugged one shoulder and said, "Why not? Everything has changed."

"Nothing's changed." Tom spoke too loudly.

After a pause, Ben said softly, "I'm afraid that's not quite true, Tom. At least not for you. You won't be twenty-one until December. And didn't you tell me once that part of your estate, when you came of age, would include manors your grandfather bought from the dissolution of Tarrant Abbey?"

"Church properties?" Francis asked. "That does indeed change your circumstances, Tom. You are now a ward of the queen."

Trumpet nodded. No doubt she remembered some part of what he'd taught them about wardship. Tom hadn't paid much attention to his studies back then, being distracted by the multitudinous diversions available in London. "Perhaps you should refresh our memory," she said diplomatically.

Francis nodded. "When King Henry dissolved the monasteries, church lands were sold into private hands under terms of knight service. Originally, such feudal duties obliged the landowner to supply a specified number of knights when called upon to defend the realm. Over time, that obligation was commuted to a monetary payment, which has now devolved to a nominal annual fee, often paid in the form of a New Year's gift to the queen. The feudal relationship still obtains, however, which means the monarch has certain rights with respect to wardship and the marriages of heirs."

"Marriages of heirs," Trumpet said. "Is that why the queen gets to approve my choice of husband?"

Francis flapped a hand at her foolish question. "The monarch's approval is a matter of course for a person of your rank, my lady."

A broad smile creased the stranger's face as he regarded Trumpet with frank interest. "This England is very different from my home." He had apparently not discerned her actual sex until this moment. That made Francis feel better for not apprehending it earlier himself.

"Never mind that," Tom said. "What does it mean to be a ward of the queen? I don't want to get married; not yet. Not for years. I want to stay at Gray's. She won't send me home, will she? I can't miss a whole term!"

"You will stay here, I'm certain —" No, in truth, he could not be at all certain. A man needed a good sixty pounds a year to reside in an Inn of Court with dignity. Tom's new guardian might put him on a too-tight allowance, forcing him to return to Dorset. Although if the guardian were to alter the ward's circumstances so noticeably to his detriment, the Master of Wards — who happened to be Francis's uncle, Lord Burghley — might object.

Francis groaned inwardly. Wardship cases were always complex and acrimonious. He smiled at Tom to excuse the long pause. "I believe you will be allowed to remain at Gray's in more or less the same condition, although you should probably prepare yourself for some reduction of funds. The queen herself will not be your guardian, Tom. Your wardship is a marketable commodity. Your father's estate is worth how much? A thousand pounds per annum, wasn't it?"

"Seven or eight," Tom said. "What do you mean by 'marketable'?"

"I mean it will be sold. Wardships are a steady source of income for the crown." And for Francis's uncle, who had built his palace at Theobalds with fees from the Court of Wards.

Tom shrugged. "I'll lose a few hundred pounds, then. There are always fees. But it would only be for a few months. When I turn twenty-one, it will all become mine, apart from my mother's jointure and my sisters' portions. There are some other small bequests, but the bulk of the estate comes to me."

Francis pursed his lips and hummed a cautionary note. Ben cleared his throat and got up to fill cups again. Trumpet clucked her tongue and said, "I don't think it's always quite so simple."

"What do you mean?" Tom glared at each of them individually. The Indian, from some partisan impulse, mirrored the look, making Francis distinctly uncomfortable.

He kept half a wary eye on the stranger as he explained. "Once a guardian gains control of your properties, he or she can be difficult to dislodge. In a case such as this, when you have little influence and your guardian will likely be a person of considerable influence, you may be compelled to sue for your rights. As you know, such suits can drag on for years."

"That's not fair," Tom said.

Francis shrugged. Surely the lad had learned by now that fairness and the law were the merest acquaintances. "You might be able to buy it back, but the guardian will demand a healthy profit. I would expect to pay twice his expenditures, which in your case will be a year's income plus an entry fine of several hundred pounds."

"So all I have to do between now and December is come up with two thousand pounds in ready money?" Tom sounded as if he believed that was possible.

Francis rolled his eyes at the impertinent tone. He had no responsibility for the outcroppings of archaic practice dotting the landscape of the English legal system. If he had, rest assured, the common law would include more common sense.

"Who do you think will get it?" Ben asked. "And when will the bidding start?"

"It's started already," Francis said. "I'm sure someone down there in the yard has already run to Burghley House with the news."

Everyone turned to stare out the windows as if they could see the rumors flying past. Francis wished he could be the messenger; this plum was very juicy.

Wait — why shouldn't he be? It wouldn't take long to dash down to Burghley House. He could drop by Leicester House on the way back and leave a message for his Lord of Essex, or even speak with him, if luck should so transpire. What purpose would it serve for him to sit here with the others all evening? He wasn't really a member of their intimate circle, and he was useless in matters of strong emotion, as they well knew.

"When?" Tom asked. "I mean, what happens next?"

"Nothing but rumors and letters to my uncle for a week or two until the survey of the estate is completed. Then my uncle will consider all the proposals and grant the wardship to the winner. As for who, it will certainly be a courtier. By tradition, only courtiers can address the Master of Wards on such matters, so they tend to get in first. For an estate of this size, I would expect a member of the nobility to win out. The size of the bribe is important, but other factors such as favors owed and favors performed also have weight." Francis shifted in his chair, half turning toward the door. "You know, I really ought —"

"Mr. Bacon!" Trumpet scolded, but Tom said, "Go. Get me a good one."

THIRTY-ONE

After Bacon left, Tom got up and paced around the room. His heart felt too big for his body. He needed to walk off some of the pressure. He wished he had someone to fight or something big to break, but he didn't want to alarm his friends. They were already worried enough. He took his lute off its peg and hung it back; he took down a pistol and flipped it in his hand a time or two, then put it back too. He wandered over to the shelves and ruffled through a stack of Ben's broadsides until he saw an illustration of a mermaid with a beard. That didn't help at all. His friends watched him in silence.

Then an idea came to him. He clapped his hands together, the smack of sound echoing off the plastered ceiling and walls. "I want a feast! I want a pheasant. A big, fat one, roasted, with four different sauces. And brawn and pigeons and rabbit pie, and —" He snapped his fingers at Trumpet. "Marzipan for the lady. Lots of it, with raspberries and sweet cream."

The others gaped at him as if he had lost his mind. He put his hands on his hips and scoffed at them. "Have you never heard of a funeral feast? My father's been dead for . . ." He swallowed hard. "Gone for four days. It's time for his feast — past time. Let's go to the Antelope." He strode to the door and opened it wide.

Dirimara walked out without pause or fuss, possibly thinking the antelope would be *on* the table instead of housing it. Ben and Trumpet grumbled about like old people while they collected their hats and oddments. What did they need? He would pay for everything. Best to enjoy himself while he still could, hey? He'd leave the bill for his future guardian to settle up.

He herded them down the stairs and through the back passage to Holborn Road. Mrs. Sprye met them as they filed into the tavern. She watched him with concern in her wise hazel eyes as he ordered the best of everything to be served as soon as might be, in the same room they'd used the week before. She led them up the stairs. Tom flung wide the door and ushered his guests inside with a cheery, "Let the feast begin!" Then he closed the door behind them and turned to Mrs. Sprye. "My father's dead."

He burst into tears, gushing like a bilge pump. She wrapped her arms around him and held him for a long time, patting him on the back and whispering, "There, there, now, Tom. Shh, shh, shh." Gradually, the flow abated. Tom stepped back and cleared his throat. He started to wipe his nose on his sleeve, but she pulled a handkerchief from her sleeve and gave it to him. "Keep it. You may need it again tonight."

He thanked her and shook himself, squaring his shoulders. He found his smile and went in to join his friends, flinging the door open with a flourish. "Holla, ye pampered jades of Asia!"

They laughed far longer than the overused quote from *Tamburlaine* deserved. He supposed they'd heard him out there sobbing like a girl, but somehow it seemed to have made them feel better too.

Mrs. Sprye said, "I'll see what I can do about a pheasant."

"One more thing, Madam, if it please you," Tom said. "No, two. First, would you send one of your men to Gray's to invite Mr. Bacon to join us as soon as he returns? Tell him that if wants to be the chief counsel in my future suit against my future guardian, he'll be sure to accept." He grinned his cheekiest grin at her and she slapped him lightly on the shoulder.

"What else, Mr. Clarady? Would you like the Lord Treasurer to join you as well?"

"No, Mistress, I imagine he's busy. But would you have your man go on to Chadwick House to bring back Catalina Luna? Ask her to bring Trumpet's craftswoman's clothes, the ones she wore in Cambridge." He turned the cheeky grin toward Trumpet. "My favorite."

Mrs. Sprye left, closing the door behind her. Tom's friends had saved him the seat his father had occupied the last time they'd supped in this chamber. He nodded his approval as he took his place. Ben sat across from him with Trumpet at his side; two better friends no man had ever had. Dirimara sat next to Ben, seeming as much at ease in this well-appointed dining room as he had been in Tom's chambers. The dark little man had an air of self-sufficiency — quiet, nonthreatening, but not a man you'd choose to meddle with.

Tom studied him from across the table. "Tell me, Dirimara. What can I do for you? You went to some trouble to bring me this hard news, instead of leaving me to hear it through gossip or from some cold authority. It would have been bitter indeed to learn of my father's death only when my new guardian showed up to throw me out of my rooms."

"You owe me nothing." Dirimara rose to his feet and bowed. "I place myself at the service of the son of Captain Valentine Clarady, a man who saved my life when I nearly died from melancholy."

"Oh. Ha. Well, that's generous of you." Tom fingered his earring, but the touch of it made him sad again. "The thing of it is, my friend, I'm not so much in a position to accept your service at the present juncture. I mean to stay at Gray's until they drag me out in a cart and our chambers are a bit cramped as it is."

"I comprehend you. I will feast with you this night and then continue on my own quest." Dirimara sat down again.

"What is your quest?" Tom asked.

"That is a long story, son of my captain. Not fit for tonight. Perhaps one day I will tell it to you." Dirimara's black eyes glittered with some private fervor.

"When did you join my father's crew?"

"Last year, in a place near the Sea of the Antilles called Maracaibo. That too is a long story."

Tom met his obsidian gaze again and nodded. They would meet again, he had no doubt, and then he would hear these stories. "You'll know where to find me."

The servers came in with wine and cups and plates of bread and savories to tide them over while the main meal was being prepared. Tom waited until they had gone, then raised his cup. "To my father — the greatest privateer who ever sailed the seven seas!"

The others raised their cups and cried, "To Captain Clarady!"

Tom and Dirimara traded stories about the times they'd each spent with the captain aboard the *Susannah* or in the many ports they'd visited. Ben and Trumpet listened with evident pleasure, asking lots of questions, even about stories they'd heard before from Tom.

During a pause while the servers brought in a course of boiled meats and pigeon pie, Ben asked, "Do you want to talk about the wardship?"

"No. I'll wait and see who I have to deal with."

Trumpet asked, "Do you trust Mr. Bacon to look out for your interests?"

"I do," Tom said, "especially when they march together with his. He benefits from my prosperity in all sorts of little ways, from my tutoring fees to the books I buy for him, knowing he'll never pay me back. And deep down, in his own way, I believe he cares about my general welfare."

"I'm glad you can see that," Ben said.

Trumpet made a rude noise. "He keeps it well hidden."

After half an hour or so, Catalina arrived with a chest of clothing. She'd ridden over with one of the grooms from Chadwick House. She and Trumpet withdrew to the bathing chamber downstairs. When they returned, Trumpet was wearing a green worsted kirtle with a modest farthingale and a ruffled collar on her Holland smock. Her shining black hair was bound under a crisp white coif. The simple costume allowed her freedom of movement, thus displaying her agile grace as well as her womanly shape. Best of all, her heart-shaped face was clean, obscured by neither courtly paints nor fake moustaches.

She offered Tom a curtsy and he smiled, nodding, letting his admiration show.

The first course was removed and the second brought in. They didn't get pheasant — Tom hadn't really expected it on such short notice — but the board groaned with baked chickens, moorcock pie, roast lamb, rabbit pie, soused pig, and a variety of tarts. For drink, they had claret, malmsey, and a big pitcher of sweet white sack from the Canaries.

Francis Bacon came in with the second course, hesitating on the threshold the way he always did. Tom waved him to the seat at the head of the table between him and Ben, making sure he got a cup of malmsey and a plate with a taste of every dish. "Any word about my guardian?"

"It's too soon, Tom. But my Lord Burghley condoles with your loss and wishes you to be assured that he will keep your best interests in mind as he reviews the candidates. None had arrived as yet, but I saw Sir Avery Fogg waiting in the lobby as I went in."

Tom and his friends exchanged a round of shrugs. Sir Avery was the treasurer of Gray's Inn, so he would probably allow Tom to continue to live in a style befitting a gentleman. But he had a volatile temper and hungered for a judgeship. Appointments to the higher courts could cost upwards of a thousand pounds.

The race had begun.

Bacon said, "My lord uncle remembers the service you performed for him last year. That will help, I hope." He picked at the morsels on his plate and settled on a bite of rabbit pie. He swallowed and smiled as if surprised by its tastiness. "He also graciously relieved me of my work on the recusancy commission. I'm free. Apparently, my mother wrote to her sister, my lord's wife, detailing the ill effect the work was having on my health. However, since I will now have more time at my disposal, he has charged me with putting a stop to the recusant murders by identifying the perpetrator, *whomever I might suspect that person to be.*" He leaned toward Ben with a significant look as he spoke those last words.

Tom followed the look with satisfaction. He tapped Trumpet's ankle with his foot. Now, finally, they would get whatever it was Bacon had been keeping from them.

Tom said, "When you spoke to the Andromache Society, I got the feeling you were worried that the Lord Treasurer already knew about the murders."

"I got the feeling you knew who it was," Trumpet added, "but were afraid to pursue him."

"Both impressions were correct," Bacon said, "although I have no certain knowledge, only suspicions." He ate another bite of pie and took a long draught of wine, plainly continuing some debate with himself. Then he sighed and put his cup down. "I feared to share my suspicions for both of the reasons you mention, but my lord uncle's injunction — the particular words he used — suggest to me that my aunt, Lady Russell, may have communicated my suspicions to him in private. He either knows whom I suspect and wants me to expose him, or he does not know, but recognizes the probable source of my reluctance and has given me to understand that he does not approve and wants the matter resolved regardless of where my investigations might lead."

Poor Dirimara hadn't followed any of that, but the others were used to Mr. Bacon's rhetorical style. Tom caught the Indian's eye and translated. "His uncle is the most powerful man in the kingdom. Mr. Bacon thinks some high-up gentleman has done these murders we're worried about, but he feared his uncle might have ordered them done, not straight out, but hint-like and hugger-mugger. Mr. Bacon's no cackler, so he's been biding his time, keeping a weather eye and giving the gentleman in question a wide berth. Now His Lordship has cleared the braces, so we can crack on."

"You are *constablularios*?" Dirimara asked. "My captain say his son study law."

"We are lawyers," Bacon answered, "who sometimes, under extraordinary circumstances, are asked to inquire into suspicious deaths."

Trumpet pounded her small fist on the tabletop. "Are you ever going to tell us who this high-up gentleman is?"

Bacon nodded once. "Yes, I am. Perhaps you've heard me speak of one of my co-commissioners, Sir Richard Topcliffe?"

He told them about his growing doubts and the foreboding sense that the murders suited Sir Richard's zealous and vengeful temperament all too well. He then told them about the manacles and rosaries he and Ben had found in the hidden room off Sir Richard's library. Last, he told them in the briefest terms about his unwilling visit to the rack room under the White Tower.

After a short interval in which everyone took long drinks to wash the sourness from their throats, Trumpet said, "He sounds utterly vile and odious. I believe the man you describe could definitely have performed those murders."

"I'm not so sure," Tom said. "He sounds to me like a man who likes to use the power of the state to satisfy his cruel tastes. He wouldn't work in secret."

Bacon shook his spoon back and forth. "He can't use the state to punish these particular victims. He would need my signature as well as those of the other commissioners. We wouldn't supply them. The state has no reason to torture those men. I've reviewed my notes from those interviews and in truth, these victims seemed only mildly interested in religion. They cared far more about their ancestry and family traditions. We did, however, suspect all the wives of taking an active part in the smuggling of priests and banned texts. We can't torture women — the idea is unthinkable. We can't prosecute them since they have no standing in a court of law. We can't even bring them in for questioning, not ladies of rank and wealth. They're untouchable. The best we can do is impose sanctions on the husbands and wait for them to bring their wives under control."

Tom and his friends laughed. Dirimara looked bemused. He had little to contribute to the discussion, but he listened to every word with rapt attention, as if storing up facts he might find useful later.

Bacon gestured for the soused pig and spooned some on to his dish while the others joked about the putative controllability of wives. Trumpet told a bawdy tale she'd stolen from Chaucer, and Ben topped it with a cautionary tale ripped from the broadsides. Tom rose to call for more wine and refilled everyone's cups. His feast was a great success.

When the jocularity tapered off, Bacon said, "The problem is that I don't know where to go from here. I had hoped you would turn up something useful in the pawnshops, pick up some thread we could follow, but that failed to transpire."

"Ah," Tom said. He cocked a brow at Trumpet. "Your choice, my lady."

Trumpet waved her cup, sloshing wine on the tablecloth. "That's all water under the bridge. We're laying our cards on the table now. Lay mine out as well." She fixed her eyes on Bacon with some difficulty. "My uncle is the upright man behind the chapel burglaries."

"Nathaniel Welbeck!"

Tom laughed out loud at the tangle of expressions on Bacon's face. Astonishment, disbelief, recognition, outrage: he used up a week's worth of emotional responses in less than a minute.

"Welbeck," Bacon said. "I never would have guessed, but now that you tell me, it makes perfect sense. How can he have been living in the Savoy with no one ever seeing him?"

"I'm sure someone saw him," Tom said, understanding he meant barristers. "Just not anyone who would spread the news widely enough for you to hear it."

Ben said, "The Savoy is the ideal location, both for a barrister who wants to conceal his whereabouts and for the organizer of the chapel burglaries. His thieves could bring the goods right up to the protected wharf there and carry them straight up to his rooms."

"He's a very intelligent man, my Uncle Nat," Trumpet said. "But he's not a murderer. The thieves didn't know about the murders and they clearly did not like them. They said Uncle Nat wanted to quit because of them."

"What thieves?" Bacon asked. "Our thieves? How do you know this?"

"Ah." Tom grinned at Bacon apologetically. "We haven't gotten to that part yet. We've met the chapel burglars, or at least some of them. And we had a long chat with Mr. Welbeck." He proceeded to tell Bacon about the pawnshop in Southwark, their visit to the Savoy, and their meeting with Coddington at the Dolphin. Trumpet threw in a detail from time to time.

Bacon listened in attentive silence, the way he did when he was analyzing your vocabulary, syntax, and meaning all at once, relating it to everything else he had ever heard or read. Many people found his fixed gaze disconcerting, but Tom was used to it.

"I see," Bacon said when they finished. "Good work, though you should have told me. But then I was keeping secrets myself, and Welbeck, though a scoundrel, is Trumpet's uncle."

Ben said, "It seems clear that Welbeck and his gang are responsible for the burglaries. I also agree that Sir Richard may have committed the murders. But I can't see any connection between the two."

"Maybe there isn't one," Trumpet said.

"I refuse to believe that," Bacon said. "It's as implausible as two explorers leaving from different countries on different days and arriving at the same time on the same island in the Spanish Main."

"That is not possible," Dirimara said. "The sea is most *caprichoso.*"

Bacon gestured at him with an open palm. "My point, supported."

The servers came in to clear away the second course and bring in the third — plates of gingered bread, honeyed almonds, sugared violets, and tiny cheese tarts. Mrs. Sprye had sent up no fewer than four small cakes of marzipan, decorated with rose petals and tiny sprigs of thyme.

Tom slid one of them in front of Trumpet. "They must be connected through the clerk," he said, picking up the thread of the discussion. "Coddington confirmed my guess. He said the clerk got paid after the goods were sold. Maybe the clerk in question is Sir Richard's secretary."

"He's every bit as vile as his master," Bacon said. "I believe he's been with Sir Richard for many years. What is his name?"

"Walter Kemp," Ben said. "But remember, the recusancy commission has never been a secret. Welbeck might have learned about it from one of his friends at Gray's."

"Or one of his friends in gaol," Tom said. "You send most of the ones you interview back to Bridewell or wherever you found them."

"That's true," Bacon said. "And stories of that nature travel like wildfire inside a prison. I'm satisfied that we can connect the crimes. However, Kemp seems devoted to Sir Richard. I doubt he would sell that list without his master's knowledge. Then again, Sir Richard is a devious man. If Welbeck approached his secretary, and the secretary informed him of the attempt, he might see an opportunity to wreak a bit of private vengeance. He hates to let anyone he deems guilty slip through his grasp."

"I still don't like the private vengeance part," Tom said. "Why private? Sir Richard has prisons full of Catholics he can torture with impunity and the wives suffer all the same."

"Never with impunity," Bacon said, looking exasperated. "England is a civilized nation. We have procedures. We have laws. Torture is abhorrent, true, but in times of great peril, it is necessary."

"We understand, Francis." Ben patted his hand. "We don't need to debate the whys and wherefores here. But I must say I tend to agree with Tom. These murders seem both too covert and too gentle for Sir Richard. From what we've managed to learn, none of the victims struggled much. Doesn't that suggest they experienced little pain? Topcliffe enjoys inflicting pain. Furthermore, if the victims were paralyzed, they wouldn't be able to speak."

The others shook their heads at him, not comprehending. "What would they speak about?" Trumpet asked.

"About other Catholics," Ben said. "Remember those strings of files in his closet? Sir Richard loves amassing information about Catholics as much as he enjoys hurting them. Our victims couldn't have told him anything."

Bacon frowned. "I wish we knew more about that poison. All I managed to do was rule out the drugs I'm familiar with."

"You did better than that," Ben said. "You tracked down references to arrow poisons used in the New . . ." His voice trailed off as everyone turned to face the stranger from the New World.

The stranger regarded them warily.

"I wonder, Dirimara," Bacon said, "if you might happen to know anything about a poison called, if I'm pronouncing it correctly, curare?"

"*Wourari*, in my language," Dirimara said. "Yes, I know it. Do you want some?" He took out his pocket and withdrew a small chunk of some blackish-brown stuff, like a lump of clay.

"God's death!" Bacon cried. Everyone gasped and flinched away, pushing their chairs back from the table.

Dirimara grinned, his gold tooth glinting in the candlelight. He tossed the lump in the air and caught it. "It is no danger in this form. I could swallow this and suffer no harm. It must enter the blood. You must pierce the skin with an arrow, a knife, a spear." He grinned again. "Or for lawyers, perhaps, a quill."

Everyone seemed to inhale the same long breath and exhale it with an audible rush. Then they settled back at the table, returning to their ordinary postures. Tom took a long draught of wine. "How do you apply it?"

"It must be warm, soft and thin, so you may spread it upon the blade."

"Does it take a lot?" Tom asked. "I mean, how thick do you spread it?"

"Not thick. Very thin. Very powerful."

Bacon asked, "How many minutes, or fractions of an hour, if you prefer, are required to effect a complete paralysis?"

Dirimara blinked at him, so Tom translated. "How long does it take to work?"

"Ah." Dirimara nodded. "I did not know minutes until I came to the English ship, but it does not take long." He tilted his head and thought for a moment, then said, "One day, I went to hunt monkeys with two men of my tribe. One was young, not so skillful. He missed the monkey and shot the other man. This man looked down at the dart in his chest and said, 'Now I must die.' He lay on the ground and folded his arms upon his breast. We start our prayer for him. After one round, he cannot move even his eyes. We carry him back to our village. Soon after, his heart no longer beats."

Bacon asked, "Is it a long prayer?"

Dirimara shrugged, then began a soft chant. When he finished, Bacon said, "Thank you. I estimate about two minutes for incapacitation. From what we know, death apparently takes the better part of an hour after that. Curious." He smiled at Trumpet. "The murderer may have left only a few minutes before your maidservant entered Lord Surdeval's bedchamber."

Trumpet grimaced. "That's a frightening thought. I don't believe I'll share it with her. She has enough superstitions as it is."

Tom patted her hand, letting his cover hers for perhaps a moment longer than necessary. She didn't object.

Ben's gaze flicked to their hands, hesitated, then moved on to the Indian. "Can you eat an animal that has been killed with this poison? I should think it would be tainted."

"Oh, no," Dirimara said. "It is delicious. The poison must enter the blood, not the belly."

Bacon asked, "Could you make a paste from the veins of the poisoned animal and use it in the same fashion?"

Dirimara tucked his chin in surprise. "I do not know."

Tom and Ben traded looks of fond amusement. Tom asked, "Where could one buy this *wourari*? Only from a man like you?"

"A man like me would not sell it," Dirimara said. "This is for me to use." He displayed the lump one last time and tucked it back into his pocket.

Tom remembered that the Indian had his own quest and suspected that poison would be used at the end of it. He had only just met the man, but the captain had trusted him, so Tom did too. He knew that whoever that poison was meant for had earned it. Dirimara must have his own Jacques Le Bon to serve with wild justice — Bacon's apt term for revenge

"We believe someone in England possesses this substance," Ben said. "Where could they have gotten it?"

"From the men who trade in New Spain," Dirimara said. "One man comes to a village and buys what he finds. He sells to another man and that one to another. Someday, these things — bark from trees, skins from snakes, many things — travel all the way to England."

"Merchants," Ben said.

"St. Jean de Luz," Tom said.

"Yes," Dirimara said. "Everything from everywhere is there."

"Is that where you're going next?" Tom asked.

The Indian smiled but didn't answer. Tom hoped he would be all right, so far from his native land, and that his quest would succeed.

Bacon had been consuming a raspberry tartlet in small bites, his face thoughtful, plainly digesting the new facts about the poison and relating it to everything else they'd learned about the method of murder employed. "It sounds like a very quiet way to kill," he said at last. "I can believe that the thieves heard nothing. It does seem too quiet for Sir Richard, however. I had the sense the other day that he rather enjoyed the screaming."

Dirimara shook his head. "With *wourari*, there is no scream."

"I have another extremely interesting idea!" Trumpet cried. Her words were only slightly slurred. She had been sipping cream sauce as if it was soup. Now she waved her spoon to get their attention. "I know why your nasty old Sir Richard does what he does the way he does it. The husbands aren't the guilty ones, the wives are. And so he murders the husbands *because* the wives are untouchable. That'll punish 'em right enough!" She drained her cup and plunked it on the table as if her argument was complete.

Ben and Bacon stared at her, dumbfounded, but Tom grinned. Trust Trumpet to come up with a completely novel solution! He watched her spoon up another mouthful of sauce, losing a trickle down the side of her chin. He felt a sudden urge to lean over and lick it off.

Then Ben chuckled, nodded, and wagged his knife at her. "Very clever, Trumpet. Very clever indeed." He grinned at Tom and Bacon. "The wives can't be punished directly; it's true. But when their husbands die, after having been entered on a list of known recusants, their estates are liable to confiscation. The wives lose their standing, their wealth, and most pertinently, their ability to foster priests."

"That is a very intriguing idea," Bacon said. He and Ben started debating the whys and wherefores of punishing recalcitrant wives. Tom stopped listening, entranced by Trumpet and her raspberries, which were almost exactly the color of her lips. She licked the bottom of her spoon, then smiled that bow-shaped minx's smile when she caught him watching her.

Tom's heart overflowed with a powerful affection. He loved her, whether in a tradeswoman's kirtle or a street urchin's galligaskins. A sigh rose out of his overburdened heart and escaped his lips. He would always love her first and foremost, though she could never be his. One day soon, she'd be married off to some potbellied sot with a title and carted off to some crumbling manor to produce heirs. Tom might see her now and then when she came to court in her husband's train, but he wouldn't get to watch cream sauce dribble down her chin.

If she was a widow with a house of her own on the Strand — handy, not two jogs from Gray's — he could slip up the river path to her garden window. They could drink claret and play primero, or maybe other games. Her case would be decided tomorrow. She should win it. Then she'd get the house and the jointure she'd worked so hard for. That was what she wanted. And why shouldn't she get what she wanted?

Why shouldn't everyone? Ben should marry that tasty widow, Mrs. What-d'ye-call-um, the one in the Andromache Society. The widow was rich — very rich. The couple could buy a fine big house in Holborn and have Tom over for dinner every Sunday, along with Mr. Bacon.

Mr. Bacon would never change, of course. Nothing could alter good old Mr. Bacon. He would stay on at Gray's Inn, and Tom would stay right along with him. They would become great barristers in the public view and wily intelligencers outside of it. Tom leaned toward Bacon, tempted to grasp his hand and shake it out of pure brotherly feeling.

The thought crossed his mind that Trumpet wasn't the only one getting a little bit drunk.

"Your proposal has merit, Trumpet," Bacon said. "Although it seems a most indirect way of exacting vengeance. What we have, gentlemen and lady, is an elegant theory, or perhaps two alternate theories. We have our opinion of a man's character and a few articles in his house related to the crimes in what one might call a thematic association, but nothing in the way of proof. We have no clear evidence against Nathaniel Welbeck either. Your abruptly terminated conversation in that tavern will not impress a judge, nor will the testimony of the clerk in the pawnshop, assuming you could obtain it."

"If we could lay our hands on that Jack Coddington," Ben said, "we might find a way to persuade him to bear witness against Welbeck."

"Never," Tom said. Trumpet echoed the word twice, shaking her head emphatically. Tom went on, "He admires him greatly. Welbeck takes care of his men, paying them promptly and bailing them out of gaol. We need witnesses outside his circle."

"We may have to wait for another murder," Ben said.

"Unacceptable," Bacon said. "We can't let another man die while we sit on our hands and do nothing."

"We should get out ahead of them," Tom said. "Then *we* could be the witnesses."

Ben nodded at him. "We could hide in the house if we knew where and when. Can we figure out who's next by studying your list, Francis?"

Bacon shook his head. "Sir James Lambert wasn't on our list. We didn't know about him — or I didn't. Sir Richard could have learned something and kept it to himself."

Ben said, "Negative evidence is evidence of a sort. If a name is not on your list, it can't have been —"

"Hey ho!" Trumpet cried. "I forgot! What Coddington said, remember, Tom? He said, 'The master has another —' and then the other whoreson knave came along, the superior one, and stopped him."

"You're right," Tom said, smiling at her. "That means the list of recusants isn't Welbeck's only source of information."

"What else could he have?" Bacon asked.

Trumpet said, "I've been thinking they might have been his clients. You know he knows a lot of Catholics, and he also knows other people like him, who are sometimes sympathetic and sometimes not. Maybe one of them is helping him choose the victims for a share of the profits."

Bacon said, "Now that is a useful idea, Lady Alice. Our list says nothing about when the houses are most likely to be empty. Someone who knew these families more intimately would be more likely to have that additional knowledge. Unfortunately, I can think of only one way to pursue your useful notion." He wrinkled his nose as if sampling a sauce over seasoned with verjuice. "We'll have to pay a call on the Savoy Solicitor."

THIRTY-TWO

Trumpet sat up in bed, twisted around, and whacked her fist into her pillows to plump them up. She flopped down on her back again and then immediately rolled onto her left side. Now the lace edgings tickled her nose. She sat up and stacked on another pillow, then pulled up her covers and closed her eyes. Two seconds later, they popped open again.

She groaned and said, "I am wide awake," to no one. She glowered at the waning moon, which mocked her sleeplessness from outside the window. She could get up and close the curtains and also pour herself a cup of wine, but then her feet would get cold and she had already had quite enough wine for one night.

The men had sent her and Catalina home with a couple of grooms around sunset to make sure they got inside the city walls before the gates closed. She'd been pleasantly tipsy at that point — Tom said ape drunk — but by the time she'd cleaned her teeth and gotten her hair brushed, while telling Catalina the news about Tom's father and explaining the thorny matter of his impending wardship, the drink had worn off. Now she lay tossing restlessly in her bed with nothing to do but worry about appearing in the bishop's court tomorrow morning.

No one had said anything about her case during that whole long supper. Not even Ben, not even when he'd helped her onto the horse behind Catalina. "Sleep well, my lady," was all he'd said. He'd forgotten about it! Tom had leered at her — well beyond ape drunk himself — and mumbled something about setting things right, but then he'd staggered off to the jakes without a kiss or a comment.

Granted, the little problem of her marital status paled in comparison to the loss of a beloved father. She wasn't a monster; she understood the gravity of Tom's loss. She grieved for him and with him and would for many months to come. But tomorrow was the most important day of her life so far and not one of her supposedly dearest friends had so much as wished her luck!

She growled into her pillow. Luck wouldn't help her now anyway. No one had believed her nap story. They'd scoffed at it. In fairness, when she remembered how cranky Surdeval had gotten whenever anyone was ten blinks of an eyelash late, she could hear the implausibility herself. Without that story, she had nothing. She would lose the case, the marriage would be annulled, and she'd be right back where she'd started. No house, no independent widowhood. All lost, after all her careful planning, thanks to some murdering religious lunatic.

She sighed hugely, ending in a little bark of frustration. She should concede the case. She could at least spare herself the indignity of the maidenhead examination.

Her door opened, revealing a thin line of yellow candlelight. Her maidservant whispered, "My lady! Are you awake?"

"Come in, Catalina. I was just wishing for something to drink. Maybe a warm posset. Something to help me sleep."

"You do not wish to sleep, my lady." Catalina sounded as if she were choking back a spate of giggles. "You have a visitor."

"At this hour?"

The next thing she knew, her covers were thrown back and Tom's strong arms lifted her up, pulling her onto his lap. His moustache tickled her neck as he nuzzled her. Was she dreaming?

But her skin flashed hot wherever his hands touched her through the thin cambric nightshirt and his breath still smelled of red wine and cinnamon. He lifted her again, cupping her arse, and shifted her so she straddled his legs. Then his wide, strong hands spread up her lower back, spanning her waist, tracing her shoulder blades. One stroked across her ribs and cupped a breast. She moaned and threw her arms around his neck, pressing her body against him. Then she tilted back her head and let the dream engulf her.

They broke for air, gasping, stunned. He smoothed the hair from her face and turned them both toward the light from the candle on the bedside table. He must have brought it in, or maybe Catalina had slipped in and put it there. It didn't matter. Tom was here, in her bed, alone, and gazing at her with his blue eyes darkened by desire.

"You are so beautiful." His voice was low and husky. "So beautiful. And so brave." He smiled that dimpled smile and her heart flipped. He feathered kisses up her cheek and whispered, "Let's make sure you win your case tomorrow. One of us should get what they want, hey?"

That wasn't quite what she wanted to hear. Had he come to effect a legal maneuver?

She sat back, opening a space between her longing and his body. She placed her flat palms on his chest and studied his face. The candle flickered, casting odd shadows, but even under that, his face had changed. She knew it better than she knew her own. Hollows had formed under his eyes and a new crease marked his brow. Somehow his cheeks seemed hollow too, although it had only been a couple of hours. She could read every tiny sign written on the beloved canvas. Grief moved him more tonight than desire.

Her ardor cooled as if someone had opened a window. "What changed your mind?"

"Hmm?" He tried to pull her toward him, but she resisted, palms braced against his hard chest.

"You refused me on my wedding night for the true and valid reason that if anyone ever found out, my father, my lord's kinsmen, and my Uncle Nat would have you whipped, or worse. You've also said, along with everyone else, that you think my nap time story is quite possibly the stupidest thing you've ever heard. That's not an exact quote, but you remember the main thrust."

"What's wrong, sweetling? Isn't this what you wanted?" Tom stretched his neck toward her, lips puckered, ready to dust more kisses across her cheeks.

She looked at him the way you look at a painting of some fabulous place you long to visit but know you never can because it isn't real. "What changed your mind?"

Tom slumped, running a hand through his golden curls, sorrow and irritation mingling in his eyes. "Ben, I guess. When we got back to our rooms, we started talking about my future guardian, who it was going be, wondering where Mr. Bacon went before he came to the Antelope. It doesn't take an hour to deliver a bit of news to Lord Burghley, you see. He's too busy to give you more than a couple of minutes and it only takes ten to get there and back. So Ben thought Bacon might have stopped by Leicester House to pass the intelligence on to the Earl of Essex."

"Oh, dear."

"That's what Ben said. It's not all bad though, Ben said. My Lord of Essex has enormous influence. He could do a lot for me. On the other hand, he might throw my whole estate into the sea to finance some mad venture to impress the queen." Tom hung his head. "My life is over, Trumpet. At least the life I had. I'm thinking I might leave. Dirimara is going to Spain to look for his father; maybe I'll go with him part of the way. Or I could join the Dutch sea beggars." He raised his head to meet her eyes and laid his hand along her cheek. "Let me give you what you want before I go. It doesn't matter what happens to me afterward."

Her heart broke fair in two. She wanted him more than she wanted health or happiness, but not like this. Not as an act of despair. She leaned in and kissed him for one long, delicious moment, then pulled back before he could make it more amorous. "I love you," she said and sent him away.

He'd argued a little and made another half-hearted attempt to draw her back into an embrace, but she knew that he knew as well as she did that their time had not yet come. She'd asked Catalina to have one of the stable boys follow him to make sure he found somewhere safe to sleep it off. The tavern around the corner was the most likely spot.

After he'd gone, she let Catalina give her a draught of valerian and settled back into her bed. She curled around the spot where Tom had sat, breathing in the lingering smell of him, cuddling a pillow in her arms.

In the morning, she would allow the bishop to annul her marriage without protest. She would surrender all rights to Surdeval House and her jointure. And then she would insist on being examined that morning by the eight matrons of good repute to prove to all and sundry that she remained *virgo intacta*. The gossipmongers would have nothing more to whisper about and the scandal about the old man, the young bride, and the handsome retainer would die.

She could do that much for Tom.

THIRTY-THREE

Francis paused for a moment outside the gate at the Savoy Palace to adjust his robes. He'd worn them to impress Nathaniel Welbeck — or to bolster his own courage. These legal robes were distinguished by tufts of silk velvet around the shoulders. Only benchers, members of the governing bodies of the Inns of Court, were allowed to wear the tufts. As a bencher, Francis had a vote in all decisions concerning Gray's Inn: admission, calls to the bar, adjudication of disputes between members, and decisions with respect to the distribution of chambers. Welbeck was merely an outer barrister, but he was a good dozen years older and had spent those years arguing cases in court. Francis hadn't quite gotten around to that yet.

He did have a full retinue to support him this afternoon. Ben and Tom, of course, wearing the legal garb of inner barristers, the sleeveless robes with flap collars and small flat caps. Trumpet, who had met them at Gray's gatehouse in her aunt's carriage, had dressed with her usual sense of occasion in stark black broadcloth with a huge white widow's coif. The five of them, including Trumpet's maidservant, had squeezed into a coach to drive the quarter mile from Gray's Inn to the Strand. An absurd degree of pomp to visit a man Francis regarded as little better than a charlatan, but this charlatan had something they wanted and no reason to give it to them.

The gatekeeper bowed them in without question. They filed through the yards and alleys of the Savoy precinct in silence. Francis had done little to prepare for the meeting beyond reviewing the list of leases coming due at Gray's.

Welbeck wanted to return to the Inn; in truth, nothing stood in his way. He'd left before any connection could be drawn between him and the murdered man in the field, leaving behind his "nephew" to tender his excuses. They had proved adequate. As far as everyone else was concerned, Nathaniel Welbeck had been recalled to his family estate in Devonshire to care for his elderly parents. He'd said he intended to build a practice in Exeter and had been successful in so doing. His reputation was untarnished. He could return whenever he pleased.

Chambers were another matter, and there Francis might have an advantage. Like every other educational institution in Queen Elizabeth's burgeoning realm, the Inns of Court were stuffed to bursting. Many incoming students and even some barristers were obliged to take lodgings elsewhere, like the Antelope Inn or the profitable Bentley's Rents. Chambers within the bounds of Gray's Inn went for quite a tidy sum, even when the applicant enjoyed the support of a majority of benchers.

The group mounted the stairs and found the door open. They were expected since Trumpet had arranged the meeting in advance. Welbeck remained seated at his desk as they entered, a petty stratagem. He waved them toward various stools and benches. Francis took the armed chair directly in front of the desk, with Ben seated at an angle to one side. Tom and Trumpet sat on stools, not far apart, but not together. Trumpet's maidservant sat on a bench near the door.

"Francis Bacon." Welbeck steepled his fingers. "It's been what — two years? You still look too young for those velvet tufts."

"Yet I wear them." Francis had long ago ceased to be affected by jibes about his youth. He gazed around the room with an air of barely restrained distaste. The walls boasted oak wainscoting, but the paint was peeling and a whole section had been bleached to a grayish brown by sun streaming through the poorly glazed window. "I expected you to be wise enough to remain in Devonshire."

"Too wise to be wasted in a backwater. A man of my capacities belongs at the center of things. You must understand that, Bacon, else you'd retire to your hunting box in Twickenham and spend your days tinkering with your vaunted philosophical investigations."

Francis had to concede the validity of that observation. The income from his two small properties was adequate for the life of a modest country gentleman, although paltry for a courtier; hence his endless scrambling to cover one debt with another. He loved Twickenham, with its herb garden, orchard, and ponds, but his sense of duty always called him back to court. "Gray's Inn is my home."

"Mine too," Welbeck said. "And soon I'll be dining among my colleagues in the hall."

"That remains to be decided."

They smiled thinly at one another — the grounds for negotiation had been staked. Welbeck turned to Trumpet and his smile warmed. "Well, Niece, I see you're dressed as a widow. Does that mean you won your case?"

"I wore black because I knew everyone else would. I conceded my case. The marriage is annulled."

That created a small stir as Ben and Tom expressed varying degrees of dismay or approval. She lifted her chin as she accepted their responses, a prideful gesture meant to cover her evident disappointment.

What made her change her mind? Ben must have finally persuaded her of the futility and risk of pressing an impossible suit. It must have been a bitter deed though; Allen Trumpington had hated to lose, even the informal mock trials after supper.

Welbeck said, "I am sorry, Alice, but you made the right decision. And you spared yourself a thoroughly unpleasant examination."

"I insisted on the examination." Trumpet lifted her chin a notch higher. "To put an end once and for all to rumors about what might or might not have happened on my wedding night."

"Ah, Trumpet," Tom said. "You didn't have to go through that."

"It's done." She waved it away with a black-gloved hand. "And now the world knows without a shred of doubt that I am a virgin. Why the world cares remains a mystery."

Blood would tell; she had her father's courage. Francis admired her in that moment. He wouldn't willingly submit to so intimate an examination of his person by eight matrons, or eight gentlemen for that matter. He had almost rather be racked.

Welbeck chuckled at her composure. "Well done, my lady." He then turned a steely gaze on Tom. "Let's be certain you continue in that condition until your next marriage."

Tom met the gaze with steel in his own blue eyes. He seemed to have aged overnight. He'd regained some of his balance since the funeral feast, but his mood remained volatile.

"Perhaps we should turn to the reason for this meeting," Francis said. "We know you're responsible for the chapel burglaries, Welbeck. We know enough to have you arrested, and I believe we know enough to convict you." He didn't, but one always opened a negotiation with the strongest possible statement of one's position.

Welbeck regarded Francis with a half smile, then turned again to his niece. "You've betrayed me, Alice. Again. I thought you didn't care about the chapels."

"I don't. But they do. And it's got to stop, Uncle."

"By 'they,' I suppose you mean Bacon and his long shadow, Benjamin Whitt. I can't imagine Clarady here posing any objection. My little venture is no worse than what his father's been doing these many years."

Tom was off his stool and pointing his knife at Welbeck's throat before anyone else could frame a response. "One word about my father — one word, Welbeck — and I'll cut you to the bone."

Welbeck quailed, leaning as far back as he could, raising his hands, his eyes riveted on the blade. "I meant no disrespect."

Ben rose and gently steered the knife away, then guided Tom back to his stool. He stood behind him with a hand on his shoulder, more to comfort him than restrain him.

Francis said, "Tom's father died in a powder explosion at Dieppe a few days ago."

Welbeck's shoulders sank. "Ah, lad, I'm truly sorry. I wish I could have known the man. His name had weight in the West Country." He shook his head, his brown eyes filled with seemingly genuine sorrow. "That's a grave loss, especially for a man your age. You're too old to go home to your mother's comfort, but not yet launched in a life of your own. You'll miss your father's guidance, but you're a man of parts, Tom. I know you'll stay the course."

The perfect speech. Tom's expression showed how well it struck him.

That was the trouble with Nathaniel Welbeck. He was a scoundrel, calculating and artful, a flouter of authority and believer in nothing, but he had the gift of fellow feeling. He liked people, he understood them, and they liked him. Skills Francis had never mastered.

Tom answered him gravely. "Apology and condolence both accepted."

Welbeck said, "I truly meant no disrespect, Tom. All I meant was that robbing those secret chapels is much like raiding Spanish ships at sea. We take from the Catholics to give to the English. A large portion of the proceeds from my ventures goes to feed the sailors and soldiers who fought off the armada."

"He has a point," Trumpet said. "Strictly speaking, the goods they steal are illicit. It's like taking booty from pirates."

Welbeck folded his arms across his chest, a smug smile on his almost handsome face. "You can't argue with that, Bacon."

"Of course I can. Your analogy is specious at its core. Privateers are licensed by the queen. They disable ships and take supplies from our enemies; ships and supplies that would or could be used against us, whether here or in the war in the Low Countries across our sea. Yes, they make a profit, but they hinder our enemies in so doing. You, on the other hand, steal family heirlooms from the homes of loyal Englishmen. There is no comparison whatsoever."

"I agree," Tom said. "And I retract my acceptance of your apology, though your neck is safe for now. From me at least."

"That qualification is pertinent," Francis said. "Your actions are felonious and can lead to only one result: hanging."

"Except that you have no proof of my involvement," Welbeck said. "Not a scrap. Jack Coddington told me about these two rascals' caper at the Dolphin. You have no proof of my supposed retainers' involvement either. All you have is a couple of men making idle boasts in a tavern. No jury in England would convict on such *evidence*, if you could even bring so frivolous a case to court."

Unfortunately, he was right. They couldn't threaten him; he knew the ways of the law too well. Time to begin the bargaining.

Francis said, "Lady Alice has stated the central theme: these crimes must stop. You evidently feel no remorse about the burglaries you've abetted. Very well; let that remain between you and your conscience. But for all your many flaws, I do not believe you would condone, abet, or otherwise knowingly facilitate cold-blooded murder."

Welbeck's smug expression turned sour. "I had nothing to do with those."

"But you know who did," Francis said.

Welbeck pursed his lips, then relaxed them; purse, relax, and again. "*Know* is too strong a word. We men of the law learn to choose our terms more carefully, don't we, Bacon? Rather say that I believe I *may* know, or that I suspect, or that I fear . . ." His eyes were shadowed by sadness or disillusionment, as if his suspicions had shorn him of something valuable.

That was not what Francis expected. No one would spare any such feelings for Sir Richard Topcliffe or his clerk. "You must give us the name, Nathaniel. These murders are the work of a lunatic. You know it as well as I do. They must stop."

"What good would the name do you? I'll wager you have less evidence against the killer than you have for the burglaries."

Another indisputable fact. "Then tell us the name of the next victim," Francis said. "We know you bought a copy of the list of recusants my commission has been interviewing, probably from one of our clerks. We also know that you have another source."

"God's bollocks, Bacon! Your underlings are more effective than I thought."

Francis smiled. His underlings would not appreciate that term, but they managed to suppress their objections. "You've chosen your victims deftly, Welbeck, I have to grant you that. But Sir James Lambert wasn't on our list, nor was his house beside the river. I confess I am unable to predict your next target with confidence. If we knew, we might be able to apprehend the murderer in the act."

"I see." Welbeck picked up his penknife and tapped it on his desktop in an irritatingly irregular rhythm. After a long moment, he said, "I want immunity for me and my men."

"Not if I discover that you had any part in the killings."

"Naturally."

"And the burglaries stop now, Welbeck. From this day forward, I will pursue."

"Understood."

Francis had known from the day he had talked to the sheriff that the chapel burglaries would be hard to prosecute in this year, of all years. Sending the coins and the note to the Earl of Essex had been a clever ploy; now a peer of the realm could attest that the profits were meant for the poor. Much as he loathed to see a crime go unpunished, he must sacrifice the lesser evil in order to end the greater one. "Agreed."

Welbeck's swift grin betrayed his relief. He hadn't been sure he'd win that round. "That's the first thing I want. The second is a lifetime lease on practicing chambers on the first floor of Ashton's Building."

Francis laughed out loud. "Please limit your demands to those that can be achieved in this world." Ashton's Building, like Bacon's own, was backed by green fields and orchards, so that one's chambers — especially one's bedchamber — received wholesome breezes free of the dust of Gray's Inn Road and the noise from the courtyards on the other side. A bencher had to die for chambers to become available in Ashton's. And Bacon owned his building, which his father had built, together with his brother Anthony. He leased the ground floor rooms but was extremely particular about his tenants.

Welbeck shrugged. "It was worth a try. Then the first floor in Stanhope's Building."

"Not the first," Bacon said. "Possibly the third."

"Never."

They dickered for a while, working through every building at the Inn. Good practicing chambers — those suitable for entertaining clients — were hard to come by. The first floor was the most desirable, being situated above the dust and bustle of the yard, but with only one flight of stairs to climb. Ground floor was next, second floor a distant third, and all other options out of the question for a man with a flourishing practice.

They finally settled on ground floor rooms in Ellis's Building in Coney Court. It backed onto Gray's Inn Road, noisy some days, but handy for a man who might need to abscond in the middle of the night.

"Now," Francis said, "who is your second source?"

"I won't give you a name."

"Then what have we been bargaining for?"

"My cooperation," Welbeck said, "to be provided on my terms. I can't just supply you with the name of the next victim and wave you down the stairs. That choice is a matter of discussion between me and my, shall we say, consultant. We consider the options together and choose the best available at the time projected."

"My cooperation with the bench with respect to your preferred chambers is contingent on that name."

"I know. I'll give you better than a name, but not today. Tomorrow afternoon, Monday at the latest. Then I'll give you the victim's name, the place, and the date."

"That date had better be soon," Francis said. "I suspect your consultant has begun operating independently since the last murder did not coincide with a burglary. We cannot allow another man to die."

"I agree. Two days at most. We had tentative plans already. But what do you have in mind? If you post extra guards around the property, you're liable to scare the individual off. I don't know how this person gains entrance, nor even exactly when." Welbeck placed a hand on his chest. "I never intended harm to anyone, Bacon. I swear it on all that I hold sacred."

As if there were any such thing. Francis had vaguely planned to enlist the Westminster constables to watch the house once they knew which one it would be.

"Constables are no good," Tom said as if Francis had spoken aloud. "They'll talk or whistle or wander off to take a piss. We'll have to set a trap."

"What do you have in mind?" Francis asked.

"Let Mr. Welbeck and his *consultant* set up their usual game. Let Coddington and crew show up on schedule, pick their locks, and slink on into the chapel the way they've been doing. Let it all look the way it's supposed to look so the murderer will feel safe enough to come in."

"It's too dangerous," Francis said. "I grant you catching the killer in the act is the surest means of obtaining a conviction, but this one kills with the touch of a poisoned blade. We'd be putting the householder's life in terrible jeopardy."

"Not the householder," Tom said. "Me." He gave them a smile so cold it sent a chill up Francis's spine.

THIRTY-FOUR

Tom peeked out the windows of Baron Strachleigh's bedchamber in Lambeth one last time, pretending to bid good night to the sliver of moon rising over the walled orchard. He wore a flannel nightshirt and a snug coif tied under his chin, doubtless looking the veriest fool close up. From outside the windows, he hoped he looked like an old man getting ready for bed.

He hobbled to the bedside table and pretended to pour a few drops of something into a cup of wine, then pretended to drink, not trusting any cup filled by another hand in this house. Then he knelt by the bed and said a genuine prayer, asking God to preserve his life that night.

He climbed into the bed and snuffed the candle, then lay on his back in the dark, waiting. Somewhere out there in the depths of the house, Jack Coddington and William Buckle crept toward the chapel. Sam Pratt, the boatman, rowed silently up and down the river, waiting for their signal to return. The thieves were playing out their regular roles, only this time they'd be leaving with sacks stuffed with twigs.

Tom felt the change in the air before he saw the shadows shift across the windows. He tensed, ready, but still flinched when he felt someone crawl onto the bed. Someone lighter than he'd expected.

Then the whispering started, barely audible, but chilling in its intensity. "You filthy, murdering Catholic swine. Where were you when my husband's life was riven from his body?"

Moonlight glinted off a silver blade and cold fingers grasped at Tom's collar. He shouted, "No!" Panic lanced through him so sharp he feared for a moment he'd been cut. *Don't touch that blade!*

His hand shot out to grasp the wrist, gripping it with all his strength, forcing it away. His assailant screamed — a high, feminine wail of pure frustration. Tom bucked her off and leapt from the bed.

Every inch of his skin prickled with fear of that knife. Where was it? Where was she? Had the bed curtain shifted? Was she there, sidling behind it, reaching for him?

He took a step toward the window and felt something brush against him. He cried, "Light! Light!" as he leapt aside, stumbling into a chair, nearly falling. Why hadn't they cleared this chamber and taken down those cursed, flapping curtains?

Ben and Trumpet burst through the door, each bearing a large candle. Ben put his on the nearest table while Trumpet held hers in front of her like a blazing sword. The three of them spread out, blocking the exits, and slowly backed the woman into a corner while she hissed her curses and slashed her gleaming knife at them.

"'Ware the blade!" Tom cried unnecessarily. They couldn't get near her.

Then Ben snatched a cloth off the bedside table, sending its contents crashing to the floor. He threw the cloth around the knife, flipping it over to cover it twice. Tom nipped in and grabbed the woman's arm, twisting it until she let go her grip with a cry. Ben bundled up the cloth, the knife safe within its folds.

Now the murderess lunged for the window. Tom caught her around the waist and dragged her back. She kicked and shrieked, but the game was over. He held on tight and carried her down the corridor to the baron's library, where Mr. Bacon and Mr. Welbeck had been waiting in the dark.

They were lighting their candles with long splinters of wood as Tom kicked open the door, hoicking his captive onto his hip. His pains that night were paid in full by the look of perfect astonishment on Bacon's face. He dropped his spunk and cried, "Mrs. Palmer!"

She ignored him, turning her face to her collaborator. "Why, Nathaniel? Why?"

Welbeck offered her an apologetic shrug, holding his hands palms up. "It had to stop, Sarah."

"They'll hang me. You'll lose me."

"You're lost already."

She wilted in Tom's arms. He let her go and she ran straight to Welbeck. He hugged her close, his eyes shining wetly, then set her aside, stepping away from her. Tom and Ben planted themselves in front of the door, although she seemed to have given up hope of escape.

She pulled off her knit cap and shook out her hair. Her doublet and hose fit her to perfection; she must have had them tailored to her form. She studied the faces of her captors one by one. Bacon got a wrinkle of the shapely nose. Tom got a wry half smile. Trumpet got a blink of surprise and a nod of approval for her boys' costume. The survey stopped at Ben. She tilted her head. "I thought you liked me."

He didn't answer.

She sniffed at his rudeness and turned back to her confederate. "Those men had to die, Nathaniel."

"No one was supposed to get hurt, my sweet. We agreed on that from the start."

"No one of *us*. No one of *us*, Nathaniel. But these . . ." She gestured vaguely at the rich furnishings and the gilded oak paneling. "These people are our enemies. These are the ones who killed my husband. They must pay for what they did to him."

"They have paid. We emptied their chapels and sold the goods abroad, as we planned. We rid England of those

Catholic gewgaws. You gave your share to the sailors; I gave some of mine too. Our plan worked perfectly, Sarah."

She shook her head and kept shaking it. "Not enough. Not enough. We took away their instruments of idolatry, but they have more. They still have their houses and their priest holes. They have their lives. They should suffer, as my husband and my brother did."

Welbeck spoke to the others. "She lost her husband to the Inquisition, you see. Then her favorite brother was killed in a skirmish with the Spanish off the coast of France. I knew she grieved for them — too much, for too long — but never realized the grief had strained her wits."

"How did she help you choose the victims?" Bacon asked.

"Her mother's diary," Welbeck answered. "That woman knew every Catholic family in England, I believe. She was part of the secret community who smuggled priests, passing them from house to house."

"*My mother!*" Sarah shrieked. "She was one of them, with her so-called music masters and the silver crosses dangling between her breasts. Feeding them, hiding them, those slithering, sneaking, viperous priests, conspiring with her friends to hold their secret Masses. That's all they ever thought about, plotting and scheming for the masters in Rome. So clever they thought they were!"

"Why murder the husbands?" Trumpet asked. "If it's the women you hate, why didn't you kill them?" Bacon frowned, but she shrugged. "I want to know if I was right."

Sarah flicked her finger at Trumpet's costume, as if picking out effective details. "You should know, better than they do. You've been through it. What happens when a Catholic dies? His widow loses most of her property. I didn't want these traitors to die; I wanted them to suffer. I wanted them to live in poverty, gnawing their knuckles over the ruins of their devilish machinations, watching their precious priests desert them when the soft beds were carted away and the barrels of sweet wine ran dry."

"Then why kill *my* husband?" Trumpet asked. "I've never even met a Catholic priest, much less kept one hidden in my house."

Mrs. Palmer shrugged. "I assumed you'd be like his other wives. And the chapel was so rich and the house so conveniently situated."

Trumpet's eyes narrowed wrathfully. Tom understood. She'd suffered — not as much as the others of course — but with no justification whatsoever.

"Where did you get the curare?" Bacon asked.

"My husband brought it back from Galicia. I don't know why; he seldom hunted. He liked to collect curiosities from the New World. I have the loveliest necklace of blue opals." She stroked her hair, looking at Welbeck but talking to someone else as she listed the odds and ends her husband had collected with the knowledgeable details of a merchant's wife.

Tom watched her with sickened fascination, unable to reconcile her pale beauty with the ugly deeds she'd done. By their harrowed expressions, the others were experiencing the same conflict of emotions.

Except for Trumpet. She put a hand on her hip and clucked her tongue sharply, then she strode across the room and drove her fist into Sarah Palmer's finely boned jaw, knocking her right down to the floor. "That's for ruining my chance to be a widow, you raving, frenetical, moon-mad bitch!"

THIRTY-FIVE

One week later, Francis Bacon stood at his study chamber window, watching the hurly-burly in the yard below. Michaelmas term would begin at the end of the week, and the men of Gray's were returning to the legal fray. He scowled as Nathaniel Welbeck waved at a friend and trotted up the steps to the hall. At least Francis was no longer obliged to share a table with him.

The compromise they'd reached still rankled. He wished he could have found a way to convict both Welbeck and poor, distempered Sarah Palmer, but without the barrister's cooperation, Baron Strachleigh would have surely died.

She was due to hang on Saturday. The field at Tyburn Tree would be crowded. Broadsides had been flying off the presses with the most exciting story since the Spanish had been driven out of the British Sea. Everyone liked to watch a murderer hang, especially a woman.

Francis would not be there. The whole affair had left him sick, in body, mind, and spirit. He meant to go to Twickenham for a few weeks of recuperation after this morning's interview. He also preferred to skip the speech-making and hearty hand-shaking that inevitably marked the start of the autumn term.

The expected knock came on the door. "*Intro!*"

Tom came in, hesitating after closing the door. "Sit, sit," Francis said, moving to the chair behind his desk.

"Has he decided?" Tom asked without preamble. None was needed. He'd asked the same question every time they'd met for the past week.

"He has. My Lord Burghley has granted your wardship to my aunt, Lady Russell."

"Your aunt?" Tom slid into the chair. "When you said 'a courtier,' I assumed you meant a lord, not a lady." He fingered the pearl in his ear, frowning, then recovered his characteristic buoyancy with characteristic speed. He grinned broadly at Francis. "There isn't an aunt in England I can't charm."

Francis gave him a cautionary look. "I've heard stories at court from men who knew my lady aunt when she was your age. From what they've said — always with that wry little smile — I suspect she must have been very much like your friend Lady Alice."

That deflated him a little. Francis didn't mean to be unkind, but only a reckless fool would confront his redoubtable aunt with a dimple as his only shield.

Tom, however, was unsinkable. "Then I've had plenty of practice. Besides, she's better than the Earl of Essex, isn't she?"

"I can neither affirm nor deny that assertion."

Tom chuckled. "Understood."

"My aunt will not sell your lands to buy ships, which is partly why she was the first person I told on the day we received the sorrowful news. She is strict, but reasonable in the main. Thrifty, on her own account, but litigious."

Lady Elizabeth Russell was one of the most strong-minded, combative, stubborn, and haughty women Francis had ever known, and he been attending upon Queen Elizabeth and her cronies since his earliest childhood.

"Litigious doesn't sound good," Tom said.

"It isn't. She has far more experience in court than you and I combined. But she liked the look of you."

Tom grinned.

Francis tilted his head to acknowledge the obviousness of that result. "She has a son your age, also named Thomas. She was favorably impressed by your experience in

Cambridge, both the intelligencing and the exposure to Puritan teachings. She will insist on taking a hand in your further education."

"No more Bible study groups." Tom held up a flat palm. "I draw the line at that."

"Your legal studies will keep you too busy in any event. She wants me to continue as your tutor and expects you to serve as my secretary for part of each week in partial compensation."

"I can live with that."

"Good." Francis had not expected him to agree so easily. "Your allowance will be reduced by some as yet undetermined amount. It can't be helped, I'm afraid. No guardian would be as generous as your father was, especially not when the monies are spent on trinkets and ah, light-skirted companions."

Tom scowled, then tossed it off with a shrug. "I'll manage. It's only for a few months anyway. I turn twenty-one on December second and then my properties come under my control."

Francis said nothing.

"Won't they?"

Francis grimaced.

"All right, maybe not that very day. But soon after Hilary term starts in January, don't you think? Or a month or two after that." Tom waited, brow creasing. "A *year*?"

Francis fingered the embroidery on his flat cuff and summoned a crooked smile. "Let's cross that bridge when we come to it, shall we?"

HISTORICAL NOTES

First, I must mention one change in the Bacon series universe and apologize for an error in an earlier book.

In *Murder by Misrule*, Nathaniel Welbeck hails from Derbyshire. I chose it because the northern counties were strongholds of Catholicism, being far from the capital and thus both culturally conservative and hard to control. Also, my fictional characters must come from Areas of Outstanding Natural Beauty, in case I ever decide to follow them home for some future tale.

But as I was writing The Widows Guild, I changed my mind. I needed Uncle Nat to have smuggling connections, more plausible for a West Country man. Then it occurred to me that although I don't write dialect, it wouldn't hurt for me to know that Trumpet is natively attuned to Tom's West Country burr. So I moved the Welbeck family seat to Devonshire, a place I would love to have an excuse to ramble in once more.

Again in *Murder by Misrule*, my lads attempt to visit Essex House, but it isn't Essex House yet. My mistake! It's known as Leicester House before the Earl of Leicester's death in 1588. Then his stepson, the 2nd Earl of Essex inherits the place and changes the name.

On to the real historical persons who appear in this book. I include the regular cast for completeness.
- Francis Bacon.
- Lady Anne Bacon, Bacon's mother.
- Lady Elizabeth Russell, Bacon's aunt and true friend of the queen.

- Robert Devereux, 2nd Earl of Essex.
- Sir Richard Topcliffe, diligent servant of the queen, really assigned to the recusancy commission. That fact was the wellspring for this story, as it happens.
- Sir William Waad (brief mention), statesman and diplomat, also really assigned to the recusancy commission.
- Sheriff Thomas Skinner, one of the two sheriffs in 1588. The other was John Catcher, whose name was too apt for fiction.

I did not deliberately alter the past in any way for this story. Dates and places that touch reality are as they were. My characters moved around the greater London area quite a bit; for that, I rely on the magnificent and indispensable work, *The A to Z of Elizabethan London*, complied by Adrian Prockter and Robert Taylor.

If you're interested in reading more about these people and places, come visit my blog at www.annacastle.com/blog. I review history books and write posts about the fascinating things I learn that can't be put in the books, where Story is King. If you have questions or complaints, please feel free to let me know at castle@annacastle.com.

ABOUT THE AUTHOR

Anna Castle holds an eclectic set of degrees: BA in the Classics, MS in Computer Science, and a Ph.D. in Linguistics. She has had a correspondingly eclectic series of careers: waitressing, software engineering, grammar-writing, a short stint as an associate professor, and managing a digital archive. Historical fiction combines her lifelong love of stories and learning. She physically resides in Austin, Texas, but mentally counts herself a queen of infinite space.

BOOKS BY ANNA CASTLE

Keep up with all my books and short stories with my newsletter. www.annacastle.com.

The Francis Bacon Series

Book 1, Murder by Misrule. 2014

Francis Bacon is charged with investigating the murder of a fellow barrister at Gray's Inn. He recruits his unwanted protégé Thomas Clarady to do the tiresome legwork. The son of a privateer, Clarady will do anything to climb the Elizabethan social ladder. Bacon's powerful uncle Lord Burghley suspects Catholic conspirators of the crime, but other motives quickly emerge. Rival barristers contend for the murdered man's legal honors and wealthy clients. Highly-placed courtiers are implicated as the investigation reaches from Whitehall to the London streets. Bacon does the thinking; Clarady does the fencing. Everyone has something up his pinked and padded sleeve. Even the brilliant Francis Bacon is at a loss — and in danger — until he sees through the disguises of the season of Misrule.

Book 2, Death by Disputation. 2015

Thomas Clarady is recruited to spy on the increasingly rebellious Puritans at Cambridge University. Francis Bacon is his spymaster; his tutor in both tradecraft and religious politics. Their commission gets off to a deadly start when Tom finds his chief informant hanging from the roof beams. Now he must catch a murderer as well as a seditioner. His first suspect is volatile poet Christopher Marlowe, who keeps turning up in the wrong places.

Dogged by unreliable assistants, chased by three lusty women, and harangued daily by the exacting Bacon, Tom risks his very soul to catch the villains and win his reward.

Book 3, The Widow's Guild. 2015

In the summer of 1588, Europe waits with bated breath for King Philip of Spain to launch his mighty armada against England. Everyone except Lady Alice Trumpington, whose father wants her wed to the highest bidder. She doesn't want to be a wife, she wants to be widow; a rich one, and the sooner, the better. So she marries an elderly viscount, gives him a sleeping draught, and spends her wedding night with Thomas Clarady, her best friend and Francis Bacon's assistant. The next morning, they find the viscount murdered in his bed and they're both locked into the Tower.

Lady Alice appeals to the Andromache Society, the widows' guild led by Francis Bacon's formidable aunt, Lady Russell. They charge Bacon with getting the new widow out of prison and identifying the real murderer. He soon learns the viscount wasn't an isolated case. Someone is murdering Catholics in London and taking advantage of armada fever to mask the crimes. The killer seems to have privy information — from someone close to the Privy Council?

The investigation takes Francis from the mansions along the Strand to the rack room under the Tower. Pulled and pecked by a coven of demanding widows, Francis struggles to maintain his reason and his courage to see through the fog of war and catch the killer.

The Lost Hat, Texas Series

Book 1, Black & White & Dead All Over. 2015

What happens when the Internet service provider in a small town spies on his clients' cyber-lives and blackmails them for gifts and services?

Murder; that's what happens.

Penelope Trigg moves to Lost Hat, Texas to open a photography studio and find herself as an artist. Things are going great. She's got a few clients, some friends, even a hot new high-tech boyfriend. But when Penny submits some nude figure studies of him to a contest, she gets hit with a blackmail letter in her inbox. "Do what I want or your lover's nudie pix get splattered across the Internet." The timing couldn't be worse, so Penny is forced to submit to the blackmailer's demands. Then people start dying and all the clues point to her. She has to rattle every skeleton in every closet in Lost Hat to keep herself out of jail and find the real killer.

Book 2, Flash Memory. 2016

Nature photographer Penelope Trigg has landed the job of her dreams: documenting the transformation of over-grazed rangeland into an eco-dude ranch and spa, owned by her boyfriend Tyler Hawkins. Then a body is found on the ranch and Ty is arrested. The victim was fooling around with Ty's baby sister Diana, but so was the senior deputy sheriff. Determined to prove Ty's innocence, Penny stirs up Diana's old flames, trying to shed enough light on the mystery to develop an alternative suspect. She mainly learns how to lose friends and annoy people, until she realizes someone has been manipulating the evidence. But is Ty the framer or the framee? Penny uses her eye for detail and her camera's memory to put the picture together and reveal the killer.

CPSIA information can be obtained
at www.ICGtesting.com
Printed in the USA
LVOW11s0812090117

520240LV00001BA/120/P